PRAISE FOR *THE RESCUE*

"Steven Konkoly's new Ryan Decker series is a triumph—an action-thriller master class in spy craft, tension, and suspense. An absolute must-read for fans of Tom Clancy, Vince Flynn, and Brad Thor."
—Blake Crouch, *New York Times* bestselling author

"*The Rescue* by Steven Konkoly has everything I love in a thriller—betrayal, murder, a badass investigator, and a man fueled by revenge."
—T.R. Ragan, *New York Times* bestselling author

"*The Rescue* grabs you like a bear trap and never lets go. No one writes action sequences any better than Steve Konkoly—he drops his heroes into impossible situations and leaves you no option but to keep your head down, follow where they lead, and hope you make it out alive."
—Matthew Fitzsimmons, *Wall Street Journal* bestselling author

"Breakneck twists, political conspiracy, bristling action—*The Rescue* has it all! Steven Konkoly has created a dynamic and powerful character in Ryan Decker."
—Joe Hart, *Wall Street Journal* bestselling author

"If you are a fan of characters like Scot Harvath and Mitch Rapp, this new series is a must-read. Steven Konkoly delivers a refreshingly unique blend of action, espionage, and well-researched realism."
—Andrew Watts, *USA Today* bestselling author

"An excellent source for your daily dose of action, conspiracy, and intrigue."
—Tim Tigner, author of *Betrayal*

"Fans of Mark Greaney and Brad Taylor, take notice: *The Rescue* has kicked off a stunning new series that deserves a place on your reading list. Ryan Decker is a must-read character."

—Jason Kasper, author of *Greatest Enemy*

"*The Rescue* immediately drops the reader into a well-drawn world of betrayal, revenge, and redemption. Ryan Decker is a flawed, relatable hero, unstoppable in his quest for justice."

—Tom Abrahams, author of *Sedition*

THE RAID

ALSO BY STEVEN KONKOLY

RYAN DECKER SERIES

The Rescue

THE FRACTURED STATE SERIES

Fractured State
Rogue State

THE PERSEID COLLAPSE SERIES

The Jakarta Pandemic
The Perseid Collapse
Event Horizon
Point of Crisis
Dispatches

THE BLACK FLAGGED SERIES

Alpha
Redux
Apex
Vektor
Omega

THE ZULU VIRUS CHRONICLES

Hot Zone
Kill Box
Fire Storm

THE RAID

STEVEN KONKOLY

THOMAS & MERCER

Text copyright © 2019 by Steven Konkoly
All rights reserved.

No part of this book may be reproduced, or stored in a retrieval system, or transmitted in any form or by any means, electronic, mechanical, photocopying, recording, or otherwise, without express written permission of the publisher.

Published by Thomas & Mercer, Seattle

www.apub.com

Amazon, the Amazon logo, and Thomas & Mercer are trademarks of Amazon.com, Inc., or its affiliates.

ISBN-13: 9781542091428
ISBN-10: 154209142X

Cover design by Rex Bonomelli

Printed in the United States of America

To Kosia, Matthew, and Sophia—the heart and soul of my writing.

PART ONE

PART ONE

CHAPTER ONE

Agent Joe Pittman concentrated on the twisty jeep trail unfolding in the headlights. "Dude. Slow the hell down," said Sal Contreras from the passenger seat.

Even at fifteen miles per hour, accidentally driving off one of these trails could put their vehicle out of commission. Worst-case scenario— he rolled the SUV navigating a sharp turn. Neither of them needed that on their records. They were two of the newest Border Patrol agents assigned to the El Centro sector.

"I don't think I can go any slower than this," said Pittman. "I feel like I'm driving in a school zone."

"Better than driving us off a cliff," said Contreras. "I think it's time to stop and figure out exactly where we are. We might be able to triangulate our position with the map."

"What does the GPS say?"

"Nothing useful. It has us on the other side of the border now," said Contreras. "Back at Signal Road."

"We're definitely not on the other side of the border," said Pittman.

Contreras had been assigned to the El Centro Station a few weeks ago, spending most of his time north of the city, searching vehicles headed away from the border toward Brawley. Pittman had been driving these roads most of that time. Not that this made him anything close to an expert on the area. The jeep trails all looked the same at night.

"How long has the GPS been screwed up?" said Pittman.

"I don't know exactly. Less than ten minutes," said Contreras. "The last time you asked, our position seemed fine."

"Is the GPS locked on to any satellites?"

"Three—according to the screen," said Contreras.

Pittman thought about it for a few seconds while squinting at the rutted trail ahead of them. Was it possible that he'd taken a wrong turn and driven them into the military exclusion zone he'd heard other agents talking about? Was it this close to his assigned zone? That might explain the GPS issue. The military could be spoofing the signal out here, discouraging curious trespassers by making navigation difficult.

If that turned out to be the case, they were screwed. El Centro's station chief would transfer the two of them north to Indio Station, placing them as far away from the border as possible without having to pay for them to move. As far as Pittman was concerned, the border was the only place to be in this job. On top of that, his fiancée would probably call it quits if they had to move again. He'd dragged her across three states in the Southwest over the past year and a half before finally landing this job a few months ago.

"Next chance I get, I'll turn us around," said Pittman. "Head back the way we came until we get a GPS signal. We might have accidentally driven into a restricted area."

"Restricted area? Here?" said Contreras. "Isn't this our area of responsibility?"

"I thought I heard a few of the desk jockeys talking about a military exclusion zone," said Pittman. "I think the military tests new surveillance technology on the border. Kind of the perfect test lab—they can use the stuff on live subjects."

"Then they're probably radioing our station right now, reporting us," said Contreras, opening the map in his lap and turning on his flashlight.

"I can't see the road with the light on," said Pittman, his attention drawn to the map.

"We need to figure out where the—*watch out!*" said Contreras, grabbing the steering wheel.

Pittman instinctively slammed on the brakes, the SUV skidding to a halt less than a foot from a small cluster of migrants who had stepped into the road. The headlights illuminated the group, now shrouded in a cloud of dust kicked up by the sudden stop. Something was off here.

They were barefoot, dressed in bras and underwear. As the dust swirled around them, slowly settling, he saw the real problem. Five girls, ages ranging from early high school to late grade school, stood huddled in the road—none of them eager to leave. This didn't resemble anything he'd seen before out here.

"Grab them before they run!" said Contreras, scrambling out of the SUV.

Pittman followed but without the same sense of urgency. These kids showed no interest in escaping. Quite the opposite. Their desperate looks and trembling bodies gave him immediate pause. Like they were on the run from something far more sinister than the cartels or Border Patrol. For the first time since he'd started patrolling the border a few weeks ago, he rested his hand on his holster and approached them cautiously.

"Don't touch them!" said Pittman as Contreras circled around them with his flashlight up. "Something isn't right."

Contreras must have finally sensed it, because he stopped in his tracks and brought his unoccupied hand to his holster.

"What is this?" said Contreras. "Why are they half-naked?"

"Can you tell if they're carrying anything?" said Pittman.

Contreras moved the flashlight up and down and in between the kids. "Nothing I can see. They're not even wearing shoes."

As Pittman got closer, the dust having mostly cleared, he noticed that two of the kids didn't look like any of the migrant children he'd seen on the job. He pulled his flashlight and pointed it at one of the kids, directing the beam at her dirty, bruised face. What the hell? The kid had light hair and blue eyes. She looked starkly European, which made no sense at all out here.

"*¿Hablas español?*" he said, getting no response. "English?"

A few of the kids shook their heads.

"Do you speak any other languages?" said Pittman, glancing at Contreras.

"I was born in Tucson, Arizona—to two migrant workers. English was my foreign language."

"Funny."

Pittman turned his flashlight toward the side of the road where the group had presumably emerged, following the scrub beyond the jeep trail to a small rise. He pointed in that direction.

"Did you come from there?" he said, a few of the kids following his gesture. "Over there?"

The kids quickly looked down and shook their heads.

"*Sprechen sie Deutsch? Parlez-vous français?*" said Pittman.

"How many languages do you speak?"

"That's all I know outside of *español*," said Pittman. "Speakie Russki?"

Two of the children glanced at him furtively, including the blonde-haired, blue-eyed kid. He examined the group again, determining that the other kid who stole a peek at him also looked European—or possibly Russian? *Russki* must have translated to something the kids recognized. Upon further inspection, the other three didn't look like Central American or Mexican migrants. They had somewhat dark skin and black hair, but now he wasn't sure. Something about them looked more European.

"They don't look like the kind of migrants we get coming through here," said Pittman.

"You've only been on the job for a few weeks. How do you know what comes through here?" said Contreras. "Let's get them back to the station. We can sort out their situation after we get them cleaned up and dressed."

Pittman stared in a southerly direction, toward the pitch darkness of the border. He'd studied the maps back at the station and knew that very little lay directly south of the Jacumba Wilderness area. A continuation of low mountains and sharp hills like those surrounding him, punctuated by long stretches of sandy desert. A few sparsely inhabited towns with intermittent electricity and half-paved roads.

The sleepy, discarded impression left by the Mexican side was deceiving. The desolate stretch of border served as one of the busiest crossing points in the El Centro sector. The hiding places and difficult-to-patrol terrain offered by the hills attracted migrants, bused in from Mexicali or points farther south. But this was something entirely different.

The migrants who crossed here came prepared for the harsher landscape, carrying extra water and wearing durable shoes sold to them at a markup by the coyotes. The coyotes, or human smugglers, insisted. Not only did they make more money from the last-minute sales, but they also cut down on the risk of leaving an injured migrant behind—like bread crumbs for Border Patrol agents.

"But how did they get here—dressed like this? A few of them look like they've been beaten. The blood is crusted. This doesn't look like a border crossing."

"They were probably robbed during the crossing," said Contreras.

"Five kids? Without any adults?" said Pittman, flashing his light past the side of the road again. "I'm going to have a look over that rise."

"Dammit, Joe. Let's just get out of here. We've caught five fence jumpers. We did our job," said Contreras. "I don't want to get canned from work because we're in the wrong place."

"Call this in while I take a quick look," said Pittman, already headed for the back of the SUV.

"Call this in? When we don't know where we are?"

"Then don't call it in!" said Pittman. "Put them in the back of the vehicle so they're not standing around in their underwear. I'll be right back."

While Contreras mumbled curses and corralled the children around the other side of the SUV, Pittman opened the rear cargo hatch and retrieved a pair of night-vision goggles from a plastic crate. After tightening the head straps, he lowered the AN/PVS-14 monocular over his right eye and set off through the brush toward the crest of a low hill just south of the trail. About halfway to the top of the rise, he heard a car door slam shut behind him. Pittman turned to see Contreras walk in front of the SUV, glowing in the headlights like he was on fire. He hit his radio mic transmitter.

"Sal. Kill the lights. No point in advertising if we're smack-dab in the middle of where we don't belong."

"Good idea," said Contreras. The hillside around him went dark a few seconds later.

Now Pittman could actually see with the night-vision goggles. A few minutes later, he crested the hill, crouching like he wasn't supposed to be here. For some reason, maintaining a low profile on the hill felt right in this case. On the downslope, he paused for a moment, scanning the vast swath of artificially green landscape beyond the hilltop. A distant hot spot, or bright point in the monochromatic green panorama, grabbed his attention.

The light source wasn't focused or pinpoint bright, like a flashlight or headlight. It looked more like background lighting, which struck him as odd. Pittman stared at the unmagnified image for several seconds, trying to make sense of it. He couldn't be certain, but it looked like someone had left the door to a house open somewhere down there—except it couldn't be a house. Not out here.

Whatever it was—it didn't belong. Could be the exit to a tunnel crossing under the border. Maybe worse. He'd read an article on the internet about rape camps. Isolated places where human traffickers brought kids they had kidnapped. A mercenary team of ex-military and former CIA operatives had found one in Tucson, Arizona, off a desolate stretch of highway. What if they'd stumbled on the same thing?

Pittman raised his night-vision goggles and stared in the direction of the light with his naked eyes, just barely able to find it again. At this distance, without binoculars, he wasn't going to learn anything useful about the odd light source. He lowered the night-vision goggles into place again and took another look at the enhanced image. A shadow passed in front of the light, vanishing just as quickly.

The kids must have come from there. It was the only thing that made sense. They were all barefoot, but from what he could tell, none of their feet looked bloodied. Anyone traveling any appreciable distance out here without shoes couldn't possibly make it very far without tearing their feet to shreds. What the hell was down there? What if there were more kids? He triggered his radio.

"Sal. I need you to call this in right now. There's something out here. Some kind of light coming out of the ground or the hillside. Maybe a tunnel? I don't know, but you have to trust me on this," said Pittman. "Tell station that we found five girls. Teenagers. At least two are Caucasian. Possibly all of them are European. And we think we may have stumbled on some kind of sex-trafficking camp. I'll take full responsibility if we're in a restricted zone."

"I don't know, Joe," replied Contreras. "Can't you just hustle your ass back and we drive out of here? Report this once we're back in our assigned territory?"

"We can't even set an accurate GPS marker. What if we can't find this place again?" said Pittman. "Please call this in."

"All right. I'll make the call," said Contreras. "Just get back to the SUV."

"On my way," said Pittman.

He stood in the dark, observing the light for at least a minute before starting back up the hill. When he reached the top, Contreras called over the radio net, sounding frantic.

"Where are you? I only got part of the call out. I have nothing but static on the vehicle radio now. El Centro Station never—hold on—I think there's someone out here."

"What? Where?" said Pittman, picking up the pace.

"I don't know. It's too dark. I thought I heard—"

The transmission cut off before Contreras finished.

"Sal?" he said, waiting for a response. "Come in, Sal."

Nothing.

"Sal. Come in. Can you hear me?" said Pittman.

No response.

His radio crackled with a faint, staticky voice.

"Sal. Is that you?"

His earpiece crackled with more white noise, punctuated by an occasional word. Multiple rapid pops echoed through the hills, reaching his ears from different directions. He drew his pistol and moved cautiously to the top of the hill, barely raising his head high enough over the rocky crest to view the SUV.

Several heavily armed dark figures in full tactical kit were busy around the vehicle. He lifted his body a little higher, in time to see one of the "soldiers" pull a limp body from the back seat of the SUV and drop it on the side of the road like a bag of mulch. A quick flash drew his attention to the front of the car, his mind barely processing the sniper set up behind the hood—before a jackhammer blow to his upper chest knocked him backward.

He rolled halfway down the hill, losing his pistol and night-vision goggles, before slamming to a stop against a couch-size boulder. Pittman lay motionless on his back for several seconds, the ground soaking up far too much of his blood. Realizing his time was nearly up, he reached across his shattered chest to trigger his radio.

"Agents down. Ambushed by soldiers," he said, his chest radiating pain with every word. "Jacumba Wilderness Area."

He turned on his side, jamming his hand against the radio microphone transmit button. He barely heard the bullets chip away at the rock around his head before it all went black.

CHAPTER TWO

Jesús Serrano stopped his group on a flat, open stretch of pebbly sand squeezed between two towering rock formations. They had crossed the border ten minutes ago, having unceremoniously stepped over a sagging, rust-covered string of long-forgotten barbed wire. The hike to the border, from their drop-off point on the far outskirts of La Rumorosa, had taken about two hours in the pitch darkness, over very uneven terrain. Normally he would keep them moving away from the border until they crossed Interstate 8, but he wasn't worried about getting busted tonight.

For reasons still unknown, the US Border Patrol had quit watching this stretch of the border about a month ago. Based on what he had learned from other coyotes working the Jacumba area, not a single crossing within a one-and-a-half-mile stretch of border immediately west of the San Diego County line, on the United States side, had been stopped. What had previously been a relatively busy but dangerous crossing area had turned into a cash cow for the coyotes and the Jalisco New Generation Cartel. A free-for-all attracting migrants from as far away as Tijuana and areas south of Yuma.

Now the only threat to his journey came from Sinaloa Cartel *sicarios* sent to infiltrate groups of migrants—and murder the coyotes. The Jacumba crossing sat close to the constantly shifting territorial border between the two cartels, and up until a month ago it hadn't attracted much attention from the Sinaloa bosses. With human-smuggling revenues quadrupled in the area, it had quickly become one of the more hotly contested geographic points on the border.

He waited for the stragglers to catch up before directing the two dozen or so ragtag travelers to take cover in the low brush on the side of the small river. Despite nearly thirty days of zero hassle, he still took basic precautions in case anyone was out looking for them. It wasn't a major problem in this area, but armed civilian vigilantes patrolled parts of the border in New Mexico and Texas. Keeping the group concealed as much as was practical, without slowing down the trip, made sense to him.

Jesús also wanted to take a moment to examine his cargo after the strenuous first leg of the journey. Anyone who didn't tend to basic needs, like sitting down to drink water, going to the bathroom, or adjusting their footwear, went on his short list of infiltration suspects. He had been doing this for three years and had never seen a legitimate migrant pass up an opportunity to rest, rehydrate, and adjust their gear. Then again, until recently, they rarely got the chance.

He walked up and down the tight cluster a few times, not detecting anything out of the ordinary. After draining one of the water bottles he carried in his backpack, he checked the time. A few more minutes and they'd get back on the trail. The next three miles were the most difficult, pitting them against uphill, rocky terrain until they reached one of the dry creek beds that would lead them to the interstate, where Jesús's leg of their long journey ended.

A car would pick him up and drive him to Calexico, thirty-five miles to the east, where he would cross back into Mexico to lead another group of migrants over the border. The sooner he got to the drop-off point, the better. He'd been running two groups a night for the Jalisco New Generation Cartel since the Border Patrol vanished, and Mexicali was still under Sinaloa Cartel control. It would take him a little while to run countersurveillance on the streets of Mexicali before his Jalisco New Generation contact could pick him up.

If it took too long, he'd have to really push the next group of migrants to reach the interstate before dawn. Failing to reach the drop-off point before sunrise meant he had to spend the day out there with them, under the blazing sun—until nightfall. The setback would cost him a second run the next night, and a few thousand dollars.

"Okay. Time to get moving," said Jesús. "Tie your shoes. Take another sip of water. We won't be stopping for—"

The ground shook violently, followed immediately by a series of sharp crunches that reverberated off the canyon's rock walls and echoed for several eerie seconds. At first he thought it was the start of an earth-quake, but the thunderclaps were like nothing he'd ever heard before. His second thought was a suicide bomber. He wouldn't put anything past the Sinaloa Cartel.

Most of the migrants scattered, only a small cluster of dark shapes remaining with him. Unsure what had just happened and reluctant to draw attention to himself by yelling at the others, Jesús melted into the prickly bushes between two families and assured them everything would be fine. They'd wait for ten minutes and continue if the area remained quiet.

After a minute of silence, he pulled out a satellite phone and called Ramón, his Jalisco New Generation contact on the Mexican side, who answered immediately.

"You okay?" said Ramón.

"Yeah. I'm good. Most of my group bolted, but that's their problem," said Jesús.

The migrants paid for their transit in advance with the understanding that nothing was guaranteed once they crossed the border.

"What was that? Sounded like an explosion," said Jesús. "Sinaloa?"

"No. Everyone checked in. You're the last," said Ramón. "The hills will be crawling with migrants tonight."

"Only eight stayed with me," said Jesús. "The rest are probably headed in your direction."

"They're stuck on the US side," said Ramón. "We're moving back from the border. I suggest you start moving north. Put as much distance between you and the wall as possible. If the Americans heard that explosion, we may have seen our last night of easy money."

"I don't like the sound of that," said Jesús.

"I'm sure my boss won't like it, either," said Ramón. "Follow the same procedures tonight unless you hear otherwise. If the border stays quiet, we'll try to squeeze another wave through tonight. We'll pick up as many of the stragglers from the first wave as possible. The last thing we need is a hundred migrants trying to hitch a ride on the interstate tonight."

"Okay. I'm heading out right now," said Jesús.

"Keep your phone on. Just in case there's more to this than reported," said Ramón before disconnecting the call.

Jesús urged the huddled group to stand up and started walking north. The sooner he got out of there, the better.

CHAPTER THREE

Border Patrol Agents Ocampo and Cruz had just finished securing the hitch that connected the mobile observation tower to their SUV when a series of flashes illuminated the distant hills to the west—in the presumed direction of Pittman's distress call.

"It's good," said Cruz. "Let's get the hell out of here."

"Should we ditch the tower?" said Ocampo.

Cruz gave it a quick thought. They could move a lot faster without this damn thing, but there'd be hell to pay if it got damaged or stolen. Then again, if someone was out here ambushing Border Patrol agents, the trailer would make it near impossible to execute any kind of effective evasive maneuver. In fact, one excessively sharp or poorly timed turn could tip the trailer and pin them in place.

"We need to get moving," said Cruz. "Raise the closest team with our Motorolas."

"What's wrong with the vehicle radio?" said Ocampo.

"No idea," said Cruz. "You're driving."

The fact that they couldn't communicate with either El Centro or Calexico Station worried Cruz more than anything. Signal jamming was something new. Not a welcome development out here. The cartels didn't take kindly to the Border Patrol's diligent efforts to cut off one of their main income sources. Maybe the Mexicans had finally decided to go on the offensive. A chain of thunderclaps hit him before he opened the passenger door.

"Undo the hitch!" he yelled, scrambling toward the back of the SUV.

"What the hell was that?" said Ocampo, fumbling with the chains connecting the trailer to the hitch.

"Nothing good," said Cruz. "High-order detonations following the flashes. I don't get it. Maybe Pittman and Contreras drove into a military operation. That exclusion zone is out there somewhere."

"Station shouldn't have put two newbies together," said Ocampo.

Cruz frantically turned the winch, raising the coupler off the hitch ball.

"We don't know what happened out there," said Cruz, giving the winch a few more spins. "It's clear. Let's go."

Several minutes later, while Ocampo navigated the winding dirt roads at a borderline unsafe speed, Cruz made contact with a nearby team that had heard the distant explosion. A few minutes after that, El Centro sector headquarters vectored every available Border Patrol unit within twenty miles of the Jacumba Wilderness Area to the missing agents' assigned territory. At nearly the same time, an MQ-9 Predator assigned to an aerial racetrack pattern somewhere in Arizona turned west, its pilot in Yuma pushing the drone's speed to the limit.

"Should we turn around?" said Ocampo.

He had no intention of driving into a possible ambush alone.

"Keep driving east. Until we link up with another team," said Cruz. "And Pittman's radio transmissions stay between the two of us."

"But you already—"

"Whatever you just heard me say on the radio is all either of us is ever going to say about this," said Cruz. "I don't need any guys with face tattoos showing up at my house. We heard Pittman's distress call and tried to contact El Centro Station, but the vehicle radio was nothing but static. Then a huge explosion. That's it."

"Nothing about the kids?"

"They got the word out about the kids," said Cruz. "We got the word out about an ambush. That's it."

"What about the tunnel?" said Ocampo. "That's pretty important. And the kids being Caucasian?"

"Mike. Trust me on this. The cartels don't mess around," said Cruz. "They were probably listening to our radio transmissions, and they have people on their payroll at the station, headquarters—even out here. I'd rather not pique their curiosity. Are we on the same page here?"

"Yes. We're on the same page."

"You don't even tell your wife," said Cruz.

"Got it."

"You better. The cartels show zero mercy when it comes to protecting their money. Nothing is off-limits, including family."

PART TWO

CHAPTER FOUR

Ryan Decker rubbed his irritated eyes with a dusty, gloved hand before lazily returning them to his binoculars. He scanned the two visible sides of the structure for several moments, fighting off another yawn until he was finished. Nothing had changed at the target house. He slunk a few feet backward along the rough ground and turned onto his back, staring at the desert camouflage net several inches above his head. He jolted awake a moment later.

"Where the hell are they?" he muttered.

Decker took a long pull from the CamelBak hose hanging over his shoulder, swishing the warm, lemon-flavored electrolyte solution around his mouth to clear the grit before forcing it down. He'd give anything for real water at this point. Even settle for one of Harlow's diet sodas. Anything but this "lab-created perfect balance of electrolytes and water" that had admittedly kept him feeling slightly human after roasting in hundred-degree-plus temperatures for the past few days.

This mission couldn't come to an end soon enough. Not because it was miserably hot out here, or because he was sleep deprived to the point of hallucination—but because he had spent nearly three full days inside his own head, with nothing to do but periodically glance at the target house. His occasional chats with Brad Pierce, who lay in a similar observation position several hundred yards to his left, did nothing to dull the inner monologue.

Nighttime had been the worst. As desert temperatures rapidly plummeted, the increased risk of detection by handheld thermal-imaging devices curtailed surveillance of the house, leaving Decker to stare at the star-filled sky above—and relive every misstep and mistake that had landed him here. Every missed birthday party, soccer game, and school open house. Every moment spent away from his family in the service of building World Recovery Group. Countless memories that should have been but would never happen. A parade of regrets on continuous play in his head. Another day of this, and he might lose his mind.

His satellite phone buzzed, momentarily sparing him the launch of another pity party. Keeping the phone below the lip of the shallow arroyo to avoid electronic detection by the Russians, he examined the LED screen before answering.

"I'm ready to go home," said Decker.

"I was ready two days ago," said Pierce. "Any news?"

"Nothing yet. I expect to hear from Harlow any minute now," said Decker. "They should be getting close to the interstate turnoff."

"I can't wait to see the looks on their faces when the FBI drags them out in handcuffs."

"Or in body bags," said Decker. "This has the potential to go really bad, really fast."

"That part is out of our control," said Pierce. "Reeves made that abundantly clear. We positively identify Drozdov and stand down. We were never here."

Decker paused long enough for Pierce to continue.

"I don't like it when you go silent."

"Just thinking," said Decker.

"I don't like that, either," said Pierce.

"I keep running all of the scenarios."

"All of the scenarios? I count two, Ryan," said Pierce. "We either ID Drozdov or we don't. That's it."

"What if Drozdov doesn't show, or we can't ID him?"

"Two scenarios," said Pierce. "We call Reeves with good news or bad news. That's it."

"You know what I'm saying," said Decker.

"Trust me, I know exactly what you're implying," said Pierce. "But we agreed to very strict rules of engagement when we took this job. Surveillance only. If we go off script, we jeopardize everything."

"The thought of leaving those kids behind doesn't sit well with me," said Decker.

"I feel the same way, but this is just one house and one set of kids," said Pierce. "We have to focus on the bigger picture. Nailing Drozdov could shut down the entire operation, saving hundreds, possibly thousands, more."

"I keep coming back to that," said Decker. "But it doesn't make this any easier."

"We both have to live with it," said Pierce.

Decker's phone chimed. "Hold on. I have a text message."

He read the message and sent a quick reply.

"Target convoy turned off the interstate on the eastern side of Indio."

"That's not good," said Pierce.

"No. It's not," said Decker. "If Harlow's team has been made . . ."

"She'll be fine," said Pierce. "They know what they're doing."

"I know," he said, disconnecting the call.

Decker turned on his side, unzipped the long, tan plastic bag lying next to him, and removed a desert camouflage–painted, suppressed MK12 SPR—special purpose rifle—identical to the semiautomatic rifle previously used by Navy SEAL snipers. Pierce carried the same rifle—an insurance policy they had both agreed upon after examining satellite imagery of their approach to the target house.

The mostly flat ground surrounding the house for miles provided little cover, putting them at a lethal disadvantage if detected by the Russians. Of course, they had neglected to mention the rifles to Reeves, who would have thrown a fit at the mere suggestion of bringing them. He'd even kept them a secret from Harlow, until the last possible moment. The look on her face at the drop-off point hadn't been a happy one.

He extended the bipod and opened the scope covers before squirming back into position to observe the house.

One way or the other, these kids were going home today.

Chapter Five

As calmly as possible, Harlow Mackenzie opened the SUV's glove compartment and removed the Scorpion submachine gun, placing it in her lap. The Russians' last-second exit from the interstate, on the far eastern outskirts of Indio, had caught her off guard—and she didn't like surprises. Based on the monthlong surveillance operation run by her firm, she'd expected them to exit near Chiriaco Summit, forty miles east of here.

"Do you really think that's necessary?" said Katie from the driver's seat.

"We've been made," said Harlow. "Why else would they get off the interstate here?"

"I don't see how," said Katie. "We've been running a continuously changing lineup of cars behind and in front of them—at very conservative distances."

"I have to go with the most obvious explanation," said Harlow. "Until another presents itself."

"Do I follow them?"

With the exit rapidly approaching, she didn't have time to give her question much thought.

"Do it. Just keep your distance. If their convoy splits up after exiting, we're out of here," said Harlow before sliding a thirty-round magazine into the compact nine-millimeter weapon.

Katie eased the vehicle off the interstate as the convoy of four black SUVs turned left onto Golf Center Parkway and sped across the overpass. The convoy had nearly reached the other side of the wide interstate by the time her vehicle squeaked through the yellow light at the top of the off-ramp. Harlow looked over her shoulder and studied the sparse traffic, finding nothing that raised a red flag. She grabbed her radio from the center console.

"All units. Target convoy exited at Golf Center Parkway. Exit 144. We're still trying to figure out what's going on," said Harlow.

"You need some backup?" said Pam, over the radio.

"Not yet," said Harlow. "If we haven't been made, this might be an enhanced countersurveillance technique, and they'll likely split up. Wouldn't surprise me, given the cargo."

"Copy that," said Pam. "How do you want us set up?"

"Let's go standard. Two units at the next exit and two at the last exit. One unit gets off at Golf Center Parkway and takes a right. Find a spot to watch the southbound lanes. We'll follow anyone that doesn't double back toward the interstate."

"I'll cover the southbound lanes and back you up if necessary," said Pam.

"Sounds good. Will advise if there's a change," said Harlow before slipping the radio back into the cup holder.

The four Bratva SUVs motored through the set of traffic lights north of the interstate, immediately turning in to a compact strip mall on the far corner of the intersection. Unsurprisingly, the light turned red just as Harlow's vehicle crossed over the interstate. Before she could analyze the situation, Katie turned the SUV right on the red light and drove them toward the entrance at the other side of the strip mall.

"What are we doing?" said Katie.

Harlow peered through the driver's side window at the line of black SUVs cruising through the parking lot. Whatever they were up to, it didn't look like countersurveillance. They would have split up at the intersection or driven past the strip mall to pull some kind of erratic maneuver a little farther down the road. That left Harlow with two scenarios. Fast food run—or a very public machine-gunning of her vehicle.

"Entrance is coming up quick," said Katie.

"Pull in," said Harlow, not seeing another option to keep the Bratva convoy in sight.

Katie guided the vehicle through intermittent oncoming traffic to enter the congested strip-mall parking lot. At least the place was busy, giving them some cover.

"There's not a lot of room to maneuver in here if they get trigger-happy," said Katie.

They wouldn't dare—or would they? Her surveillance certainly indicated that they were still on edge from Penkin's abduction and murder. Aside from these suspected side trips to the desert, the new Bratva leader rarely ventured outside their enclave in Van Nuys.

Decker's stunt had left them justifiably paranoid, graphically demonstrating their vulnerability to the wrong—or right—enemy. An enemy they still hadn't identified, who could appear when they least expected it. Maybe following them into the parking lot hadn't been one of her better ideas. They could have pulled a U-turn and sat in the gas station on the other side of the street. She'd let her enthusiasm for nailing this son of a bitch to the wall affect her better judgment. Wouldn't be the first time or the last.

"We'll be fine," said Harlow, shifting the Scorpion in her lap—business end facing the convoy.

"You don't look convinced."

Katie took her left hand off the steering wheel long enough to loosen the pistol wedged between her right hip and the center console. Harlow turned her head a few inches to the right, her eyes scanning the row of SUVs creeping along the storefronts. What the hell were they doing?

"Shit," said Katie, the vehicle suddenly stopping. "I have a car backing out. Make that two cars."

Harlow disengaged the Scorpion's safety and glanced in the side-view mirror, knowing that Katie was one hundred percent focused on the two vehicles pulling out in front of them. Until proven otherwise, they had to operate under the assumption that the convoy's unexpected detour into the strip-mall parking lot was a trap.

"Rear is still good," said Harlow, her eyes alternating between the SUVs and the mirror.

Katie's hand drifted to the gearshift.

"What's up?" said Harlow, staying focused on her sectors.

"Nothing," said Katie. "Just in case."

When the closest car in front of them straightened in the lane and started to creep slowly toward the other car, Harlow glanced over her shoulder—through the rear cargo compartment window.

"We're still clear in back," she said before reassessing the scene in front of them.

Both cars slowly drove away, opening the lane in front of them.

"False alarm," said Katie.

Harlow focused her attention back on the Bratva vehicles as Katie eased them forward. In the brief span of time she'd taken her eyes off the Russians, the line of SUVs had stopped across from a liquor store; the occupants of the rear vehicle had headed inside already. She released her death grip on the Scorpion.

"Double false alarm," said Harlow. "Liquor run."

"They must be planning to stay at the house for a while," said Katie.

"Happy to disappoint them," said Harlow, grabbing the radio. "All units. Target convoy stopped at a liquor store. We're going to reposition across the street, in case they don't head back to I-10. Pam. You pick them up if they continue their trip using the interstate. We'll catch up in a few miles."

"Got it," said Pam. "We're in position just south of the on-ramp."

"I'll let you know when they're on the way," said Harlow, putting the radio down.

"Liquor run, huh? Wish we could be there to watch that party fizzle," said Katie. "Or explode."

"I'm just happy to play a role in this," said Harlow.

Happy was an oversimplified understatement. Harlow was thrilled. She'd been naive to think that exposing Aegis Global's despicable connection to the Steele kidnapping and the Solntsevskaya Bratva would trigger a tidal wave of new interest in the war against human trafficking. The wheels of government spin slowly under the best of circumstances, and when hundreds of lawmakers have to reconcile their sordid relationships with an international powerhouse like Aegis Global . . . they barely move at all.

When Supervisory Special Agent Reeves had reached out about a month ago to ask for help with an ongoing Bratva operation, Harlow agreed on the spot. A second chance like this came around only once in a career. One of his top informants had identified a long-shot opportunity to hit the Bratva's recently installed West Coast leadership hard enough to shut the West Coast operation down permanently, but Reeves couldn't do it without covertly shadowing key members of the organization. A trick his division could no longer achieve.

Persistent Bratva countersurveillance efforts over the past several months had identified most of his division's agents, effectively relegating them to overt surveillance postures. He needed fresh blood to work the Russians. An off-the-books crew that could stay invisible, even under the most rigorous countersurveillance conditions. If the Russians suspected anyone had followed them, the unusual opportunity would vanish, never again to materialize.

That's why she had personally overseen this exhaustively comprehensive but entirely discreet surveillance operation from the beginning. Everyone was counting on her to do this right.

"At least Decker and Pierce have a front-row seat," said Katie.

"Outfield seats," said Harlow. "That's what Decker called them."

"How long has he been out there?" said Katie.

"Three days," she said, wanting to say it felt like three weeks.

"Is this the longest you've gone without seeing him since he returned to LA?" said Katie.

"What's that supposed to mean?"

"Nothing," said Katie, shrugging.

"Uh-huh," she mumbled, her thoughts no longer in the strip-mall parking lot.

CHAPTER SIX

Supervisory Special Agent Joseph Reeves pocketed his satellite phone and turned to Matt Kincaid, who leaned against the front of a black, bullet-resistant Suburban, patting his damp forehead with a towel.

"Target convoy just got off the interstate. I want to be airborne in fifteen minutes. Vehicles leave in five."

Kincaid nodded and sprang into action, walking down the line of FBI vehicles while issuing orders through a handheld radio. Reeves headed toward the small hangar fifty yards away, where he'd brief the helicopter assault team one more time before liftoff. When he was halfway to the corrugated metal building, the California Air National Guard helicopter crews emerged, jogging toward the four HH-60G Pave Hawks in the middle of the tarmac. He waved them over for a quick talk before they readied the helicopters for takeoff.

"Target convoy is thirty minutes out," said Reeves. "Any questions or concerns before we do this?"

Lieutenant Colonel Robert Baker, the group's flight leader, shook his head while glancing at the rest of his pilots and aircrew, who similarly indicated they were ready to go.

"It's a straightforward mission," said Baker. "I just need to reinforce what we talked about earlier. If we take fire on the way in, under no circumstances can your agents return fire from the helicopters. We're under strict orders to maintain a support role status. Taxi service only. If ground fire becomes too intense at the primary LZ, we'll divert to the secondary. It'll be your call whether to disembark at the secondary LZ."

"If Drozdov shows, we're hitting the house," said Reeves. "My ground team will arrive about five to seven minutes after we hit the landing zone. We'll hug the ground and wait for the cavalry."

Baker nodded. "My guess is you'll be fine. We've done a dozen raids like this with the DEA. The baddies rarely put up a fight when our helicopters swoop in. It's pretty intimidating. Loud as a rock concert. Dust blowing everywhere. They can't see far enough to tell we're flying unarmed. The only thing missing is 'Ride of the Valkyries' music."

Reeves laughed. "Now that would be something. I hope you're right."

The pilot patted his shoulder and winked. "Me, too. Crew chiefs will call your teams forward once we get spinning."

"We'll be ready," said Reeves.

Inside the hangar, four teams of six heavily armed, body armor–clad SWAT agents stood in tight clusters, restlessly checking their rifles and sweating profusely. When Reeves appeared, they straightened up and gave him their undivided attention.

"Drozdov's convoy just exited the turnpike," said Reeves. "ETA three-zero mikes. We're airborne in fifteen."

"Positive ID?" said one of the team leaders.

"Negative. The convoy fits the pattern we've identified for Drozdov's trips, but we won't know for sure until he steps out of one of those vehicles at the target house. We'll be in a holding pattern five minutes out."

"What if he doesn't show?" said the team leader.

"Then we return to base," said Reeves.

"RTB and leave the kids there?"

Reeves shrugged, suddenly feeling the heat under twenty pounds of tactical gear.

"And wait for the next time. Surveillance and intelligence strongly suggests that Drozdov makes these trips regularly. He's acquired a taste for spending time with the new arrivals."

Collectively, the agents shook their heads and muttered foul language. He didn't blame them for expressing disgust with the situation. The vast majority of agents assigned to the Los Angeles field office worked relatively straightforward jobs. Counterintelligence. Counterterrorism. National criminal enterprises. Few of them had experience in transnational crimes—dealing with the worst of the worst. Groups that didn't care about the consequences of their degenerate business ventures.

He'd lived and breathed this nightmare for the better part of three years, unable to make a dent in the Bratva's sex-trafficking business. Drozdov's depravity and insistence on "breaking in" each new crop represented Reeves's best chance of shutting down the Russians. As cruel as it sounded, he had no choice but to bail on the mission if Drozdov didn't materialize.

"I don't make this decision lightly, especially given what I've seen working this crew," said Reeves. "But if we hit that house without Drozdov, we'll never get a chance like this again. He'll go so deep underground, we'll need an oil drill to reach him."

"My bad. This is your area of expertise," said the team leader. "Same ROE?"

Relieved that he didn't have to expand a buy-in speech he didn't completely agree with, Reeves switched gears.

"Same ROE. No matter what happens en route to the LZs, you are not authorized to use your weapons until you disembark. No exceptions," said Reeves, continuing before they could respond. "If the primary is too hot, they'll drop us at the secondary. Leaves us exposed for six minutes tops, until the vehicles arrive."

"Unable to shoot back," said another team leader.

"You're cleared to fire once you get off the helicopter," said Reeves.

"Not with hostages in the house."

Reeves swallowed hard, realizing he wasn't going to slip anything past this group. He nodded slowly.

"Return fire on this mission must be precise—and strictly limited. That's why I asked for this group," he said. "That said, my money is on an uncontested landing and a swift breach of the house. With four helicopters dropping on their head out of nowhere, I don't expect any resistance."

A high-pitched, slowly building mechanical whine interrupted the team leader's response, drawing their attention to the four helicopters on the baking tarmac outside the hangar. The rotors rotated slowly at first, building speed as they watched. Reeves gave his gear a perfunctory check before leading the SWAT team out of the hangar. As the agents formed up just outside the rotor arcs of their assigned helicopters, his earpiece chirped.

"Ground convoy departing," said Kincaid.

Reeves glanced over his shoulder at the multicolored line of heavy SUVs speeding toward the Desert Center Airport access road. They'd hit the interstate in two minutes, headed west toward the Red Cloud Mine Road exit. He triggered the push-to-talk switch mounted to his tactical vest.

"Let me know when you reach the point of no return," said Reeves. "I'm going to coordinate our times on target as closely as possible without tipping our hand."

The point of no return was a mathematically derived location six miles northwest of the target house on a hard-packed jeep trail that led straight to the Russians. It represented the first point at which a relatively sharp Bratva lookout, stationed with binoculars on the roof of the one-story house, could detect an inbound vehicle. Actually, the calculated distance was 5.7 miles, but since they couldn't possibly know the real height of the lookout, Reeves had added a small buffer—just in case they put an Andre the Giant–size guy on the roof.

Ideally, the air and ground assault teams would arrive simultaneously, thrusting an obviously superior force in the Bratva's face and discouraging any rash decisions, but he didn't have that option in this case. Waiting for Kincaid's convoy to close the six-mile gap before he landed would squander the element of surprise. Reeves had to drop down on the Russians like a hammer from the sky to prevent a replay of the Alamo.

A gunfight at the target house meant casualties—kids and agents down. Reeves couldn't ultimately control how the Russians reacted, but he could try to stack the deck in favor of a swift, bloodless raid. He wished there were a safer way to nail Drozdov, but he needed to indisputably connect the Russian to the Solntsevskaya Bratva's human-trafficking business.

Grabbing Drozdov at one of the organization's remotest human-trafficking hubs, where he'd have no plausible explanation for his presence, was Reeves's best shot at dismantling the Russians' decades-long stranglehold on the human-trafficking business in California.

Two massive leadership upheavals within a year would send the organization reeling. One had almost been enough. The sudden decapitation of the Bratva's West Coast leadership last summer had left the Russians scrambling. With no explanation for the near simultaneous deaths of Penkin and his top enforcer, the remaining street bosses kept their distance from each other, unsure who had pulled the trigger.

None of them wanted to jump in and seize control if their *Pakhan*, or supreme authority, had ordered the double hit. A move like that could add to the body count, continuing until the Pakhan was satisfied that the message had been clearly received.

While they waited for directions from above, each boss prepared for war, in case the killings had been the start of an internal coup. Extremely lucrative, high-level positions like these could be a once-in-a-lifetime opportunity within Solntsevskaya Bratva. The short delay gave their Pakhan a chance to fill the void with one of his most trusted associates—before a costly, unexpected war erupted.

Ruslan Drozdov, a Solntsevskaya plank owner, stepped off a private jet at the Bob Hope Airport less than forty-eight hours after Penkin disappeared. He was immediately whisked away by a small army of muscle that had poured into the Los Angeles area ahead of Drozdov, to ensure that his appointment went uncontested. Within a week, the Bratva's West Coast operation had fully recovered, now led by one of the most notorious *mafiya* bosses to operate within the United States.

With any luck, his reign would come to a bloodless end in the next thirty minutes.

CHAPTER SEVEN

Decker closed his eyes and isolated the different sounds reaching him. A light wind whistled faintly, dragging thin tendrils of sand and dust over the edge of the arroyo. Maybe he had just imagined it, knowing that the helicopters were out there. He kept his eyes shut a few more seconds, about to open them when a barely audible, rhythmic thumping reached him. Just a few deep beats—fading away as quickly as they arrived. His satellite phone buzzed.

"You heard it?" said Decker.

"No mistake that time," said Pierce.

"I'll give Reeves a call. Switch to Motorolas for primary comms."

"Copy that. Switching to radio," said Pierce.

He scrolled through the preset list on his sat phone and dialed Reeves, who answered before Decker had retracted his finger from the phone.

"What's wrong?" said Reeves, barely audible over the whine of the helicopter's engines. "The convoy should still be out of sight, unless you're standing up."

Very annoying. Reeves had beaten them over the head with his calculations, which Decker appreciated as a former team leader—to a degree. The FBI agent had taken it to a whole new level.

"The convoy is still out of sight," said Decker. "But I can hear the helicopters."

"You shouldn't be able to hear us," said Reeves. "The pilots were pretty adamant about detection distances."

"Yeah. Well. They spend most of their time inside the helicopters and don't have a lot of experience from the ground," said Decker. "Pierce and I both heard very faint rotor chop. You need to pull them back a few miles."

"Affirmative. We'll open the distance," said Reeves. "Any movement at the house?"

"Negative. My guess is they'll get a call once Drozdov's convoy is a few minutes out. It's very important that they don't hear helicopters when they come outside to greet him."

"Message received, Decker. We'll back off," said Reeves. "You know you're relentless, right?"

"*I'm* relentless?" said Decker, catching some static in his other ear.

"Target convoy spotted," said Pierce over the radio net.

"Copy target convoy spotted. ETA three minutes or less," said Decker. "Did you get that, Reeves?"

"Got it," said Reeves. "Next call is the big one."

"Move those helicopters," said Decker. "The front door just opened."

Reeves disconnected the call without a response.

"Movement. Front door. Targets remain in the house," said Decker, triggering his radio.

"I hate this part," said Pierce.

"You always say that."

"Makes me feel better."

"Movement. Rooftop," said Decker, shifting his binoculars to the roof. "Must have climbed up from the back of the house."

"I wish we had eyes back there," said Pierce.

So did Decker, but it was just the two of them out here, and the only way they could hope to ID Drozdov was to take widely spaced positions in front of the house. When Drozdov got out of his vehicle, one of them would have fewer than ten seconds to make the identification, depending on which side he exited. Decker didn't want to think about the possibility of the convoy proceeding around the back of the house. Intelligence indicated that the SUVs parked in a line facing the house, with Drozdov's vehicle directly in front of the front door.

A man dressed in jeans and a black T-shirt—tattoos covering his arms, neck, and face—straddled the roof's shallow ridge and started looking in the direction of the approaching convoy with binoculars. Decker focused on the rifle slung over the man's back for a few moments. Not good. The lookout appeared to be armed with one of the Russian Federation's latest-generation sniper rifles.

"Rooftop observer scanning the convoy with binoculars," said Decker. "Looks to be armed with a T-5000."

"I don't like that at all," said Pierce. "They wouldn't put a rifle like that in just anybody's hands."

"I agree," said Decker, pressing his body into the hard ground to present as little of his head and binoculars as possible to the presumed sniper.

The faint thumping of helicopter rotors washed over him again. He centered the binoculars' field of view on the sniper's face, detecting no change in the man's behavior.

"They're going to blow this," said Pierce.

"The lookout didn't seem to notice," said Decker.

"This time," said Pierce.

"The whole thing will be over in a few minutes," said Decker, pulling his rifle a little closer to the top of the arroyo. *One way or the other.*

Three heavily armed, serious-looking men walked through the front doorway and formed a loose perimeter around the concrete-block stoop. One of them talked into a handheld radio, spurring the rooftop sniper to remove the radio attached to his belt and respond. Decker could hear the vehicles now, a faint rumbling behind him.

"Three targets just stepped outside, sporting some serious hardware," said Decker. "They're talking to the rooftop lookout."

"Convoy is less than a minute out," said Pierce. "Time to earn our paycheck."

"We're getting paid?"

"Funny," said Pierce. "Keep an eye on that sniper."

"Yep," said Decker, and the frequency went quiet.

Mindful of the sniper, Decker inched his body up a little farther to ensure a full view of the ground in front of the house. He trained his binoculars on the space soon to be occupied with SUVs, frequently tilting the powerful optics upward far enough to confirm that the sniper rifle still hung on the lookout's shoulders. Any change to that posture indicated a problem—mostly for Decker and Pierce.

The deep hum of powerful vehicle engines crescendoed, joined by a discordance of crackling rocks, as the four-SUV convoy sped past Decker's left side and barreled toward the house. He took another quick look at the sniper, confirming that he posed no immediate threat, before turning all his attention to the convoy's arrival.

The SUVs skidded to a halt in front of the house, fanning out into a tightly spaced line. Most of the car doors opened before the vehicles had come to a complete stop. Instinct told Decker that Drozdov would be one of the last to get out. Even at a presumably secure site in the middle of nowhere, the crime boss would take precautions. That's how you survived for as long as Drozdov had in the Solntsevskaya Bratva.

His instinct proved correct. Four of Drozdov's dozen or so bodyguards broke free from the line of vehicles and brushed past the three men standing guard outside the front door, compact assault rifles ready. They emerged ten seconds later with their weapons pointed downward, one of them nodding at the vehicle directly in front of the door. *The moment of truth.*

A pair of legs swung out of the SUV's door, followed immediately by a short, wiry man with thick black hair and a tight goatee. *Bingo.*

Decker stared at the man for a few seconds just to be sure—but there was no mistaking Ruslan Drozdov.

"I have Konstantin Trukhin exiting the SUV on my side," said Pierce. "Please tell me they didn't send him instead of the big kahuna."

Trukhin was Drozdov's second in command, one of his most trusted *Bratok*, or crime lieutenants. Instead of promoting one of Penkin's Los Angeles–area Bratok, he'd brought his own from the East Coast. Trukhin had come up the ranks with Drozdov, reportedly paving Drozdov's way to the top of the US organization with bodies. Bringing him west was a not-so-subtle message to Penkin's men. Bringing him to this house was about the biggest mistake Drozdov could make.

"The big kahuna just stepped out of the SUV on my side," said Decker. "Number one and two in the same place. I hope Reeves is strapped in for my call. Keep an eye on the situation."

"Got it."

Decker slid out of sight and took the sat phone out of his vest pocket, immediately dialing Reeves.

"Please give me some good news," said the FBI agent.

"Drozdov is here," said Decker. "Along with Trukhin."

"You're kidding me," said Reeves. "Hold on a second."

Reeves yelled over the helicopter racket, instructing the pilot to turn toward the target house.

"We're inbound. Time on target is roughly two minutes," said Reeves.

"The Bratva can't sustain another one-two punch," said Decker. "This is going to be huge."

"Are you one hundred percent on the IDs?" said Reeves.

"Nothing's one hundred percent," said Decker. "Could be two body doubles."

"Funny," said Reeves. "Observe the target house and report any changes."

"We're not going anywhere," said Decker. "By the way, their roof-top lookout is armed with a T-5000. Latest generation—"

"Sniper rifle," interrupted Reeves. "I'm familiar with it. Any other significant hardware?"

"Lots of assault rifles."

"Let me know right away if you see anything heavier."

"Copy that," said Decker, his confidence in the operation suddenly waning.

The numbers bothered him. The Russian convoy had delivered close to sixteen heavily armed men to the target house, raising the total count to around twenty-four—a formidable threat under the best of circumstances. Reeves's helicopter assault team was comprised of the same number, and they'd be operating without cover or concealment the moment they set foot on the ground.

Decker edged his way back up the rise and settled in behind his rifle, scanning the house through its scope. The front door was closed, and most of the Russians had disappeared inside. He counted a total of five men standing around the door stoop, none of them looking particularly vigilant. The sniper seated on the rooftop looked similarly relaxed, taking a long drink from what looked like a metal flask. Maybe he had overreacted.

A few moments later, the distant echo of helicopter rotors confirmed that he hadn't.

CHAPTER EIGHT

The rooftop sniper reacted immediately, speaking excitedly into the handheld radio. A few seconds later, he unslung his rifle and shouldered it to scan the horizon. The Russian should have stuck with the binoculars. The rifle scope's field of view was too narrow for a 360-degree search, and there was no way to determine the direction of the helicopter sounds until it was too late. The simple decision gave Decker hope that the man wasn't very well trained. The last thing they needed right now was a competent sniper.

"Sniper is active," said Decker into the radio. "Watch yourself."

"Copy. The security team just ran inside—and the front door is still open," said Pierce. "I predict a mass exodus very shortly."

"That's not good," said Decker.

"The FBI ground team will grab them before they get too far," said Pierce.

"Drozdov and Trukhin can't be three miles away from the target house when the helicopters arrive. They need to be in the house or right outside so there's no squirming out of this in court."

"Should we warn Reeves?" said Pierce.

"Drozdov isn't getting away," said Decker, shifting his aim from the sniper to the SUV Drozdov had arrived in. "Start shooting out the tires. Work left to right. I'll hit Drozdov's vehicle."

"Dammit, Decker. Reeves was very clear—" started Pierce.

The rifle bit into Decker's shoulder, flattening the rear right tire of Drozdov's SUV.

"I better not go to jail for this."

"We were never here. Remember?" said Decker, taking out the other rear tire with a single shot. "Flat tires are part of life in a place like this."

"As long as we stick to flat tires," said Pierce.

Decker hit the partially obscured right front tire next, firing two shots to be certain. At this angle, he couldn't see the left front tire, so he moved on to the next SUV, disabling it before any of the security detail rushed out of the house.

"Watch the door," said Decker, quickly reacquiring the rooftop sniper with his scope.

The sniper had correctly guessed the threat axis and had taken cover behind the top of the roof, leaving Decker with little more than a head to target. The man slowly panned his rifle left, toward Pierce.

"Brad. Take cover right now," said Decker, placing the tip of the ACOG scope's red reticle a few notches to the right of the sniper's head.

"Do not engage the sniper," said Pierce.

"That's up to him," said Decker, pressing the trigger.

The sniper flinched, instinctively glancing upward, searching the empty sky for a bullet that was long gone. Definitely not well trained. Decker shifted his aim to the other side of his head—and sent another bullet downrange. The man ducked below the rooftop a moment later.

"You're clear," he said to Pierce.

"I'm not even going to ask," said Pierce.

"My guess is he won't be a problem."

To ensure that message was received crystal clearly, he shifted the scope reticle to a point directly above the man's last known position and fired again, the bullet clipping the top of the roof and knocking a shingle into the air. If the sniper showed his face after that, Decker would have little choice but to remove it.

"Any sign of Drozdov?" said Decker, keeping his scope aimed at the rooftop.

"Negative," said Pierce. "The door is still wide-open."

"I think we effectively discouraged any escape attempt," said Decker.

"I don't know," said Pierce. "If I were Drozdov, I'd still get in one of those SUVs. Any distance away from the house is better than no distance."

Pierce was right. It still made sense for Drozdov to get as far away from the kidnapped children as possible, even if it meant shambling down a dirt road on three flat tires at five miles per hour. As the deep, rhythmic song of the approaching helicopters continued to strengthen, time was running out for the Russians. If they planned on making a run for it, they'd do it shortly.

"Cover the rooftop," said Decker. "I'll make sure they don't go anywhere."

"In for a penny," said Pierce. "Rooftop is covered."

Decker centered his scope's reticle on the back of Drozdov's SUV and considered peppering the vehicle with the rest of the rifle's magazine. No. The tires would be hard enough for Reeves to explain. He needed something less obvious to forensics experts, but just as impactful. His options were limited, and the clock was ticking. The helicopters sounded like they were thirty seconds out. He caught some motion in the doorway, deeper inside.

"Fuck it," he muttered, moving the tip of the reticle to the door's upper right jamb.

He pressed the trigger slowly, letting the recoil surprise him. At this distance, Decker couldn't see the bullet's entry point. The 5.56-millimeter projectile barely measured wider than a pencil eraser. The exit point could be an entirely different story. He just hoped that the door casing's thick wood had stopped the bullet or slowed it down enough to prevent overpenetration. His goal was to dissuade anyone from rushing out the door until the FBI arrived.

The doorway remained empty as the helicopter rotor sounds grew louder by the second. A pair of outstretched, empty hands emerged from the shadows; Decker unconsciously shifted his aim and applied a few pounds of pressure to the trigger. When Drozdov stepped into full view, raising his hands over his head, Decker removed his finger from the trigger well. The Bratva was finished.

CHAPTER NINE

Reeves hopped down from the helicopter and drew his pistol, keeping it aimed at the huge gaggle of dust-swept Russians, as he ran with his agents toward them. Rotor wash from the two helicopters that landed in front of the house pelted the back of his neck with tiny rocks, launching dead scrub and debris past him at the surrendered crowd.

He absorbed the inexplicable and completely unexpected scene. Close to two dozen unarmed Russians stood in a cluster in front of the four SUVs, hands high in the air and heads turned to protect their faces from the artificial dust storm. What the hell was going on here?

"Back door. What's your status?" said Reeves, triggering his radio.

"Negative contact. Back and sides are clear," said the lead agent, who'd been dropped off behind the house. "Moving to breach."

"Proceed with breach. I want those kids on the helicopters and out of here in five minutes," said Reeves. "Be advised. Most—if not all—of the Russians appear to have surrendered. I have about twenty military-aged males in front of the house."

"Request permission to skip the explosive breach," said the agent. "I'd hate to hurt one of those kids."

"Good call," said Reeves. "Let me know when you're in."

He slowed his pace about twenty feet from the Russians and holstered his pistol, letting the SWAT team leader deploy the twelve agents in a "hasty 180," or semicircle, around the Bratva crew. With the agents in place, rifles at the ready, Reeves moved forward, scanning the crowd for his prize. Drozdov worked his way to the front of the pack, as if he'd read his mind.

"Agent Reeves!" said Drozdov, lowering his hands to shoulder height and holding them forward—like he might be contemplating a hug. "Thank God you're here."

Here we go. He couldn't wait to hear Drozdov's spin on the situation.

"I learned about this place just the other day," said Drozdov. "Got out here as fast as I could to see it with my own eyes. Unbelievable what's happening here. I put a quick end to it."

Reeves made it clear that they wouldn't be hugging by placing his hand on top of his pistol.

"Hands over your head," said Reeves, staring into Drozdov's lifeless, ice-blue eyes. "Stay right where you are."

The Russian's faux smile dissolved, the thin veneer replaced by the murderous stare that had earned him his position as one of the Bratva's top executioners.

"Back door. What are you seeing?" said Reeves into his radio mic, his eyes searching the crowd for Trukhin.

"The kids are secure. Eleven total. We're searching them for surprises before we load them on the helicopters," said the agent. "I also have a stack of rifles in the foyer—and four men tied to chairs in the kitchen. Beaten senseless. The blood is fresh."

"Copy that," said Reeves. "Get the kids out of here and form a perimeter in back with the remaining team. The ground convoy should be here shortly with the EOD detachment."

"Kids are on the move," said the agent.

Reeves shielded his eyes with one hand and signaled the helicopters behind him to take off with the other. When the dust started to settle, the helicopters fading in the distance, he beckoned Drozdov. The Russian took several steps forward, stopping when Reeves held up a hand.

"On your knees," said Reeves. "Cross your legs and place your hands on your head."

"Is this really necessary?" said Drozdov. "I'm the hero here. I saved those kids."

Reeves didn't take the bait. He had no intention of engaging him on any level outside of his official capacity as an FBI agent.

"Ruslan Drozdov. You have the right to remain silent. Anything you say can be used against you in a court of law—"

"Yeah. I'm familiar with your Miranda garbage," said Drozdov.

Reeves closed the distance to Drozdov with lightning speed, grabbing the Russian's thick black hair and yanking him violently off balance. The crime boss dropped to his knees, but Reeves pulled again, slamming him face-first into the ground. While the closest agents helped him zip-tie the Russian, he continued with the Miranda warning.

"You have the right to have a lawyer present during questioning. If you can't afford a lawyer, one will be appointed for you."

"My lawyer is going to bend you over and—"

Reeves pressed his boot against the side of Drozdov's face, muffling the obscene threat.

"I highly suggest you shut up," said Reeves, easing the pressure on his face. "It's no coincidence that we showed up at the same time you did."

"None of this will stick," said Drozdov. "You'll see."

"My money is on the kids' testimony," said Reeves. "I'm sure a few of your colleagues here will have something to add as well. Maybe Trukhin?"

Drozdov stiffened at the name.

"Then again. What are your chances of surviving an extended period in custody?" said Reeves. "I'm sure the big boss won't be happy to find out that his number one and two men out in LA got caught at one of his kiddie houses."

Reeves stepped back and took it all in. He still couldn't believe it. The Russians had been tied up with a bow when they landed—like a present. Drozdov was smart enough to know that surrender was his best option, but Reeves had expected some kind of standoff. That was the Russian way. They rarely made things easy for law enforcement, even when it was in their best interest. He had fully expected them to barricade themselves inside the house or make a run for it when they heard the helicopters. Either way, Reeves had anticipated a long, excruciating day in the sun.

Now, barring any unforeseen complications with the house, they could be back at headquarters in a few hours, the Bratva's West Coast leadership in lockup. Not a bad day's work at all. As the FBI ground convoy approached the house, Reeves noticed something he'd missed with all the dust flying around. The rear tires on all the Russian SUVs were flat. Interesting. He turned and scanned the horizon past the arriving FBI vehicles, searching in vain. His sat phone buzzed a moment later, a message appearing on the touch screen. He shook his head slowly, unable to suppress the grin he knew his audience would hold against him.

You're welcome. When can we go home?

He typed a quick response.

Not until we're gone. A few hours.

More like nightfall, or later. Forensics would be out here for a while.

Hurry the fuck up, please. Good job grinding Drozdov's face in the dirt. Worth the price of admission.

He was once again in debt to Decker.

Chapter Ten

Senator Margaret Steele's flats clicked against the marble floor as she passed one darkened office after another. Invariably, she was one of the first senators to show up in the Hart Senate Office Building every morning when the Senate was in session. Continuing down the hallway, she nodded congenially at a few of her colleagues' staff members, who scurried to their respective bosses' offices with grease-stained fast food bags and oversize cups of coffee.

After a quick ride in an empty elevator, she reached the clear glass double doors of her brightly lit Senate office. The two desks visible just beyond the doors were empty, the bulk of her staff not expected to arrive for another hour. Deep within her office, her chief of staff was already hard at work, despite the senator's daily protest. She didn't expect Julie to beat her in to the office, especially since it was the senator's habit to arrive excessively early.

A number of months after her daughter's and husband's untimely deaths, Senator Steele made a pact with herself to outlive every one of her contemporaries and set a record for age in the Senate. Since she still had quite a way to go—fifty-three years to beat Strom Thurmond, whose barely responsive corpse was wheeled onto the Senate floor until he was one hundred—Steele had begun a strict regimen of exercise commencing at four in the morning.

After an hour of cardio, followed by fifteen minutes of calisthenics, in her home gym, she left her Georgetown brownstone at six sharp, long before the vast majority of the city started moving. Twenty minutes later, she arrived in her office to find Julie Ragan wading knee-deep through whatever had landed in the office overnight, or over the weekend in this case. Despite being "in session," she'd given most of her staff the weekend off. Nothing urgent had demanded their attention by Friday's end.

Senator Steele placed her SecureID against the card reader and opened the door after hearing the telltale click. The smell of strong coffee drew her through the thick wooden door to the right of the empty desks—into the heart of her Senate office.

"Julie?"

"In the conference room. You need to see this," said her chief of staff.

She picked up the pace, walking briskly past several dark offices until the hallway opened into a spacious, luxuriously appointed conference room. Julie sat in the middle of one of the long sides, her laptop open and a dozen or more stacks of neatly arranged files in front of her. It looked like she'd been here for the better part of an hour. As if reading her mind, Julie glanced up from the laptop.

"I got here about ten minutes ago," she said.

"Uh-huh," said Steele, placing her leather tote on the conference table. "What do you need me to see? Should I grab coffee first?"

"Maybe something stronger," said Julie, turning her screen to face the senator.

"That bad?"

"I don't know," said Julie. "There was an incident at the border this weekend. Saturday night. Actually, it was more than just an incident. Two Border Patrol agents were presumably killed in an explosion—or some kind of ambush."

"An ambush?" said Steele. "Nothing but bad news from the border lately."

"It gets worse."

"I can't see how."

"It does," said Julie.

"Wait. Why are we getting this? I mean, it's big news, but I stepped down from the Subcommittee on Border Security and Immigration over a year ago."

"Right before contact was lost with the Border Patrol agents, they reported stumbling upon five teenagers—barefoot and in their underwear."

"Could be migrants separated from their parents," said Steele, skeptically.

"The agent calling it in, identified as Salvador Contreras, mentioned a human-trafficking camp," said Julie.

That answered her initial question. As head of the Senate Judiciary Committee's Subcommittee on Human Trafficking, the report had been flagged and delivered to her office.

"He actually said that in a radio transmission?" said Steele.

"Yes. But the transcript is short. Apparently, the transmission was cut off—possibly due to an apparent ambush or explosion," said Julie. "A nearby Border Patrol team also experienced trouble with their primary radio."

"Some kind of jamming?" said Steele.

"The report doesn't speculate on that," said Julie.

"Did they find the kids?" said Steele.

"No. And the two agents are still missing," said Julie. "They found the Border Patrol vehicle near the suspected entrance to a bunker."

"Suspected?"

"Take a look at the picture," said Julie, opening one of the report's attachments.

There wasn't much to look at. Most of the SUV had been consumed by the same explosion that must have destroyed the bunker. The twisted, blackened vehicle chassis sat in front of a tangle of partially buried and splintered logs.

"No bodies at all?" said Steele.

"None mentioned in the report," said Julie.

"They didn't dig any out of the suspected bunker?"

Julie scrolled through the pages for several seconds.

"Interesting. The entrance is on the US side, but most of the collapsed structure is on the Mexico side," said Julie. "The report doesn't mention any excavation efforts."

"Something doesn't add up," said Steele.

"Nothing adds up," said Julie. "I can see the two agents finding the bunker door and going inside to investigate. Maybe they set off a trap that blew the place up, or the cartel blew it up to conceal its purpose."

"They wouldn't blow up a drug-smuggling tunnel," said Steele. "We find those all the time. They just dig three more. If the Sinaloa intentionally blew up their own tunnel, along with two federal agents—there's way more to this than drugs."

"The kids," said Julie. "Maybe the cartel has finally expanded into human trafficking. It was only a matter of time."

Steele shook her head in disgust, and with a tinge of doubt. Today's cartels and their less organized predecessors had been smuggling drugs across the US-Mexico border for more than a half century, and despite some tumultuously violent periods, the cartels were careful not to push US lawmakers and the American public too far. She hated to admit it, but the war on drugs had dragged on for so long, most Americans were numb to it—the new status quo that the cartels worked hard to maintain.

Intentional cartel violence north of the border was almost unheard of, and violence in the Mexican border towns rarely claimed American lives. State Department travel warnings highlighted the ongoing, brutal war between the cartels south of the border, but the threat to tourists was nearly nonexistent. The last thing the drug lords wanted was to energize and outrage their customers.

They'd even started to take precautions with their latest money-maker, migrant smuggling. The days of finding padlocked, abandoned cargo trucks filled with dead or dying border crossers had mostly passed. It still happened, but not frequently enough to stir the kind of outrage north of the border that could make life difficult for the cartel bosses.

The senator had a hard time imagining that the cartels had graduated from human smuggling to trafficking, but the circumstances surrounding this incident strongly suggested it was possible. Why else would they bury that tunnel complex under several tons of rock and dirt? Whatever the reason, they'd made a calculated decision that the fallout from the murder of two Border Patrol agents was preferable to a search of the tunnels by US authorities.

One thing was certain. If she discovered that the cartels had brought human trafficking to the United States, she'd make it her mission to take them down.

"I'm sure Customs and Border Protection is on the scene with its full investigative might, but I'd like to augment their efforts in any way we can," said Steele. "Specifically, I'd like to send a team to sniff around. There's definitely more to this story."

"That's going to be difficult," said Julie.

"What do you mean?"

"CBP isn't running the investigation. Department of Defense has authority," she muttered, pointing at the document on her screen. "Damn. I missed that on my first read-through. The incident took place in a military exclusion zone on the border."

"Two Border Patrol agents wandered into a military exclusion zone?" said Steele.

Julie shrugged. "Another thing that doesn't add up."

"How long has the exclusion zone been active?"

"Doesn't say," said Julie. "You know how they are about that stuff."

"Need-to-know basis. Even for me," said Steele. "Especially for me."

Senator Steele's reception by Pentagon leadership was best described as frosty, if not borderline hostile. For the past several years, she'd been critical of proposed military budget increases, citing their staggering impact on the federal deficit—not to mention inflation and the requisite shifting of funds away from domestic programs.

To cap it all off, she'd not only triggered but also driven Aegis Global's meltdown after discovering Gerald Frist and Jacob Harcourt's stunning betrayal last year. Aegis's financial influence turned out to be more pervasive around town than she'd initially guessed—the corporation's tentacles wrapped tightly around DC's power brokers. These Beltway bandits thrived on the military-industrial complex, fueling another layer of subtle, unspoken disdain.

She didn't care what they thought. So far, her outspoken work on several other high-profile committees had kept her from losing the seat, though the margins in last year's vote had noticeably contracted.

"I can start working my contacts," said Julie. "Call in a few favors. This is too important to get swallowed by the Pentagon swamp."

Steele nodded. "You do that, and I'll reach out to Paul Duncan. The military exclusion zone specifics undoubtedly crossed his desk at some point."

CHAPTER ELEVEN

Congressman Bob Saling waved off his assistant and scurried down the hallway before the rest of the working group emerged. Two days of intense negotiations, marginally edible food, and subpar hotel accommodations had left him yearning for the flight back to DC, even if it meant flying economy class out of Yuma. If he never saw El Centro again in his life, he'd die a happy man. Happier at least.

When he reached the far end of the hallway, he ducked into a side corridor and dialed Senator Paul Duncan, the man who had sent him on this unsavory but necessary task.

"How did it go?"

"A regular goat rope. But I think I managed to kick the can down the road for now," said Saling in a thick Texas drawl.

"How far down the road?" said Duncan.

"All the way to Me-hi-co," said Saling. "Since it appears that the vast majority of the underground structure lies south of the border, it only seemed appropriate to involve the Mexican government."

"And Homeland didn't grumble?"

"Oh, they grumbled," said Saling. "But I convinced our friends at Fort Bliss to let US Customs and Border Protection investigators take possession of the missing agents' vehicle."

"That makes me nervous," said Duncan.

"Me, too. But the Joint Task Force North folks didn't balk at the suggestion," said Saling. "If anyone should be nervous, it's them."

"I saw the pictures. Can't imagine CBP discovering anything useful."

"That seems to be the general consensus," said Saling. "CBP didn't walk away happy, but I think this bought JTF North some goodwill."

"I don't care about goodwill," said Duncan. "We need time."

"All the same, from what I could tell," said Saling. "I got a tour of the site this morning. What the hell were they thinking? Looks like they detonated one of those mother of all bombs out there."

"They needed to bury stuff—fast."

"Yeah. Well. They certainly accomplished the mission," said Saling. "Question now is how the hell are they gonna dig it all up and get rid of it for good? JTF North can't hold on to this stretch of border forever."

"I'm sure they have a plan, which will no doubt involve their Mexican friends to the south," said Duncan.

"It ain't exactly hospitable terrain—on either side of the wall," said Saling. "I think they got nervous and screwed the pooch on this one. The ambush was a total shit show, but this is something else. Kind of makes you wonder about the folks calling the shots out there."

"I voiced those concerns with McCall," said Duncan. "The team sitting on the bunker had to weigh a lot of factors in a very short span of time. The operation is in good hands."

"Trigger-happy hands," said Saling, peeking around the corner at the gaggle of uniformed men and women who had spilled into the hallway. "Not to mention the other small oversight. Is it safe to say that the other sites have been cleaned up?"

"No kids at the other locations," said Duncan. "McCall confirmed that with Jupiter."

"I guess we have to trust what he says," said Saling. "What were the *Mexi-cans* thinking?"

"Nobody knows. They were buried along with everything else," said Duncan. "Everything has run very smoothly until now. We were due for a hiccup."

"More like a projectile vomiting," said Saling.

"We might have one more *little* hitch to deal with."

"*Little* sounds awfully big right now," said Saling.

"Margaret Steele called this morning, fishing for information about the incident."

"Senator Steele? Why the hell—of course. The kids," said Saling, remembering that she chaired the Senate Subcommittee on Human Trafficking.

As head of the House Judiciary Committee's Subcommittee on Border Security and Immigration, Saling had crossed paths with her a number of times, always ending on a congenial note. They both sought the most updated intelligence regarding Mexican cartel activity along the border. Senate and House committees rarely worked directly together, but they frequently shared information and sometimes attended each other's hearings.

"She can be persistent," said Duncan. "But I think I steered her clear of this mess. I shared what I have, which is more than she had."

"And that was good enough?"

"Nothing's good enough for her when it comes to this kind of thing."

"I have a little hole in my retirement portfolio to remind me," said Saling.

"Her hands are pretty much tied on this one," said Duncan. "She doesn't have many friends in the Pentagon. I'll keep passing along whatever information my committee receives—to prevent her from having a meltdown."

"Have our friends at JTF North been notified?" said Saling. "I can pull Colonel Souza aside before I skedaddle."

"Probably not the best idea. CBP and Homeland might think you're playing favorites," said Duncan. "I'll get in touch with McCall directly. JUPITER needs to make sure the cartels maintain a lower profile."

"Works for me," said Saling. "I'll make my farewells and get the hell out of here."

"You don't like El Centro?"

He couldn't tell whether Duncan was serious or sarcastic.

"Have you been here?" he said.

"God, no. I hate the desert," said Duncan. "I have no idea why anyone would choose to live like that."

"Neither do I," said Saling.

Duncan chuckled.

"What?" said Saling.

"Isn't your entire congressional district a desert?"

"Pretty much, but there's one big difference," said Saling, waiting for Duncan to respond.

"I'll take the bait. What's the difference?"

"It's Texas," said Saling. "And everything's better in Texas."

"Don't you mean bigger?"

"That, too," he said, glancing around the corner again. "I gotta run and say adios to some folks."

"Handshake and a smile, Bob. Doesn't take much to keep them happy. Handshake and a smile."

"And a promise to support the next CBP budget increase."

"If everyone plays their cards right, that'll be out of our hands," said Duncan, ending the call.

I sure as hell hope he's right. With the final phase of Southern Cross set to commence in less than a month, the incident's timing couldn't be worse. Operation Southern Cross had always been a bit of a stretch, in his opinion, but he'd deemed the payoff to be worth the minimal risk of exposure they'd each incurred.

Duncan chaired the Senate's version of the Subcommittee on Border Security and Immigration. Together, they had gently guided their respective committees to support Joint Task Force North's smokescreen request to test new infiltration-detection equipment at a few unobtrusive, remote locations along the border. Nothing that might alarm a public predisposed against domestic militarization—until it was too late.

Saling took a moment to put on his meet-and-greet face before stepping out of the side corridor to put a few more finishing touches on the critical damage-control job he'd been sent to chaperone. All because some idiot desk jockey mistakenly put two newbies together in a sensitive patrol zone—and because the Jalisco New Generation Cartel apparently didn't have a shred of decency. He just hoped JUPITER took this seriously. Another screwup like this would cost them everything.

CHAPTER TWELVE

A persistent knock on his apartment door broke through the deep slumber. *What the hell time is it?* The light peeking through the blinds didn't give him any indication, but he figured it had to be late in the afternoon. He'd set his alarm for five to make sure Pierce made his nine o'clock flight back to Colorado. The airport was barely more than ten miles away, but the trip could take close to two hours at this time of day.

Decker turned his head, still mostly buried in the pillow, and squinted at the alarm clock beyond his pistol and phone. Three twenty-two p.m.? He put the pillow over his head and prayed the uninvited interruption went away. To say he was exhausted would be a gross understatement.

Harlow had dropped Brad and him off at Decker's apartment around midnight after picking them up at a prearranged roadside GPS coordinate several miles away from the Bratva site. Reeves had been wrong about the timeline. The FBI forensics crew was still at work inside the house at sunset, and Decker had no intention of fighting off tarantulas and scorpions for a fourth night. They'd slipped away from their observation posts about an hour after the sun went down.

The seven-mile forced march to the rendezvous point took two and a half bumbling hours in the darkness, fueled by the promise of a bag full of In-N-Out Double-Doubles and cheese fries. The burgers were cold by the time they arrived but tasted heavenly, nonetheless. Same with the Diet Coke. Then again, Decker would have gladly eaten Taco Bell after spending three days slurping electrolytes and nibbling energy bars.

The knocking stopped, and for the briefest of moments, he thought they were off the hook. Decker couldn't have made it clearer to Harlow that he had no interest in "doing brunch" to celebrate. He could barely walk up the stairs to his apartment last night. His phone started buzzing a few seconds later. *She's relentless.* He grabbed the phone and rolled onto his back, still feeling the rocks that had dug into him in the desert.

"Happy hour is out of the question," said Decker, putting the call on speaker.

"Good afternoon to you, too!" said Harlow. "We have reservations for four. That gives you more than thirty minutes."

"Reservations for happy hour?"

"It's a little more than that," she said.

"Harlow. I'm serious," said Decker. "I can barely get out of bed, and I have to take Brad to the airport. How about happy hour tomorrow?"

"Brad won't be here tomorrow," she said. "It wouldn't be right to celebrate without him. Would it?"

"I'm sure he won't mind."

"I'm not going anywhere without the two of you," said Harlow.

He could tell by her tone that he wasn't going to win this one.

"Hold on. I'll let you in," said Decker, sliding out of bed onto the cool hardwood.

Decker searched for a pair of shorts or pants to pull over his skivvies but only found the same crusty desert-camouflage pants he'd worn on the mission. He'd apparently gone from the front door to his bed without any detours—including a shower. He pulled them on and grabbed a T-shirt from the laundry basket at the foot of the bed, wrestling it over his muscular frame. Halfway over his head, the shirt's pungent odor told him he'd also picked the same shirt that had clung to his body for the past four days. Too tired to sort out a wardrobe change in the dark, he made his way through the apartment, still trying to come up with an excuse to bail on Harlow's get-together.

He opened the door, immediately regretting his choice to recycle last night's outfit. The less-than-happy expression on Harlow's face confirmed his assessment. She was dressed in T-strap sandals, blue capri pants, and an off-white, cold-shoulder lace top, holding two coffees. Despite the annoyed glare, she somehow looked more amazing than usual.

"Wow. You slept in those clothes," she said, wrinkling her nose.

"You want to come in?" he said.

"As long as you haven't changed the bathroom policy, too," she said, handing him the coffees.

"Not that I recall," said Decker, backing into the apartment. "But that's no guarantee of anything. I honestly don't remember going to bed last night."

"Do you at least remember showering?" she said, heading toward the kitchen.

"He definitely took a pass on personal hygiene last night," said Brad Pierce, standing in the guest-room doorway in boxer shorts. "I called dibs on first shower when we got back, and that was the last I saw of him."

"You didn't call dibs. You literally pushed me and ran to the shower."

"I felt like I had sand mites or something in my underwear. I needed to—"

"TMI! The two of you are like children when you get together," interrupted Harlow. "And Brad? You're in your underwear."

"Oh. Sorry," he said, disappearing.

"At least I'm not in my underwear," said Decker.

Harlow examined him for a moment before shaking her head. "Actually, I'm not sure which is worse."

"I threw these on to answer the door," said Decker. "First thing I could find."

"Did you fire the housekeeper I arranged?"

"No. But I don't make her do laundry."

"I don't make my housekeeper do laundry, either. I pay her to do laundry. Pay her well, actually," said Harlow, glancing at her watch. "Shower time? The clock is ticking."

"It's up to Brad," said Decker, cringing at the obvious cop-out.

"What's up to me?" said the newly attired Pierce.

"A little get-together in Santa Monica with the crew," said Harlow. "We're celebrating yesterday's success."

"I don't know," said Pierce. "My flight's at nine."

"We'll get you to the airport with plenty of time to spare," said Harlow. "Do me a favor and say yes. We couldn't have done this without you."

"She's good," said Pierce.

"Too good," said Decker. "I'll be ready in ten minutes."

"Five. Skip the shave," she said. "I'll put together an acceptable outfit for you, if that's even possible."

He wasn't getting out of this, no matter how hard he tried.

"Relentless," muttered Decker.

"I'll take whatever you just said as a compliment," she said.

CHAPTER THIRTEEN

Harlow led the two reluctant but admittedly exhausted-looking men-children to the table she had reserved in a private, glass-enclosed atrium overlooking Santa Monica beach. The sound of boisterous laughter drifted through the double french doors separating the sun-drenched room from the main restaurant space. The crew was already a few drinks into happy hour. Decker heard Sophie's inimitable cackle and made a face.

"It won't be that bad," Harlow said, shaking her head. "Let loose and have a few drinks. Maybe even laugh a little."

"Just smiling is kind of a big ask right now," said Decker. "My lips are still cracked—from my three-and-a-half-day desert vacation."

"And I feel like I have bedsores from lying on the ground," added Pierce.

"Jesus. You two are a barrel of monkeys," she muttered, pulling one of the doors all the way open.

Hoots and hollers filled the room, nearly wiping the forced smiles off both of their faces. Harlow quickly closed the door behind them to keep the noise from disturbing the restaurant's other patrons—and to prevent Decker and Pierce from beating a hasty retreat. The pair looked miserable. Then the applause started, and she wondered if she might have to handcuff them to the table.

Katie Murphy stood up and pulled out the chair next to her. "I saved a seat for you, Decker!" she said a little too loudly.

He glanced at the two empty seats on the other side of the table, broadcasting his intentions. Harlow blocked him before he could claim the seats.

"Not so fast," she said. "I'm not letting the two of you sit together and sulk for the next hour. Decker sits between Katie and Sandra. Brad sits next to me so I can somewhat shield him from the madness."

"Works for me," said Pierce.

"Why don't I get a shield?" said Decker.

"Because you've been working with the team on a daily basis for the past year and can handle them," said Harlow. "Brad might need the help."

"They can't be that bad," said Pierce.

Harlow raised an eyebrow moments before Katie and Sandra pounded the table in front of Decker's reserved seat.

"Come on, Decker! We don't bite," said Katie. "At least I don't! Not sure about Sandy!"

The entire table broke into laughter, and Brad smiled for the first time that day.

"Better you than me," said Pierce, leaving Decker stranded.

Harlow nodded at the empty seat. "Might take a few drinks to catch up with them, Decker. Better get a move on."

Their waiter opened the door on cue, and Decker didn't skip a beat.

"Can I get a dirty vodka martini?"

"I'll have what he's having," said Harlow.

She could afford to unwind a little after the past few weeks. They all could, and judging by what she saw at the table, tomorrow was looking more and more like a day off for the entire firm.

The firm had a full load of ongoing cases, but with the exception of Jessica, their perpetually booked attorney, none of them *had* to be anywhere tomorrow. They had intentionally left the calendar clear of appointments and commitments for the next two weeks to accommodate a possible extension to the FBI operation. Given the rare opportunity to take some time off, she'd considered floating the idea of taking a trip down the Baja coast to Decker—and had just as quickly chickened out.

They'd spent a lot of time together over the past several months, on the job and off, but Harlow knew the time still wasn't right to step across the unspoken line they'd drawn between each other. Thankfully, it wasn't a friend-zone situation. Decker simply wasn't ready to let go of the past, and she couldn't blame him. Not after what he'd been through. She didn't expect him to ever fully let go, but so far, he'd barely shown any signs of pulling away.

Decker's long-distance relationship with his daughter, Riley, had further complicated matters. He spoke frequently with his daughter, the rift between them mostly repaired from what she could tell, but with Jacob Harcourt still at large, Riley had to remain in hiding—a decision neither of them relished.

He flew once a month to visit Riley, who stayed with his parents at a secure, isolated lakeside house in Idaho, always returning in an uplifted mood—only to nose-dive back to ground zero within a few hours. Decker wouldn't be truly happy until Riley was a permanent part of his life again, and that couldn't happen until someone put Harcourt into a coffin. A feat easier said than done.

In the aftermath of the attack on his estate, Jacob Harcourt had disappeared, along with a substantial chunk of Aegis Global's money. Government agency efforts to find him yielded nothing. Senator Steele's expensive private investigation came to the same conclusion. Harcourt had gone deep underground, taking Decker with him—and Harlow couldn't do anything about it right now.

She could see a future with him, somehow. They clicked brilliantly when hanging out together, but the emotional wall Decker had built was too high for her to climb, and even if she managed to get over it, a minefield of fear, grief, and regret waited on the other side. Harlow's instincts told her that Decker was worth the wait. His facade showed cracks. She'd seen *that look* from him enough times to know that she wasn't pining away on a lost cause.

Mercifully, the party hadn't taken a turn for the worse by the time Pierce's airport-run clock ran out. The well-timed arrival of their food, halfway through the hour, had significantly slowed the drinking and somewhat quieted the boisterous group, which didn't surprise her. Everyone was exhausted from three weeks of rotating day-and-night surveillance of the Solntsevskaya Bratva.

She got Decker's attention and tapped her watch—not a moment too soon. Two martinis had taken their toll. Despite the constant chatter around him, he looked like he was about to pass out in his seat. Same with Pierce. A few minutes later, after bowing out of the festivities, she walked an exhausted Decker and Pierce out of the restaurant and sat them down on a bench next to the restaurant's street-side entrance.

"Be right back with the car," she said.

A car door closed on the street behind her, eliciting a groan from Decker. She turned to see Supervisory Special Agent Joseph Reeves standing on the curb in leather sandals, pressed khaki shorts, and an untucked red button-down shirt.

"You look like you just stepped out of a J. Crew catalog," said Decker.

"You look like the dump my dog just took in the backyard," said Reeves, putting his hands on his hips.

Harlow couldn't help but laugh at Reeves's comment. Maybe it was the tiny bit of alcohol remaining in her system—more likely it was the gruff hilarity that ensued whenever Decker and Reeves occupied the same space.

"I'm too tired to think of a comeback," said Decker.

"And I'm completely neutral in all of this," said Pierce, neither of them moving to greet Reeves.

Reeves considered them for a moment. "Would either of you care to explain why nearly every Russian tire was flat when we got to the target house?" said Reeves.

"Seriously?" said Decker. "You're here to—"

"They all popped on the way in," said Pierce. "Craziest thing ever. Probably ran over a cactus patch or a bunch of nails left over from construction."

"That's what I guessed. I'll let the US attorney know that the quality of road was questionable, likely contributing to the dozen or more flat tires. You know, because we certainly didn't have anyone on the ground observing the house—armed with sniper rifles that I expressly prohibited."

"We certainly didn't," said Harlow.

Reeves approached their small group, the tense look normally stretched across his face slowly easing into a smile.

"Nice work out there," he said. "Aside from handing me Drozdov and his top lieutenant on a platter, we rescued nine kids from that house."

"All we did was sunbathe and drink electrolyte juice behind a pair of binoculars," said Decker. "Harlow's crew did the real work."

"The compliment was meant for Ms. Mackenzie," said Reeves, breaking into a full grin.

"It never ends with the two of you," said Harlow.

"Fortunately, we don't spend a lot of time together," said Decker.

"I think the word you're looking for is *thankfully*," said Reeves.

"See. He doesn't stop," said Decker.

"Yeah. It's all him," said Harlow, needing to move this little rendezvous along so she could get Pierce to the airport in time. "I assume you didn't drive out here on what appears to be a day off to hand out compliments?"

"Correct. Something urgent came up earlier this afternoon," said Reeves. "I didn't want to interrupt your party, so I thought I'd wait out here."

"I need to run Mr. Pierce to the airport right now. Is this something you could run by Decker really quick, and we could talk about later? Preferably tomorrow?"

Decker shot her a confused look and started to protest.

"Senator Steele insisted I reach out to you immediately. She needs a favor. A rather timely favor," said Reeves. "Mr. Pierce. Is there any way I could convince you to stick around a little longer? This is right up your alley."

"How long?" said Pierce.

"I'd say less than twenty-four hours if we start planning right now," said Reeves. "But given your current condition, after three days of extensive sunbathing, I'm thinking more like forty-eight. We could begin the planning phase tomorrow, midmorning, and have you back in town by the next morning. Maybe earlier."

"Can this be done without me?" said Pierce. "My wife won't be happy with a last-minute extension to an already overextended absence."

"The site is somewhat remote, about halfway between Tecate and Mexicali, on the US.-Mexico border," said Reeves. "Walk in. Walk out. No direct support. Rough terrain. Has to be done at night. Not much different than the last op."

"That's cartel country," added Decker.

"Correct. One of their prime migrant crossing spots," said Reeves.

"Anna's gonna kill me," said Pierce.

"Oh, I know the feeling," said Reeves. "My wife barely looked at me when I stepped into the garage a few hours ago."

"Is this related to the Border Patrol agents killed recently?"

"Directly," said Reeves. "You'd be examining the same site."

"Wow," said Decker.

Harlow thought it over for a few moments, not liking the implications. Steele's interest in the site could only mean one thing.

"Please don't tell me the Sinaloa Cartel has brought my least favorite illegal activity to the United States."

"That's why Steele wants eyes on the site. The Border Patrol agent specifically used the words *possible sex-trafficking situation* over the radio before headquarters lost contact. Five kids."

"Could be anything," said Harlow, not playing a very convincing devil's advocate. "Kids cross on their own all the time."

"He identified two as Caucasian," said Reeves.

"Motherfuh—" she grunted. "Doesn't sound right at all. Does it?"

"Nothing about what happened out there sounds right," said Reeves. "Which is why Steele wants to get a second opinion. Preferably an objective one."

"Can't she just send a fact-finding team to the site? Coordinate with the Border Patrol?" said Pierce.

"She tried. The incident occurred deep inside a recently activated military exclusion zone, and US Northern Command—specifically Joint Task Force North—hasn't let anyone take a meaningful look at the crime scene. Just a quick site visit for a few top officials, and they agreed to let CBP take possession of the agents' SUV, which was incinerated down to the chassis. This is an extremely sensitive issue, as you can imagine."

"Which means the military will have it locked down hard," said Pierce. "I'm not tangling with real soldiers."

"You're right. JTF North will have the US side locked down. At the very least, they'll have it under some serious surveillance," said Reeves. "But not the Mexican side."

"Mexican side?" said Harlow, glancing at Decker and Pierce. "How big of a crime scene is this?"

"That's where this gets really interesting," said Reeves. "Most of the site lies on the Mexican side of the border."

"Wait," said Decker. "What kind of a site are we talking about?"

"A massive bunker complex. Possibly a few hundred yards long," said Reeves. "Only about five percent of it is estimated to be on the US side."

"And you want us to come in from Mexico and infiltrate a working cartel bunker?" said Decker. "We might be better off trying to slip through JTF North's stranglehold on the US side."

"I'm not doing either," said Pierce. "This is crazy talk."

"The only cartel presence in the area will be the coyotes taking groups across the border," said Reeves. "The bunker was destroyed in a massive explosion several minutes after the agents made their last transmission."

"Someone's hiding something," said Decker.

Harlow unconsciously pressed her lips together, a subtle tell that she was weighing all the information Reeves had presented. Was the bunker some kind of human-trafficking way station? The cartels never destroyed their drug laboratories or product distribution hubs—but she could see them trying to bury something like this. Then again, why blow it up if most of it lay in Mexico? Why not just evacuate the kids on the Mexico side and abandon the place?

"Shall we meet in your office around ten a.m.?" said Reeves.

They nodded in unison. Something was off, and judging by the looks on Decker and Pierce's faces, they sensed it, too.

CHAPTER FOURTEEN

Decker examined the satellite photo displayed on the ninety-inch high-definition LED dominating the conference room wall.

"Sophie, can you switch to Google Maps? Satellite view with roads," he said.

"Don't you want to take a closer look at the images?" said Reeves.

"I assume all of this satellite imagery has been cleared for release by the military?" said Decker.

"I believe that's what the file indicated," said Reeves.

"The same military that doesn't want anyone looking too closely at the site," said Decker. "We won't find anything particularly useful in these images. Right now, I'm more concerned with getting close enough to the site to walk in without drawing *Federale* or cartel attention. You weren't kidding when you said the area was isolated."

"Is there any reason for two gringos to be in La Rumorosa at night?" said Pierce. "That's a hell of a lot closer to the site than Tecate."

Decker craned his head toward Sophie, who typed furiously at her laptop. She shook her head a few seconds later.

"I can't find a restaurant in the town open past nine," she said. "Federal Highway 2D has a lot of scenic vistas, which would give you an excuse to be in the area during the day—but that doesn't really help us."

"No. It doesn't. But that winding stretch of highway north of La Rumorosa is the ideal kickoff point," said Decker.

Pierce shifted in his seat, a critical look on his face. "It's the only kickoff point, unless we're willing to risk a serious off-roading adventure."

"I wouldn't recommend that," said Harlow. "The Sinaloa Cartel has the area locked down. Migrant smuggling is big business for them. Two gringos off-roading it near one of their key crossing points is begging for trouble."

"We could parachute in," said Pierce.

"No pilot in their right mind is going to fly us over the border and let us jump into the night," said Decker. "And forget about Bernie. We're not spending six figures to poke around in the sand."

"Senator Steele doesn't mind spending the money," said Reeves.

"We can figure this out," said Decker.

"It's a three-hour drive to Tecate," said Reeves. "If you can't figure it out, I suggest considering the option."

"No way we'd get Bernie lined up by tonight, anyway," said Decker.

"What about pushing the timeline back twenty-four hours?" said Sophie. "Don't tell your wife it was my idea, Brad."

"Don't worry. I will," said Pierce.

"If we push this trip to tomorrow night, that gives us more options," said Decker.

"The more I look at this, the more I think we need to go with the plan I suggested at breakfast," said Harlow.

Her plan was solid, but he wanted to explore options that involved as few people and moving parts as possible. He just wasn't seeing an alternative that didn't involve aircraft. Decker tapped the table with his fingers, his brain vapor-locked on the screen. Harlow must have sensed he'd run out of ideas, because she continued a few seconds later.

"The only way this works is with a roadside drop-off. If we leave here by noon, we can be in Tecate by four at the latest. That gives us time to study road maps and grab an early dinner before heading out for a scenic sunset drive on Federal Highway 2D, north of La Rumorosa. We dump you on the side of the road as close to the border as possible and head back to Tecate. That puts you two and a half, maybe three miles from the site. We pick you up in the morning and drive back to Tecate for huevos rancheros—after the two of you clean up."

Pierce closed his laptop and nodded at the satellite-view road map on the screen.

"Sounds like this is our plan. I don't see any other way to reach the site without drawing a lot of attention or hiking ten to fifteen miles over shitty terrain. And I like Tecate beer. So there we go."

Decker swiveled in his chair toward Harlow. "See. I knew you were right."

"Uh-huh," she said, raising an eyebrow.

"You came up with this plan at breakfast? Damn. What have we been doing for the past hour?" said Reeves, casting a sly look at Decker.

Decker shook his head, well aware that Reeves had just thrown him under the bus.

"Based on the general location you gave us yesterday, I looked at some maps last night," said Harlow. "But what do I know?"

Reeves turned to Decker with a feigned look of surprise, trying to elicit some kind of ill-advised retort, but Decker took a deep breath instead—and let it go. The lecture about comprehensive mission planning could wait. Maybe indefinitely.

"Let's take a good look at the satellite imagery of the site and start packing. The sooner we get to Tecate the better," said Decker.

They spent the next twenty minutes scouring the digital imagery, identifying the best approaches to the site. The bunker complex had been built underneath one of the relatively few flat stretches of land touching the border in that area. They eliminated the easiest routes, guessing they'd either be used by the coyotes or blocked by the cartel. After settling on a rather difficult path, Decker and Pierce extracted rough GPS waypoints from the imagery.

"Sophie. Can you zoom in on the bunker complex only?" said Decker. "Fill the screen with the collapsed area."

"I knew you saw it," said Pierce. "They did one hell of a job with the demolition."

The image came into focus on the huge screen, looking like an evenly collapsed fault line. The section of border wall crossing the northern edge of the complex lay flat on the ground, dropped by the sudden implosion beneath it.

"Massive, simultaneously detonated underground explosions that instantly compromised the structure," said Reeves. "That was JTF North's assessment."

"It's just so neatly done," said Pierce, clearly admiring the work.

"I'm going to assume you know what you're talking about," said Reeves.

"Brad saw his share of tunnels in Afghanistan."

"And permanently put them out of commission," said Pierce. "It's not a simple task, and it requires a ton of explosive power—distributed evenly throughout the tunnel. Nothing we demolished looked like this."

"What are you implying here?" said Reeves.

"The cartel went out of their way to make sure this place was buried," said Pierce. "Which brings us back to another great point Harlow made during breakfast."

"Sounds like Ms. Mackenzie was on a roll this morning," said Reeves. "What were you doing at breakfast, Decker?"

"Eggs benedict," said Pierce. "Hold the egg. Who does that?"

"And home fries. Don't forget the home fries," said Harlow.

"Drowned in ketchup," added Pierce. "Until you can barely see them."

"Too funny. All of you," said Decker, shaking his head.

"What's your theory?" said Reeves.

"It's not really a theory. I just don't see the Mexicans destroying something like this to cover their tracks. If it was a sex-trafficking feeder point into the US, they could just yank the kids out of there and leave the tunnels. Major drug-distribution center? Move the drugs out and leave the tunnels. They could do that in plain sight of the border, and there's nothing our government could do to stop them. Why would they bury the place?" said Harlow.

"Bury the evidence," said Reeves.

"I don't think this is about selling kids," said Decker. "You don't destroy a bunker that big to cover up a sex-trafficking operation, and you certainly don't kill Border Patrol agents. The Sinaloa Cartel is up to something entirely new. Something they did not want discovered under any circumstances. And if I had to guess, I'd bet JTF North has a good idea what they're up to. Why else would they have activated a military exclusion zone right on top of the site?"

"I hadn't thought of that," said Reeves. "Still doesn't change the fact that kids are involved."

"No. It doesn't. It just ups the stakes," said Decker, still scrutinizing the satellite image. "Does that look like a road running up to the bunker on the US side?"

"Looks more like a wash to me," said Pierce. "Dry riverbed."

"Zoom out a little, Sophie. Slowly," said Decker, following the wash as the image expanded. "Stop. Check that out. Connects to a nearby jeep trail. I don't think that's a wash."

"It looks natural enough," said Pierce.

"But it leads directly to the bunker," said Decker. "How big was the entrance?"

Reeves flipped through the file on the table in front of him.

"Doesn't say," said Reeves. "Just that they found chunks of timber sticking out of the ground."

"Timber sounds big to me," said Decker.

"What about the Mexican side?" said Pierce. "Any evidence of a road at the other end?"

Sophie moved the satellite image along the north-south axis of the collapse area, until the southern end of the bunker appeared on the far left of the screen. Decker couldn't believe they had missed this a few minutes earlier. The Mexicans hadn't bothered to conceal the fact that a road led right to the former mouth of the underground complex.

"Follow that jeep trail, please," said Decker.

Sophie zoomed out far enough to keep the jeep trail easily visible before moving the digitally merged satellite image until it connected to a bizarre spiderweb of dirt roads roughly three miles southeast of the bunker. She tightened the image's scale, filling the screen with the roads.

"What is that?" said Reeves.

"It's a wind farm," said Decker. "Maybe we should be examining that area instead. Has to be some kind of staging area for whatever they're bringing up to the border."

"It's your call," said Reeves. "Senator Steele wants to get to the bottom of this."

"She's pursuing this from the human-trafficking angle," said Harlow, turning to Decker. "If you really think this is something different, we might be overstepping if we start snooping around the wind farm."

Decker rubbed his face and eyes with both hands, like it was going to bring him the answers.

"I say we start with the bunker," said Decker. "If that's a bust, we consult with Senator Steele and see if she wants us to press this further. Frankly, neither site is likely to prove fruitful. The cartel isn't stupid. If they're working on a game changer, like I suspect, both sites will be sanitized."

"And they'll be closely watching each site," said Pierce. "Probably keeping an eye on all of the nearby ports of entry for US intelligence agents."

"Brad's right. We'll need to be extremely cautious the moment we cross into Mexico. The cartel has built an extensive intelligence network over the years, focused on the border areas. They'll be on high alert, if my guess about the site is even close to being right."

"Should we consider traveling under false identities?" said Harlow. "Some of us might trigger an alert, given our work on this side of the border."

"Without a doubt. If we attract the cartel's attention in Tecate, the mission is scrubbed," said Decker.

"I don't want to hear this part," said Reeves, putting his hands to his ears. "Maybe I should bow out at this point."

"Not a bad idea," said Decker. "We'll be discussing weapons next."

"Definitely leaving now," said Reeves. "I'll let Senator Steele know you'll submit your findings by close of business tomorrow. Keep me posted of any significant changes to your itinerary. Use the voice-mail box we set up for this stuff."

"You don't want me to call your FBI-issued cell phone from a Mexican police station?" said Decker.

"Please don't," said Reeves. "And I know this goes without saying, but—"

"You're going to say it anyway," said Decker.

"Yes," sighed Reeves. "Please exercise restraint. Observe, investigate, and report. If you run into a problem out there, I can't help you, and neither can Senator Steele."

"If we get caught by the cartel, nobody will ever hear from us again," said Decker.

"Or find us again," said Pierce. "Acid-bath spa treatments for everyone."

"Or the heated lye barrel plunge," said Decker. "I hear they have to pour you back into your room afterward."

Sophie rolled her eyes and closed the laptop.

"It's going to be a long ride to Tecate," said Harlow.

"Better you than me," said Reeves, already headed for the door.

CHAPTER FIFTEEN

Decker drove the rental car out of the duty-free parking lot and pulled into the leftmost of the two lanes leading into Mexico. He stopped their modest, four-door sedan behind a rust-spotted Jeep Wrangler, three vehicles from the customs and immigration booth, and lowered his window. Border traffic had been lighter than expected, putting them slightly ahead of schedule—even after negotiating the somewhat round-about process of obtaining tourist visas and a vehicle permit. Now came the fun part.

To say that Mexican customs officers performed their duties inconsistently was an understatement. He'd watched them wave five cars through without getting out of their chairs, and stop the sixth for a full inspection. Decker hoped for a wave through but more realistically figured they'd get a cursory look inside the trunk and passenger cabin, which wouldn't reveal anything suspicious.

At the very worst, the officers might remove the luggage to examine the trunk. Still not a problem, since they had broken down the weapons and evenly distributed the pieces, along with ammunition, throughout the suitcases. If customs inspectors decided to open the suitcases, they had a critical problem—with only one not-so-great solution: bail out of the car and sprint back into the United States, roughly a hundred feet away. They could sort things out on the US side.

"Everyone's good with the bailout plan?" said Decker.

"It won't go down that easy if the officers get aggressive," said Sandra from directly behind him.

"We'll be dealing with two or three of them—at most," said Decker. "Nothing the Tasers can't shake loose."

"If they go for the formal vehicle search, they'll direct us to a small inspection area on the other side of the customs booth and have us get out of the car," said Harlow. "If that happens, I say we walk calmly toward the US and bolt when they figure out what we're up to."

"Probably get halfway before they realize we've bailed," said Pierce. "This looks like a pretty laid-back port of entry."

"It is," said Harlow. "Tecate is still a sleepy little town."

The line started to move, and Decker eased off the gas.

"Undo your seat belts," he said, putting a hand on Harlow's wrist as she reached for her belt latch. "Not us."

The officers waved the cars in front of him through, and for a few seconds, Decker thought they might slip into Mexico with the magic wave of a hand. A uniformed customs officer stepped into the lane before they reached the covered declarations area and motioned for them to stop. Two seat belts clicked behind him as he eased into place next to the serious-looking officer. The man considered Decker for a few moments before doing the same with the rest of the vehicle's passengers.

"The purpose of your visit?" said the officer.

"Winery tours near Guadalupe," said Decker. "But we're staying right in Tecate."

"Where?"

"Santuario Diegueño. For two nights. Just a quick getaway."

"Which wineries?"

"Lechuza . . . Trevista," said Decker, thankful he had taken a quick look at wineries on Google. "Which others?"

Harlow took his cue, though she struggled for a few seconds. "Uh . . . I kind of wanted to see Tres Mujeres?"

"Whatever you want, sweetie," he said, squeezing her hand.

The officer continued his rather stern visual sweep of the occupants, taking a step back when he was done. Decker feigned a smile while the officer looked up and down the car, his eyes settling on the trunk. Crap.

"Open the trunk, please."

"Yes, sir," said Decker, his smile fading.

Decker searched to the left of the steering wheel, trying desperately to locate the lever or button that opened the trunk. He looked up at the officer, his hand fumbling under the dashboard.

"Sorry. It's a rental," he said, really wishing he had thought of this earlier.

"Maybe it's on the dashboard," said Sandra.

"It's not on the dashboard," said Decker, glancing at the controls. "Definitely not on the dashboard."

"Well, it has to be there," she said offhandedly.

"I'm looking for it," he said, glancing at the officer again. "Do you mind if I open the door? It might be on the side of the seat."

"It's not on the side of the seat," said Sandra. "You're somehow missing it."

"Would you like to find it?" said Decker, stealing a glance at Harlow and mouthing, "WTF?"

Harlow shrugged. "It's there somewhere. You want me to look in the manual?"

"*Está bien.* Have a nice visit," said the officer, waving them through.

"Are you sure? I'm sure I can—" he started, the sudden kick to the back of his chair clueing him in to the charade. "Oh. Okay. Thank you, señor. *Buenas tardes.*"

Decker drove them out of the customs zone and onto Avenida Presidente Lázaro Cárdenas, a wide, four-lane road separated by a sparsely landscaped median.

"Jesus, Decker," said Sandra. "I thought you were going to blow it back there."

"Took me a little while to catch on," said Decker.

"A little while?" said Pierce.

"And what was up with 'Whatever you want, sweetie'?" said Sandra. "That was about as natural as an old Arnold Schwarzenegger line."

"Acting isn't my specialty," said Decker.

"You did fine," said Harlow, touching his hand. "But the first thing we're going to do at the hotel is find the trunk release."

"Please!" said Sandra. "I almost had to relive my track days back there."

"You ran track in high school?" said Harlow.

"Not really. I was on the team, but I mostly watched my boyfriend run."

They all laughed a little as the car cruised toward the first stoplight. A black, wrought iron TECATE sign spanned the street on the other side of the intersection, held aloft by tall redbrick columns. Decker glanced in the rearview mirror, the road behind them clear all the way to the customs area. He continued through the green light, scanning the few cars waiting on each side of Avenida Revolución for anyone suspicious. It wasn't hard to spot Sinaloa muscle. Face tattoos tended to stick out, even down here.

"I don't mean to be a buzzkill," said Decker. "But we need to shift into countersurveillance mode. At least until we get settled at the hotel. We're probably less than five minutes away. If we pick up a tail that quickly, we may as well turn right around and drive home."

"We'll have to keep an eye on things at the hotel, too," said Harlow. "If the customs officer is on their payroll, they'll stake us out after we check in."

"I say we go for a quick turnaround at the hotel. Assemble the weapons, prep the gear, and head east. We can run an extensive SDR—surveillance detection route—before we commit to the drop-off. Kill some time at a restaurant and visit a few gift shops while we're at it. Should be really obvious if we've somehow piqued their interest," said Decker.

"I don't see how or why we would have drawn any attention," said Pierce.

"Better safe than being lowered feetfirst into a tub of acid," said Decker.

"See what I mean?" said Harlow, glancing back at Sandra.

"Really inspires confidence," said Sandra.

"I meant it to be a scare tactic," said Decker.

"It worked," said Sandra.

Decker cruised through another green light at the next intersection, taking a left on Route 2—the same road they would take out of town later in the afternoon. A few minutes later, they passed through the manned security gate at Santuario Diegueño, a boutiquey-looking hotel on the eastern edge of Tecate's downtown area. He purposefully parked them as far away as possible from the valet station, so they could handle their own luggage.

"Nice place," said Decker.

"Too bad you won't get to enjoy it," said Sandra. "I'm looking forward to a relaxing night swim after we dump the two of you on the side of the road. The pool looked wonderful."

"A couple margaritas," said Harlow. "Kind of be like a mini vacation."

"Don't forget to bring the satellite phone down to the pool," said Decker, getting out of the car. "You know, in case Brad and I need to pass important information along before we're captured and beheaded."

"What happened to the acid bath?" said Sandra.

"I'm suddenly feeling optimistic," said Decker. "Found the trunk release. On the door."

Fifteen minutes later, after filling out several seemingly unrelated hotel forms and repeatedly turning down a barrage of time-share presentation offers, they finally stood in the elevator with their bags.

"Second floor, please," said Pierce.

The hotel only had two floors.

"Funny," said Decker, pressing the button.

"If nobody is watching, we should start with everything in one room," said Harlow. "Assemble the weapons and prep your mission gear first. Then trick out the luggage in case the turn-down maid gets nosy."

"Works for me," said Decker.

They got off the elevator and followed the open-air walkway to their side-by-side rooms.

"Too bad they don't have connecting rooms," said Harlow. "Make this a lot easier."

He looked around, not seeing anyone on the long second-floor terrace or in the dense courtyard garden below.

"The place is pretty much empty right now," said Decker, reaching into his back pocket. "Time for the gloves."

They quickly and quietly slipped on thick, clear vinyl gloves as they walked. Sandra stopped just ahead of them and put her card against the reader before pushing the door open. She held it open as they rolled their luggage inside, pulling it shut after them and engaging the security latch.

"Let's go to work," he said.

They spread the four carry-on-size pieces on the king bed and started to remove the weapons parts, placing them on the wide, marble-topped desk. Pierce examined one of the pieces in his hand, shaking his head.

"You really need a better selection of untraceable weapons," he said.

"We don't run across many abandoned rifles. Pimps and dealers prefer the concealable stuff. Just be glad I didn't give you a pair of beat-up pistols," said Harlow. "I did not want to part with these."

"Pistols would be more accurate," said Pierce, handing the piece to Decker.

Decker winked at Harlow, who rolled her eyes. He joined the two halves before pushing the thick receiver pin through a hole near the front. Satisfied that the two pieces were firmly locked together, he pulled the top-mounted bolt handle back, cocking the weapon and pulling the trigger. The click sounded about right for a functional firing pin.

"This is about as good as it gets when it comes to compact firepower," said Sandra, handing him the weapon's iconic one-foot-long, two-inch-diameter suppressor. "And quiet."

"We'll attach these after drop-off," said Decker, placing the "can" and the MAC-10 nine-millimeter submachine gun on the desk.

"It's a mean weapon, I'll give you that," said Pierce, assembling the second gun. "Not much use in a space bigger than this hotel room, but it'll definitely keep heads down."

Pierce was right. The weapons would be mostly useless against targets more than fifty feet away. A small team of cartel goons armed with AK-47 rifles would have them seriously outgunned in the open. They'd have to rely on the weapons' suppressors and insanely high rate of fire to either maneuver closer or break contact altogether. In light of the weapons' limitations, their most effective tactic tonight would be to avoid contact in the first place. Easier said than done in the dark, even with top-of-the-line night-vision gear.

Sandra produced the second suppressor, which went on the desk, along with the MAC-10 Pierce had just assembled. Harlow created a pile of thirty-two-round magazines at the foot of the bed, which Decker and Pierce divided evenly among them. Six magazines each. One hundred and ninety-two rounds of nine-millimeter ammunition sounded like more than enough until you took into account the MAC-10's cyclic rate of fire. At twelve hundred rounds per minute—roughly twenty rounds per second—an undisciplined shooter could dump a magazine in less than two seconds.

Even disciplined shooters like Pierce or Decker would have a hard time conserving ammunition. A brief trigger pull fired several bullets. He'd get four, maybe five bursts per magazine, and they'd all have to count. Thirty or so trigger pulls would go fast in a serious gunfight.

Harlow yanked two lightweight, coyote-tan backpacks out of the luggage, each preloaded with night-vision goggles, prefitted desert camouflage gear, and an individual first aid kit. A twist tie attached to the shoulder strap of one of them identified it as Decker's.

"This is yours," she said, tossing it to Decker. "And yours."

Pierce caught his and unzipped the top, slipping the MAC-10, the suppressor, and the magazines inside.

"I should have gone with the larger pack," said Harlow. "They're going to be stuffed."

"It's fine," said Decker. "We're ditching them a few hundred yards from the drop point. They just need to carry our gear from point A to point B and pass a quick visual inspection if the *Federales* pop our trunk."

They finished loading the rest of the equipment, spreading it as evenly as possible between the two packs—knives, foldable hand shovel, thermal scope, flashlights (infrared and standard), hand-portable radio frequency detector, two military-grade smoke grenades, zip ties, Taser, satellite phone, binoculars. Decker jammed the binoculars in his pack, barely pulling the zipper shut.

He held up his hiking boots. "We'll have to wear these now."

"Sorry, guys," said Harlow. "I'm guessing that we won't be able to fill the CamelBaks built into the packs."

Pierce shook his head, forcing his pack shut. "Not until we offload after drop-off."

"We'll grab a bunch of bottled water on our drive," said Harlow.

They spent the next few minutes inflating plastic travel pillows and stuffing them in the bottom of the bags that had held the backpacks. A few layers of clothing covered the pillows, creating the impression that the suitcases were full. Decker transferred Harlow's suitcase and his to the other room to complete the illusion.

Everything they had brought into Mexico was disposable and untraceable, including the car, which they'd wipe down with the package of baby wipes they'd left in the back seat. If they picked up a tail on the way to the drop-off, they'd dump the backpacks and head for the border without returning to the hotel.

If things really went sideways, they'd ditch the car and split up into groups of two—and try to cross on foot. Failing that, they'd regroup and head deeper into Mexico by whatever means they could arrange. Each of them carried five hundred dollars, a second set of identification, and a credit card matching the second ID. Plenty of money to discreetly make things happen down here. He hoped.

CHAPTER SIXTEEN

Harlow glanced in the rearview mirror and muttered a few choice words. The headlights following them remained at the same distance, despite her lower speed. She'd gradually slowed down over the past mile, hoping the vehicle trailing them would close the distance and pass them on the last stretch of relatively straight road.

They'd first noticed the lights a few minutes after turning onto the northern, westbound part of the Highway 2D scenic loop. The highway split into two roads separated by rocky crags and deep valleys, forming a north-south loop between La Rumorosa and the military checkpoint east of the hills.

They had been alone on the eastbound run, and no vehicles waited on the westbound side of the checkpoint, when they reversed direction at the gas station. The car had undoubtedly originated from the gas station or the tourist shopping mall parking lot next to the checkpoint.

"No change," said Harlow.

"Concur," said Pierce.

"We're running out of passable road," said Decker.

"I'm already under the speed limit," she said, glancing at the speedometer.

"Could be a cautious driver," said Sandra. "Last thing anyone wants is an accident out here—or anywhere in Mexico."

The Raid

"We'll know soon enough," said Decker, playing with a handheld GPS unit. "You're coming up on a gradual left curve. The last decent straightaway until the drop-off point begins after the long bend, when the road turns right again. I'd start dropping speed as soon as we hit the curve. Come out of the turn at half the speed limit."

"What if they don't pass us?" said Harlow.

"Then we stop the car and wave them on," said Decker. "Force them to make a move."

"If it's the cartel, they'll wait for us in La Rumorosa," said Sandra. "When they see two people in the car instead of four, we'll definitely have their attention."

"And the two of you will drive right straight to the border crossing in Tecate," said Decker.

"I'm not worried about us," said Sandra. "They'll be looking for you out there."

"It's a big desert," said Decker. "We'll be fine."

"They can probably guess where you're headed," said Sandra.

"Good point," said Decker. "If you pick up a tail in La Rumorosa, let us know. We'll reassess the situation on our way to the target site. If we detect an unusual amount of activity, we'll abort the mission and camp out somewhere safe until you can send someone down to get us."

"I better not have to spend another night sleeping on the ground," said Pierce.

Everyone laughed, except Harlow, who was too focused on the winding road, two sets of mirrors, and the gravity of their situation to process any humor. The cartel could just as easily pull them over, practically guaranteeing an acid bath for all of them—or they could just riddle the car with bullets without warning, having already assumed they were up to no good.

The guardrail's white reflectors curved left at the limit of her headlights, and she slowed the car for the shallow turn, intending to continue decreasing speed until they hit the straightaway. Harlow momentarily lost the headlights in her mirrors when her line of sight was blocked on the curve by a jagged rock wall on the left side of the road. A few seconds later, the lights reappeared.

"That's a good sign," said Pierce.

"We'll see," said Harlow, taking her foot off the gas pedal.

She let the car slow on its own, without using the brake, until the rock wall curved to the right, following the road. *Here we go.* Harlow lightly depressed the brake as she eased the car into the right turn that would deposit them on the last stretch of passable road before they reached the primary drop-off point.

"They appear to be slowing with you," said Pierce.

A quick glance in the rearview mirror confirmed the vehicle appeared to be dropping back. Not good. The road straightened ahead of her, their car once again pointing at the last blue remnants of a nearly faded sunset.

"I'm thinking we should consider aborting the mission. Try again in a few days. Maybe the weekend, when it's busier. We've been the only car on the highway since La Rumorosa."

"Let's give this a chance," said Decker. "We'll know in a few seconds."

Harlow shook her head imperceptibly, frustrated by Decker's tunnel vision. Or was it stubbornness? Sometimes it was hard to tell with him.

"Fuck it," she muttered, drastically reducing her speed.

"You don't have to—" started Decker.

She stuck her arm out of the window and waved the vehicle on, slowing to a crawl along the right shoulder of the road.

"We'll know in a few seconds," she said under her breath.

The headlights grew in the side mirror, shifting lanes a few car lengths behind them. The short distance and direct angle magnified the light, blinding her. Harlow craned her neck toward the center of the car to avoid the reflection, watching the vehicle with her peripheral vision.

She eased her head back as the reflection moved, coming face-to-face with the occupants a few seconds later.

"Everything okay?" said a very normal-looking middle-aged woman from the passenger seat of a luxury SUV.

"We're fine," said Harlow. "Thought you might be the *Federales*. We hadn't seen a car since we left La Rumorosa."

"Neither have we!" said the woman. "That's why we followed you out of the parking lot. My husband didn't want to drive back alone. Safety in numbers, right?"

"I guess so," said Harlow. "We drive this all the time and never have a problem."

"Sorry to give you a scare," said the woman. "We'll lead the way back. We're going to stop for dinner in Tecate and head back across before they close the border for the night."

"Close the border?" said Decker. "That would have been nice to know."

Harlow gave him a *not now* look.

"Yeah. The Tecate port of entry closes at eleven p.m.," said the husband. "We live in Spring Valley, so it's only an hour drive from there."

"We never stay in Mexico," said the wife. "I don't think I'd be able to sleep at night."

"Well. We don't want to hold you up," said Harlow. "We'll keep you in sight. Safety in numbers."

"Sounds good," said the wife. "We know a great place for margaritas in Tecate if you're interested. Hole in the wall, but they don't skimp on the tequila."

"We'll play it by ear," said Harlow. "We drove down from Temecula for a few days. Been a long day in the car."

"Without a sunset," said Decker.

"I'll never hear the end of it," said Harlow.

As soon as the couple pulled away, Pierce chimed in with the obvious. "You're gonna have to ditch them on the way back."

"Yep," said Harlow. "Big-time."

"Maybe recheck the port of entry closing time while you're at it," said Decker.

"I'm not the only one that had internet access while we were planning this op," said Harlow, silencing Decker.

As they neared the drop-off point, it became obvious they still had a problem. The couple kept adjusting their speed to keep the two cars no farther than ten car lengths apart, sometimes slowing drastically when they lost sight of each other on a sharp turn. Decker stared at the GPS screen the entire time, occasionally looking up to match the actual road to the digital map. They'd experienced a few drops in GPS coverage while driving through the steep rock formations.

"This'll have to be a quick stop," said Decker, glancing into the back seat. "Ready?"

"Not really," said Pierce, unbuckling his seat belt.

"Start slowly drifting back," said Decker. "We should be passing a scenic overlook with several parking spaces in about fifteen seconds. The drop point is about a thousand feet beyond. We should see a white sign on the right side of the road that says ARROYO LA GLORIA. At least that's what Google Maps showed."

"Google Maps didn't show a shopping center or gas station at the military checkpoint," said Sandra.

"I have a waypoint. Just in case," said Decker.

"There's the overlook," said Harlow, her lights illuminating a blue information sign ahead.

The car ahead of them passed the empty turnoff, not appearing to have noticed that the distance had opened between them. Just when she finished that thought, the car's brake lights illuminated road.

"Here they go again," said Harlow.

"That's fine," said Decker. "There's a sharp turn right after the drop-off point, so we'll be completely out of sight—unless they put the car into reverse and look for us."

"I wouldn't put it past them," said Harlow, suddenly feeling more at ease.

When they reached the overlook, Decker tucked the GPS receiver in one of his cargo pockets.

"Maybe twenty seconds," said Decker, undoing his seat belt.

They traveled in complete silence until the white sign appeared—and the SUV vanished behind a two-story chunk of rock. Harlow pressed the brakes, nearly screeching the tires to stop them on the shoulder in front of the sign. She popped the trunk and turned to Decker, who unexpectedly gave her a peck on the cheek.

"Stay safe," he said before sliding out of the car. "First sign of trouble—you get over the border. Don't worry about us."

Harlow managed a nod and a barely audible *yes* before he disappeared. The trunk thumped a moment later, and she caught a quick glimpse of them in the red light cast by the brakes—hopping over the guardrail with their backpacks. Those two were crazy. They were all crazy. Sandra hopped into Decker's seat and shut the door, snapping Harlow out of the trance.

"Did he really just kiss you?" said Sandra.

"I guess so," said Harlow.

"You gonna start driving any time soon? Our friends are probably waiting for us."

"I guess so," she said, with a smirk—and hit the gas.

Chapter Seventeen

Decker landed on an uneven heap of rocks, pitching forward into Pierce, who somehow managed to stay upright and keep them both from tumbling into the arroyo. The same couldn't be said for the over-strained plastic bag in Decker's left hand, which had broken open and spilled its contents over the rocks. They scrambled around, managing to find half of the bottled water before deciding to move on. Neither of them wanted to break out their flashlights this close to the road.

"Sorry about that," said Decker, searching the darkness ahead to regain his bearings.

"That was your water we lost," said Pierce.

"I told you the bag was overfilled," whispered Decker.

"It would have been fine if you hadn't taken the guardrail in one leap," said Pierce, pausing for a second. "Trying to impress your girlfriend."

"Funny," said Decker, making a face his friend couldn't possibly see.

"I wasn't really joking," said Pierce. "About Harlow or the water."

They stumbled through the rock-filled gap for several difficult minutes before Pierce abruptly stopped. Decker glanced over his shoulder, still able to see the outlines of the guardrail in the distance.

"We need to keep moving," said Decker.

"I'm breaking out a flashlight before one of us blows out an ankle," said Pierce, kneeling in front of his backpack.

Decker didn't argue. The steeply pitched, rock-jammed gulch was a disaster waiting to happen, particularly with the oversize backpacks. One misplaced step and they'd have to ditch the mission, putting Harlow and Sandra in the difficult position of repeating the Highway 2D loop to pick them up. They'd undoubtedly draw the wrong kind of attention on the return trip.

He shifted the backpack onto one shoulder and dug through the main pouch, barely managing to pull the flashlight free from the bulging monstrosity. Covering the lens with one hand, he turned it on, adjusting his fingers to get a thin stream of usable light. Uncovered, the six-hundred-lumen flashlights could be seen for miles in the valley below.

Hopefully, they'd only need to use them to get out of the arroyo. If the jagged bed of rocks continued beyond that, he wasn't sure they could rely on night vision alone to proceed. The head-mounted devices they'd brought on the mission, like most night-vision goggles, significantly impaired depth perception. Walking over rough terrain with NVGs wasn't much better than without. Sometimes it was worse.

They continued down the rock bed for several minutes until the highway was no longer in sight. Pierce halted them again, calling Decker forward.

"I say we gear up here, lighten these packs," said Pierce. "We have at least another thirty minutes in the rocks. I thought we'd be out of them by now based on Google Earth images."

"Probably a good call," said Decker. "I suspect we'll be dealing with this shit for longer than thirty minutes."

They dropped their packs and started unloading the gear, careful not to lose anything in the dark. Within a few minutes, the transition was complete. They set off with their pockets full, night-vision goggles raised, and the MAC-10s dangling loosely by one-point slings—to free their hands to use the flashlights. The rock dance continued as predicted for the next forty minutes, until the ground finally gave way to short stretches of hardened sand and thick scrub.

Decker turned off his flashlight and checked the GPS unit. As he suspected based on the geography, they had overshot the first waypoint by about two hundred meters. Not a big deal in the grand scheme of things. They had also underestimated the amount of climbing it would take to get out of the arroyo to head straight for the target site.

He tapped Pierce's shoulder to get him to stop. "GPS puts us point-two clicks past Alpha One."

Pierce turned his head toward the imposing rise on their left flank. "That's not happening. Let's go with Route Bravo. I'd rather add another hour or two to the trek than struggle over that crap."

"I agree," said Decker, calling up the secondary route on the GPS.

Route Bravo took them due east after the next bend in the arroyo, where they'd turn almost due north into what had looked more like a traditional high-desert wash in the satellite imagery.

"Bravo Two is point-five clicks away," said Decker, pocketing the GPS. "We should switch to night vision. We probably won't be the only people out here tonight with the same idea."

The easier approach carried the additional risk of running into migrants headed for the same stretch of border. They'd have to move quietly and deliberately, pausing frequently to scan their surroundings with the thermal-imaging scope. The process would be tedious and slow, but it would prepare them for the final approach to the collapsed bunker site—when their lives would depend on absolute stealth.

Decker lowered his night-vision goggles, taking a few seconds to adjust to the monochromatic green image before stepping off to trail Pierce. A few steps later, he raised the MAC-10 submachine gun, cradling its oversize suppressor in the crook of his left elbow to keep it from banging noisily against his thigh.

The terrain eased up on them halfway to the waypoint, the ground more sand than rock. The prickly desert bushes grew thicker as the arroyo widened, evidence of occasional water retention. He suspected that this area would flood in a heavy rain, the water carried swiftly down the craggy ravine they had just descended—along with anything not part of the natural landscape. Flash floods killed dozens of migrants every year in foothills like these.

He stopped them a few hundred meters from Bravo Two and carefully scanned the landscape in every direction with the thermal scope, not finding any hot spots indicating body heat.

"Looks clear," said Decker.

"I figure it won't get busy for another hour, when we merge with the main crossing routes. Most of the coyotes probably depart from the northern outskirts of La Rumorosa—to our west," said Pierce. "It's too risky to pull the same trick we did."

"The cartel can do whatever it wants out here," said Decker.

"I don't plan on letting my guard down," said Pierce, patting his submachine gun.

"Didn't think so," said Decker.

CHAPTER EIGHTEEN

Harlow glanced at the rearview mirror, convinced they had picked up a tail on the outskirts of La Rumorosa. Unlike their meandering late-afternoon drive, which took them through several dusty, local towns, Harlow had followed the couple from Spring Valley onto Highway 2D, a four-lane tollway that avoided every town between La Rumorosa and Tecate. The headlights had first appeared about a minute west of the town, suddenly materializing out of the pitch blackness behind them.

"What do you think?" said Harlow.

Sandra looked over her shoulder. "Seems like they pulled off the side of the road. Like they were waiting."

"Routine cartel surveillance?" said Harlow.

"That's what the intelligence package suggests," said Sandra.

"That package was a little light on specifics," said Harlow. "And heavy on cost."

"I balked at the price tag, but nearly all of the intelligence is based on comprehensive external surveillance," said Sandra. "Inside sources are rare. The cartels always manage to buy a copy of the same package, which they use to modify their tactics—and identify moles. They've been pretty ruthless about this, even targeting the company's field operatives."

"Looks like they haven't changed this tactic," said Harlow.

"If it ain't broke . . . ," said Sandra, checking again. "And I don't think we'll be able to shake them between here and Tecate."

"I don't think we should try," said Harlow. "They might do more than follow us."

They drove in silence for the next several minutes, Harlow running every scenario she could imagine through her head. They all pointed toward one solution. Drive straight across the border and head east on Interstate 8 to Calexico, where they would wait until tomorrow to cross back into Mexico to pick up Decker and Pierce. Sandra studied the road map on her phone while Harlow plotted.

"Right after we hit the highway split just outside Tecate," said Sandra, "I say we break off from our margarita-seeking friends and turn north on José María Morelos Boulevard, or whatever it is. That'll take us straight to US customs, but if they don't follow us, it also passes right by our hotel."

"Tecate is a small town," said Harlow. "They'll find us within the hour if they're so inclined, and we won't know how inclined they might be until it's too late. We're done here for now. It's too risky to stay."

"You're right," said Sandra. "According to the expensive intelligence I bought, they've completely infiltrated Mexican customs—and can get whatever they want out of the local businesses. Nobody opposes them. If we really piqued their interest, it won't be long before they know that four people crossed into Mexico. We're two short of that number right now."

"They can't follow us into the US customs line, so they might not be able to visibly confirm the number of people in our car. The sooner we get across the border, the better. Keep them guessing until they visit our hotel," said Harlow.

"I'll call Decker with the bad news," said Sandra, grabbing their satellite phone from the center console.

"Let him know we'll cross in Mexicali first thing tomorrow morning," said Harlow. "Pick them up and head right back across."

Sandra hit the speed-dial number for Decker's sat phone and waited.

"Right to voice mail," said Sandra, before leaving a message outlining the possible cartel problem and their proposed plan.

Less than a minute later, the satellite phone buzzed, its touch screen illuminating. Sandra read the text message aloud.

1–2 hours behind due to detour. Will call after site visit. Be careful. Cartel active on both sides of border.

Harlow didn't like hearing that they were behind schedule. If the cartel moved fast and discovered that only two of them crossed the border tonight, Decker and Pierce could be headed into an ambush.

"Send him a quick reply to consider aborting the mission," said Harlow. "They were looking at a two-hour trek to start. If they take three to four hours to reach the site, the cartel might be alerted to their presence. I mean, it's a long shot that the cartel will put this together so quickly, but if Decker is right about them being up to something new—better safe than sorry."

"Yep," said Sandra, composing a response.

Cartel might discover only two of us when we cross in approx 1 hour. Possible they might put 2&2 together fast and warn site.

Several seconds later, a reply arrived.

We'll be extra careful. Let me know what happens at border.

An hour and twenty minutes later, after ditching their presumed cartel tail and crossing the border, Sandra typed the last message they'd send until they reached Calexico.

Status of suspected tail still unknown. Crossed border without incident or tail. En route Calexico.

Decker's response was unusually abrupt.

K. Out.

Out, meaning the conversation was over.

"Do you think they're in trouble?" said Harlow. "Unless they made up for lost time, they should still be an hour or more away from the border site."

"I think they're one hundred percent focused on their surroundings," said Sandra. "We should leave them alone for now."

Harlow surrendered to the first yawn of what promised to be a much longer night than either of them had anticipated. The drive east on Interstate 8 would take them at least two hours, landing them in Calexico around midnight. Right around the time Decker and Pierce should be finishing up their inspection. She'd be lucky to get an hour or two of sleep worrying about their exfiltration from the site and next morning's south-of-the-border extraction. A lot could go wrong between now and then.

CHAPTER NINETEEN

A gust of cool wind washed through the dry streambed, rattling the dense grove of bushes next to Decker. *Cool* was a relative term out here, even at night. Anything less than eighty degrees felt welcome compared to the hundred-degree scorcher this afternoon. After this mission, he was done with the desert for a while. The three days spent roasting outside the Bratva house had ruined it for him.

He raised his night-vision goggles out of the way and pressed the thermal scope's eye cup tightly against his face, to prevent any light from escaping. He activated the device and waited a few seconds for the scope's grayscale image to appear.

Once the digital picture came into focus, Decker reduced the magnification by pressing the rubber buttons on the top of the scope, giving him the widest possible field of view. He rose slowly from a crouched position behind Pierce, keeping the scope aimed directly ahead of them. Pierce had picked up a radio frequency signal thirty seconds ago that had stopped them in their tracks—a little more than two hundred feet from the southernmost point of the collapsed bunker.

The multichannel radio frequency detector had flagged a short-frequency burst at 1622 MHz—in the L-band used for satellite phone communications. The burst puzzled them. A person using a satellite phone would emit a steady signal for the duration of the call. Even a single line of text data would create a longer radio frequency event than they'd detected. All they really knew at this point was that the signal didn't belong, and that was enough to halt their approach.

Decker slowly panned the scope from left to right, looking for any hot spots that would appear white on the dark background. He gave it another minute before kneeling next to Pierce.

"I don't see anything," whispered Decker.

"Something's out there," said Pierce. "The signal's too strong to be background noise."

"And it can't be someone making a call, right?"

"Not unless it's some kind of new—There it goes again! Same direction. Same frequency."

"How long between bursts?"

"About two minutes," said Pierce.

"Let's see if we can triangulate this thing," said Decker. "I'll take the RF detector as far east as I can reasonably move in two minutes and mark my GPS position, along with the direction of the next burst. I'll do the same in a westerly direction. It won't be the best triangulation, but at least we'll get some sense of the signal's distance."

"Better than nothing," said Pierce, handing him the detector.

Decker gave Pierce the thermal scope before climbing over the short rise to their immediate right. He activated the stopwatch function of his wristwatch and started walking briskly, carefully studying the terrain ahead of him for trip hazards. When the stopwatch read ninety seconds, he stopped and plotted his position on the GPS receiver, unsure if the 260 feet he'd traveled would be enough.

He crouched and waited for the next burst, which appeared on the RF detector a few seconds later. Definitely a regularly timed signal. Maybe some kind of automatic check-in? But what was checking in, and with whom? Decker entered the direction in the GPS, creating a direction line from his current point to the mystery object. A quick mental calculation told him that the object wasn't very far away. A few hundred feet at most. They'd know for sure after the next direction line.

Decker hustled back to Pierce, pausing briefly to let him know that he thought the signal source was at the southern edge of the site. Now he was starting to suspect it was some kind of passive surveillance device, which regularly checked in with its tracking station—in case an intruder disabled it. If that were the case, they'd have to expedite their investigation at the site.

He took off and repeated the GPS trick on their western flank. The direction of the next burst confirmed what he'd guessed about the distance. The source was nearby. Decker made his way back to the creek bed, crossing the jeep trail he had missed the first time. He settled in next to Pierce and showed him the GPS.

"Same result. I think it's dead ahead. Maybe two to three hundred feet," said Decker. "I crossed the jeep trail. Looks well worn."

"I couldn't find anything out there," said Pierce, handing him the scope.

"I think we're looking at an automated check-in signal," said Decker. "As long as it keeps transmitting, the tracking station knows it's still operational."

"Some kind of newest-generation surveillance device?"

"That's my guess," said Decker. "The cartels have a lot of money, and they're not afraid to spend it on gear."

"We won't be able to spend much time at the site," said Pierce. "Not if the signal goes straight to the Sinaloa."

"How long?"

"Twenty, maybe thirty minutes. Tops," said Pierce. "I can't imagine them taking more than an hour to get out here. Gives us some time to disappear."

"That's not going to buy a lot of distance," said Decker. "They'll be all over us with Jeeps and ATVs. All kinds of stuff."

"Or not," said Pierce. "Maybe they'll just assume it was a group of migrants passing through."

"If this place is important to the cartel, I'm willing to bet it's off-limits to the coyotes," said Decker. "If we trigger an alarm, we can expect company."

"It's your call," said Pierce.

"Don't give me that again."

"I say we do it," said Pierce. "Take ten minutes to look around and get the hell out of here. I mean, what are we expecting to find up there? A notebook the cartel accidentally left behind describing the contents of the bunker?"

"Probably not," said Decker. "We'll locate the signal source, neutralize it, and do a quick site survey. I never expected to find anything out here. Figured this would be an easy job to keep Senator Steele happy. A walk in the park."

"Through cartel land?" said Pierce. "You have a funny concept of *easy*. I need to remember that the next time my phone rings and I see your number."

"I'll be sure to remind you," said Decker.

"That doesn't even make sense," said Pierce. "You can't remind me if I don't answer your call."

"No. It doesn't make sense because I'd never remind you if you actually did answer my call," said Decker. "That would mean you'd forgotten."

"I'm not even going to try to figure out what you just said," said Pierce.

"Good call. I don't think you're not smart enough to figure it out," said Decker, fueling their nervous humor.

Pierce shook his head and mumbled something out of earshot before moving out—with the MAC-10 pointed in the direction of the signal. They walked guardedly in a staggered column down the shallow wash, pausing every twenty paces or so to search the landscape ahead of them for signs of something that didn't belong.

Antennae. A blinking light. Reflective camera lens. Anything. If they didn't locate the source by the time they'd reached the edge of the bunker, Decker would suggest they assume the alarm had gone out to the Sinaloa and start the investigation of the site. Ten minutes and gone. Hopefully it would be enough.

Decker watched the GPS receiver, stopping them when they had reached a point thirty feet from the southern edge of the collapsed bunker. From what he could tell, the site lay just beyond the stubby rise directly in front of them. The jeep trail sat about a hundred feet to their left, running parallel to the creek bed they had used to approach the site.

"My bet is it's just over the rise," said Decker.

"Odd place to put a surveillance device," said Pierce. "Not exactly outward facing."

"For all we know, it could be facing the bunker entrance," said Decker. "This is a well-concealed approach. You ready to take a peek?"

"Hold on," said Pierce, pausing to check the RF detector again. "Shit."

"What?"

"I have a second, much fainter signal," said Pierce. "Same frequency. Different direction—but not by much."

"Point, please," whispered Decker.

Pierce pointed directly ahead of them and then moved his arm to the one o'clock position.

"Still blocked by the rocks," said Decker.

"Or at the other end of the site," said Pierce.

Decker considered his statement for a moment, suddenly realizing their mistake.

"We have this backward," said Decker.

"I don't—" started Pierce. "Ah. Satellite comms are line of sight."

"Right. The first signal source is probably located at the far end of the bunker, on high enough ground to be within line of sight. The second, fainter signal is on the other side of these rocks. The detector finally registered the extremely limited ground wave associated with the ultra-high-frequency signal."

"Time to rip off the Band-Aid," said Pierce.

Decker shoved the GPS in one of his pockets and hurried to catch up with Pierce, who had already started climbing the small rise. He'd nearly reached the rocks when Pierce yelled an obscenity—and a long burst from his MAC-10 stitched over the quiet night.

A second, shorter burst immediately followed.

"All good," said Pierce.

Decker scrambled up, reaching him a moment later. "What happened?"

"Take a look," said Pierce, pointing at a bizarre, mechanical-looking device on the other side of the rocks. "I'm pretty sure I killed it. Whatever it is. It started to come after me."

"Seriously?"

"That's what it looked like," said Pierce, slamming a fresh magazine into his weapon.

Decker shouldered his weapon, keeping it aimed at the object as he moved forward to take a closer look.

"Can you hit it with your flashlight while I keep it covered?" said Decker.

He took a few hesitant steps forward, preparing to jump down from the short ledge, when Pierce's light illuminated the machine.

"Oh. Shit. Get back. Get back," said Decker, yanking Pierce behind a half-buried boulder.

"What was it?" said Pierce. "You blocked my view."

"Spider Networked Munition. A version I've never seen before," said Decker. "Looked highly mobile."

"Armed spider bots? We're out of here," said Pierce. "Right now."

"I didn't see any grenade canisters. They might just be using it as a very high-tech sensor," said Decker.

"It transmits via satellite," said Pierce. "And it moved really fast. That's not an off-the-shelf item. It's military grade. If the cartel—"

Decker held a finger to his lips, quieting Pierce. Something was moving out there, the sounds coming from the site.

"If I look over this rock and see a hundred spider bots," said Pierce, "I swear . . ."

"Swear what?" said Decker, rising to a crouch.

"Swear I'll never talk to you again," said Pierce, raising his submachine gun.

"I can live with that," said Decker, patting his shoulder. "Ready to do this?"

"Not really," said Pierce.

They rose at the same time, immediately spotting the source of the noise. A single spider bot moved steadily across the sunken void created by the sudden collapse of the bunker—still at least a hundred yards away.

"Fucking creepy," said Pierce.

"At least there's only one," said Decker.

"That we know of."

Without warning, the spider bot raced straight for them, somehow picking up speed over the uneven, buckled terrain. Decker couldn't believe what he was seeing. The latest version of the Spider Networked Munition had been advertised as static. Soldiers had to plant it in the ground. This thing was several generations ahead of anything he'd read about.

"Oh. Hell no," said Pierce, extending his MAC-10's flimsy wire stock.

Decker did the same, nestling the weapon into his shoulder. They'd be lucky to hit this thing outside of fifty feet. More like thirty. The firearm was more of a spray-and-pray phenomenon favored by gangbangers.

"We empty a mag each at max range," said Pierce. "Reload and go with short bursts. You sure these things aren't armed?"

"Not sure about anything at this point," said Decker, resting the bottom of the long suppressor against the top of the boulder.

"Say when," said Pierce.

Decker tracked the cat-size spider bot as it clattered toward them, trying to gauge fifty feet through the night-vision goggles. He resisted the temptation to lift the goggles. By the time his eyes adjusted to the darkness, it would be too late. The thing moved too damn fast.

"Stand by," said Decker, waiting a little longer. "Here we go. Three. Two. One. Do it."

He kept the crude weapon pointed at the spider bot for the 1.5 seconds it took to empty the magazine—praying for a high percentage of hits. The moment his weapon stopped firing, he dropped the spent magazine and inserted a new one, reacquiring the spider bot, which appeared to have slowed down. Pierce and Decker alternated bursts for the next few seconds, hearing metal tear through metal, until the thing stopped moving altogether. They dropped behind the boulder and reloaded.

"That wasn't so bad," said Pierce.

Before Decker could respond, a massive explosion shattered the night, knocking them flat. They remained pressed against the ground, ears ringing as a heavy shower of rocks and sand pelted them from above. When the last of the debris kicked up by the explosion had fallen, they sat up and very carefully looked around the boulder. A fifteen-foot-wide, five-foot-deep crater sat where the spider had stopped—less than fifty feet away.

"Can we go home now?" said Pierce.

Decker stared at the crater without answering. It almost looked like the explosion had opened a section of the bunker, or maybe his eyes were playing tricks.

"Does that look like an opening to you?" said Decker.

"Yeah. It looks like the ground opened up and tried to swallow us," said Pierce, walking past Decker.

He followed Pierce to the far right edge of the ledge, where the other spider bot lay motionless.

"That thing had me dead to rights," said Pierce.

Decker stared at it for a moment. If it had detonated when Pierce climbed over the rise, there wouldn't have been anything left of his friend.

"I think the self-destruct feature is remotely activated," said Decker. "You killed it before it received that signal. I want to take a look at the crater."

"You can't be serious," said Pierce. "That explosion could probably be heard as far away as Mexicali. This place is about to get busy."

"I don't think so," said Decker. "That was a latest-generation US military robotic device. My guess is that even the cartel isn't welcome here."

"That doesn't make sense."

"None of this does," said Decker. "Which is why I want to check out that crater. Just in case I can get a glimpse of whatever they buried."

"Ten minutes," said Pierce. "I'll get some pictures of the intact spider."

"Don't touch it," said Decker. "We don't know why it didn't detonate."

"Seriously? Like my mom used to say," said Pierce, "touch with your eyes."

CHAPTER TWENTY

Decker approached the crater like it could expand and drag him under at any moment. While half of him focused on the bunker, the other half worried about another suicide bot skittering out of the bushes surrounding the site—hell-bent on delivering its lethal payload. The RF detector convinced him that only two spider bots had been deployed to the site, but he found it impossible to shake the thought of another lurking in the dark. Watching and waiting for the right moment.

When he reached the recently blasted cavity, he took a deep breath and slid down the side of the crater, his feet landing solidly at its jagged bottom. A one-foot-by-two-foot-wide breach in the side of the hole, framed on one side by a splintered wooden beam, revealed a pitch-black interior. Decker raised his night-vision goggles and took out a flashlight before kneeling in front of the gap.

He stuck the light inside and turned it on, peering through the gap. A thick cloud of suspended dust particles reflected the powerful beam, allowing him to see barely more than a few feet into the hole. Aware that time was running out, he took off his backpack and dug out the foldable shovel, known as the e-tool, or entrenching tool, to Marines. He snapped the two pieces open and locked them together to form a sturdy, compact shovel, which he jammed into the earth several inches from the left edge of the hole.

The shovel sank into the dirt far enough to encourage him. He lifted a foot and struck the shovel's shoulder with the bottom of his heel, driving it all the way through and breaking off a large chunk of earth. Decker repeated the process several more times until he had formed a hole large enough to fit through. He shined the light inside again, still unable to determine how far the space extended. Only one way to find out.

Decker removed his night vision and weapon, placing them on top of his backpack, before scooting feetfirst into the hole. He snaked through the opening until his feet struck something solid. A series of kicks in different directions determined that the space didn't extend any farther than his legs. One of the kicks had struck a piece of wood that felt different from the heavy beams that had once held up the structure. He turned onto his stomach and pulled his legs out of the hole, curious about the hollow sound the wood had made.

"Five minutes," said Pierce, who watched over him from the nearest cluster of boulders.

"Yeah. Yeah," muttered Decker, turning himself around to face the hole.

A crazy thought flashed through his head, which he just as quickly dismissed. A few moments later, it was back.

"Bad idea, Decker. Really bad idea," he muttered, unable to shake it.

He couldn't leave without giving it a try. Decker stood up and whispered to Pierce, "I'm going in the hole. If I'm not back out in three minutes, come get me."

"No! Absolutely not!" hissed Pierce, but Decker had already dropped to both knees. "Dammit, Decker. If you get stuck, I'm leaving you!"

"No, you won't," he said to himself.

Decker gripped the flashlight between his teeth and stuck both arms through the opening, feeling for the rubble below. When his hands found the bottom, he crawled forward until his hands found the long plank of wood. Before he could take the flashlight out of his mouth, he started to cough uncontrollably from the dust. The flashlight dropped and rolled into a crevasse to the left, stopping just out of his reach.

He really didn't want to pull his legs into the hole, but he didn't see any way around it. Without the light, he couldn't examine the hollow piece of wood. He tried for the flashlight again, extending his hand as far as he could stretch it but falling a few inches short.

"Screw it," he whispered, bringing his legs inside.

Crammed into a painfully uncomfortable fetal position, he grabbed the flashlight and twisted his torso to face the plank that had drawn Decker into a constricted space barely large enough to fit him. He ran the light along the surface of the wood, immediately recognizing it as a section of a military crate. His hand froze when he read the black stencil identifying the crate's contents.

NSN 1430-01-433-8019
EQUIPMENT SET, CLU (COMMAND LAUNCH UNIT)
M98A1 (JAVELIN WEAPON SYSTEM, COMPLETE)

No wonder they buried this place in a hurry—whoever "they" turned out to be. He dug into one of his camouflage jacket's pockets and removed a thin digital camera, taking a dozen or more pictures of the stenciled nomenclature. A brief attempt to loosen the side of the crate with his hands yielded nothing, so he decided it was time to get moving.

For the next few minutes, Decker tried to work his way into a position where he could grip the beam on the side of the hole to pull himself out, but he couldn't move his arms into a position to gain enough leverage to fully turn around. A mild panic took hold until he heard a string of obscenities from above and someone slid into the crater.

"Decker?" said a familiar voice.

"I'm kind of stuck!" said Decker.

A dark face appeared in the opening above his legs. "We have company. I registered another signal a few seconds ago, originating from the north. I think they may have remotely activated a third spider bot."

Decker extended a free hand, and Pierce pulled him free. He crawled onto the floor of the crater and turned onto his back.

"How much time do we have?"

"No idea," said Pierce, raising the RF detector. "But the signal is getting stronger."

Decker grabbed his night-vision goggles and peeked out of the crater, catching movement at the far northern end of the stretch of sunken field. The third mechanical suicide bomber skittered into view, moving deftly across the broken ground.

"Spider bot headed our way," said Decker.

Pierce took a quick look. "It's not coming directly for us. We could draw it toward us and use the crater as cover."

"I don't think the remote operator will make the same mistake twice," said Decker. "They'll probably detonate it while we're up and firing, hoping to catch us in the blast. We need a different strategy."

"Hide in the hole?" said Pierce.

"Only one of us will fit."

"I know."

Decker smiled, then rapidly scanned the landscape around them. "I think I have an idea, but you're not going to like it."

"That's a shocker," said Pierce. "Let me hear it."

A few seconds later, Pierce just shook his head. "Your plan doesn't leave a lot of room for error."

"There's no room for error," said Decker. "But I don't see any other way. We'll never shake this thing once it starts tracking us."

Pierce shrugged. "Lead the way."

Decker shouldered his backpack and climbed out of the crater, pretending to examine his GPS unit. Pierce knelt next to him and pointed his MAC-10 south, in the opposite direction of the inbound threat. The robot responded immediately, turning toward them and picking up speed.

"It's coming right for us," said Decker. "Two hundred yards and closing fast."

"This is crazy."

"It'll work," said Decker. "The bot's camera is at ground level."

"What are the options if it doesn't come directly at us or stops short?"

"Do exactly what I do," said Decker. "I'll come up with something."

"That's reassuring."

When Decker estimated the spider bot to be about fifty feet away, he shook Pierce's arm, and they both dropped to the ground, pointing their weapons at the robot. They fired wildly at the spider bot, purposefully emptying their thirty-two-round magazines without scoring a single hit. While they scrambled to reload the MAC-10s, the remotely guided machine charged mercilessly forward—before abruptly dropping into the crater.

Decker and Pierce finished reloading the moment it disappeared, both of them immediately angling their weapons' long suppressors down into the crater and firing a long burst into the spider bot. The sound of metal striking metal convinced him they had accomplished the mission. The robot had sustained too much damage to climb out of the crater on its own.

They'd managed to crawl several feet away from the edge of the hole when the spider bot's explosive charge detonated—violently shaking the ground beneath them. As Decker had predicted, the depth and shape of the crater directed the bulk of the blast skyward, shielding them from the potentially lethal shock waves and fragmentation. Ears ringing, Decker lay on his stomach with the backpack pulled over his head until the shower of dirt and rocks kicked up by the blast stopped pelting him. He turned onto his back to find Pierce already sitting upright—RF detector in hand.

"It's clear," said Pierce. "For now."

"You'll never guess what I found down there."

"El Chapo?"

"Funny," said Decker, standing up and dusting himself off.

"I hope it's worth robot nightmares for the rest of my life," said Pierce.

"Javelin missiles."

"Jesus, Decker. This isn't a cartel bunker."

"Maybe it is," said Decker. "Connected to a road on the US side, which just happens to be controlled by our military. Time to get as far away from here as possible."

CHAPTER TWENTY-ONE

Out of breath and aching from a relentlessly paced hour of hiking and climbing, Decker started to look for a concealed place to rest. They had put more than two miles between themselves and the bunker site, over rough terrain that would make it extremely difficult for anyone to track them.

Their original plan had been to parallel the border toward Mexicali, cutting south a few miles east of the military checkpoint, where they'd hide in sight of the highway and wait for an early-morning pickup. The surprising discovery in the bunker convinced them to do precisely the opposite.

The eastern route was too exposed, half of it a flat desert wasteland, broken up by small clusters of widely separated, low-lying hills. Easy pickings for a well-equipped cartel and whoever they were in business with up north—especially given the distant aerial buzzing that had started several minutes ago. Decker had immediately recognized the sound. So had Pierce. An MQ-9 Reaper, likely armed with a full payload of guided missiles, had been deployed from a nearby US air base to investigate their run-in with the spider bots. If they'd chosen to travel east, they might be dead already. The Reaper could carry up to four Hellfire air-to-ground missiles.

Instead, they had traveled southwest, away from the border and into some of the most punishing terrain near the US-Mexico border. Terrain they could use to hide if the drone expanded its search beyond the area immediately adjacent to the bunker site. On top of that, it pushed them deeper into cartel-controlled land, the last place anyone would expect to find them.

The decision came with a few drawbacks—the increased risk to their lives being the most obvious. They'd have little margin of error traveling on the cartel's home turf. Harlow and Sandra would face the same challenge on the pickup, which would most likely be delayed by more than twenty-four hours. Another drawback.

Decker highly doubted they could reach La Rumorosa by dawn. With the cartel alerted to their presence, daylight travel was impossible. Two dirty gringos sneaking around the hills would draw the wrong kind of attention. They'd lie low in an isolated arroyo north of the town and wait for tomorrow night. The delay's overall impact on the risk of Harlow's return trip could go either way. Ideally, someone else would do the pickup, in a different car.

He guided them down the side of a rocky ledge into a wide gulch thick with tall desert shrubs. After checking both directions for signs of human activity, he eased the pack off his shoulders.

"This looks good," said Decker, breathing heavily. "Fifteen minutes?"

"Works for me," said Pierce, heading for the bushes.

They pushed deep into the abrasive foliage until it ended at the arroyo's rock-strewn western edge. Neither of them spoke for several minutes while they sipped stingily from their CamelBaks and split one of the extra energy bars Decker had stashed in his backpack. They faced a long twenty-four hours without any hope of a resupply.

"I should call Harlow," said Decker. "Let her know the new plan—and pass along what we found."

"All right," said Pierce, getting up. "I'll keep watch."

Pierce disappeared, rustling the bushes in the darkness for a few seconds, before going still. Decker checked the signal on the satellite phone, thankful the antenna wasn't blocked by the rock wall on the other side of the stream bed. Harlow answered the call before he heard the first ring tone.

"You're out of there?" she said. "On the way back?"

"Sort of," said Decker. "I need to make this quick, so let me talk."

"Is everything okay?"

"Yes and no. We're fine, but everything is not okay, which is why I need to keep this short. Do you have a pen?"

"Yes. Go ahead," said Harlow.

"We encountered and neutralized two Spider Networked Munitions at the site. Satellite communications capable. L-band. Sixteen hundred and twenty-two MHz. Highly mobile. One was equipped with a powerful explosive device, which detonated near us. Resembled a robotic spider. The crater left by the detonation led to a hole in the bunker. I briefly entered the hole and found part of a military crate. Crate contained the M98A1 Javelin antitank missile system. I did not see an actual launcher or missiles. Just read the nomenclature stenciled on the side of the crate. Got it?"

"Got it," said Harlow. "What the hell is that place?"

"No idea," said Decker. "We were lucky to get a look inside. Make sure you pass this on to Senator Steele immediately. Like right now."

"We'll pass it along," said Harlow. "How far are you from the pickup area? We'll cross at first light and get you out of there."

"That's not going to happen tonight," said Decker. "We opted to head southwest, over more difficult terrain. The western run was too exposed."

"Wait. You're headed toward La Rumorosa?"

A faint bird chirp kept him from answering. He disconnected the call and sent a quick text message before turning off the phone.

> Busy. Pickup following AM. La Rumorosa. Different car and driver. Stay safe.

Without making any noise, he moved silently toward the edge of the scrub, where he found Pierce, his MAC-10 shouldered and pointed south. He knelt next to Pierce and readied his weapon.

"What do you have?" he whispered, his voice barely audible.

"Movement. Lots of it. Can't ID."

"You want me to spread out?"

Pierce shook his head and gave him a hand signal indicating he had "eyes on." Decker peered through the thick tangle of branches and leaves, catching a glimpse of a dark figure walking down the middle of the arroyo. A few moments later, several more indistinguishable figures appeared, trailing the first by at least twenty feet.

The lead figure stopped and yelled at the group. *"¡Vámonos! ¡Llegamos tarde! ¡El camión no espera!"*

"Coyote," whispered Decker.

Pierce nodded and continued to track the leader with the business end of his weapon. Decker checked his watch. One thirty a.m. *Kind of late for one of these runs.* They could be pushing sunrise by the time they reached *el camión*, or the truck. As the group drew closer, Decker had his second really bad idea of the night. One he needed to share immediately before the opportunity slipped away.

"This guy can get us over the border," he whispered.

Pierce shook his head emphatically.

"The border can't be more than a mile and a half due north. Maybe less," said Decker. "Interstate 8 is just a couple miles past that. We could be eating breakfast at Denny's in a few hours."

More head shaking.

"It's the perfect cover," said Decker. "We'll look like migrants to a drone pilot."

Pierce turned his head. "Decker. No."

"Too late," said Decker, nodding at the lead figure, who now stood motionless. "Trust me. This is a good idea."

He stepped into the open, pointing his weapon at the man's chest. The man raised his hands. A few of the migrants immediately behind him gasped and held their hands high. Most of them couldn't see what was happening in the dark.

"Dammit, Decker," mumbled Pierce, joining him in the open.

"¿Habla inglés?" said Decker.

"Sí," said the man, nodding. "I mean, yes. Yes."

"We need to get over the border," said Decker. *"Muy pronto."*

"Okay," said the man.

"You'll take us?" said Decker.

"Sí. Yes."

"What's your name?"

"Jesús."

"Jesús. Is this your usual route?" said Decker. "Regular route?"

"Ah. Yes. Every night. Twice."

"Twice?" said Pierce. "You mean, like you return to Mexico and do it again?"

"Yes. No problems here. No Border Patrol," said Jesús. "We go fast."

"Wait. No Border Patrol?" said Decker.

"Sí. Yes. No problems for a month. Very easy."

"They probably cross inside the exclusion zone," said Pierce.

"Makes sense," said Decker. "Especially if JTF North is doing business with the Sinaloa."

"No Sinaloa here," said Jesús. "No Sinaloa."

"Uh-huh," said Pierce. "There's no cartel out here."

"There's no Sinaloa," said Jesús.

"Qué cartel?" said Decker.

"Not the Sinaloa," said Jesús.

Decker had a few more questions before they took off.

"Can you cross anywhere along the border?"

"No. Not in the middle," said Jesús.

"Middle? What do you mean?"

"One kilometer of the border is off-limits. We have a kilometer on each side. No more than that or we have Border Patrol problems."

"What's in the middle?" said Decker.

"I don't know, and I don't ask questions," said Jesús. "Can I lower my hands? I can't walk far like this."

Pierce stepped forward. "Keep your hands up. Do you have a phone?"

"Just a cell phone," said Jesús.

"There's no cell reception out here," said Pierce. "Is it a satellite phone?"

"That's too expensive," said Jesús.

"Jesús? I'm only going to ask one more time," said Pierce. "Do you have a satellite phone? I can lead these good people to the border on my own, especially since you just told me exactly where I can cross without any—problems?"

"*Sí.* Back pocket," said Jesús. "But it's not mine. They'll make me pay for it if you smash it. Or worse."

"I'm not going to smash it. Just going to make sure you don't send out some kind of warning," said Pierce. "Turn around and keep those hands high. Got him?"

"I got him," said Decker, pointing the MAC-10 at Jesús's head.

Pierce retrieved the phone, which appeared to be a basic model. He stepped back and quickly examined the settings before stuffing it in one of his pockets.

"Jesús? I need you to remember something *muy importante*," said Decker. "Can you remember one thing?"

"Yes. Yes. What is it?"

"If you lead us into a problem, you'll never hear the bullet that kills you. *¿Comprende?*"

"*Sí,*" said Jesús in a flat voice. "No problems. I'm the only one out here."

"You better be," said Pierce, motioning for him to move.

"What do I tell them?" said Jesús, nodding at the two dozen or so people huddled behind him.

"Tell them we're here to make sure you do a good job," said Decker. "And they can never speak of us, to anyone."

"Very good idea," said Jesús. "We don't want that happening."

While Jesús instructed his flock, Pierce took Decker aside.

"He's going to rat us out the first chance he gets. Probably right after we part ways north of the border."

"Nothing we can do about that," said Decker. "Harlow and Sandra will pick us up as soon as we hit the interstate. We'll be fine."

"Don't underestimate the cartel's capabilities on the other side of that wall," said Pierce. "And don't forget about that mystery bunker's still-unidentified patron—who I'm almost certain has free rein up there."

"I don't want to sign that guy's death warrant," said Decker.

"Better than Harlow's or Sandra's—or mine," said Pierce.

"You forgot to include me in there."

"I didn't forget," said Pierce, before switching to a whisper. "We have to smash the phone. There's no other way. He can say he tripped and dropped it. We can give him enough money to buy a new one. That's my final offer."

"Accepted," said Decker.

"Ready, amigos?" said Jesús, headed in their direction.

"Lead the way," said Decker.

A few minutes later, the Reaper drone's distinctive buzz intensified, echoing off the canyon walls. Decker lowered his head to conceal the night-vision goggles, praying that the drone pilots wouldn't bother to look too closely at a group of Mexicans trudging north toward the border.

Chapter Twenty-Two

Harlow slowed the car, easing them off the interstate at the In-Koh-Pa Park Road exit. They passed a cluster of darkened, squat buildings on their right, which appeared to be the only structures within sight.

"We're screwed if Border Patrol is watching," said Harlow.

"Nothing illegal going on here," said Sandra.

"I'm talking about Decker and Pierce," said Harlow. "They've been walking right through a heavily patrolled area, wearing night vision."

"Maybe the Border Patrol figured they're with one of those militia groups watching the border," said Sandra. "If CBP hasn't checked them out by now, they should be fine."

"Don't count on it," said Harlow.

"It'll be fine," said Sandra. "CBP will run our info through their database and search the car—finding nothing suspicious. We're good to go."

"Let's just hope they ditched the MAC-10s," said Harlow.

"Yeah. That would kind of be a showstopper."

She turned left at the end of the off-ramp, headed south along an unlit access road that paralleled the interstate. A quarter of a mile down, she turned again and cruised through the interstate underpass, coming to a stop sign that marked the start of Old Highway 80.

"This is the middle of nowhere," said Harlow.

"Pretty damn close to it," said Sandra, checking Harlow's phone. "They're at the trailhead, sitting in the bushes."

"Tell them to ditch the guns if they haven't already," said Harlow.

"I'd rather not put that in writing," said Sandra. "You know. In case Border Patrol picks us up."

Harlow drove a few hundred yards down Old Highway 80, almost missing the unmarked turnoff for the Valley of the Moon trailhead. She slammed on the brakes, the car skidding on the sand-coated road.

"It's like they're trying to hide this," she muttered, putting the car in reverse.

She pulled into a wide, semicircular sand lot imprinted with tire tracks and anchored by a covered information board that stood in the center of the trailhead parking area. Harlow turned off the headlights and parked next to the information panel as Sandra pressed "Send" on a text. A few seconds later, Decker and Pierce appeared about fifty feet beyond the edge of the lot, deep in the waist-high scrub.

They got about halfway before lights appeared in the hills behind them and to Harlow's left, down a dirt road connected to the parking area. Decker and Pierce started to run.

"You should turn us around," said Sandra.

Flashing red and blue lights on a vehicle approaching from the left killed that idea.

"Shit. Border Patrol," said Harlow.

They rolled down their windows, exposing their ears to an incomprehensible barrage of distant megaphone commands.

"Should we get out?" said Sandra. "Wait for them with our IDs ready?"

"Probably not a bad idea," she said, turning off the car and getting out.

Decker and Pierce arrived, huffing from the sprint. They looked dirty, ragged, and completely out of place in their camouflage outfits. The original pickup plan, on the other side of the border, had included a change of clothes and a box of baby wipes to clean up.

"Please tell me you got rid of the guns," said Harlow.

"Good to see you, too," said Decker. "We broke them down into pieces and scattered them before exiting the military exclusion zone."

"The one good decision he's made all night," said Pierce, dropping his backpack on the ground. "This should be fun."

"Not a problem. We got lost on our way back from the Valley of the Moon," said Decker.

Pierce stared at him incredulously. "Do you even know what that is? Could you describe it if they asked?"

"Winding trail surrounded by giant boulders and rock piles that resemble the moon's surface. You probably came up on the border, which is marked by a few strings of neglected barbed wire someone could step over. Scenic vistas into Mexico. That kind of stuff," said Sandra. "Pulled that off the internet at the hotel."

"Sounds about right to me," said Decker.

"You do realize we're dressed in camouflage," said Pierce.

"Better for watching the wildlife?"

Pierce shook his head and checked his watch. "And it's four in the morning."

"Just stick to this story. We dropped you off for a late-afternoon hike and went back to Calexico for margaritas. Enjoyed them a little too much and kind of forgot about you until the sun went down. We got worried and tried to call but couldn't get through. Didn't want to drive drunk, so we took a nap and woke up to your messages."

"It's thin," said Pierce. "But we're all US citizens. No drugs. No weapons. What can they do?"

"We're about to find out," said Harlow, turning to face the SUV racing in from the north. "Stay cool."

A white-and-green Chevy Tahoe skidded to a stop a few feet behind their car's rear bumper, effectively blocking their departure, as two ATVs raced down the hill along the Valley of the Moon's trail. Border Patrol agents in the tinted-window SUV hopped out of their vehicle, one walking down the opposite side of the car—the other approaching them directly.

"What's going on here?" said the agent, blinding them with a flashlight.

"Just picking up these two idiots," said Sandra, obnoxiously enough to get an eye roll from Decker.

Sandra ran her concocted story past the agent while his partner peered through the windows of the car with a flashlight. When Sandra finished, the stocky agent shook his head.

"Anything?" he yelled to the agent on the other side of the car.

"Inside looks clean," she said, stepping around the hood of the car. "Mind popping the trunk?"

"I'd like to take a look in those backpacks, too," said the burly agent.

The ATVs arrived, mostly drowning out Decker's answer, which Harlow construed to be a little more adversarial than necessary, particularly given their desire to expedite the encounter and get as far away from here as possible this morning. She hit his leg with her hand while the agent told the ATV patrol to shut down their vehicles.

"We consent to a brief look inside the trunk for immigrants, but that doesn't extend to opening the suitcases," said Harlow. "The backpacks are off-limits as well."

"Sounds like an ACLU lawyer," said the agent who had inspected the vehicle.

"No. An ACLU lawyer would have more sense than to be out here at four in the morning," said the stocky agent in front of them. "And they certainly wouldn't let us look in the trunk without putting up a fight."

He examined each of them from head to toe with his flashlight before turning off the light and stepping forward.

"I'm gonna run your driver's licenses," said the agent. "If you wouldn't mind producing them."

He took the licenses and compared them to their faces, pausing longer to examine Decker and Pierce.

"Nice outfits," said the agent before turning for the Border Patrol SUV.

The ID check lasted several very long minutes, made even longer by a constant barrage of questions from the other three agents—which they answered carefully and concisely. When the agent returned with their driver's licenses, Harlow could tell he was annoyed.

"Everything looks good on this end—Ms. Roberts—and the rest of you," he said, holding the IDs out for her to grab.

When she reached out to take them, he pulled them just out of her grasp.

"But your story is one hundred percent, grade-A bullshit," said the agent, singling out Decker and Pierce. "I don't know what the two of you were doing out there, but you sure as hell weren't hiking. We don't need a bunch of yahoos out there pretending to do our jobs for us."

A seemingly endless silence ensued.

"Screw it," said the agent, handing Harlow the IDs. "If we run into you again, outside of trail hours—sunrise to sunset—we'll take you back to the station for detailed questioning. The forty-eight-hour-long version. I suggest you get moving before I change my mind."

Decker and Pierce tossed their backpacks in the trunk, purposefully giving the Border Patrol agents a quick look inside to leave them somewhat reassured that releasing them had been the right decision. Harlow backtracked through the underpass and drove south on Interstate 8, which would wind west in a few miles, taking them into San Diego County.

"You guys okay?" said Harlow. "You're awfully quiet back there."

"Just tired," said Pierce.

"We needed that Border Patrol stop like a hole in the head. Won't take much digging to figure out who took a close look at their bunker," said Decker. "This is going to come back at us pretty fast."

"That ship sailed the second we nailed the spiders," said Pierce. "Now it's just going to be easier for them to connect the dots."

"How fast did those things move?" said Sandra.

"Fast. Like jogging speed," said Decker. "Over broken ground."

"That's really creepy," said Sandra.

"Yeah. Especially when you discover they can blow you to pieces if they get close enough," added Pierce.

"We did some research into Spider Networked Munitions," said Harlow. "I couldn't find any reference to a satellite-controlled version or anything mobile. This is new tech."

"New and highly classified tech," said Decker. "It looked similar enough to the older variants that I'm guessing it's military—which means we have a really big problem on our hands."

"This is way bigger than one of the cartels breaking into the human-trafficking business. Not to downplay that," said Pierce.

"I understand what you're saying," said Harlow. "As nauseating as this sounds, the kids were probably a sideshow out there."

Without looking, she could feel them shaking their heads in disgust. Nobody spoke for another mile, a combination of sheer exhaustion and deep thought holding their words at bay.

"So—how long do we have until they come after us?" said Harlow. "That's probably the most important question right now. We need to protect ourselves."

"Sorry this happened again," said Decker.

"Why would you be sorry?" said Harlow.

"I keep dragging the firm into the mess I created," said Decker.

"Oh boy," said Sandra.

"We can talk about this later, but for the record, I don't get dragged into anything I don't ask for. Same with the rest of the firm's partners," said Harlow. "We weighed the risks of bringing you on board against the rewards—"

"Isn't it usually the other way around?" said Pierce, chuckling a little. "Rewards against the risks?"

"Not in his case," said Sandra.

"Thanks," said Decker, kicking her seat.

"We decided the risks you brought to the firm would ultimately be the reward," said Harlow. "After taking down Harcourt, Frist, and Drozdov, I think it's fair to say we made the right call."

"For what it's worth, Decker, I still think you're worth keeping around," said Sandra. "It's a close call after tonight, but . . ."

"We just need to get past this little setback and we're back on track," said Harlow.

"I think this is going to be more than a little setback," said Decker.

"Which brings us back to—what's coming after us and when?" said Harlow.

"Depends on how fast the cartel moves, on a few different fronts," said Decker. "It won't take them long to put two and two together and guess that we were dropped off on the Mexican side. Did they get close enough to read your license plate outside Tecate?"

"Yeah. They came right up on us before we reached the highway split," said Harlow. "I think it was routine surveillance. They probably caught up to the couple in the SUV after we turned for the border."

"They have the resources to track down the license plate," said Decker.

"Which is a dead end," said Sandra. "We used your fake ID to rent the car, which is linked to a completely different picture in the DMV system. Facial recognition will give them nothing."

"But the rental agency probably has video of me in the branch," said Decker. "They'll lean on their contacts inside LAPD to run the image."

"Reeves scrubbed us from the system to keep any of Harcourt's surviving goons from tapping into it. Right?" said Harlow. "Your face won't trigger a match."

"I guess if they don't know who I am from the start, they can't really use the system."

"Let's assume they have their own facial-recognition database. One with all of our faces in it," said Pierce. "They could grab images from the Mexican immigration office. We all sat in front of their cameras for twenty minutes."

"I give it twenty-four hours before they start kicking in doors," said Decker. "Could go faster than that."

"That's not a lot of time," said Harlow.

"We need to go to ground when we get back to LA. Noon at the latest, in case they can move faster than we think," said Decker. "Brad needs to get out of town as soon as possible. There's no link to his house as far as anybody knows."

"I'll have one of our cutouts buy a car in San Diego and deliver it this afternoon. You should drive back to Colorado instead of taking a flight, so they can't possibly identify you. I don't know if they can investigate that deeply, but I don't want to take the chance," said Harlow.

"I appreciate that. Seriously," said Pierce. "I wouldn't be surprised if they could."

"Even if they can't—whoever supplied them with antitank missiles might have that kind of reach," said Decker. "We have no idea how deep this little conspiracy runs."

"Hard to imagine anything worse than Harcourt's treachery," said Harlow, immediately regretting her choice of words.

Harcourt's name still hit Decker like a punch to the gut. Sometimes he was tensed and ready, barely skipping a beat. Most of the time it knocked the wind out of him for a few hours, leaving him in a somber mood. Occasionally, it laid him flat—and he spiraled into darkness for days. She could never tell which scenario would unfold.

"He . . . uh. Yeah . . . well," said Decker, momentarily struggling for words. "Harcourt isn't the only poisonous snake in the system."

"*Was* in the system," said Pierce.

"Trust me. He's still out there, planning his next coup," said Decker. "We just haven't sniffed him out yet."

Harlow wasn't sure what to make of his last comment. He'd agreed not to actively pursue Harcourt while working at the firm, unless Senator Steele's network of contacts provided a promising lead. That had been one of the few nonnegotiable terms her partners had insisted upon when she proposed bringing him on board.

The reasoning had made sense to her. Not only did they want him focused on embracing their present business model, which represented a significant departure from what he had built at World Recovery Group, but they also needed him to keep as low a profile as possible.

Harcourt had gone deep underground, presumably into a world filled with similarly desperate thugs and psychopaths who would be happy to lend him a helping hand. Until they received vetted, actionable intelligence, Harcourt had to be off-limits—for the sake of the firm.

Judging by Decker's sudden silence, she wondered if he hadn't already stuck his nose where it didn't belong. She started to spin up inside her head, knowing no good would come of it. Pierce saved her from saying something she'd undoubtedly regret.

"Speaking of sniffing things out, how do you plan on hiding from people that would skin children alive to find you?"

"We're pretty good at disappearing," said Sandra. "And we've been dodging the Bratva for a number of years while mostly working in plain sight."

"This is different," said Pierce. "May I make a suggestion?"

"Sure," said Sandra and Harlow at the same time.

"Pack up your team and follow me out to Colorado," said Pierce. "Your cartel problem isn't going away any time soon. They collapsed a bunker that probably took them a year to build—at the drop of a hat to hide its contents. Who knows what else is buried out there?"

"We couldn't possibly put your family at risk like that," said Harlow. "And I'm sure your wife wouldn't appreciate the sudden appearance of ten guests."

"As long as you don't leave a note with our grid coordinates on the refrigerator, nobody will ever find the place. Anna won't mind at all. Seriously," said Pierce. "Fair warning, though. The nearest sushi place is an hour drive."

"The nearest restaurant is a thirty-minute drive," said Decker.

"It's hidden away very nicely, and I have plenty of room," said Pierce.

"If you don't mind sleeping on an air mattress in the basement," said Decker.

"Finished basement—and you're about to be uninvited," said Pierce. "Give it some thought. You can set up your SCIF in one of the spare bedrooms. Maybe consider doing this until we get a better handle on who's behind the weapons in the bunker."

"We?" said Decker.

"Well. Unless you planned on reporting this to Senator Steele and walking away, I just assumed there'd be some follow-up," said Pierce.

"What's your idea of follow-up?" said Harlow.

"Shaking the bushes a little," said Pierce. "Maybe scare a snake or two out of hiding—and stomp on them."

Harlow liked the way that sounded.

CHAPTER
TWENTY-THREE

A persistent knock at the door drew Decker away from the half-stuffed suitcase on his bed and toward the main living area of the apartment—pistol drawn. Pierce's absence in light of the noise could only be explained by what had to be the longest shower in human history. Before stepping into the living room, he glanced toward the patio sliders, not detecting a shadow beyond the closed curtains. Decker walked softly through the spacious room, careful not to make a sound on the way to the kitchen, where he checked his phone for a missed call or text message from Harlow. Nothing.

Now he wished he had taken her suggestion to install a wireless peephole camera. The thought of putting his face up to the door with the cartel on the prowl didn't appeal to him. He'd never hear the bullet that ripped through the door and punctured his skull. Then again, it wasn't exactly the cartel's style to knock.

"Hello! Who is it!" he said, quickly moving to the other side of the room—just in case.

"Decker. It's Reeves."

"Supervisory Special Agent Reeves?"

"Do you have more than one Reeves in your life?"

Decker opened the door. "One is more than enough. What's up?"

"May I come in?" said Reeves.

"Kind of like a vampire asking to be invited inside," said Decker.

Reeves laughed.

Decker stepped aside, motioning for Reeves to enter.

"We're in the middle of packing," said Decker. "Heading out shortly."

"That bad?" said Reeves, peering into his apartment from the short foyer.

Decker nodded. "I think so. We're assuming the worst and going completely off the grid."

"I won't ask where you're headed," said Reeves.

"I wouldn't tell you."

"I just hope it's nowhere near LA, or any major city, for that matter. The Sinaloa Cartel has a vast network of people on their payroll, and whomever they don't own they strong-arm—or worse."

"I'm not sure we're dealing with the Sinaloa," said Decker. "The coyote that took us across insisted there was no Sinaloa in the area."

"They all deny cartel involvement," said Reeves.

"I know, but this guy didn't deny that a cartel was involved—just that it wasn't the Sinaloa," said Decker. "Can you check into this? Maybe the cartel landscape recently changed. El Chapo's capture shook things up down there. Right?"

"I'll ask the lead agent in California's drug enforcement task force," said Reeves. "Jalisco New Generation and Tijuana cartels are constantly competing for strategic territory on the border."

Decker stepped into the kitchen and opened the lightly stocked refrigerator. "Diet Coke. Seltzer. Orange juice. Beer?"

"Seltzer water would be great. Thank you," said Reeves.

"Grab a seat."

When Reeves had settled onto a stool on the other side of the counter, Decker handed him a can of lemon-flavored seltzer. He leaned against the closed refrigerator and opened a beer.

"A little early, wouldn't you say?" said Reeves.

"Not after last night," said Decker, holding the can up. "Cheers."

"Cheers," said Reeves, and both of them took a sip. "What can I do to help, Ryan? I feel a little helpless here."

"You and me both," said Decker. "Do you know what a Javelin missile is used for?"

"I did a quick internet search and watched some videos. Scary stuff," said Reeves. "I'm glad those got buried."

"Fire and forget, antitank missile, with close to a three-mile range. It can also be used against fortified positions. The operator locks on to the target, fires, and scoots—as soon as the missile leaves the tube. The warhead does the rest. Someone could launch this from the back of a pickup truck and drive away, or fire a dozen of them from the top of a building, wiping out a presidential convoy. The possibilities are endless," said Decker. "And I'm sure replacements are on the way. The cartel wouldn't have buried them like that otherwise."

"Shit," said Reeves.

"*Shit* is a bit of an understatement," said Decker. "We have no idea what other goodies got buried out there. The spider bots we encountered were absolute cutting-edge technology. We stumbled onto something huge out there. Something that might even somehow be sanctioned by the government."

"The military," said Reeves.

"Very likely. You can't buy a Javelin on the black market," said Decker. "And you can't buy Spider Networked Munitions. Certainly not the variation we encountered. In a way, Brad and I got lucky. The older variants are equipped with miniature grenade launchers, or maybe we just ran into the suicide bomber version. Can you imagine a few of those chasing down a cartel case witness outside the federal courthouse, or climbing into a federal prosecutor's backyard the night before a big trial?"

Reeves shook his head, looking overwhelmed. "So. What's the next step?"

"I don't really know," said Decker. "I thought about going to the newspapers with pictures of what we found, but my guess is it won't generate a lot of interest. A stenciled crate and a mangled robot, wrapped into a wild conspiracy theory about the US military selling sophisticated weapons to the cartels? Not exactly the most compelling reason to send a news crew to the border, and even if they could gain access to take a look from the US side—which I highly doubt—I guarantee the crater has already been filled and the robot removed."

"And nobody is getting there from the Mexico side," said Reeves.

"Right," said Decker. "The cartel will have the area locked down hard. Whatever they have planned for those missiles is too important to them to risk any further exposure."

"Do you think Senator Steele could launch an inquiry into the missing Javelin missiles?" said Reeves.

"I have no idea how that works. Once we get situated in our new digs, I'd like to arrange a conference call with the senator," said Decker. "She might be our only hope of moving this any further, if it's something worth pursuing."

"What do you mean by *that*?" said Reeves, looking surprised.

"That didn't come out right," said Decker. "What I meant is that this might not be worth exploring if we're looking at a legitimately authorized operation."

"How could arming the cartels with sophisticated weaponry be legitimate?" said Reeves.

"Our country does it all the time—all over the world."

"We don't sell weapons to drug lords," said Reeves.

"We've been arming some of the nastiest people around the world for years," said Decker. "Why not the Sinaloa, if it serves our interests? I'm speaking hypothetically, by the way."

"Because they operate right here in our country," said Reeves. "And they can't be trusted."

"All valid points," said Decker. "I'm just saying that this might have high-level support in DC. The kind of support that doesn't easily frighten—especially if the reward is big enough."

"The American people won't tolerate it."

"I don't know. We've all seen the news," said Decker. "People seem to put up with a lot when it comes to border issues. Real or not."

Reeves nodded sympathetically. "Good point. I guess we'll have to wait and see what Senator Steele is willing to stir up. How long until the crew is back up and running?"

"I think we could be ready by noon. Tomorrow," said Decker.

"All right. I'll get in touch with the senator," said Reeves. "Schedule something for tomorrow afternoon. I'll get the information about the cartels to you in advance of the meeting. Same emails and contact methods?"

"Same email. We're ditching all phones and starting over," said Decker. "One of us will call you at the office with new contact info."

Brad Pierce appeared in the doorway leading to the bedrooms, dressed in jeans and a T-shirt. He rolled a suitcase into the living area and looked up.

"Sorry to interrupt," he said, eyeing Decker's beer. "I'll take one of those."

"You're not interrupting anything," said Reeves, standing up. "I was just about to leave."

Decker tossed a cold can of beer across the room to Pierce, who snatched it out of the air with one hand.

"Before I go, I wanted to thank both of you again for everything you've done," said Reeves. "And apologize for the way I treated both of

142

you in the past. I don't think I've ever formally apologized. Actually, I know I haven't. I'm . . . uh . . . not good at this."

"Joe. It's fine. Apology accepted," said Decker. "Even though you really have nothing to apologize for. You were doing your job—maybe a little too well."

They all had a brief laugh, Reeves visibly relaxing.

"I appreciate you saying that," said Reeves. "Maybe I'll take one of those beers after all."

"Probably not the best idea at nine in the morning. My guess is the FBI frowns on that sort of thing," said Decker.

"Probably," said Reeves.

"How about when I get back?" said Decker, offering Reeves his hand for the first time—ever.

"Deal," said Reeves, grasping his hand. "Drinks are on me."

"Careful with that," said Pierce. "He's an expensive date."

"Two-drink maximum, and dinner's not included," said Reeves. "That's the fine print."

"Nice," said Decker. "Don't let the door hit you on the way out."

"Be careful, Decker. You, too, Pierce," said Reeves, opening the apartment door. "The Mexicans don't mess around."

"Neither do we," said Decker, well aware that they didn't stand a chance against an organization like one of the cartels.

Chapter Twenty-Four

Rafael Guzmán wiped the thick sheen of sweat off his forehead and contemplated the remnants of the man hanging upside down in front of him. A thick, frayed rope ran from his tightly bound ankles to a wooden rafter above, keeping the top of Jesús Serrano's battered head suspended a few feet above the rapidly expanding pool of bright-red arterial blood beneath him.

Guzmán didn't relish losing one of his more productive coyotes, but Serrano had initially lied about the new satellite phone found in his possession, and the stakes were too high right now to risk that he might be hiding something else.

Shortly, he'd bring every coyote who had worked near the border site over the past month into the warehouse, where they'd stare at Serrano's naked, brutalized corpse while his interrogators posed a few questions. Nothing brought the truth to the surface quicker than the sight and smell of a rotting colleague. He'd seen friends rat out friends, brothers turn on brothers, and children sell out their parents—all to avoid the twisted fate on display in front of them.

He handed the knife he'd used to cut Serrano's throat to Raúl, one of his top lieutenants. There was still work to be done on this one before the other coyotes arrived. Serrano hadn't required his interrogators to go beyond a single finger to satisfy their inquiry.

"Skin one of his arms from elbow to wrist and remove a few more fingers. This doesn't look bad enough."

"Yes, boss," said Raúl, wiping the knife partially clean on his jeans.

"I need to make a call," said Guzmán. "When I'm done, we'll start to bring the others in."

"How hard do you want to go on them?" said Raúl.

"Nothing over-the-top. We already have a pretty solid picture of what happened out there. I'm just trying to fill in any gaps that Serrano may have taken with him."

"I don't think Serrano held anything back," said Raúl.

"I don't, either," said Guzmán. "But we can't take any chances. We're too close to the finish line. I'd just as soon kill every coyote that has ever worked within a hundred miles of the site rather than risk a leak."

"That would mean every coyote working for us right now," said Raúl.

"Coyotes can be replaced," said Guzmán. "Our deal with the Americans can't."

Raúl raised an eyebrow.

"Get rid of them," said Guzmán. "And no replacement for now. That crossing is closed until further notice."

"I'll take care of it," said Raúl, turning to the pair of *soldados* standing by the wall. "Cut this one down. Then bring the others in one by one and cut their throats."

"What do you want done with the bodies?" said one of the soldiers.

"Bury them somewhere," said Raúl, looking to him for approval.

Guzmán nodded. There was no need to send an over-the-top public message. The sudden and permanent disappearance of the six coyotes would be enough. Anyone wanting to cross the border would have to take their business west of La Rumorosa for now, or risk vanishing like the coyotes.

He stepped out of the sweltering warehouse and into the cool, mesquite smoke–laced evening to make an overdue call. Guzmán had wanted to be sure of the situation before passing along a final update to the Americans. He couldn't give them any reason to pull the plug on the Jalisco New Generation's share of the operation. His organization would not survive without a seat at the table after the war.

Guzmán dialed JUPITER and waited for the satellite call to connect.

"Rafael. I was just about to call you. Our friends north of the border are getting a little nervous," said the man he'd never met.

JUPITER had worked through an American proxy to make his proposal in the beginning. Guzmán suspected the proxy was CIA, but all efforts to identify him during the early phase of the operation had failed. Locating him after the deal had been struck proved equally futile. Like JUPITER, he was a ghost, and all they knew for certain about JUPITER was that he had powerful friends in the United States—and that he kept his word. Until now.

"I needed to close out one additional lead before making a final report," said Guzmán. "I like to be thorough."

"We're cut from the same cloth, Rafael," he said. "What did you uncover?"

"Working backward from the time of the incident, we were able to identify several possible leads. One of them panned out rather quickly. A car known to have traveled after dark, on a stretch of Highway 2D immediately south of the site, crossed into the US at the Tecate port of entry at nine twenty-two p.m., abandoning their luggage in a Tecate hotel. They must have been spooked by one of our vehicle surveillance teams.

"Hotel staff confirmed that four people—two couples—had checked in under the car registration, and one of our police contacts stationed in the outbound US customs lanes verified that only two people departed Mexico in the vehicle. Two women."

Jupiter interrupted. "My surveillance assets detected two intruders at the site."

"Right," said Guzmán. "Mexican customs documents and video confirmed that four had crossed into Mexico, using this vehicle."

"I assume they didn't use their real names."

"At first we thought they did. The licenses popped up in the California Department of Motor Vehicles database," said Guzmán. "But a quick run through another source presented conflicting information."

"You're killing me with the suspense, Rafael. What are we looking at?"

"I got hits on three of the four," said Guzmán. "The two women are Harlow Mackenzie and Sandra Volpe, both associated with an unnamed private investigative firm out of Los Angeles. The third is Ryan Decker, also based out of LA, who has an interesting history. None of them came up in the LAPD database, which we found odd."

An uncomfortably long pause ensued, giving Guzmán the feeling that Jupiter recognized the names.

"No headway on the fourth?"

"None so far," said Guzmán. "And the three we've identified have left Los Angeles. In fact, everyone known to be associated with the private investigative firm has disappeared. The last anyone saw or heard from any of them was around eleven this morning."

"You guys work fast," said Jupiter.

"There's a lot at stake here," said Guzmán. "I made this my top priority, and we've left no stone unturned. My associates interviewed a couple that had been on the same stretch of highway. They verified that four people were in the car. Two positive photo IDs. Mackenzie and Decker. Are you familiar with either of these people?"

"Vaguely. The name Ryan Decker sounds familiar."

"He ran World Recovery Group, an elite VIP hostage-recovery firm that botched the rescue of an influential US senator's daughter," said Guzmán. "His world went to shit after that."

"That's right. I remember it. A high-profile case involving the Russians," said JUPITER. "He went to jail for that."

"Apparently, he's out of jail and nosing around my business," said Guzmán. "One of my coyotes claims that two heavily armed men wearing night vision jumped him a few miles southwest of the bunker site and forced him to take them across the border. My contact at the US Border Patrol confirmed his story.

"Agents tracked two men approaching Interstate 8, west of the military exclusion zone. They met two women at the Valley of the Moon trailhead, where Border Patrol intervened. IDs matched the four that had entered Mexico at Tecate twelve hours earlier. Do I need to be concerned about this?"

"I can't see why at this point. Nobody is getting through from the US to take a look, and I sure as hell hope we can say the same about your side."

"I've closed the loop on all witnesses," said Guzmán, letting his anger get the better of him. "I don't appreciate being lectured to. Your suicide robots opened the damn bunker for them."

"Rafael. Need I remind you that none of this would be an issue in the first place if your people didn't like to rape little kids."

He clenched his teeth, unable to respond for a few seconds. He couldn't prove it, because JUPITER's team had brought the entire bunker down on his people's heads, but rumor suggested that the gringo mercenaries had imported the trafficked kids. Guzmán made the strategic decision to let the comment slide. No good would come of getting into a pissing match over something neither of them could change.

"I have this side under control, and my associates will keep digging in Los Angeles," said Guzmán. "What do I do about a replacement shipment? We lost the bulk of our heavy-duty stuff last night."

"I'll figure something out," said JUPITER. "We obviously don't have time to dig another bunker."

"If you deliver a similar shipment by sea to Veracruz or Puerto Vallarta, I can fly it north," said Guzmán.

"I'm not sure we have the time for that, and the sea lanes are risky. If this happens, we'll most likely deliver by air."

"If?" said Guzmán. "We need that advanced equipment to take and hold Mexicali. Same with the other Sinaloa strongholds in the Golden Triangle. We're bearing most of the burden in this war. Without us, the plan falls apart."

"I understand, Rafael. We'll get you what you need to pull this off. I just need to be careful on my end. Your organization is under a lot of scrutiny right now, from both sides of the border."

The American was right. Guzmán had already fielded a few calls from "concerned" Mexican politicians regarding the cartel's alleged involvement in the killing of the Border Patrol agents. He fully expected to hear from contacts in the Federal Public Ministry, expressing similar worries. The mostly feigned concern would likely lead to nothing but a few worthless public statements condemning the cartels, but given the right set of political circumstances up north, something like this could explode in his face. If that happened, he had no doubt that JUPITER would drop him like a hot tamale.

"We'll play it cool on our side," said Guzmán. "You keep us in the game, and we'll hold up our end of the bargain."

What he wanted to say was, *Keep us in the game, or I'll feed you to my sharks.* Guzmán owned an enclosed cove north of Puerto Vallarta stocked with several tiger sharks. He'd lost track of the number of rivals who had been torn to shreds in front of his eyes. Guzmán himself often descended beneath the water in a custom shark cage to watch the blood-bath up close and listen to the muted underwater screams.

"I'll be in touch shortly," said JUPITER. "If your associates in Los Angeles get lucky, I need to know immediately. And make sure they exercise discretion if an opportunity presents itself. The last thing either of us needs is more attention directed at your organization. I plan on sending my own people to LA in the next day or so. They'll take over from that point."

"Fair enough," said Guzmán. "Let me know when they arrive, and I'll call my people off."

"I doubt they'll find anything," said JUPITER. "Your people don't strike me as the kind to miss much."

Finally. The conciliatory olive branch. He'd take it, even if he knew it could be rescinded just as quickly.

"They don't miss anything," said Guzmán. "If you need them to take care of something north of the border, just say the word."

"I'll keep that in mind."

The call ended, leaving Guzmán feeling uneasy about the entire situation. He'd call a leadership meeting in the next day or two to discuss a contingency plan—in the event that JUPITER cut Jalisco New Generation out of the deal. It was hard to imagine the Americans moving forward without his organization's support, even if they couldn't deliver a new shipment of weapons, but he had to plan for it.

The other cartels were unlikely to hand back the weapons already delivered, and Guzmán certainly had no intention of returning the vast quantity of small arms, light machine guns, grenade launchers, and military night-vision gear he'd received. The Americans would have no choice but to move forward with or without Jalisco New Generation, or face the consequences of putting some of the United States military's most sophisticated weapons in the hands of the Mexican cartels. The Americans needed this war to happen, if only to ensure the weapons were used only against other Mexicans. Regardless of their decision, Guzmán would ensure his organization survived—and reaped the rewards of whatever remained when the smoke cleared.

CHAPTER TWENTY-FIVE

Freya Walker had just settled down for the night in front of the television—overfilled glass of Chardonnay in one hand and Fire TV Stick remote in the other—when her phone buzzed. She took a long sip of wine before glancing at the device's screen. *JUPITER.* Freya straightened up on the couch, placing the wine and remote on the low glass table in front of her.

She quickly navigated to an application on her phone, inputting a nine-digit code and memorizing the six-digit string of numbers and letters it returned before answering the call. A synthetic voice greeted her.

"Authenticate. Juliet Foxtrot Whiskey."

"Seven Alpha Echo Five One One," she said.

Three short clicks followed, connecting her to JUPITER's cutout, whose voice was altered just enough to prevent voice recognition. Freya had no idea who she was talking to at the moment, and there was no point in speculating. That's how he wanted it.

"Good evening, Freya. I hope I didn't catch you at a bad moment."

"Actually, this is perfect timing. I just finished a miserably boring job in Memphis. Good barbecue was the only highlight. I hope you have something for me."

"I do, but it's more of a Mexican food kind of situation."

"You know I love Mexican food," said Freya. "South of the border?"

"I don't anticipate that. It's a top-priority coffin trace originating in Los Angeles."

"You haven't passed one of those along in a while," she said.

Coffin trace was JUPITER's code for a skip trace ending in a termination.

"Thanks to you, I ran out of enemies—until now. This won't be an easy one, Freya. Fair warning."

"I can handle it," she said.

"This job will require the largest team you can assemble. What do you have at your disposal?"

"Depends on the pay," she said. "What am I looking at?"

"Top floor. Doubled upon completion," said JUPITER.

Holy mother! Six figures. Something big was in the works.

"For everyone on the team?" she said.

"No. Straight up top floor for the team. Plus fifty percent for a good secondary. Permanent salaried employment on the same floor for top performers, if things go well on my end in the next month."

"Nick will definitely walk off his current job for this," said Freya.

"That's good to hear. Nick is a solid team leader."

"I can think of at least a dozen more that will fall in line fast. Another dozen within a week. Does that sound about right?"

"Twenty K walk-on bonuses. You'll need more than a dozen to start."

"I can make it happen with that," she said, shaking her head in disbelief. "Trail goes cold in Los Angeles?"

"Correct. I'll send you the files and support documents shortly. Eight skips."

"Eight," she said, shocked by the number. "I'll definitely need a sizable team. Any chance they're still in LA?"

"Very doubtful. This group made that mistake once. I can't see them making it again."

"I'll start making calls as soon as I get the files and make an initial assessment," she said.

"One word of caution. Do not under any circumstances underestimate this crew, particularly Decker and Pierce. You'll see what I mean. Whatever resources you think you might need to deal with them—triple it."

The name Decker rang a bell, but she couldn't place it.

"I'll factor that into my planning. Anything else?"

"Not at the moment. Payments will be processed through the same anonymous portal we've used before. You'll receive all of that information in the support documents."

"Easy enough," said Freya. "I'll feed you team updates and equipment requests as they develop. I look forward to getting started."

"I'm glad you were available."

"For you, and your top-floor pay, I'm always available," said Freya.

"Always the mercenary," said JUPITER. "That's one of the reasons I keep hiring you. I know exactly where you stand. Keep me posted."

"I will," she said, but the call had already been disconnected.

Freya grabbed the glass of wine and sat back on the couch, rigid from the call. She was looking at a onetime payment of close to two hundred thousand dollars for this job, plus the prospect of a quarter-million-dollar-a-year salary, with bonuses, after that. Her day had gone from shit to platinum with one phone call. A long drink from her glass warmed her head and lowered her shoulders a few centimeters.

At last. The opportunity she had been chasing for six long years had finally been delivered, and not by chance. Hard work and loyalty—before and after Aegis Global's implosion—brought her to this point. Without a doubt, the job outlined over the phone moments ago was critical to Jacob Harcourt's plan to resurrect Aegis, and she'd been chosen to spearhead the effort. For all Freya knew, she may have been talking to Harcourt himself on the phone. Just the thought of it gave her goose bumps.

Freya had started working at Aegis Global after a short stint as a vice cop in Philadelphia, where she spent most of her time posing as a street prostitute. John after john—night after night—the grimy work quickly wore her down to a point where she turned to alcohol to cope with the misery. The booze trip made it worse, no surprise there, and she started to wake up from blackouts with her pistol on the bed, couch, or floor next to her. She bought a small safe for the gun, but somehow the pistol kept showing up after a long bender.

A year into the job, she didn't see an end to the work. Her sergeant dodged every one of her attempts to transfer out of vice or shift to a different detail within the division. She had found her niche in the department—bait for the seemingly endless supply of johns cruising the streets. Despite the utterly demoralizing and frequently dehumanizing year, she hadn't given up on herself. The first time one of her fellow officers called her the squad's "looker hooker" in a roll-call meeting, Freya cleaned out her locker and walked out of the station. She had no intention of spending the rest of her career as a cop trying to dig out of that hole.

Ironically, she jumped right back into the same line of work at Aegis Global, accepting a temporary job in their national "honeypot" division—the only real difference in the work being that she was paid four times more than she ever saw as a cop. The scenery similarly improved. She'd traded trash-strewn alleys and shadowy park benches for five-star hotel lobby bars and upscale jazz clubs. Anywhere one of Aegis's indiscreet and vulnerable adversaries could be lured into a compromising situation that could be leveraged for gain.

The temporary position stretched to a year and looked like it would go on indefinitely. Once again, Freya felt pigeonholed in a job she did well but utterly despised. She'd almost quit after a rough night with a less-than-happy target, but thought better of it on the drive home.

Would they really let her walk away from this job alive? She was a witness to more than fifty ongoing blackmail operations, some involving top DC politicians and federal cabinet members.

Rather than signing her own death warrant, Freya decided to take her chances with the occasional out-of-control target. She kept her eye on internal job postings, though she suspected she'd made the same mistake again, boxing herself into a corner that would be impossible to escape. Literally impossible.

She got lucky a few months later, working a French politician with unsavory ties to the international arms business. She'd lured him back to his room after a few drinks in the hotel's swanky, mahogany-paneled bar to find two serious-looking men with Russian accents waiting for them in the suite's marble foyer. Freya started to back out of the room, meaning to leave the Frenchman to answer for his own sins, but the Russians had no intention of letting her escape.

Ten seconds later, both Russians lay bleeding out on the white marble floor, Freya having taken them completely by surprise with the razor-sharp Microtech automatic knife hidden in her purse. The next morning Aegis reassigned her to the personal protection division, where she stayed for three years, until her application to the special activities division was approved.

She spent half of the next year in Aegis Global's elite SAD training program, followed by several hectic months of field apprenticeships. All designed to prepare her for a junior leadership role within SAD, the first step toward running an independent operation. Aegis Global collapsed a month before she was due to graduate, forcing her to compete against several hundred far more experienced SAD contractors for a dwindling number of field jobs.

Freya downed the rest of her wine and put the glass in the trash, along with the bottle of Chardonnay. She wasn't going to fuck this up. She'd worked too hard to get this far.

CHAPTER TWENTY-SIX

Jeff McCall set his phone on the desk in his study and muttered a few choice words. He knew the breach at the Jalisco New Generation site was bad news—he just hadn't expected it to be this bad. He imagined the news had hit Jacob even harder. They could deal with a nosy journalist or a profiteering coyote, but this was completely different, threatening the entire operation and everything McCall had worked hard to build over the past two years.

The crew suspected of penetrating the site had been directly responsible for Aegis Global's downfall, taking a sizable chunk of McCall's nonpension retirement investments with it. Even worse, Aegis's death spiral had killed any chance of McCall riding off into the sunset with a cushy, six-figure advisory board position with the company—something he'd counted on to make up for the money sacrificed over a twenty-four-year career in the army.

Many of his West Point classmates, like Jacob Harcourt, had left the army after five years, climbing to the top of their excessively lucrative professions by the time McCall retired from active duty. His military pension and health benefits, guaranteed for life, were still a pittance compared to the investment portfolios and real estate empires accrued by these classmates.

Fortunately, classmate loyalty extended beyond West Point, and Jacob Harcourt, his roommate at the academy and longtime friend, had stepped up to make things right—contingent upon McCall's help. More like dependent on his help, because without it, Harcourt's bold plan was dead in the water, along with McCall's hopes of retiring in the kind of comfort he deserved. Their fates were once again intertwined.

He glanced at his watch and decided to hold his call to Bob Saling until the morning. There was no point in keeping their other classmate up all night worrying about Decker. McCall would catch him early, on the way in to the Capitol, to strategize next steps for Saling and Duncan in light of recent events. For now, he didn't envision them doing more than trying to keep an eye on Senator Steele's activities in the Senate, particularly any attempts by Steele to access sealed, highly compartmentalized information regarding the impacted military exclusion zone.

McCall wasn't overly concerned about her lifting the veil from the site in California, since the initial request to authorize the exclusion zone and all subsequent updates submitted by JTF North to the Pentagon had maintained the original cover story. JTF North was testing new surveillance technologies against seasoned infiltrators in one of the most challenging landscapes found along the border.

He'd be far more worried if Steele started looking into the rest of the exclusion zones JTF North operated along the US-Mexico border. If that occurred, he might have to call on Saling and Duncan to do more than keep an eye on her. Harcourt had thus far refrained from dealing with Senator Steele, convinced that the US authorities would declare him a terrorist and put a price on his head. Money bought him safety in Mexico, but no amount of money could keep him safe from a dedicated special operations mission. Once Southern Cross kicked off, Harcourt could do whatever he wanted. Despite the legal hand-wringing that was bound to ensue in DC, he'd be unofficially heralded as the architect of a new era of border security and the mediator who reined in the cartels.

McCall planned on basking in that same glory from his desk, located just down the hallway from the two coconspirators he'd recruited at Harcourt's request—General Colin Hooper and Colonel James Souza, the commanding general and deputy commanding officer of Joint Task Force North. Dragging them both into Southern Cross had been a major coup, even if it hadn't required much more than a few nights on his patio with good Cuban cigars and a few bottles of rare-batch bourbon he'd special ordered for the occasion.

The two senior officers couldn't have been a better match for the proposal, which probably hadn't been a coincidence. Harcourt was a meticulous planner, and McCall got the sense that Southern Cross had roots going back long before Aegis Global folded. His friend probably had a dozen plots like this hatched around the world, waiting for the right set of circumstances to ripen. The trifecta of McCall, Hooper, and Souza in the top leadership positions at JTF North undoubtedly triggered the plan.

He hoped they didn't get cold feet when he told them the news. Neither of them had looked thrilled by the prospect of sending a replacement shipment to the Mexicans. The bunker site had represented the least risky way for JTF North's Special Activities Proliferation Group to deliver weapons and equipment to the cartels. Sending another load through the exclusion zone was out of the question at this point. They'd have to drive it across, where prying eyes like Decker's could see it.

Flying it in appeared to be the only feasible option to meet the approaching deadline, and that required bringing the Air Force into the fold. The SAPG had plenty of ground vehicles but no airlift capability. More unwitting accomplices to testify against them later. McCall would have to bring out the cigars and bourbon again, ready to reignite their deep-seated fears of an inadequately protected and incompetently controlled border.

It would be a long, boring night, but the payoff was more than worth it. His two percent share of the "tax" agreed to by the cartels in exchange for new border access represented a minimum of two million dollars a year. More than enough to indefinitely fuel his exile if the hammer dropped on JTF North for illegally funneling arms to the cartels.

CHAPTER TWENTY-SEVEN

Senator Steele picked up the phone, half grunting into the receiver.

"I was hoping he'd cancel."

Her secretary didn't skip a beat; the unwanted guest was probably standing right in front of her. "Senator Paul Duncan just arrived. Shall I bring him back?"

"Yes, Sheryl. Thank you," she said, replacing the receiver.

Steele clasped her hands and lowered them to the desk, taking a series of deep breaths. A knock at the door came far too quickly to be Duncan. Before she could answer, Julie Ragan pushed it open and stepped halfway inside.

"Suddenly he's fucking available—and making house calls?" she said. "Do you want me to sit in on this?"

The senator chuckled. Julie was in rare form today, not that foul language was something she avoided.

"I'll be fine. Should be interesting," said Steele.

"That's one way of putting it," said Julie. "Careful with this one. The last time he reached across the aisle—scratch that, he's never cooperated with us."

"Maybe it's some of that southern hospitality," said Steele.

"Oklahoma?" said Julie.

"Close enough," said Steele.

"I wouldn't repeat that outside of closed doors," said Julie.

Steele waved her off. "Then you better close those doors and act like you never heard me say that. Five minutes and you call me with something that needs my immediate attention. I don't want to be in here with him for any longer than that."

"Copy that," said Julie, shutting the door.

Copy that. Every once in a while, Julie inadvertently reminded her that she'd started out her government service in the Navy. Seven years as a pilot before walking into Steele's Annapolis office and volunteering to work for an upcoming campaign. Five years later, she was running the senator's show as one of the youngest chiefs of staff in the Capitol.

A long minute passed before the dreaded knock arrived. Steele opened the door and cordially welcomed the senior senator from Oklahoma inside with a handshake. Before Duncan took a seat, he scanned her sparse walls, politely smiling without comment. Not surprising, since she knew from the hundreds of pictures Duncan's staff posted that barely a square inch of wall could be found between the hundreds of signed pictures, awards, and animal heads collecting dust in his office.

"Margaret. I want to thank you for seeing me on such short notice. I apologize for not being available earlier. As you can imagine, the, uh . . . incident on the border has monopolized my time."

"I can only imagine," said Steele. "The reports are, uh . . . surprisingly low on details."

"Which is why Bob Saling and I took an unannounced trip down to the site as soon as we received the news."

Duncan's statement didn't exactly square with what she already knew. They had flown in on Tuesday, three days after the incident, and flown back to DC on Thursday. Her inability to reach either of them by phone or email all week had led her to contact Reeves and make alternate arrangements to investigate.

"I hope you managed to pry something loose from the Department of Defense," said Steele. "They're extremely tight-lipped on this one."

"I agree. We think they're embarrassed that something like this happened in one of—in their exclusion zone," said Duncan.

"I can see why. Especially if all of the new surveillance technology they were testing couldn't shed any light on what happened smack-dab in the middle of the exclusion zone."

Duncan shifted in his seat, nodding in agreement. "I imagine they're somewhat protecting the companies that provided the experimental systems," he said. "It's understandable under normal circumstances, but this is a different story."

"Entirely different," said Steele. "I caught your update last Friday but haven't seen anything since. Did CBP ever submit their findings after examining the agents' vehicle?"

"As a matter of fact, they just sent the results," said Duncan. "Unfortunately, the vehicle had been subjected to intense heat from the explosion that destroyed the bunker."

"I thought the bunker was demolished from the inside," said Steele, immediately wondering if she'd read that in one of the reports or had mistakenly repeated something she'd heard from Decker's assessment.

"I don't know the specifics," said Duncan. "The SUV was found right outside the northern bunker entrance—incinerated. No bodies. Pretty much nothing left but the chassis and melted tires."

"Have we approached the Mexican government? Asked them to dig up their side of the bunker?" said Steele.

"It's complicated, from what I understand," said Duncan. "The cartels—"

"To hell with the cartels, Paul," she said. "They killed or kidnapped two of our federal agents, and we both know what they're up to with those kids."

"I know. I know. It's unforgivable," said Duncan. "But—"

"But what? We owe it to the families of the two missing agents to investigate, not to mention the families of the children."

"Maybe we could work together to gain some traction with this," said Duncan. "Joint Task Force North barely budged on handing over the vehicle."

"I'm listening," said Steele. "But I have to warn you that I'm not exactly one of the Pentagon's favorites."

Duncan gave a hearty, forced laugh. "Leave that part to me. If you start making some noise from the human-trafficking committee, I might be able to pull the ol' good cop–bad cop routine on them."

"Where I'm the bad cop?" said Steele.

"Where you're the noisy cop," said Duncan. "The more noise you make, the more everyone will want to come to the bargaining table."

Steele wasn't buying it. This wasn't a negotiation. The White House could reach out to the Mexican president this morning and request permission to cross the border with excavation equipment and retrieve the bodies, leaving whatever the cartel had hidden to the Mexican authorities.

The cartel wouldn't like it, but aside from threatening their *presidente*, which would not be well received, there wasn't much they could do about it. José Lopez Peña was far from a pushover, having taken the most active stance against the drug cartels in Mexico's drug-war history.

Steele decided against pushing this any further with Duncan, opting instead to play along. His sudden willingness to meet with her was suspiciously timed, to say the least. After Frist's betrayal, she had lost all trust in her colleagues, with very few exceptions.

"It's a start," said Steele. "I'll convene the committee as soon as possible to discuss releasing a statement. I don't want to reach out to the White House directly, or they'll be all over the members within the hour, pushing back."

"Yeah. They have a well-oiled machine over there," said Duncan, reaching into his suit coat pocket and removing a thumb drive. "I've put everything I have related to the El Centro Sector incident on this drive. I also took the liberty of including the latest cartel activity assessment report prepared by my committee. That's hot off the presses, so please don't distribute it outside your office. It contains intelligence provided by more than a dozen agencies dealing with the cartels. I also tracked down some human-trafficking intelligence you may not have come across yet. DEA and CBP statistics, assessments, and projections based on what they've encountered. It's not the smoking gun you're looking for, but at least you'll be armed with the most updated information."

She took the drive and placed it on the desk, right next to her laptop, Duncan's eyes following it the entire way.

"I can't thank you enough for this," said Steele, straining to look sincerely appreciative. "I feel like we've found some common ground. I'll let you know when I'm ready to start pressing buttons at the White House."

"You should really take a look at CBP's report on the vehicle," he said, leaning forward and nudging the thumb drive. "Sounds to me like the cartel torched it separate from exploding the bunker. That might be something to highlight."

Her phone buzzed twice. Saved by the bell.

"Hold on for a second," she said, one hand on the thumb drive, the other picking up the phone. "I'm still in—I see. I'll be right out."

She pushed her chair back and stood up. "Sorry to do this to you, Paul, but I have a very displeased constituent waiting for me on the line. A very influential constituent. I apparently didn't use enthusiastic enough terms when speaking about Patuxent River Naval Air Station's future. Time for some damage control."

"We've all been there and will be there again," said Duncan, getting up from his seat.

He glanced furtively at the thumb drive, seemingly unable to control himself in front of her, before following Steele to the door. They shook hands, and she promised to get back to him shortly with her plan.

"Julie. Do you mind walking with Senator Duncan?" said Steele.

"Not at all, ma'am," said Julie, getting up from the conference table.

"Thank you, but I'm fine," said Duncan. "It's a straight shot to the door. Not like the byzantine network of hallways in my office. Like something straight out of an old hotel basement."

"Small price to pay for that huge office," said Steele. "And you have a fireplace."

"Decorative fireplace, but I suppose you're right. Look forward to hearing from you, Margaret," he said, shaking her hand again.

Senator Steele returned to her office and grabbed the thumb drive, emerging several seconds later.

"Is he gone?"

Julie nodded. "Just walked out the front door."

"Good," said Steele, holding the drive out to her. "Do you know anyone that can discreetly examine this thumb drive? Senator Duncan seemed a little too eager for me to insert this in my computer. I don't trust him for a second."

"What's supposed to be on the drive?" said Julie.

"Updated intelligence on the cartels and CBP's vehicle investigation report," said Steele. "He was just looking for an excuse to give this to me, I can feel it."

Julie took the thumb drive. "I'll find someone on the outside to take a look."

"Thank you, Julie. I also need to clear my schedule for the late afternoon. Say, three o'clock onward."

"I'll make the adjustment to your calendar."

"And let's sweep my office for bugs again after lunch," said Steele. "Duncan's visit wasn't a reach-across-the-aisle goodwill measure. He's up to something."

"I couldn't agree more," said Julie. "I'll ask Scott to arrange a sweep."

Steele returned to her office, keeping the door open while Julie started making calls to rearrange her schedule. Her chief of staff still hadn't asked her a single question about why Duncan had shown a sudden interest in Steele's affairs or why she had started to block off private office time a few days ago. Steele felt bad keeping her out of the loop on what had been discovered at the border site, but it was for Julie's protection—and her own.

While she trusted Julie implicitly, Steele suspected that the people behind the buried weapons wouldn't hesitate to take extreme measures to keep it a secret, including kidnapping, torture, and murder. She'd seen this ugly side up close and personal. If things started to heat up any further, she'd take steps to safeguard Julie and the rest of her staff, without releasing the details. Anyone in her office could be a target—which gave her an idea.

She walked to the door and waited for her chief of staff to finish a quick call canceling one of her afternoon appointments.

"Julie? I think this afternoon would be a good time to hold an office-wide operational security refresher. Everything from cybersecurity to basic counterespionage and surveillance. Maybe a half hour."

Julie gave her a concerned look.

"Anything I need to be overly worried about?" said Julie.

"Not yet," said Steele. "If it gets to that level, I'll take care of it."

CHAPTER
TWENTY-EIGHT

As the team's caravan departed Interstate 25, a thin blue strip of light stretched across the seemingly endless flat horizon to the east. The exit merged with an unlit, two-lane county road that took them northwest into Aguilar. Decker barely noticed when they entered the town's outskirts, the darkened structures blending with the surrounding trees to form amorphous shadows along the side of the road.

"You picked one hell of a place to hide," said Harlow. "Do they cut off electricity to the town at night?"

"We should pass some streetlamps on Main Street," said Pierce. "If they still work. The place seems to fade away a little between every visit."

"How often do you visit town?" said Sandra.

"Every couple of weeks. Sometimes longer. There's nothing much to see," he said. "At least you can see the stars out here. I don't think I've seen one since I left."

Sandra didn't respond, but Decker knew what she was thinking—*How did I let them talk me into this?*

"It's gorgeous out here. Wait until later," said Decker, turning them onto Main Street. "Looks like three lights still working."

The four vehicles motored through the mostly vacant and boarded-up downtown, rumbling onto the hard-packed dirt that would fork into two jeep trails about a quarter of a mile away. Decker slowed the SUV, remembering that the road conditions worsened significantly the farther they drove. A single porch light shone ahead, up near the fork. Pierce's guardian angel was up before the dawn.

"Is Gunny waiting for us?" said Decker.

"He insisted," said Pierce.

"Gunny?" said Harlow.

"Gunnery Sergeant Fowler. United States Marine Corps. Retired," said Pierce. "He's taken it upon himself to watch the road for me. Nobody lives beyond his house."

"He knows your story?" said Harlow from the back seat.

"I trust him with my family's life," said Pierce.

Decker snaked around and through a long series of potholes deep enough to throw a tire, hoping the drivers behind him were paying attention. After emerging from the natural minefield, he eased them right at the fork in the road and pulled up to Gunny Fowler, who stood on the side of the road next to a wheelbarrow. Decker rolled down his window.

"Good to see you again, Gunny," said Decker.

"Decker," he said, nodding the rest of his greeting. "Welcome back, Brad. Looks like you brought half of LA with you."

"Good to be back," said Pierce. "You didn't have to get up on our account."

"Nonsense. I figured you'd all be starving after the drive and didn't want Anna to have to bother with making anything," said Gunny, glancing toward the wheelbarrow. "The missus and I got up early to put together some bag nasties."

"Bag nasty. What the hell is that?" whispered Sandra just a little too loudly.

The question brought Gunny to the rear driver's-side window, where Harlow was seated.

"This should be good," said Decker, and Pierce chuckled.

Harlow lowered her window. "Morning, Gunny. I've heard a lot about you. I'm Harlow. This is Sandra."

"Pleasure to finally make your acquaintances. Heard a lot about you, too. Mostly good," he said. "So. You ladies aren't hungry?"

"No. Yes. I'm just not sure I'm sold on the bag nasty idea?" said Sandra. "But I won't turn it down. Not after you went through the trouble."

"They'll be delicious," said Harlow. "Everyone will love them."

Gunny Fowler laughed, slapping the side of the SUV a few times.

"These ain't the typical bag nasties enjoyed by Uncle Sam's misguided children."

"United States Marine Corps," said Decker, matter-of-factly.

"Okay," said Sandra. "So the bag nasties are actually good?"

"Mine are. Grilled ham and cheese sandwiches. Apple-smoked ham, pan fried until crisp. A thick layer of sharp cheddar cheese. All pressed between two slices of homemade sourdough bread. I also threw in a bag of kettle-cooked chips, freshly cut apple slices, a can of sparkling Pellegrino, and a hard-boiled egg. I couldn't resist the egg, sorry. Old habits die hard."

"Sounds incredible," said Harlow. "Is the egg wrapped or anything?"

Gunny broke into another fit of laughter. "That's Los Angeles for ya! Don't worry. The missus made me put the eggs in a Ziploc."

"Thank you, Gunny," said Sandra. "I think you and your wife went above and beyond the call of duty here."

"We'll have the two of you up to the house to thank you properly once we get settled," said Pierce.

"Someone has to man the observation post here," he said.

"I'm sure the road can go unguarded for a few hours," said Pierce. "I'll call you later today. I'm not sure we'll be here for more than a few days."

"Look forward to it," said Gunny, reaching into his wheelbarrow and pulling out four overstuffed paper sacks. "Bon appétit!"

Decker pulled forward to make room for the other vehicles, stopping to wait for Gunny to distribute the rest of the meals. His mouth started to water from the savory grilled cheese smell, followed by a series of low stomach growls. For security reasons insisted upon by Decker himself, they'd decided to drive straight through from Los Angeles, only stopping briefly to refuel. Each vehicle carried a cooler packed with the food and drinks required for the trip. Out of sheer road boredom, he had eaten his share by Flagstaff. A rookie mistake that turned the remaining nine-hour trek into somewhat of a nightmare.

"How long to the house?" said Decker. "I'm tempted to pull over right here and dig into one of those sandwiches."

"I wouldn't be opposed to that," said Harlow. "My stomach is only an hour behind Decker's."

"Hold on," said Pierce, before speaking into his handheld radio. "Hey. Don't let the crusty guy handing out bag lunches intimidate you. Just take what he gives you and move on. We're thirty minutes from the house."

Thirty long minutes.

"A thank-you would be nice," he heard over the radio.

"Thank you, Gunny," said Pierce, shaking his head.

"He's one hell of a character, that's for sure," said Sandra. "Looks a hundred years old."

"Don't let that fool you," said Pierce. "He kicks my ass hiking these hills."

"I'm not surprised," said Harlow. "That was really nice of him to put these together. I really don't want to inconvenience your wife. Make sure she knows that we'll take care of everything. Food. Cooking.

Washing. Whatever the eleven of us add to the Pierce household burden. We really appreciate this. I'll probably annoy the hell out of Anna repeating that."

"She'll appreciate hearing it, but honestly, she's beyond excited to have the company. So are the kids. Before Decker showed up last year, the only guests we'd had at the house were Gunny and his wife. Anna may talk your ear off about the outside world. We lived in a swanky Annapolis neighborhood. House on the water. Summers at the country club. A very active social life—until it all came crashing down on our heads. Anna and the kids were immediately moved into FBI protective custody. Isolated from everyone. They've been on the run or in hiding ever since. I promised them we'd leave here once Harcourt was gone for good. I'm not sure she can wait that long."

"She can talk my ear off all day and night," said Harlow. "I can't even begin to imagine what they've been through."

"Careful what you ask for," said Pierce.

A blanket of melancholy smothered Decker. Anna and his wife, Marley, had been good friends. They'd spent a lot of time together when Decker and Pierce were out of town, which was often. The kids hadn't been as close, because they were in different school districts, but the families had spent time on each other's docks, boats, and at the country club. A decade of memories that had all but faded to a point where they felt unreal. Pierce's words briefly pulled them into focus, leaving Decker conflicted. He wasn't sure he wanted to remember it in any detail.

Pierce squeezed his shoulder. "You good?"

Decker snapped out of it, not sure how long he'd been staring through the windshield at nothing.

"Just tired—and hungry. Are we ready?"

"Why don't you let me drive the rest of the way? The trail can be a little tricky in the dark," said Pierce.

Pierce knew where his head had been. He was perceptive like that.

"Sure," said Decker, avoiding his eyes.

171

"I'm breaking open one of these—did you really call these bagged nasties?" Harlow said.

"Bag nasties. Military speak," said Decker. "Traditionally, they came with a plain bologna and cheese sandwich on white bread, a popped, hand-size bag of Lay's potato chips, a juice box, and . . ."

"And a half-crushed hard-boiled egg," said Pierce.

"What if you were a vegetarian?" said Sandra.

"We didn't allow those in the Marine Corps," said Decker, and they all laughed.

He caught Harlow's glance while climbing into the passenger seat, holding it for a few moments. She winked at him and took a bite of her sandwich. Decker smiled and returned the wink, feeling slightly better already. Like Pierce, she seemed to understand how his mind worked, having taken the brunt of his erratic mood swings over the past year. Through all of it, Harlow never once showed the slightest bit of annoyance.

Pierce carefully navigated the uneven network of jeep trails deep into the foothills of the Sangre de Cristo Mountains, until the towering ridges surrounded them and blotted out the expanding blue sky. Progress through the dozens of draws and ridgeline breaks proceeded slower than anticipated, the three drivers behind them both unaccustomed to true off-roading and terrified of negotiating the trails in the dark. When they finally arrived at Pierce's home, it was still too dark to appreciate the post-and-beam masterpiece nestled in the protective draw.

A light appeared in one of the second-floor windows, followed shortly by two floodlights pointed at the gravel driveway. Decker got out of the SUV and directed the other vehicles to form a line to the right, where they wouldn't block the garage. Pierce met his wife at the front door, where they kissed and held each other tightly.

He'd never forgive himself if anything happened to Pierce or his family. Part of him wanted to repack the convoy while the Pierces slept and disappear without a trace. Save his friend's family from the danger that was bound to catch up with Pierce if the two of them kept on kicking hornet's nests together.

Decker turned to retrieve his suitcase from the back of the vehicle, nearly knocking over Harlow when he spun around. He grabbed her to keep her from stumbling backward, finding himself not wanting to let go. A few awkward seconds later, after he'd steadied her, Decker took a few steps back, the bright light revealing that she was blushing.

"Sorry about that," said Decker. "I don't know whether I'm coming or going right now."

"For a second there, I thought you were going to give me another peck on the cheek," said Harlow.

Now Decker's face felt flushed. "Kind of a spur-of-the-moment thing."

She considered him for a second before nodding at Pierce, who had broken free from Anna. "Time for our bunk assignments."

Our bunk assignments? His mind raced to interpret the statement, instantly determining that he needed to recalibrate.

"More like floor space," said Decker, turning to his friend. "How are Anna and the kids?"

"The kids are asleep. She didn't want them up all night waiting, so they'll wake up to a surprise. Anna couldn't sleep. She's tired but excited to host," said Pierce. "I was going to put the SCIF team in the two spare bedrooms upstairs, but Anna doesn't want to wake the kids. The walkout basement is pretty much one big room, so it would be a bit of a slumber party to stuff everyone in there. Anna set up our tents in the backyard. I figured maybe the guys could take the tents?"

"Works for me," said Decker. "I'm sure the SCIF guys won't mind."

"Might be their first camping trip," said Harlow. "They don't get out much."

"I'll break the bad news to them," said Decker.

"Sleeping bags are already unrolled," said Pierce. "Anna put a few eye pillows in each tent so everyone can catch a few hours of sleep after the sun comes up."

"She really put some thought into this," said Decker.

"I wasn't kidding when I said she was excited to have guests," said Pierce. "She specifically mentioned that they were lavender-scented eye pillows."

"Fresh mountain air and lavender eye pillows? Maybe I'll sleep out in the tents," said Harlow, once again momentarily confounding Decker's overly active mind.

"You can have my tent," said Decker, hoping that had come out right. "If you want to sleep outside."

"I'd take you up on that if I didn't think I'd be getting up in an hour to go to the bathroom. And the hour after that," said Harlow. "Too many Diet Cokes."

"Harlow, if you want to grab the ladies, I'll take you around back to the basement slider. Get you set up. I think we should leave all of the gear in the vehicles for now. Just suitcases and backpacks. Decker, you introduce Joshua and his geek squad to the tents."

"Don't use the term *geek squad*," said Harlow.

"I know. The last time I made that mistake, they sent me on a seven-hour-long wild-goose chase through some of the worst neighborhoods in LA," said Decker.

"I can't believe it took you that long to realize they were messing with you," said Harlow.

"I was a lot more focused on not ending up dead in a gangbanger's backyard."

"I haven't heard this story," said Pierce.

"It's a good one," said Harlow. "Anna and the kids would get a kick out of it."

"I'm not sure it's kid friendly," said Decker.

"You'll have to leave the ass kicking you took in the strip club out of it," she said.

"Wow. No wonder he kept me in the dark," said Pierce.

"It wasn't my finest hour," said Decker.

"More like day," she said.

"Good night, Harlow."

"Sleep tight, Decker."

"See you in a few hours," said Pierce.

"Make sure you come get me," said Decker. "I anticipate crashing hard."

Chapter Twenty-Nine

Freya Walker sipped at the steaming-hot cup of coffee, her tenth since speaking with JUPITER the night before. She'd immediately gone to work studying the files, her first goal to decide the composition of the team she needed to assemble so she could finish the recruitment as quickly as possible. Gathering everyone in one place would take some time, especially since team members would have to bring their own equipment to the mission. Equipment that would require discreet transport to the staging area.

Based on JUPITER's warning about two of the targets and her early plan concept, she decided the team should be skilled-shooter heavy, which left her to draw from a woefully short list of former special operations and SWAT types who hadn't forsaken Jacob Harcourt. Availability had been somewhat restricted, many of the operators currently working jobs they couldn't or wouldn't leave. Their loss.

By the time the sun had peeked into her Indianapolis apartment, she'd recruited twenty-one operators, whose skill sets tipped very heavily in favor of tactical field operations. Freya was a little concerned that JUPITER would object to the one-sided nature of her selected operators, but she was convinced that the solution to his problem would come down to a single, decisive engagement. Decker and his associates had no choice but to surface in one of two locations, identified in the files, where no amount of electronic trickery could save them.

Freya studied her notes for a few minutes and reexamined the maps displayed on the triple monitor setup in her apartment office. Satisfied that she'd accounted for every possible contingency, she dialed JUPITER's cutout number, navigating the verification process.

"Freya. I hope you had a productive night," said JUPITER.

"Very productive, sir. I have solid commitments from eighteen contractors formerly aligned with Aegis Global. Three new freelancers also signed contracts. I'm still waiting to hear from seven more."

"Sounds a little thin."

"Given what we discussed last night, it would be extremely thin, but I don't intend to send anyone to Los Angeles," she said.

"No?"

"I estimate it would be a complete waste of time," said Freya. "Even if Decker and company stayed in LA, we don't have the necessary organic or local resources to find them if they go to ground like before. The list of remaining LAPD contacts is slim. Federal law enforcement support nonexistent. On top of that, I don't think they stuck around LA. One, it's too risky. Two, there's no nexus to your operation in Los Angeles."

"I didn't mention an operation."

"Of course. Let me rephrase that. There's no connection to the only known points of vulnerability that you made known to me. I can easily cover all of them and bring everyone to bear on whichever location pays off. They're just a few miles apart."

"How good is the team you've assembled?"

"It's a highly skilled direct-action crew. Point and shoot," said Freya.

"Team leaders?"

"Nick is on board, and I have a former Army Special Forces master sergeant."

"Dale Gibson?"

"He started driving south from Washington State thirty minutes after I ended my call with him," said Freya. "Sent me a text."

"He's a solid operator. Have you picked a staging area?"

"Yuma. I'll split the team into two groups, and we'll head to El Centro," she said. "It's about an hour away. I'll grab several motel rooms in that area and rent a house for final gear prep and mission briefings. I found one on the eastern outskirts that would work well. A very private location."

"El Centro is a long shot, but it may be our only chance of wrapping this up quickly without leaning on an extremely risky and unreliable partner. Is it possible to pull this off discreetly?"

"I don't see how," said Freya. "We'd have to find Decker's team well in advance of them making a move on the listed addresses and nail them at their hotel or wherever they're staying."

"They won't make the mistake of staying in a nearby hotel or gathering in one place. Your best bet will be a direct-action mission at one of the identified addresses. And I don't care how messy it gets. If they show—I want them dead. I don't care who gets caught in the crossfire."

"Understood. If the opportunity presents itself in El Centro, we'll close the deal," said Freya.

"I'm counting on it."

CHAPTER THIRTY

Harlow ascended the stairs, searching for Decker. She'd just finished a quick shower and figured he'd rolled in from his tent while she was in the bathroom. Joshua and the other guys had long ago given up trying to sleep in what one of them called a convection oven. Scanning the two-story great room and the kitchen area, she didn't see him.

Anna sat at a long, rough-hewn table next to the kitchen, eating lunch with her two teenage kids. They looked up when she emerged on the main level of the house.

"Anna. Have you seen Decker?" she said, heading straight for the coffee maker.

"We haven't," she said, getting up. "I saved him some soup and a few sandwiches."

Pierce stepped inside the open slider that led to the deck. "He just got up. Said he'd take a quick shower and be ready in a minute."

"It's going to be quicker than he imagines," said Harlow. "I got the last of the warm water."

"A cold shower will do him good. He looked like death warmed over," said Pierce, nestling in behind his wife and kissing her head.

"You all looked pretty rough around the edges this morning," said Anna.

"It's been a long couple of days," said Harlow, her eyes darting to the coffee maker.

"So I've heard," said Anna, breaking free from her husband's embrace. "I just made a fresh pot. Two, actually. The other is in the thermos."

"We should probably brew a few more before we kick off our planning session," said Pierce. "Maybe fill up one of the stockpots and keep it warm on the stove."

"That'll work," said Anna, starting to dig through one of the cabinets under the kitchen island.

"I'll take care of it, Anna," said Harlow. "You've been at it for most of the morning. We really appreciate all of this."

"It's no trouble. Seriously," said Anna, placing a tall stainless steel pot on the stove. "And I had plenty of help this morning. All the time, actually. They've taken all of this in stride."

Pierce glanced at Anna and nodded somberly. "They've been troupers. Probably got that from their mother."

Harlow sensed a little tension, which she assumed had to do more with their continued "exile" here than the rather sudden arrival of nearly a dozen guests. Or maybe it was a bit of both. Their presence here certainly suggested a continuation of Brad's involvement, which would put him at risk.

"Nicki and Thomas," said Harlow, turning to the two teenagers, "I'd ask you some questions, but your dad talked about the two of you for at least ten out of the sixteen hours on the drive out here."

Nicki, the older of the two by a year, got up from the table with her plate and brought it to the sink without looking at Harlow. She turned on the water and started rinsing the dish.

"Nicki," said Anna in a soft but stern voice.

"What?" said her daughter, keeping her back turned to them.

"It's totally okay," said Harlow. "Seriously. As much as I'd like to say I completely understand, I can't—and I won't pretend to. Show me where to find the coffee, and I'll get that going."

"I really don't mind taking care of it," said Anna, starting across the kitchen.

180

Nicki turned off the water. "Does all of this mean Dad isn't staying?"

Their son turned to Pierce, who stood behind him. "I really don't want you to leave."

"Who's leaving?" said Decker, suddenly appearing at the top of the stairs.

"Dad," said Thomas, getting up from the table. "You're heading back out with him, right?"

"It looks that way, Tommy," said Decker. "I'm not going to lie. I need your dad to keep me out of too much trouble."

"He's very good at finding trouble," said Pierce, squeezing his son's shoulder. "That's for sure."

"Does this have anything to do with Jacob Harcourt?" said Nicki.

"It doesn't appear to," said Decker. "But it could be something worse."

"I don't see how," said Nicki. "What happened to Harcourt? Is he gone?"

"We don't know, Nicki," said Pierce. "He's gone off the grid, and we haven't been able to find him. You know this. We've talked about this at length."

"Maybe he's not looking for us anymore," said Thomas.

"I wish I could believe that," said Pierce. "But people like Harcourt never forget."

Harlow recalled the venomous words Harcourt had spewed at them when he realized he'd been played. Horrifyingly personal threats that had haunted her ever since.

"I need the two of you to understand something," said Decker, approaching the kitchen. "I don't forget, either. When Jacob Harcourt decides it's safe to show his face, I'll be there to put an end to all of our worries."

At least he didn't say "put a bullet in Harcourt's head."

"I'll be there, too," said Pierce. "Just to make sure he doesn't screw it up."

"The bottom line, kids?" said Decker. "We're working on it. My daughter is in the same situation. She's tucked away somewhere with shitty internet. Sorry. Crappy internet."

"The internet is fine here," said Pierce.

"No. It's not, Dad," said Nicki. "But I've gotten used to it. Like a lot of things."

"As I was saying, before your dad interrupted me," Decker said, winking at Thomas. "My daughter is living with her grandparents and a twenty-four-hour security detail in a place just as isolated as this—but it's not her home. This is a real home. You two are lucky, even if the internet sucks."

Neither of the Pierce kids offered a rebuttal, which Harlow assumed had more to do with their knowledge of what had happened to Decker's wife and son than his closing argument.

"Sorry. I didn't mean to drop an atomic buzzkill bomb on the two of you," said Decker, eliciting a few strained smiles from the kids. "We've all been through the wringer with this. Three years of uncertainty, fear, and . . ."

Decker took a deep breath and blinked a few times, one of his tells. He was on the verge of breaking down. Harlow glanced at Pierce, who looked just as helpless. She'd known coming here would be tough on all of them—particularly Decker. The sooner they got on the road, the better. Distraction seemed to be the only strategy that worked. One of these days, it wouldn't be enough. She checked her watch.

"We have an hour until the teleconference with Senator Steele," said Harlow, hoping to shift gears.

"How long until the water heats up?" said Decker. "I feel like crap. Pardon my language."

"You look like crap," said Pierce. "Twenty minutes."

"All right. Let's get everyone together in thirty," said Decker. "Go over a few things before kickoff."

And just like that, Decker was back in the game.

CHAPTER THIRTY-ONE

Decker slipped on a gray T-shirt and gave his hair another round with his damp towel before tossing it in an overflowing laundry basket. He took a look at himself in the mirror and sighed. Pierce was right. He looked like crap, and the brief shower hadn't improved the situation. A quick shave might help his overall roadkill appearance, but nothing could hide the bags under his eyes and the wear on his face. He was simply exhausted from the past week and needed at least a week of regular sleep to start looking and feeling right again. Decker didn't see that happening any time soon. A glance at his watch scrapped the shave idea. He could take care of that after the videoconference.

He grabbed the basket of wet towels and walked it to the laundry room next door, setting it on top of the washer. Anna stepped in as he was leaving.

"Hey, Anna. I left the towels on the washer," he said. "Not sure if you bleached them every wash or whatever. Marley didn't allow me to touch the household towels."

"She trained you well. Brad's not allowed to touch anything except his own clothes. We have a utility closet full of off-color towels that justify his ban."

"I quit buying white T-shirts and white towels," he said. "It's easier that way."

She considered him for a moment, smiling warmly. "How are you doing, Ryan?"

"All right. I guess," he said. "I mean. It is what it is."

"It is what it is?" she said. "That's not much of an answer."

"It's the only answer that doesn't drive me crazy," said Decker.

His reply was a casual lie he'd crafted to sound like he'd come to terms with what had happened—which he hadn't. Not a day went by that he didn't spend time thinking about his wife and son. Thinking about the horror Jacob Harcourt had brought down on them, for no reason other than to irreparably break Decker and World Recovery Group. Michael, a few years away from being a teenager, murdered and mutilated in front of Marley. What they'd done to his wife was unspeakable. The kinds of things you could never come to terms with.

"Sorry. I just—" she said, looking like she had something difficult to say.

"What's wrong?" said Decker, suspecting the answer.

"I'm worried about losing Brad," she said. "I know that sounds selfish after what you've been through, but I—"

"It's not selfish, Anna," said Decker. "Not at all. Taking Brad from you guys is the last thing I'd ever want to happen."

"Then why are you dragging him into this?"

"I have this strange feeling that whatever we found in Mexico is related to Harcourt," said Decker. "Nailing that fucker to the wall is the only way we'll be able to live normal lives again."

"Harcourt isn't behind every conspiracy out there," said Anna. "In fact, I wonder if you won't be making a new enemy by pursuing this. Brad told me what you found out there. If the US government is behind it, the number of enemies has multiplied. One is enough for all of us."

Decker wasn't sure what to say next. It didn't sound like Brad had given her a complete picture of the situation, or maybe she'd simply chosen to ignore it, knowing that her family was safe here—as long as they remained vigilant.

"I think it's safe to say that we've all been identified by whoever is behind the weapons in Mexico, and the cartel involved," he said, laying the facts straight out.

"I knew that last job was a mistake," she said. "I know why he agreed to help Senator Steele, but deep inside, I knew it meant bad news."

"None of us, including Senator Steele, had any idea it was this bad," said Decker. "We knew the cartel had to be involved but figured the risk was minimal. Honestly, I expected to walk around the site for a few minutes and conclude our investigation."

She shook her head slowly, a competition between tears and anger playing out in front of him.

"I guess there's no going back from this one," she said.

"Brad doesn't have to go with us," said Decker. "If he stays here, the connection is severed."

"No. It's not," she said. "I know you'd go to your grave with our secret, but I just served lunch to ten other people that know where we live. As soon as you drive out of here, I have to take the kids to our bug-out spot."

"I don't want to know where that is," said Decker.

"I didn't plan on telling you."

"Damn, Anna. I didn't think this through," he said.

"Neither did Brad," she said. "I think the two of you have been running on fumes for too long at this point."

The laundry room door squeaked open, revealing Pierce. "We're ready to start. Why the sullen looks?"

"Anna pointed out something I had completely overlooked," said Decker.

He explained the problem Anna had identified, which hit Pierce hard. He buried his head in his hands and muttered a string of self-deprecating foul language.

"I say we throw this into Senator Steele's lap," said Decker. "She has the money to hire the right people to protect your family. We'll select a crew with no possible connection to Aegis Global. No chance of compromise. Bring them in just in case things go sideways down in El Centro. If she won't do it, I'll make it happen."

"I'm still bugging out until I know it's safe," said Anna. "I won't take any chances with the kids."

"I won't, either," said Pierce. "Ryan, I hate to do this, but I'm staying here."

Decker nodded, knowing his friend had made the right call. He'd dragged Pierce far enough into his mess, potentially endangering his family without realizing it.

"I understand. We'll still arrange a protective detail," said Decker.

"Hold on," said Anna. "What makes you think Harcourt is involved with the weapons?"

"It's just a hunch," said Decker. "Aegis Global had unsavory ties around the world, particularly in Mexico and Central America. Rumor has it that Harcourt bought off hundreds of Mexican politicians, police officials, and the Sinaloa Cartel so he could operate black-ops training camps and store equipment he needed to ship worldwide—without questions. I don't have any proof of this, but Harcourt disappeared a little too neatly. I've always suspected that he fled south, where he was untouchable."

"And you think this might somehow lead to him," she stated.

"It's not the reason I agreed to the job," said Decker. "But in the back of my head, I hoped we might dig something up. Anything. I know it's a total long shot, Anna, but it's all I've come across in the past year. If I develop a lead from this, I'll let Brad know. The two of you can decide if you want to pursue it."

"Screw it," said Anna. "Brad's going with you to El Centro."

"What do you mean?" said Pierce.

Decker shook his head. "We can manage without him. Seriously. He should stay."

"I very much doubt you can manage without him," said Anna. "Which is why he's going. Brad keeps you and Harlow's crew out of enemy hands, which keeps the enemy out of our little valley. I think that's a far more efficient and effective use of his skills to protect us."

"She's always been the more practical of the two of us," said Pierce. "I still want a team here to provide security."

"I'll call Bernie first thing after the videoconference," said Decker. "He'll know people we can trust."

"We should have used him for the last mission," said Pierce. "Hindsight twenty-twenty and all, it would have been worth the money and the wait. In and out in less than thirty minutes."

"Yeah. Remind me not to skimp on spending the senator's money next time," said Decker.

CHAPTER THIRTY-TWO

Decker took the front-row seat Harlow had saved for him between her and Pierce. A tripod-mounted video camera sat just below a live digital image of the group projected on the wall behind it.

"Looks okay," said Harlow, not sounding satisfied. "Should we close the blinds a little more? I feel like the picture is a little washed out."

Joshua got up from the computer station just out of the camera's view and to their right to examine the picture head-on.

"If we close the blinds any more, you'll wash out even more on their screens," he said. "This is the best we can do under the circumstances. You'll look crisp to them."

"That's fine," said Harlow. "As long as they can see us."

Decker laughed. "I'm not sure we want the senator to get too good a look at us. She might think twice about who she's pinning her hopes on."

"Did he just call me a mess?" said Jessica, generating a feigned uproar from the group.

Decker turned to address her question. "I apologize. Flannel shirts and designer camouflage are a good look for you."

Harlow elbowed his shoulder, both of them well aware that Jessica was further out of her element than anyone in the room, including the SCIF team. She fought her battles in a power suit, unwinding at the end of the day with a Kir Royale in the black-and-white-themed bar across the street from her Westwood apartment.

"I had to scrounge to put this outfit together," said Jessica.

"I'm just kidding," said Decker. "I mean, they do suit you, but—"

"You should probably quit while you're not too far behind," said Harlow.

"Good idea," he said, nodding at Jessica. "There's a Walmart in Trinidad. We'll get you a more appropriate wardrobe before we leave."

"Nice," said Jessica. "I'll remember this."

"Behave yourself, please," said Harlow.

He looked over his shoulder at Jessica, who glared at him. "Sorry."

"Keep digging, Decker," said Pam, who sat directly behind him.

He was about to engage his favorite target on the team when Joshua flagged their attention. "Reeves and the senator have joined the video-conference," he said. "Shall I take us live?"

"Do it," said Harlow, squeezing Decker's knee and whispering, "Behave."

The projected image on the wall in front of them blinked, changing to a split screen featuring the contrasted images of Supervisory Special Agent Reeves in a dark hotel room and Senator Steele in a brightly lit office.

"Before we get started, I'm truly sorry to have put you in this precarious and inconvenient position. If there's anything I can do to alleviate the situation, please do not hesitate to ask," said Steele.

"Ma'am," said Decker, "I'd like to upgrade the security posture at the Pierces' homestead. Whether we hunker down here for a few weeks or head out tonight, I think it's only fair that we give Brad and his family that added peace of mind."

"I agree," said Steele. "I'll trust you to make the arrangements, which will be covered by the account I established for our mutually agreed-upon operations."

"Thank you, Senator," said Pierce.

"It's the least I can do, Mr. Pierce, and please pass on my sincerest thanks to your wife and children," she said. "Mr. Decker?"

"Yes?"

"Please do not skimp on the security detail," said Steele. "If armored SUVs and a helicopter gunship would make Pierce's family feel safer, then I expect to see a serious dent in that account. Understood?"

"Understood, ma'am."

Brad whispered without moving his head, "Thank you, man."

"I would have paid for it myself," Decker whispered back.

"If you don't mind, I'll kick things off, since I suspect my recent revelations will heavily influence our path forward," said Steele.

After everyone nodded and agreed, the senator continued.

"I had an interesting visit this morning from Senator Paul Duncan of Oklahoma, chairman of the Senate Subcommittee on Border Security and Immigration. Bottom line? Duncan, a man with the personality of a snake oil salesman, offered his full support of my human-trafficking inquiry, even going so far as to provide me with a thumb drive jam-packed with the latest reports on the border incident and fresh intelligence regarding the cartels' human-trafficking influence."

"That sounds encouraging," said Harlow.

Decker knew there was more to this. He could feel it in the senator's tone, and so could Harlow.

"In a vacuum, yes," said Steele. "But Duncan hasn't spoken more than ten unscripted words to me in the fifteen years he's been a senator. He's stuck in what I like to call the 'white-haired man's time warp,' where my gender doesn't count for much. Naturally, I was a little suspicious when he scheduled an appointment to meet with me, and I wasn't the least bit surprised to learn that the thumb drive he provided contained a rootkit virus."

"Jesus," said Joshua.

"That's what I said when I found out what Duncan had attempted to install on my computer," said Steele.

"Joshua?" said Harlow.

"Wow. So many variations of the rootkit," said Joshua.

"Ten-second version," said Decker.

"A rootkit virus buries itself deep in a computer, granting remote access to the attacker," said Joshua. "Complete and undetectable access and control."

"*Jesus* is right," said Decker.

"I think we can safely assume that Senator Duncan is directly involved in the cover-up on the border," said Steele. "And whatever greater conspiracy is linked to those weapons."

"Very sophisticated weapons," said Reeves. "Game-changing weapons if they were aimed north."

"I can't imagine the cartels would be that stupid," said Pierce. "One Javelin missile fired on US soil, and that would literally be the end of the Sinaloa Cartel."

"Maybe that's the goal," said Decker. "Artificially create an excuse to do what our government has wanted to do for decades—conduct direct military operations against the cartels. Win the supposed war on drugs."

"It's too overt," said Pierce. "Our government has a long history of working this kind of stuff well behind the scenes. It's not our style. Not to mention the fact that our government has no interest in winning the war on drugs. It's a budget booster for a number of federal agencies. No offense, Joe."

"None taken," said Reeves.

"I completely agree, Mr. Pierce," said Steele. "We're totally missing something here."

"Have you looked into Duncan? Past connections. Present connections. Proposed legislation. The kind of things that helped us connect the dots between Senator Frist and Jacob Harcourt?" said Harlow.

"I took a page right out of your book, Harlow, and dug into Duncan's record," said Steele. "I also took the liberty of researching Bob Saling, who accompanied Duncan on a fact-finding trip to the border a few days after the border incident. The two of them have been thick as thieves. Bob is the House chairman of the Subcommittee on Border Security and Immigration."

"They sound like twins," said Harlow.

"In person and in politics," said Steele. "Both of them are anti-immigration and pro–border militarization. Surprise, surprise."

"But they'd be the absolute logical choice to send down to El Centro—to fact find on a border-security issue," said Decker.

"Correct," said Steele. "They also had financial ties to Aegis Global—once again, not a shocker. Three-quarters of Congress took money from Harcourt on some level."

"But you didn't," said Decker.

"No. Ironically, I didn't," said Steele. "I just unwittingly advanced Harcourt's agenda."

"Not your fault," said Decker, a long pause ensuing. "So. What's next?"

"I want to send you to El Centro."

"What's in El Centro," said Decker, "that can compete with Javelin missiles buried in the desert?"

"I'll be entirely frank with you," said Steele. "Nothing can compete with what you already found out there, but that's an avenue we can't pursue for a number of obvious and frustrating reasons. Your presence in El Centro would serve one purpose."

"Bait," said Pierce.

The room broke out in a discordance of murmurs.

"I know how that sounds, but hear me out," said Steele. "After extracting the data from the thumb drive on an air-gapped computer, we identified a discrepancy in the testimony provided by the two-agent Border Patrol team located a few miles east of the missing and presumed murdered agents. The fleeing agents reported the explosion when their Motorolas came within range of the next border patrol, three minutes after the explosion was recorded by several teams in the area, but there's no way they could have driven that far, that quickly.

"They were towing a mobile observation tower, which takes at least ten minutes to take down. Either they never deployed the station and took off as soon as they heard the explosion, or they heard something over the Motorolas that prompted them to lower the tower and get out of there. I can only presume that the people behind the murders and the weapons buried in Mexico arrived at the same conclusion."

"Why wouldn't they have killed the witnesses?" said Pam.

"Probably because they had access to the same frequencies," said Decker. "Whatever they heard wasn't enough to justify another big mess."

"That's what we think," said Steele.

"We?" said Decker.

"I've already shared this with Special Agent Reeves," said Steele.

"The timeline doesn't work out," said Reeves. "Something spooked the two agents, but it didn't warrant their execution."

"Back to the bait idea," said Decker. "It's a long shot."

"I don't expect it to pan out," said Steele. "But it's all we have right now, other than pursuing Duncan."

"We go to El Centro and poke around, hoping to draw whoever is behind the buried weapons into the open?" said Harlow.

"Something like that," said Steele. "It'll either be a nonevent or the fight of your life."

Decker laughed. "You really covered both ends of the spectrum with that statement."

"Just being honest," said Steele.

"What if it doesn't pan out at all?" said Harlow.

Steele raised her hands in a surrender posture. "We have a few more avenues to consider, but they're even less defined. I'll let Joe cover those."

"All right. Here's what we have. First, the cartel was sniffing around all of your digs in Los Angeles. I put surveillance teams on most of your apartments, and you definitely had visitors," said Reeves.

"Did they break in?" said Harlow.

"I can't say," said Reeves. "My surveillance teams remained on the street to avoid detection, but there's no doubt that they showed up."

"What time did they arrive?" said Decker.

"We first picked them up entering Harlow's apartment around one fifty p.m."

"Damn. They didn't waste any time," said Decker.

"No. They didn't. You were smart to get out of town as soon as possible," said Reeves. "Frankly, I thought you were being paranoid. Lesson learned."

"The Sinaloa has its shit together," said Harlow.

"They do," said Reeves. "But this wasn't the Sinaloa. The head FBI liaison to the joint FBI-DEA task force based out of LA told me that the border west of Mexicali is under Jalisco New Generation control. It's been a hotly contested area over the past few years, but the Jalisco cartel runs things now."

"Is that a relatively new cartel?" said Pierce.

"Sort of. The Jalisco New Generation Cartel sprang from the Milenio Cartel in 2009," said Reeves. "They rose to power quickly, expanding their operational network from one side of Mexico to the other in under a year. They've previously aligned with the Sinaloa to attack common rivals, but the two cartels have mostly fallen out at this point. Jalisco New Generation is currently fighting four different cartels for control of strategic border areas and ports around Mexico."

"So the weapons were bound for this Jalisco cartel?" said Decker.

"Assuming that you were identified at the Tecate port of entry, well inside their territory, I'd say that's a solid theory."

"Let me interrupt for a moment," said Senator Steele.

"Absolutely," said Reeves.

"The Sinaloa Cartel is still the dominant Mexican cartel, right?" said Steele.

"That's right," said Reeves. "Jalisco New Generation controls a hundred-mile stretch of the border between Mexicali and Tijuana, plus a wide swath of the country extending from Guadalajara to Veracruz. The Juárez Cartel controls a small pocket around Ciudad Juárez, which is extremely profitable. Los Zetas controls about half of the Texas border, competing with the Gulf Cartel. Everything else is controlled by the Sinaloa."

"Why would someone on our side of the border ship advanced weapons to one of the underdogs?" said Steele.

"Maybe our government is trying to weaken the Sinaloa?" said Jessica. "Even out the power distribution?"

"That's a possibility," said Steele. "But a risky one. The Sinaloa will quickly guess that the US supplied the missiles, and that won't sit well with them at all. I can see them capturing missiles and exposing US involvement or, worse, using them against us."

"Either scenario would be a nightmare," said Reeves.

"What if the missiles are a deterrent to prevent the Sinaloa from knocking this New Jalisco group out of business?" said Harlow. "Keep the Sinaloa from consolidating even more power."

"I'd agree if Decker had only found rifles and machine guns," said Steele. "Javelin missiles, guarded by the most advanced surveillance robots on the market, suggests something different. Is that a fair assessment, Mr. Pierce or Mr. Decker?"

"I can't think of any other explanation," said Pierce. "If I wanted to stabilize a cartel's hold on an area, I'd flood the defending cartel with military-grade rifles, light machine guns, unguided rocket launchers, grenades, and antipersonnel mines."

"I agree," said Decker. "I might also provide training on the construction and employment of remotely detonated improvised explosive devices. Area denial weapons."

"Remind me not to wage a street war against the two of you," said Harlow.

"The question is, why Javelins?" said Steele.

"I'd use those to strategically target enemy leadership—in their vehicles, homes, or places of business—from a safe, standoff distance. Nobody in their right mind would give chase."

"These people are out of their minds," said Reeves. "Don't forget that."

"Good point. But even most loyal and crazy cartel soldiers tend to get discouraged by a twenty-pound high-explosive warhead," said Pierce.

Decker continued the theoretical war game. "I'd also target production and distribution facilities from a distance. A focused and persistent targeting campaign, backed by street-level attacks, could subdue an area. Leadership would be terrified to leave any stronghold that can't be penetrated by one of those warheads, which would lead to a loss of control on the ground."

"The two of you would use it as purely an offensive weapon," said Steele.

"Right," said Pierce. "The system could have a defensive role down there, possibly to defend an isolated, high-value target from vehicle attack, but that's about the extent of how I see it being used defensively."

"That pretty much sums it up," said Decker.

"We're definitely missing something," said Senator Steele.

"Maybe we'll get lucky in El Centro," said Decker. "Grab someone that can shed some light on this."

"I won't sanction a kidnapping operation, Mr. Decker," said Steele. "This has to be purely intelligence gathering."

"I'm very glad you said that, Senator," said Harlow. "I'm not comfortable kidnapping anyone."

"What if we return the person a little later?" said Decker.

"That's still kidnapping," said Jessica.

"But it doesn't sound as bad," said Decker.

"And what do you plan to do in between grabbing and releasing the victim?" said Jessica.

"Don't answer that, Mr. Decker," said Steele. "Intelligence gathering only. Understood?"

Decker barely heard the senator, his thoughts grappling with an idea that had sprung into his mind. Harlow tapped his leg.

"Decker," she urged.

"Mr. Decker?" said Senator Steele. "Did we lose you?"

"Yes. I mean, no. Sorry," he said. "I just thought of something."

"Before we get to that, I need you to acknowledge that this is an intelligence-gathering mission only," said Steele.

"Yes. Acknowledged," said Decker.

"Now. What managed to steal your attention away so quickly before?" said Steele.

"Joe, do you have any contacts at Customs and Border Protection?" said Decker. "Someone high up?"

"I don't regularly interact with CBP, but I'll do what I can," said Reeves. "What do you want to know?"

"I wonder if other sites exist, connected to other military exclusion zones," said Decker. "What if the US is feeding sophisticated weapons to more than one of the Sinaloa's rivals? Kind of like what Jessica said. To more evenly distribute the power. It would be far easier for the US to combat drugs if the Mexicans had a less unified and powerful front like the Sinaloa."

"That might be a tall order for someone at my pay grade," said Reeves. "Senator Steele, is there any way you could make a discreet inquiry?"

"I'll see what I can do," she said. "The only way I'd feel comfortable doing this would be to go outside congressional channels and contact CBP directly. Unfortunately, they typically like this kind of information request to go through congressional channels. I'll figure something out."

"More weapons caches would expand our options," said Decker. "If our intelligence-gathering mission doesn't pan out."

"We'll cross that bridge when we get there," said Steele. "Does anyone have any questions or suggestions?"

"Ma'am?" said Joshua, edging his seat into view. "Senator Steele?"

"Yes?"

"Joshua Keller. I'm part of the firm's technical operations team. Is there any way I could get a look at the full contents of the thumb drive given to you by Senator Duncan?" he said. "It might be possible to run a reverse rootkit on Duncan, or whoever he hired. I know some people who would love nothing more than to work on this."

"Is that safe? The absolute last thing I'd want to do is infect your computer network," said Steele. "Or compromise your safety."

"It would be perfectly safe if you overnighted me the drive," said Joshua. "We carry a few air-gapped computers with us for just this kind of thing."

"Even if we had it sent to a post office box in Colorado Springs, that would create too much of a trail pointing in this direction," said Decker.

"Yeah. I don't feel comfortable with that," said Pierce.

"What if I had someone hand deliver it to the location of your choice?" said Senator Steele. "Preferably near a major airport. I would send someone nobody could connect to my office. I could have it in your hands this evening if the flights line up."

"Denver would work," said Pierce.

"Still too risky to send one of us that close to a major city," said Decker.

"I'll send the gunny," said Pierce. "He'll love it."

"I love the sound of giving Duncan a taste of his own medicine," said Steele. "I'll send you flight information through our secure link as soon as I have it."

"I think we all have solid marching orders," said Decker. "I can't think of anything else right now."

The rest of the team murmured in agreement.

"Then let's get to it," said Steele. "We'll plan to reconvene when you return from El Centro, unless something urgent comes up. Signing off."

The senator's face disappeared, followed shortly by Reeves's, leaving them to stare at a reverse image of themselves on the wall. Decker stood up and turned his folding chair, straddling it to face the rest of the crew.

"How does everyone feel about heading to El Centro?" said Decker.

"To do what, exactly?" said Sandra. "Other than serve as bait."

"Intelligence gathering," said Harlow.

"What does that even mean here?" said Katie.

"That's the question we're going to spend the rest of the day answering," said Decker.

CHAPTER THIRTY-THREE

Before they reassembled to start planning, Decker made a quick reassessment of the gear they had transported from Los Angeles. Harlow's crew had neatly arranged the equipment, separating the items by different categories along the floor at the back of the basement. He was immediately drawn to the modest but potent array of weapons they had selected. Two short-barrel HK416 rifles constituted the bulk of their firepower. One capable of automatic fire. Both entirely illegal in California. The rifles would only be used under the direst circumstances.

Two additional upper-receiver pieces completed the set, each interchangeable with the short-barrel receivers to provide different mission capabilities. A heavy-barrel piece transformed one of the rifles into a light machine gun, capable of sustained automatic fire, and a longer, precision-barrel piece satisfied their marksmanship needs. The extra pieces gave them the ability to fluidly adapt to the threat level that emerged without carrying four rifles. Decker sincerely hoped they wouldn't be needed.

Two semiautomatic Benelli shotguns, a dozen pistols, and five Tasers rounded out the small arsenal, giving each member of the team the option to select the personal protective weapon that they felt the most comfortable carrying. An assortment of concealed holsters and discreet body armor carriers lay next to the lethal selection.

The remaining equipment fell into the communications, surveillance, or defensive-measures categories. Katie had brought her usual assortment of tricks, ranging from smoke grenades to remote-activated spike strips that could flatten tires without warning the driver. He'd witnessed the value of the spike strip firsthand last year while fleeing Gunther Ross. Decker had gladly traded space in the vehicles for her goodies. Katie's clever use of this equipment could alleviate the need for Decker's favorite tools.

He moved on to the six commercial-grade, two-by-two-foot plastic cases he'd never seen prior to packing the SUVs for the trip. They sat stacked against the wall on the other side of Katie's equipment. Decker started to play with the locking mechanism on one of them, curious to see what was inside.

"I forgot to put up the 'hands off the merchandise' sign," said Katie, startling him.

"Funny," said Decker. "Your mystery cases took up a lot of our cargo space. Care to spill the beans?"

"A little something I've been working on with our SCIF team," said Katie.

"That's it?" said Decker. "And here I thought we were friends."

"Acquaintances. When you're not bugging the shit out of me," said Katie.

"You're really not going to tell me your little secret?"

"I guess there's no point to hiding these," she said. "I've retrofitted six lift-capable drones to carry some surveillance and countersurveillance gear."

"What kind of countersurveillance stuff?" said Decker.

"Aerosolized paint bombs that can instantly cover a ten-foot-diameter circle with black paint, droppable flash bangs, and a multishot Taser package."

"Seriously?" said Decker. "That's crazy."

"Crazy with some limitations. The paint bombs disable a vehicle by instantly obscuring the windows, but we have to fly the drone directly overhead and detonate the canister while it's attached to the drone. Dropping it like a gravity bomb proved nearly impossible against a moving target."

"I assume detonating the canister while it's attached to the drone effectively kills the drone?" said Decker.

"Bingo. Turns it into a fifteen-hundred-dollar paint bomb," she said. "Still not a bad investment under the right circumstances."

"Not at all. What about the flash bangs?"

"I've had three hangers in twenty-three drops," said Katie. "One partially releasing, which resulted in the destruction of the drone. The others just sat in their cradles—useless. If I can get the failure rate down to one in a hundred, I'd take them more seriously."

"And the Taser?"

"The Taser rig needs a lot of work. Targeting is nearly nonexistent, and we keep snagging wires in the propellers."

"Who do we have trained to fly the drones?" said Decker.

"All of the SCIF techs," she said. "Kyle and Mazz are the better of the four. Sophie isn't bad, either. All of the gamers seem to have a knack for it."

"Sophie is a gamer?"

"Hard-core," said Katie. "*Call of Duty. Battlefield. Far Cry.* She goes to a couple of conventions every year."

"To compete?"

"No. She's not that good. She goes to be among her people," said Katie.

"I learn something new about this crew every day," said Decker.

"It's a diverse group, that's for sure," said Katie. "What are you thinking for the El Centro op?"

"In terms of drones, or the whole mission?"

"Both."

"I'm thinking we'll need all six of them configured with paint bombs," said Decker. "And that I should go ahead and write you a nine-thousand-dollar check right now."

PART THREE

CHAPTER THIRTY-FOUR

Freya Walker took in the vast sea of tightly spaced, indistinguishable stucco homes as they rapidly approached the cul-de-sac containing one of their two primary target houses. Brightly lit windows and porch lights cast a soft glow over the neighborhood.

"Slow us down," said Freya.

"This is our fifth pass in two hours," said Nick Adler, her assistant tactical operation commander. "I'd say it's our last in this vehicle."

"I agree," she said.

The first and only thing she really noticed while cruising through the intersection was her surveillance car parked several houses down the street. The car stood out because it was the only vehicle parked on Fieldview Avenue. Not exactly a viable long-term strategy in a neighborhood generously sprinkled with Border Patrol families and cops. They needed a short-term fix.

"This isn't going to work," said Freya, the intersection fading away behind them. "They stand out even more at night."

"Yeah. The neighborhood is quieter than I imagined, and way too tidy. Keeping a car on the streets overnight is absolutely out of the question," said Adler. "We'll be seriously pushing our luck during the day. Today was a freebie, because the surveillance is fresh, but keeping a car parked on one of these streets tomorrow, for any length of time? Someone will call it in."

"We need twenty-four-hour coverage to make this work," said Freya, reaching into the backpack nestled against her leg. "Zero gaps."

"That's not gonna happen unless we start commandeering houses," said Nick.

"Sooner than later," she said, already dialing her satellite phone.

"I wasn't expecting a call this quickly," said JUPITER. "Do we have a problem?"

"No problem. I just need to adjust our surveillance posture," said Freya. "Significantly enough to warrant a call. We need to reposition the street teams."

"Inside nearby homes, I presume?"

"Yes, sir. It's just too damn quiet around here to keep our vehicles parked for any length of time without drawing attention. We'll focus on the two primary targets. If Decker comes to El Centro, he'll end up in one of those two locations."

"Be careful not to pick a cop or Border Patrol agent's house. The same rules of engagement for the street apply here."

"Understood. I'll let you know when we're in place," said Freya.

"Let me know when Decker and Mackenzie no longer pose a threat."

She lowered the phone, immediately forming a plan.

"Turn us around," said Freya. "Time to go house hunting."

"Rules of engagement?" said Adler.

"Nonlethal measures only, unless there's no choice," said Freya.

"That's not going to be easy."

Adler executed a three-point turn in the middle of the empty road and returned them to the intersection.

"Let's start with that one," she said, pointing at the first house across from the cul-de-sac. "It has the best view of the target house and two of the three approaches."

While Nick maneuvered the SUV into the driveway, Freya reached out to the surveillance team a few houses down.

"X-Ray One. This is ATHENA. We're establishing a permanent observation post at the corner of Fieldview and Cypress," she said. "Wait for us at the Super Stop Travel Center just north of here. One of us will pick up your team in ten to fifteen minutes."

"Copy that. Proceeding to new location," said the team leader.

"You think it'll take that long?" said Adler, parking the vehicle at the top of the driveway.

"Never know what we'll find in one of these houses," said Freya. "We could find a dozen undocumented migrants living in a spare bedroom or a garage."

"We'll have to take a pass if that's the case."

"The problem is we won't know it until after we've taken steps that can't be undone," said Freya.

"That's when it becomes more of a lethal situation," said Adler.

"Fingers crossed we find nothing but run-of-the-mill families," said Freya, opening her door. "Easy to stuff in a closet for a few days."

They met at the back of the SUV to unload the kit they had assembled specifically for this situation. Fake badges with holders. Tasers. Duct tape. Zip ties. Black hoods. Electrical cords. Collapsible batons. Pepper spray. CamelBaks and PowerBars to facilitate feeding and watering prisoners.

She readied the Taser and clipped it to her belt, followed by the badge. The two new additions, combined with the concealed holster on her right hip, should be enough to keep anyone from questioning the authenticity of their story. When Adler finished gearing up, she removed the nylon briefcase containing the less friendly items and headed for the front door. Adler rang the doorbell and stepped back, both of them waiting with their hands folded at the waists.

A young Hispanic man with a tight haircut opened the door. *Possible law enforcement or ex-military.*

"Yes?" he said, examining them for a moment before scanning the dark street behind them. *Alert. Possibly hiding something?*

"Sorry to bother you around dinnertime, sir," said Freya, removing her badge from her belt and holding it up to the man in front of her. "I'm Dana Sullivan with the Department of Homeland Security's internal affairs division. This is Brett Webster of the same department. We're following up on the Customs and Border Protection investigators that took a routine statement from you two days ago regarding the murders of the two agents near the border. We just wanted to thank you in person and check to see if you had remembered anything else that might be useful."

"We were never questioned by investigators," said the man. "Unless my wife talked to them during the day."

"Is she usually home with the kids?" said Freya.

The man contemplated her question a little longer than she expected. She was getting a nervous vibe from this guy. If he called her on the relevancy of her question, they'd move on to another house. They needed someone far less observant and confrontational to make this work. He shook his head and answered her question, not showing any sign of doubt.

"We don't have kids," he said. "My wife works from home."

"Is she home now?" said Freya. "I'd like to verify this with her."

"Sure. Hold on," he said, shutting the door.

She looked at Adler. "Something's off with this guy. Pass?"

He shook his head. "No kids? Easy times. It won't get any better than this. We've seen tons of kids cruising around the neighborhood today."

"Unless he's a cop," said Freya.

"I don't think so," said Adler. "He would have said something."

Muffled, argumentative voices interrupted their conversation. The door opened a few moments later. A tall Hispanic woman with blonde hair appeared next to the same man they'd spoken to a minute earlier. The woman's chunky diamond earrings and equally impressive necklace caught Freya's eye. Either the rocks were fake or this woman ran a very successful home business.

"Nobody ever asked me any questions," said the woman, her hand moving the door a few inches closer to shutting it. "Never knew them. They're not even our neighbors. I'm not sure why you'd need a statement from me."

Freya edged closer, sensing that the woman was about to slam the door on them.

"Sorry again for interrupting your evening. One of the agents that may have witnessed something while on patrol lives in the cul-de-sac over there," said Freya, pointing in the direction of Agent Ocampo's home. "If CBP didn't interview you, we'll need to take a very quick statement. Five questions. Mostly yes and no answers," she said.

"Do you have some kind of warrant?"

"You're not a suspect, or under any kind of suspicion," said Freya.

"Then the answer is no," said the woman. "I know my rights, and I don't have to talk to you."

Something definitely going on here.

Freya glanced at Adler. "Do we really need their statements?"

"I'm afraid we do," he said, stepping behind Freya.

"Is this something we can do at the door?" said the man.

"Shut the fuck up, Gabe. Ain't happening," said the woman, attempting to push the door shut.

Freya jammed her foot in the doorway, just in time to stop the door from shutting. The door opened several inches and slammed against the woman's foot.

"I'm calling nine-one-one," said the woman. "Get some real cops over here."

The door opened a few inches again, and the man tried to kick Freya's foot out of the doorframe. When that failed to dislodge her, he stomped on her foot. Fortunately, her cross-trainers beat the man's leather sandals. She glanced over her shoulder at Nick, who was frantically twisting a suppressor onto the barrel of his pistol.

"You sure about that?" she said.

He nodded and stepped back, the suppressor firmly attached.

"Last chance to open the door," said Freya.

"Nine-one-one is on the way, bitch," said the woman. "Get your fake-ass badges out of here—and tell Raúl we're paid up. I paid his ass this morning! No bullshit. How the hell didn't this get communicated?"

"Do it," said Freya, moving out of the way with her foot still firmly planted between the door and the frame.

Adler front kicked the door, which knocked it halfway open and caused the couple inside to stumble backward, the man falling onto his hands and knees. He followed up with a second kick, the door striking the man's face straight on and snapping his neck backward. Adler shouldered his way inside and aimed his weapon at the woman, who was on her back.

"We paid! I fucking paid Raúl this—"

A small red dot appeared in the middle of her forehead, spraying the white tile floor behind her with dark-red chunks. A second shot bounced the man's head off the tile at Adler's feet. Probably an unnecessary shot given the prior sound of the door's impact against his head. Freya stepped inside, careful to avoid the pool of blood spreading from the man's head, and shut the door.

"Not the result I expected when we knocked on the door, but she didn't leave us much choice," she said.

"The nine-one-one threat was probably nonsense, but we couldn't take the chance."

"What do you think they're into?" said Freya.

"My guess is they're holding drugs that make it through the Calexico port of entry," said Adler. "And they've skimmed the product long enough to buy Mrs. Drug Runner a necklace worth more than their house. I'm going to watch the street from the front window. Make sure we don't have any nosy neighbors."

"I'll take the upstairs," said Freya. "Expand the view. If the cops don't show up within five minutes, I think we can assume our entry went unobserved."

"I'd give it ten, just to be sure," said Adler. "Never know what someone saw and reported from the safety of their home. Have one of our standby units drive through the extended neighborhood and look for a gathering of police cars. The police wouldn't rush into the situation that unfolded here."

"Sounds good," said Freya, glad to have Nick on the mission.

Her supervised time in the field had been cut short by Aegis Global's destruction, putting her in the unenviable position of leading seasoned field operators claiming far more "been there, done that" experience. Nick Adler, a seasoned Aegis operator, had so far demonstrated no aspirations of running the show. He appeared perfectly content in the number-two position, where he assumed little responsibility for a mission's outcome but played a personal, hands-on role in how it unfolded. They were well paired for operations like these.

"When we're done here, maybe they'll assume everything that happened on this street was cartel related," she said.

"Nice and tidy."

"Exactly how Jupiter prefers it," she said.

Adler shook his head and chuckled. "Harcourt is Jupiter. I don't for one second believe that he's operating through some kind of proxy. You're getting your orders straight from the source himself, which is a good thing for all of us."

"As long as we don't screw it up," said Freya.

He glanced around at the blood-splattered murder scene. "I can't imagine it getting worse than this."

"I hope not," she said before heading upstairs.

Ten minutes later, she drove the couple's Mercedes SUV to pick up one of the teams and deliver them to the house. She made one more trip before heading out with Adler to secure the second surveillance location, where they could monitor Agent Cruz's house.

The second takedown went smoothly, the unsuspecting and friendly couple inviting them inside immediately. The couple and their two elementary school–aged kids now sat under guard in the master bedroom's walk-in closet, their legs zip-tied together so they couldn't move independently.

Within thirty minutes, both of her strike teams had moved quietly into place, safely watching the two target houses. She'd assigned three three-person groups to each house, keeping one of their SUVs in each driveway. They'd use the homeowners' vehicles to move the rest of the teams when the time came. Nine operatives should be more than enough to bottle up Decker and whoever arrived with him. She'd shift forces from one house to the other, doubling that number within a few minutes if he proved more troublesome than expected.

That left her with two floating teams as a tactical backup, who would remain close at hand, plus a single operative parked in a Suburban at a nearby hotel, whom she'd deploy to pick up stranded operatives or break up a roadblock.

Satisfied that she'd deployed her teams as effectively as possible under the less-than-optimal circumstances, Freya settled at the kitchen table with a fresh mug of their imprisoned hosts' coffee—ready for a long night of watching the neighborhood.

CHAPTER THIRTY-FIVE

Harlow shifted in her seat, nearly an entire day on the road in the gray Mercedes-Benz passenger van taking its toll. They had left their four untraceable vehicles at a hotel on the western outskirts of Phoenix at nine in the morning and taken a taxi to a rental agency on the opposite side of the city to pick up the transportation they would use in El Centro. A license plate swap back at the hotel, before setting off for California, added the final layer of anonymity.

The only way the vehicles could be traced back to the rental agency was if one of them fell into the wrong hands, and even then the trail would go cold pretty quickly. Fake IDs. No video identifying their original vehicles. They'd checked the hotel parking lot and found no surveillance. Assuming none of them were captured, there was no link to the vehicles that would take them back to Colorado.

After Phoenix, a three-and-a-half-hour drive brought them to Indio, where they took rooms for cash in the most no-questions-asked motel they could find. They wasted little time at the motel, rigging each vehicle for the mission ahead of them and leaving for El Centro, where they'd spend the rest of the day running a sophisticated surveillance operation to determine the optimal course of action to accomplish what felt like a hopeless mission.

The luxury passenger van, which barely looked larger than a mini-van, took the longest to configure. Four separate antennae had been affixed to the roof, with cables run to communicate with the electronics gear inside. The third row of seats had been removed and placed in one of the hotel rooms to accommodate the equipment, which consisted of a computer to control the drone interfaces, a separate computer to process the radio signals, and a satellite-linked wireless router to provide a powerful, continuous internet connection in the van.

The gear ran on an uninterruptible power supply, continuously charged by the van's power outlets, and it was securely strapped down inside a custom-made padded box, sitting on top of a six-inch shock-dampening platform guaranteed to absorb impact against a curb. The control van and its team were arguably the most important part of the operation, an opinion even shared by Decker, who sat next to her, eyes scanning the road around them through the tinted glass.

"Last run for the night," said Harlow. "We have an hour-and-a-half drive ahead of us."

Joshua, who sat in the front seat with his laptop open, turned and nodded.

"I think we're good. We've seen the same configuration on each run," he said. "One car watching each house. A backup vehicle floating around nearby—no more than a few minutes away."

"Take us right down the middle of the neighborhood," said Decker, sounding even more exhausted than he did in Colorado.

"Again?" said Harlow. "It's a little quiet around here. We might draw attention."

"We haven't been down Cypress Avenue in two hours," said Decker.

"Feels like fifteen minutes ago," she said.

"More like five," said Decker. "One more run before we head back to the Cockroach Inn for a night of no sleep."

"I'm sleeping in the van," said Joshua.

"Me, too," said Mazzie, the driver. "My pillow smelled like vomit."

"You sniffed your pillow?" said Joshua. "We were only there for a few minutes."

"Priorities," said Mazzie.

"I've learned to bring my own pillow on any adventure arranged by Sandra," said Decker. "She has a talent for finding motels with smells."

"That rhymed," said Joshua.

"Score one for the English major," said Decker.

"You studied English—at Annapolis?" said Harlow.

"Bachelor of science in English," he said. "Try to wrap your head around that one."

"I'll pass," said Harlow.

"Coming up on Cypress Avenue," said Mazzie.

They had entered the neighborhood of tract houses from the south after traveling along a vast stretch of lush green alfalfa fields earlier in the day. It was hard to imagine anything growing here at any time of the year, particularly these brutally hot and dry summer months, but El Centro sat in the middle of one of the most agriculturally productive regions of the world—Imperial Valley. Year-round irrigation delivered by the All American Canal and fed by the Colorado River had turned what should have been an inhospitable desert into "America's salad bowl."

Mazzie eased the van into a right turn on Cypress Avenue, which ran north-south for a half mile, cutting the neighborhood right down the middle. One of the Border Patrol agents who had been situated near the ambush site lived in a cul-de-sac connected to Cypress Avenue, about half of the way up the street. After passing a few dark, empty streets, Harlow got cold feet about driving directly past one of their primary targets. Their van was too conspicuous. Even though it would remain on the fringe of the action tomorrow, she couldn't risk the chance that it was recognized at any point before or during the operation. The control van was critical to their success.

"I say we turn left on Valleyview and drive the periphery of the neighborhood," said Harlow. "This place has thinned out significantly since we last drove through it."

"I'm good with that," said Joshua. "I can ping the neighborhood from the turn and get a decent picture."

Decker scanned the streets for a few seconds and nodded his head.

"You're right," he said. "We can't afford to lose this van tomorrow."

"Lose the van?" said Mazzie.

"Yeah. As in they take note of the make and model tonight, and a roving patrol recognizes you on one of these side streets tomorrow morning, gets suspicious, and decides to investigate," said Decker. "End of van. End of mission."

"End of us," said Joshua.

"Wonderful," said Mazzie.

"You'll be fine as long as you stay out of the fray," said Harlow.

"That rhymed," said Decker.

"And I'm not even an English major," said Harlow, getting a laugh out of Decker. "We'll keep the van far enough away to run the drones and track the radio signals. I don't anticipate a problem."

The van slowed as they approached the stop sign at the intersection of Cypress and Valleyview Avenues.

"Going live with a series of pings," said Joshua. "Take the turn superslow. This is as close as we'll get."

While the van crept through the intersection, Joshua typed furiously on his keyboard for a few seconds before going completely still.

"Something has changed," he said. "Pinging again to verify."

Earlier in the day, on their initial drive around the outskirts of the target neighborhoods, they had identified an active P25 encrypted radio frequency in use near Agent Ocampo's house—a dead giveaway that the location was under surveillance. Subsequent runs near each of the remaining three houses revealed the same.

They'd spent the next hour pinging the P25 network's data layer from the van and cataloging the automated responses. Once they had isolated the unique data layer used by the network, they didn't have to wait for users to transmit a message to determine their location. Every radio in the network would instantly respond to their multiple undetectable pings, which allowed them to triangulate signal direction and determine each radio's location. Within moments of each ping, Joshua's laptop displayed a digital street map with the latest radio positions.

"What are we looking at?" said Harlow.

"I have a single, heavy concentration of radios on the southeast corner lot at the intersection of Fieldview and Cypress, within view of Agent Ocampo's house," said Joshua. "Looks like they moved into one of the houses. No other signals in the neighborhood."

"They probably made the same assessment Harlow just made," said Decker. "No way they can stay on the street."

"So they just took over a house?" said Harlow.

"Probably more than one," said Decker.

"My guess is two, but we'll have to drive by the other locations to be sure," said Joshua. "Four of the responding radios were previously located in the vicinity of Pittman's house. Two haven't been previously detected."

"Sounds like they've compressed to the two most likely targets," said Harlow.

"Or they called in reinforcements, and we're up against a force we can't handle," said Decker. "We'll have to drive by each house to make that assessment."

"I strongly suggest we consider deploying the remote pinging relays," said Joshua. "Two for each of our primary target neighborhoods. They're sat-com capable, so we can track locations and assess their movement throughout the night—from our motel."

"How far away can we deploy them?" said Decker. "There's no way we're going to get on one of these rooftops without ending up in county jail."

"Depends on how high we go," said Joshua. "I saw some unused utility poles around the water treatment plant one block north of this neighborhood. Two relays spaced a few hundred yards apart would do the trick."

"I saw a whole line of unused utility poles along California Route 86, next to the other neighborhood," said Harlow. "They're right on the road, though, and the area is wide-open. Might not be the best spot."

"We'll figure it out," said Decker. "After we figure out how to climb the poles. I didn't see any of those metal pole steps."

"We got you covered," said Joshua. "I have a lineman's climbing rig and spurs under your seat."

"Have you tested it?" said Decker.

"No. But it looks easy enough. Kind of like rappelling," said Joshua. "Amazon reviews were positive. Three point nine average."

"That makes me feel so much better," said Decker. "Have you ever rappelled?"

"Uh. No," said Joshua. "But you don't have to go too high on those poles. Two-thirds of the way up should be fine. The reviews were superpositive."

"I'm sure they were," said Decker. "This should be fun."

"Nothing you can't learn from a YouTube video or three," said Harlow.

"Funny," said Decker. "But oh so true."

Two hours later, Harlow held Decker's hand, doing her best to remove the most visible splinters while the van bounced north toward Indio. Joshua had forgotten the thick gloves essential for lineman work, and Decker's hands paid the price. Running her fingers over the palm of his bloodied hand, she felt another prickly sliver. Harlow examined it closely with her smartphone light and determined she could excise it.

"Ready for another?" she said, handing him the phone. "Looks like the last one I can get on this hand with my nails. You have a date with a pair of tweezers when we get back."

"Can't wait," said Decker, his hand stiffening as she pinched the end of the splinter between her nails and pulled it clear.

"That was a good one," she said, holding the half-inch-long shard in the light.

"I've had shrapnel pulled out of me that didn't hurt this bad," he said, giving her the other hand.

"Hands are always sensitive," said Harlow, examining his shooting hand.

Decker could shoot well with either, but he favored his right, which was why she was a little hesitant to dig too far into that hand without tweezers.

"I think we'll wait until we get back to do the rest," said Harlow. "Some of those will naturally start working their way out, so it'll be easier for me."

"Thank you," he said, squeezing her hand and wincing slightly.

"Mazzie. You good to drive all the way back?" said Harlow. "I can take the wheel or we can swap someone in from the other car."

Katie, Pam, and Brad Pierce followed them in one of the SUVs. They'd spent most of the day in a holding pattern around El Centro, in case something went wrong.

"I'm good for now," she said.

"Keep an eye on her, Josh," said Decker. "She's on her tenth Red Bull. When she crashes, we crash. Anything new going on back in El Centro?"

"No. The radios keep responding from the two houses," said Joshua.

"Our primary targets. Twenty hostiles less than a mile apart," said Harlow. "I'm having serious doubts about this."

"We'll be fine," said Decker. "I have a workable plan in mind."

"Workable?"

"That's about as good as it gets after midnight," he said. "It'll go from workable to solid in the morning."

"I hope so," she said. "Or I'm calling this off."

Chapter Thirty-Six

Decker scanned the rooftops ahead, spotting one of their drones in a stationary hover near the target area. Three more drones hovered out of sight within easy striking range—each equipped with one of Katie's paint bombs. The technical team in the Mercedes-Benz van controlled all four of the drones and could actively run three of them at a time if necessary.

Pam had parked the van on the side of an out-of-the-way road nearby, giving the dedicated UHF antenna on the vehicle's roof a clear line of sight to airspace over the cul-de-sac. Continuous line of sight would be critical over the next several minutes, as Decker tried to lure the group watching Ocampo's house into the open, where one of the drones would take thousands of high-resolution digital photos of the responding crew.

Joshua would oversee the picture taking, constantly maneuvering the drone into the right position to capture the best images and send the files back to the van. Maintaining a direct line of sight between the antenna and the drone would ensure the steady flow of data, preventing them from having to retrieve it directly from the camera's hard drive.

Decker had no intention of lingering in the area for any length of time after they kicked this hornet's nest.

"I'm really nervous about this," said Harlow, her hands tightening around the steering wheel.

"So am I," said Pierce, from the rear cargo compartment. "I'm putting my life in the hands of three video gamers."

"And three ballistic shields," said Decker. "You're in an armored box back there."

Pierce lay on his back, facing the rear of the vehicle, enclosed on three sides by Level III ballistic shields capable of stopping most bullets fired by military-style rifles. He carried one of their HK416 rifles, configured as a light machine gun, and five sixty-round drums of ammunition. With a little luck, Pierce would never fire the weapon.

"A lot of good that does me if we're run off the road," said Pierce.

"A lot more good than they'll do me up here!" said Decker, squeezing Harlow's shoulder. "We'll be fine. It's going to be intense for about a minute, then it'll all fall away behind us."

Harlow showed no signs of stopping at the last intersection before their turn into the cul-de-sac.

"Stop sign," said Decker.

She rapidly decelerated the car to the point where he thought the tires might screech, but she just as quickly let off the brake and sped through the empty intersection. Decker did a quick 360-degree scan to make sure she hadn't done that in front of a police car.

"No harm, no foul," said Decker. "Slow down a little."

"Sorry," she said. "I don't usually get this jumpy on jobs."

"This isn't a normal kind of job," said Decker. "Want to go over it one more time?"

She nodded. "Please."

"Slow us down even more," said Decker. "We're thirty seconds out."

"Forget it," said Harlow, her knuckles white on the steering wheel. "We're too close."

"Better if we talk it through," said Decker. "Right, Brad?"

"Talk it through right up until the real thing," said Brad.

"All right," she said, slowing the SUV considerably.

"You turn us at a normal speed into the cul-de-sac, park in the driveway, and we both get out," said Decker. "Then what?"

"We meet in front of the vehicle, and Josh lets us know what to do next."

"Right. If the team watching Ocampo's house reacts, we hop back in the SUV and get the hell out of Dodge. Which way do you turn out of the cul-de-sac?"

"Left."

"That's important. If the team doesn't take the bait right away, then what?"

"We approach Ocampo's house and knock on the door. Pretend we're selling something, but don't tell them why we're really there," said Harlow.

"My guess is that the surveillance house will empty the moment the door opens. Once they're on the move, we take off. Our only job is to get onto Cypress before they do. Josh will take the pictures and use the drones to help us. He'll also trigger Katie's assorted tricks."

"I still think we need to warn the Ocampos," said Harlow.

"We will," said Decker. "Which way when we get to the end of Cypress?"

"Right turn on Manuel Ortiz," said Harlow.

"And after that?"

"We listen to Josh," said Harlow.

"We take Josh's guidance under advisement," said Decker. "Feel better?"

"A little."

"Good. I was doing that more for me than you," said Decker. "We're approaching the turn. Might want to speed up so we don't look like total creepers. Ready back there?"

"No. I'm posting a selfie on Facebook," said Pierce.

"Funny." Decker triggered his wireless radio microphone. "Joshua. We're a few seconds from Fieldview. Any changes?"

"Negative. Ten radios pinging inside the corner house," said Joshua. "As soon as you make the turn, I'm bringing the camera drone into final position to snap some pics."

"If anything changes at that house, I need to know immediately," said Decker. "Our escape will come down to seconds."

"Understood," said Joshua. "I can tell if they start moving around inside."

"Eyes up. We're here," said Decker as the SUV slowed into a lazy left turn through the intersection.

CHAPTER
THIRTY-SEVEN

Nick Adler's earpiece crackled to life, jarring him out of an entirely superficial midmorning slumber. He was in that tenuous state of caffeine-fueled, sleep-deprived stakeout purgatory, floating effortlessly between wakefulness and nothingness—regardless of the time. The light pouring through the picture window no longer made a difference.

"I have a slow mover approaching from the south," said one of his second-floor lookouts. "SUV. Two occupants. Woman driving. Man in the front passenger seat."

"Copy that. On my way up," said Adler.

He shot up from the living room recliner with his rifle and dashed upstairs to the rear corner bedroom, barging into the room. The lookout held a pair of binoculars out for him. Adler snatched it out of his hands and pressed the rubber eye cups against his face, adjusting the lenses to sharpen the image. The woman wore a coyote-tan ball cap that hid most of her face. Hair not visible. Probably pulled through the back of the hat and blocked from view by her head. The man wore sunglasses and a similarly nondescript cap. Decker and Mackenzie? Still too far away to tell. He activated his radio.

"Do we have anything coming in from the north or east?" said Adler.

"East is clear."

"North is clear."

"Stand by to pounce," said Adler. "We have a possible visual ID on two targets."

Adler followed the SUV through the binoculars as it ambled along Cypress Avenue and disappeared behind a bushy tree planted in the corner of the backyard. When the vehicle reemerged, nearly even with the backyard fence, he studied the man and woman for a brief second. There was no doubt in his mind he was looking at Ryan Decker and Harlow Mackenzie—alone with no backup.

"It's them!" he said, tossing the binoculars and sprinting for the bedroom door. "Everyone downstairs! Now! Team one takes the vehicle. The rest of you sprint for the cul-de-sac once they make the turn. I want one of them alive, unless they don't give us the option. Doesn't matter which one."

By the time he'd reached the bottom of the stairs, Freya had answered his satellite call.

"I was about to—"

"Hold on! Hold on!" he said.

Phone still to his face, he called out to the lookout staring out the front living room window. "Did they turn?"

"Just turned!" said the stocky ex-soldier.

"Get to it. Everyone out the door!" said Adler.

"Nick. What the fuck is going on?" said Freya.

"Decker and Mackenzie just drove into the cul-de-sac," said Adler. "No backup in sight. Get your team over here!"

"I think you should hold back and watch, Nick," said Freya. "These people are good. Always a few steps ahead."

"Too late for that," said Adler. "My people are already out the door. This'll be over in less than thirty seconds. Get your team over here immediately for cleanup and extraction."

"Dammit, Nick!" said Freya. "Pull your people—"

Adler disconnected the call and jammed the phone in his pocket as he followed the last member of his team out the front door. This was how it was done. No hesitation. High tempo. Maintain the initiative. None of this sit-and-wait nonsense. Decker was counting on a small buffer of time to make a decision. That's probably how the guy had outsmarted them in the past. Not this time. Adler intended to collect that six-figure bonus right here—right now.

CHAPTER
THIRTY-EIGHT

As the SUV turned, Decker moved the compact rifle off his lap and stuffed it, barrel down, between his left leg and the inside of the foot well so he wouldn't have to fumble with it when he got out of the car.

"How are we looking?" said Pierce.

"So far, so good," said Decker, focused on the end of the cul-de-sac.

Harlow reached up to adjust the rearview mirror, muttering something he didn't catch. Before he could ask her what she'd said, Joshua's voice filled his earpiece.

"They're on the move. Get out of there right now!"

"I see them," said Harlow, stopping the car halfway down the short street.

"How many?" said Decker over the radio.

"All of them!" said Joshua. "Running in your direction. Heavily armed!"

Decker twisted in his seat and peered through the rear cargo compartment window, initially baffled by what he saw. Seven figures, carrying squat, black weapons, sprinted toward them. A few had already reached Cypress Avenue. The SUV in the corner house's driveway backed into the street behind the men. He hadn't anticipated an all-out rush like this, mostly because it didn't make a lot of sense—tactically. Of course, there was no way they could know about Decker's insurance policy.

"Keep driving," said Decker.

"Which way?" said Harlow.

"Forward," said Decker. "I need some space to think."

The SUV lurched forward, speeding toward the wide, circular end of the street.

"Think about what?" said Harlow.

"About how we're going to get out of here without a gunfight," said Decker, his eyes darting back and forth between the assassins still running headlong toward them. "Stop in the middle of the cul-de-sac circle."

Pierce lifted his ballistic helmet–encased head high enough to look out the back window.

"I think that ship has sailed," said Pierce.

The SUV jerked to a stop, forcefully reminding Decker that he was still wearing a seat belt. The sudden move prompted a few of the men behind them to drop into combat stances, their weapons pointing down the street. Decker disconnected his seat belt.

"Now what?" said Harlow, shrinking in her seat.

Decker ignored her question for the moment, activating his radio. "Joshua. Are the paint bombs effective against pedestrians?"

"The group is too spread out," said Joshua. "And you have that SUV to worry about. You also have three more vehicles inbound from the second house. ETA two minutes max."

He analyzed the situation for another second, only seeing one solution to their dilemma.

"Pierce. Weapons free," said Decker. "Joshua. Focus your efforts on keeping those other vehicles away from us, and keep taking pictures."

"Understood," said Joshua.

"How free?" said Pierce from an upright position, rifle barrel pressed against the tinted glass.

"Light 'em up! Left to right. I got the SUV!" said Decker, turning to Harlow. "Stay down until this is over."

A long burst of deafening automatic fire exploded inside the vehicle, and Harlow crunched down in the seat, cursing. Decker slipped onto the street with his rifle and three spare magazines taken from the door's cup holder before moving in a low crouch toward the back of the SUV. Pierce's weapon continued to unleash one burst after another, dropping the three men visible from Decker's side of the vehicle in lifeless, blood-splattered heaps on the street.

Shattered pieces of milky-blue safety glass showered Decker on his quick trip to the back corner of the vehicle, punctuated by heavy thumps against the vehicle's chassis. He tucked the spare rifle magazines into his pants pockets and disengaged the weapon's safety, ready to join the gunfight.

Decker eased himself forward, careful not to directly expose himself to the remaining shooters. He centered his rifle's holographic reticle on the SUV speeding toward them. The rifle bit repeatedly into his shoulder. Several tightly spaced white dots materialized on the SUV's windshield, obscuring the driver's face. Before he could shift his aim to the passenger side, the vehicle swerved violently to the right and slammed into a parked car.

Both of the passenger doors burst open. The disabled vehicle's armed occupants fired wildly as they frantically tried to escape the kill zone. Decker fired four times at the side of the front passenger door. The bullets passed straight through and dropped the shooter in a seated position on the asphalt, half of his body still concealed behind the door. Decker's next series of bullets stitched through the rear seat shooter as the man scrambled for cover—leaving a dense crimson stain on the vehicle's gray side panel.

Decker moved forward and peeked around the corner of the SUV with his rifle, searching for targets. A head and rifle appeared above the hood of the T-boned parked car, followed by a fusillade of bullets that lashed against the rear of the SUV. Pierce answered, peppering the sedan's grille and hood with automatic fire. A short silence ensued, his last burst still echoing back from the houses.

"Changing," said Pierce over the radio. "We might have to dig this guy out."

Rapid fire erupted, bullets pounding into the SUV again.

"Looks like it. Any possibility the guys you took down are still in working order?"

"Not a chance," said Pierce.

"Good. I don't like surprises. When you're back up, hit him with suppressive fire. I'll head for the back of their SUV and swing in behind him," said Decker, changing magazines. "Harlow. What's your status?"

"I'm good," she said. "We need to get out of here before the entire El Centro PD shows up."

"We're working on it," said Decker.

"I'm up," said Pierce, followed by a sustained volley of automatic fire.

"Moving," said Decker, bursting into the open with his rifle aimed at the bullet-riddled sedan.

Confirming that the shooter hadn't reemerged, Decker sprinted in a wide, left-sweeping arc down the street, giving Pierce room to fire and keep the man's head down. When he reached the back of the crashed SUV, Pierce stopped firing and ducked before the shooter emptied what sounded like an entire thirty-round magazine at him. Decker crept past the SUV until he reached the back of the sedan. He crouched as low as possible and listened. The guy sounded like he was having an argument with someone.

"They have a machine gun! I'm pinned down, and everyone else is dead!"

Short pause.

"Yeah! Like the kind that keeps firing and doesn't stop. Are you coming or what?"

Another pause.

"Quit thinking about it and get the hell over here. Our boss will not be happy if I end up in a jail cell."

Our boss? Decker leaned around the corner of the sedan with his rifle, catching the shooter's attention.

"Shit," said the man, dropping the satellite phone in his hand and raising his rifle.

Decker fired a single shot at the guy's upper right arm, which instantly went slack, bringing the rifle down with it. The man tried to recover the weapon with his other hand, but Decker shifted his aim and drilled a hole through it. The rifle clanked to the pavement. The man pulled the bloodied hand tight against his chest, barely making a sound. He looked up at Decker with a murderous glare.

"Eyes down. Keep your hands right where they are or the next one goes through your head," said Decker, taking his nontrigger hand off the rifle to activate his radio. "I need some help with a prisoner."

"Joshua. How are we doing for time?" said Harlow.

"Police have been notified. I don't have a fix on them yet," said Joshua. "We can handle the second set of approaching hostiles—and the police for a while, if necessary."

Decker heard a car door open and looked up. Harlow was on her way over, holding a Taser.

"What's the status at the Cruz house?" she said.

"All clear. Sandra and Pam are trying to convince the agent and his family to come along," said Joshua.

"The gunfire wasn't enough?" said Decker.

"Keep us apprised of any threats," said Harlow. "I expect to be moving in less than thirty seconds."

"Copy that," said Joshua.

Decker kept his rifle pointed at the man as Harlow approached, stepping aside when she had a clear shot.

"Left arm," he said. "He's wearing a plate carrier under the jacket."

The man unexpectedly jumped to his feet, without using his hands, and tried to charge Decker, but Harlow responded in an instant, shifting her aim for the legs and discharging the Taser. The two darts penetrated the shooter's pants and skin, rendering him immobile for a moment before he started convulsing and fell over.

"Turn the vehicle around," said Decker. "I'll have him ready for transport in a few seconds."

Harlow took off, and Decker went to work with the zip ties. The man screamed in agony when Decker pulled his shattered right arm and mangled left hand behind his back, the shrieks intensifying when he yanked the zip tie's ends, cinching the plastic restraints tight.

He dragged the man by the collar of his ballistic vest to the back of the repositioned SUV, heaving him high enough for Pierce to grab the top of his vest. With the man suspended over the rear bumper, Decker gripped the man's belt and lifted, while Pierce pulled him inside the cargo compartment until only his feet and ankles protruded. Decker quickly zip-tied the man's ankles and pushed them the rest of the way inside.

After the man's feet vanished inside, Decker took a moment to stare at the carnage they'd unleashed. The men sent to kill or capture them never knew what hit them or what had gone wrong. Running full speed to victory one moment; perforated by a dozen bullets the next. They lay in twisted, unnatural positions—utterly still except for the blood pumping out of them. *What the hell are we doing?*

When he turned to get back in the vehicle, the three or four dozen bullet holes in the cargo hatch came into focus.

"You good?" said Decker, glancing around the cargo area.

Pierce sat on a bed of loose shell casings and broken safety glass, his back against the rear row of seats. The headrests and seat tops had been torn up by the mercenaries' bullets. Pieces of foam stuffing and plastic hung loosely from the metal poles connecting them to the seats.

"You can be the one back here next time," said Pierce.

Their prisoner lay scrunched on his side, Pierce's feet pressing him face-first against the rear cargo door.

"Make sure you reload," said Decker. "We're not out of this yet."

Distant sirens echoed between the houses as Decker made his way to his seat. He hopped in and opened the glove compartment, grabbing more rifle magazines, as Harlow sped toward Cypress Avenue.

"What are we looking at, Josh?" said Harlow.

"I think we have a problem," said Joshua. "The three cars that left the Cruz house have just pulled over on the side of 86, and I have six more radios on the screen, two cars of three—moving south on 86. Looks like a rendezvous."

"Get Sandra's team out of there," said Harlow, flying past the stop sign and screeching through a left turn onto Cypress.

"Concentrate on the road," said Decker. "Josh. Push Sandra west and north, away from the hostiles. We're headed for your position to dump our vehicle."

"I can potentially take four of the five hostile vehicles out of play with the drones," said Joshua. "Just say the word."

"Do it," said Decker and Harlow at the same time.

He looked at her and nodded, the two of them riding in complete silence until they got to the end of the street. Decker's ears still rang from the gunfire.

"If Josh can't take out at least four of the vehicles, we'll have to help out," said Harlow.

Decker nodded, having already come to that conclusion. He hadn't brought it up yet, because he was still reeling from the fact that they had just gunned down nine men in broad daylight in the middle of a suburban street. The thought of doing it again in the next few minutes almost didn't register as real to him.

CHAPTER THIRTY-NINE

Freya Walker got out of the SUV and listened. The police sirens had picked up, but the gunfire had completely stopped. Not that she had heard the gun battle. They had been driving with their windows up when that catastrophe unfolded. The team in the last vehicle reported gunfire seconds before Adler's call had come through. She hoped he was dead, because she had no intention of driving directly into a shooting gallery to retrieve him.

What the hell had he been thinking—and what did Adler do with his sniper support? Dammit. She could think of a dozen ways to approach that situation better than rushing headfirst at it. Hadn't she made herself clear? Nobody moved until she gave the order. The idiot hadn't paid enough attention to Decker's file, and now she was truly screwed unless she could salvage this situation.

She stared across the green field of low-lying vegetation and pounded the hood of the vehicle. Think! Decker, or whoever was behind ultimately behind this, had obviously led Adler into an ambush. Why? What did they gain? Why come here at all? They couldn't possibly be talking to Agent Ocampo with the police en route and ten bodies littering the street. What the hell was she missing?

"Shit. The other agent," she muttered, scrambling back into the SUV. "The other house was a diversion! Head back to the house on Quail Run!"

Once her convoy of three vehicles had turned around on California State Road 86, she contacted the inbound backup vehicles.

"ZULU group. This is ATHENA. What's your position?"

"Headed south on 86. Running a red light just past the Imperial County Center."

"Change of plans," she said, grabbing her computer tablet and activating the map. "We're headed back to the target house on Quail Run. You might be able to see us on 86 from your position."

"I think I see you," said the team leader.

"I want your team to follow us into the neighborhood on Countryside Drive, but keep going when we turn off. Take Countryside until it ends and turn right. That'll put you onto the east end of Quail Run. We'll come in from the west and squeeze whoever came for the target house."

"Copy all," said ZULU team leader.

"Did everyone else catch that?" she said.

All the team leaders in her convoy acknowledged her plan.

"No fuckups," she said. "Somebody pass me something bigger than a pistol."

CHAPTER FORTY

Border Patrol Agent Al Cruz stood halfway behind his front door, one hand on the knob, ready to slam it shut, the other wrapped around the handle of his off-duty pistol, prepared for whatever these two crazies had in store for him. Thank God he was a lefty.

He'd listened to their desperate plea for a minute now, still not buying it. Pittman and Contreras had been victims of circumstance, pure and simple. They'd gotten lost and driven up on some kind of armed cartel posse playing around on this side of the border. End of story. Nobody was coming for him or his partner. Nobody had a reason to. He'd convinced Ocampo to stick to a sanitized version of the night's events. Or had he?

"Listen. I'm calling the police—" he started.

Buzz Cut interrupted him, edging forward.

"The police are busy right now with the shootout in front of Agent Ocampo's house," she said. "My associates barely stopped a team of mercenaries sent to kill them. You really didn't hear the gunfire?"

"I didn't hear anything," said Cruz. "I was dead asleep until you two woke me up."

"You're going to be dead for real if you don't grab your family right now and come with us," said the redhead next to her, scanning the street to the west.

A guy wearing glasses poked his head through the rear passenger door of the SUV idling in front of his house.

"We have like twenty seconds to start moving," he said. "Or we'll have to shoot our way out of here."

"That's not going to work," said Buzz Cut. "We don't have the firepower. Last chance, sir. I need to move my team out of here if you're staying."

A drone buzzed into view, hovering over the SUV. It carried some kind of cylinder, and for a brief moment, Cruz thought it might be a bomb—and they were right all along.

"What the hell is that?" he said, closing the door a few inches.

"That's our only real protection right now," said Red. "Paint bomb suicide drone."

He started to say something, but she cut him off.

"Don't ask how it works, but it'll completely cover one vehicle. I have three more on the way. You have five vehicles headed to your house. That leaves one SUV, bristling with rifles. Do the math."

Cruz shook his head. "This is crazy."

Buzz Cut turned to Red with a genuinely worried look. "We have to go."

Red muttered a string of curses under her breath before nodding at him. "Sir, if I were you, I'd grab your family and climb the fence in your backyard. Run and hide. I don't know what else to say," she said, grabbing Buzz Cut. "Let's go."

Cruz stood there as they jogged away, torn about what to do. The drone took off, headed west, drawing him far enough out of the house to watch it speed toward the end of the street. He glanced at the women headed back to the SUV, his hand still on the pistol. The two of them appeared to be genuinely concerned about their own safety at this point.

"Honey, what are we doing?" said his wife from the hallway behind him.

He waffled for a few seconds, until Buzz Cut shut her door.

"Grab the kids and your purse," he said. "We're going with them."

His wife had been ready for this possibility, yanking their twin eleven-year-old daughters into the hallway and running for the door. Cruz ran toward the SUV, yelling to get their attention. The vehicle lurched forward and immediately stopped, Buzz Cut hopping out of the front passenger door with a semiautomatic shotgun. His grip on the pistol tightened. Had he screwed up?

Buzz Cut opened the rear passenger door and waved him forward. "Come on! We're already pushing it!"

He waited for his family to catch up, helping them into the SUV when they arrived a few seconds later. The third row was occupied by Four Eyes, a nerdy guy in his twenties wearing thick glasses, and a very young-looking woman wearing headphones. Jailbait. Both of their faces glowed from the laptops he could see behind the seats jam-packed with his family.

"Squeeze in, Agent Cruz," said Red. "We needed to be gone ten seconds ago."

Movement to the west caught his attention. The last thing he saw before piling into the vehicle was a tight formation of three SUVs taking the turn onto his street.

CHAPTER
FORTY-ONE

Freya peered through the driver's door window with binoculars as her vehicle cleared the house on the corner of Quail Run Drive and the driver slowed for the turn. She wasn't hopeful. Too much time had elapsed since they bailed out of their surveillance nest across the street from the Cruz house.

She should have left someone behind to keep an eye on the street, but the prospect of nabbing Decker and Mackenzie, two of the primary targets identified by JUPITER, had been too tempting—by design. Now she was playing a very late game of catch-up. If Cruz was gone, Freya wasn't sure what to do next. She couldn't think of any options to recover from the mess Adler had created.

She'd correctly deduced that the Border Patrol agents had been the best lead to pursue. Unfortunately, they appeared to be the only lead. Outside of returning to Los Angeles and staking out her targets' usual hangouts, she didn't have another angle to follow right now.

When her vehicle straightened and the street came into full view through the windshield, she lowered the binoculars. Quail Run was crowded with cars, parked on the curbs and driveways, nearly all of them obscuring her view to Cruz's house, more than halfway down the street.

"Slow us down a little," she said. "We need to give ZULU some time to get in position."

"Got it," said the driver, the SUV decelerating to a crawl.

A few seconds later, the second team checked in.

"ATHENA. This is ZULU lead. We're approaching the right turn toward Quail Run."

"Copy. We're on Quail Run, headed east. No sign of—wait. A black SUV just pulled into the street, headed in your direction," she said, raising her binoculars.

A door on the right side of the departing vehicle was still partially open, a hand reaching out moments later to shut it. She was still in business!

"ZULU lead, form a block at that turn," said Freya. "Do not engage with lethal force unless they take you under fire. I need information from these people. Shoot out the tires, if possible, but that's it."

"Understood. Setting up the block right now."

"They're about fifteen seconds away from making the turn and seeing you," said Freya, tapping her driver's shoulder. "Get me behind them!"

Al Cruz squeezed most of his upper body between the two front seats, his knees pressed agonizingly against the back of the center console and his head jammed against the roof. One substantial bump and he'd probably break his neck and both kneecaps at the same time. His wife and daughters shared the two seats a few inches behind him. He could have sat with a daughter in his lap like his wife, but Jailbait said they had two vehicles moving to cut off their escape route, so he wanted to put himself between the threat and his family.

Red drove the SUV down his street like a Formula One race car, picking up speed as they approached the sharp left curve onto Blossom Way.

"You might want to slow down," said Cruz. "The roadblock will be right after this turn."

"Two hundred and seventy feet, to be exact," said Four Eyes. "This is going to be tight."

"We can't hit them with the paint before we reach the turn. Has to be at the last moment so they don't have time to get out of the vehicles and turn their rifles on us," said Buzz Cut, sticking her shotgun out the window at a forward angle.

"What about the trucks behind us?" said Cruz, unable to crane his head back far enough to see through the rear window.

"Disabled as of right . . . now," said Four Eyes. "Mission kill, bitches! Sorry for the language."

As the SUV built speed, Freya tossed the binoculars aside and grabbed the hefty UMP-45 submachine gun next to her leg in the foot well. She disconnected her seat belt and maneuvered herself far enough out of the window next to her to rest the UMP on the side mirror—just in case they didn't surrender quietly. She had no problem shooting up that vehicle and extracting whoever survived. A bullet wound or two might even expedite the interrogation process.

Parked cars flew past her head, the relative wind created by the vehicle's excessive speed pressing against her face, as they raced to catch up with the fleeing SUV. A sharp crack was the only warning Freya received before her vehicle veered left—smashing into a parked pickup truck.

The sudden left turn at over sixty miles per hour, combined with the unfortunate fact that she had disconnected her seat belt, left her body at the mercy of a significant centrifugal force, which kept her moving in the original direction of the vehicle. During the brief moment her SUV traveled left, Freya's body flew halfway out the window. If the F-150 pickup hadn't been in their new path, she would have been ejected through the window and skidded across the pavement—likely surviving.

Instead, the collision caught her half inside and half outside the open window, folding her like a lawn chair around the thick, crash-resistant windshield pillar. When the SUV settled from the crash a few moments later, she hung limp over the passenger door—her smashed body held in place by legs that protruded through the paint-covered windshield.

She remained conscious long enough to watch the other two vehicles in the convoy skid to a halt on the lawn next to her, their windshields and side windows obscured by a seemingly impenetrable coat of black paint or dye. Freya wished she'd been spared that final sight of complete failure.

CHAPTER FORTY-TWO

"What's the plan up ahead?" said Cruz.

"We have a team somewhere else running the last two—hold on," said Buzz Cut, pausing for a few seconds. "The block is at the corner of Blossom and Countryside. Two SUVs parked in a V. Plenty of room to maneuver to the left, up a driveway, and across the yards."

"Got it," said Red, increasing their speed. "Everyone get down!"

Cruz gripped the headrest posts on both sides, as Red barreled into the turn at forty miles per hour, skidding precariously close to the curb before the wheels regained traction and started propelling them forward toward the roadblock. Out of the corner of his eye, he saw two gray objects streak toward the SUVs.

A bullet hole appeared in the top left corner of the windshield, followed by a loud crack that made his kids and wife scream. A second bullet smacked into the window, just to the right and a little lower. The bullet snapped past his head and struck something hard in the back of the SUV. The kids screamed, and he craned his neck to check on them. His family lay flat on the seat, well below the bottom of the windows. They should be safe. When he turned back around, a third hole appeared in front of the driver, a bullet whipping through the right side of the headrest and grazing the top of his outstretched arm. Red never flinched.

He was about to yell something entirely unhelpful when two car-size black clouds exploded a few feet above the roadblock, instantly blotting out the SUVs and the men inside them. Red slowed and turned into the next driveway, taking them across several lawns before knocking over a mailbox to get back on the road. Buzz Cut emptied the semiautomatic shotgun into the barricade as they pulled even with it, shattering most of the SUV's side windows and extracting heinous, bloodcurdling screams from within.

A single bullet thunked into the back of their vehicle. Red jerked the wheel, and their getaway vehicle screeched through a right turn to escape the rest of the fusillade.

"Everyone okay back there?" yelled Buzz Cut.

His girls cried over Jailbait's "All good back here."

"We'll be fine, girls," Cruz said, sharing a doubtful look with his wife. She gripped his hand, which he lowered from the seat.

"You're bleeding," said his wife.

He glanced at his arm, seeing that the bullet had barely broken the skin.

"It's fine. We'll take care of it later," said Cruz, squeezing her hand.

Red slowed them down and rolled up to the stop sign just outside his neighborhood.

"Still north?" said Red.

"Yes. Still north," said Four Eyes. "I'll guide you to Interstate 8. Control wants us to head east to California 111 and take that to Brawley rendezvous point."

"I know how to get us there," said Cruz.

Red turned to say something to him, her eyes immediately diverting to the chunk torn out of the headrest.

"Shit," she whispered, glancing at him with an apologetic look.

"Shit is right," said Cruz.

Chapter

Forty-Three

Harlow drove their bullet-riddled SUV down the dusty unincorporated road toward the control van. As they pulled closer, Katie hopped out of the driver's seat, shaking her head. Joshua stayed in the front passenger seat, the top of his laptop visible above the dashboard. Mazzie and Wade emerged from the passenger-side sliding door and joined Katie by the van's front bumper, staring in disbelief as the vehicle drove past and the real extent of the damage became obvious. Harlow stopped the SUV on the dusty road just beyond the van. Multiple police sirens echoed through the vehicle's missing windows.

"You got to be kidding me," said Katie from behind the vehicle. "How the hell did any of you walk away from this?"

The two operations techs startled when Pierce shifted and raised his head, the bed of hollow shell casings rattling under him.

"Most of their fire was focused right here, striking the ballistic shields inside. They far exceeded the maximum number of guaranteed hits," he said, removing his helmet and examining its exterior. "I thought I felt a few more than that. Got a little crazy back here."

Harlow sensed that everyone was in shock at the moment, and she needed to get them moving before the police grasped the full extent of what just happened in their city.

"Decker. Pierce. Let's get our new friend situated in the van," said Harlow. "I'm going to try and run this thing through that scrub up there. Hide it as best as possible. We need to get out of El Centro before they start throwing up police checkpoints."

Decker nodded. "It's gonna be a tight fit, but we'll be ready by the time you're done. Make sure you damage the VIN so they can't track it too easily. I still think we should burn the thing. Just to be sure."

"It'll attract too much attention. We need all the time we can get," said Harlow.

"Right," he said, looking worried.

"What?"

"This is out of control. Whatever we stumbled on is huge," said Decker. "Maybe too huge for us."

"We can walk away at any time," said Harlow, not convinced she was right.

"Not from something like this," said Decker. "This'll follow us."

"Nothing new," she said. "Kind of a job hazard working with you. Get them ready."

He got out and opened the rear passenger door, collapsing the second-row seat and helping Pierce out of the vehicle. The two of them grabbed the prisoner and slid him across the broken safety glass and bullet casings, the man shrieking the entire time. His body hit the pavement with a thud and another round of agonizing cries.

"Make sure he doesn't bleed out," said Harlow. "I'd like to ask him a few questions later."

"He better be worth expending one of our med kits on," said Decker.

"I have a feeling he will be."

Harlow drove the SUV a few hundred feet down the road and pulled diagonally across the shoulder, aiming it toward a thick stand of short, bushy trees. She found an opening in the outer layer large enough to squeeze through, quickly bringing the vehicle to a stop when the branches spilling into the front seat through the missing windshield pushed too close to her face. Knowing her door was most likely blocked, Harlow climbed into the back seat and kicked one of the rear doors open far enough to escape.

She emerged from the brush to find Decker standing next to the van.

"I couldn't open the door to scrape the VIN," said Harlow.

"Doesn't matter. It's hidden pretty well. Unless someone is watching us right now."

"I'm counting on that," she said.

"We can't return any of the vehicles to the agency at this point, so it doesn't matter," said Decker. "Front seat is yours."

The three second-row seats were occupied by her operations team. Joshua and Mazzie typed on their laptops while Wade carried a stack of drone-control cases on his lap.

"I assume Pierce is with our guest in the back with the computer gear?"

"He has combat medic training from his time in the teams," said Decker. "I was more of an intelligence officer."

"He lost the coin toss—again?"

"Rock, Paper, Scissors," said Decker, lowering his voice. "He's a little too quick at the end. I beat him every time."

"I'm turning you in when we get back," said Harlow, hopping into the front seat. "Where are you sitting?"

"I was going to try and squeeze in with Josh's team somehow," said Decker, looking doubtful about the prospect.

"There's plenty of room back here, cheater!" said Pierce.

"Looks like you're busted."

"How far is it to the rendezvous point?"

She laughed and shook her head. "Get in back with your buddy. Sounds like he misses you."

CHAPTER
FORTY-FOUR

Decker waited patiently for someone to open one of the van's rear cargo doors. The rendezvous point was in the middle of the Westgate Shopping Center parking lot, the most anonymous spot in Brawley. Anonymous because it was the largest and busiest parking lot in the town, which meant Harlow and her team had to pick the right moment to let him out. The sight of a blood-splattered, partially hog-tied guy lying facedown between two heavily armed men would be a showstopper for their group.

"Maybe they forgot us," said Pierce.

Decker patted their new friend's head. "Hard to forget what's back here."

The guy tried to yell through the double layer of duct tape covering his mouth. Decker pushed his face into the hard plastic floor, and the man tried to twist onto his side. He grabbed the man's injured arm and applied pressure in the opposite direction of the twist, having an immediate effect. Their prisoner settled onto his stomach, the pain obviously too much to bear.

"I told you, I'm not ready to talk yet," said Decker.

"This guy's going to require constant supervision," said Pierce.

"Rock, Paper, Scissors?" said Decker. "To see who gets to stretch their legs first?"

Pierce looked at him and laughed. "I didn't lose my memory from today's trauma. I always knew you were cheating."

"It's not cheating if I'm better at it," said Decker.

"It's supposed to be a game of random chance," said Pierce. "Like the coin toss you rigged with your two-sided coin. Took me a while to figure that one out."

"I'm busy working on my next scam," said Decker. "You want to head out first?"

"No. You can just slide out," said Pierce. "I'd have to climb over this asshole. I'll reposition him while you're gone and try to wipe this blood off me."

The door opened without warning to reveal Harlow and Pam standing lookout and blocking them from general view.

"Hurry up," said Harlow.

Decker hopped out and examined himself for anything out of place. He'd already removed his lightweight plate carrier and slung it over the seat. Pam glanced into the van and shook her head.

"No way he's going inside covered in blood like that," she said.

"I was going to grab some wipes," said Decker.

"More like a fire hose," said Pam. "It's too risky."

"He can at least stand up right here when we get back," said Decker. "Stretch out a little. He's been on his ass in the back of a vehicle for most of the morning."

"I'm good," said Pierce, forcefully turning their prisoner's head so he couldn't see out of the van. "How long until the next stop?"

Pam indicated sixty minutes with her hands. They didn't want to give their prisoner any sense of how far or where he'd traveled.

"No problem. I can manage," said Pierce. "Get me a grande cappuccino with an extra shot?"

"You got it," said Decker, before shutting the door.

"You sure he's okay in there with that guy?" said Harlow.

"He'll be fine. The guy's pretty much immobile," said Decker. "Where is everyone?"

"Inside the Starbucks," she said, starting to walk in the direction of the coffee shop. "We need to make some preliminary decisions before we head out. Like what we're going to do with Agent Cruz and his family."

"And the guy you grabbed," said Katie. "Not saying you shouldn't have. Just saying he complicates things."

"I couldn't help myself," said Decker.

"He doesn't strike me as the kind to talk," said Harlow.

"I don't know," said Decker. "I heard him arguing with someone over his radio. Maybe we can use that against him. Either way, I'm not going to torture him or kill him, so we need to figure out where we're going to take him."

"How bad is his arm?" said Harlow.

"I can't say," said Decker. "Pretty bad, but he'll be fine for now. We'll have to drop him off at a hospital sooner than later."

Harlow reached for the door to the shop. "Then I think we need to do whatever we're going to do with him in Indio. Dump him near a hospital and call nine-one-one from one of our burners."

Decker stepped inside and immediately saw most of the crew in line for drinks. Sandra sat at a table in the back of the shop with the Cruz family.

"Katie, do you mind grabbing Pierce's drink? I want to get started with Cruz right away."

"That's fine. Do you want anything?" said Katie, turning to Harlow. "You?"

"I'm all right," said Harlow.

"I'll take what Pierce ordered," he said. "And maybe one of their panini—"

Harlow yanked his arm. "This isn't lunch. Come on."

Decker whispered over his shoulder as he was led away. "Tomato and mozzarella. Hook me up, Katie."

The look on Katie's face and the subtle head shake didn't lead him to believe he'd get the sandwich. When they got to the table, Decker extended a hand to Agent Cruz.

"No names for security reasons," said Decker, shaking his hand. "Is everyone okay, aside from the obvious shock of what just happened? Mrs. Cruz?"

"The girls are terrified, and so am I, but we're fine. Thank you," she said, looking over at Sandra. "I don't know what would have happened if you didn't show up."

"Yes," said Cruz, squeezing his hand. "I still don't know what to make of this, but I owe you one. Thank you."

"We don't exactly know what to make of it, either," said Decker, taking a seat. "I'm just glad we were there."

Harlow gave him a disapproving look before squeezing in next to the twins, who were huddled next to their mom. Most likely, if they hadn't sent Sandra and Pam to coax the Cruz family out of their house, they would be in federal protective custody right now or possibly just sitting at home, oblivious to what happened a few neighborhoods away. Decker didn't see any harm in perpetuating their "savior" status for now. He smiled at the twins, who looked a little too frightened for a family outing at Starbucks.

"How about the two brave little ladies here? Can we get you a drink? Cookie? The whole store?" said Decker.

One of them smiled. The other burrowed into her mother's arm.

"Your friends are getting them something. I hope you don't mind," said Cruz's wife.

"I'll pay them back," said Cruz.

"It's on us," said Decker. "Seriously. I'd buy them ponies right now if I could. This has been one hell of a morning."

The skeptical daughter eased up on her mother's arm.

"Do you have kids?" said Cruz's wife.

"I do. A daughter in high school . . . and a son," he said, knowing that didn't sound right.

Harlow avoided eye contact, obviously sensing the same thing—and probably not wanting to make him feel more uncomfortable than he already did.

"Where are they?" said the daughter next to Harlow.

"Far from here, where they're safe," he said. "Daddy's job can be a little dangerous."

"Our daddy's job is dangerous, too," she said.

"And we're going to make sure you're just as safe. Okay?" said Decker.

As they both nodded, Harlow discreetly tapped her watch. Time to move this along.

"Agent Cruz, can I speak with you—maybe over there?" said Decker, motioning toward a few empty stools near the window.

"Al. Just call me Al," he said, turning to his wife. "Is it okay if I step away for a minute?"

"I think we're in good hands," she said.

"We won't be gone long. Promise," Decker said to the kids before he led Cruz over to the empty stools.

The moment they sat down, the Border Patrol agent spoke.

"I need to warn Ocampo. He's in the same boat."

"Ocampo is safer than all of us right now," said Decker. "He probably has the entire El Centro Police Department and every available Border Patrol agent within fifty miles on his street right now."

"That's true. How bad was it?"

"Bad. Ten heavily armed mercenaries descended on the street," said Decker. "They didn't expect us to fight back."

"And they're all gone?"

"Every last one of them. We broke out some heavy artillery, which is why I guarantee the entire neighborhood is locked down by the police," said Decker.

"Dios mío," whispered Cruz.

"Why was Ocampo in the same boat?" said Decker.

"You don't know?" said Cruz. "I assumed that's why you were watching me. Us."

Decker had to be careful here. One wrong step and Cruz would shut down. Probably call the police.

"I know for a fact this is connected to the border incident. That much is obvious," said Decker. "But to be honest, keeping an eye on you and your partner was kind of a stab in the dark. I know you were situated a few miles away from where the agents were ambushed—and I know the reported timing of your departure doesn't make sense. I just don't know why. Actually, I think I know why."

Cruz rubbed his chin and stared out the window. "Why?"

"Because you heard something over the radio."

"The radio wasn't working," said Cruz. "It was jammed."

"Over the Motorolas," said Decker. "We used similar systems in Iraq and Afghanistan. Sometimes I couldn't talk to my Marines two houses over. Sometimes I could reach my liaison at battalion head-quarters four miles away, especially if they were in the open, at a higher elevation—like someone in a mobile observation post."

Cruz remained silent for several long seconds before opening up.

"We didn't say anything because I know how the cartels work. I've been down here for ten years. They find out everything in time," said Cruz. "A lot of good it did us."

"This is more complicated than the cartels. I can't say any more than that," said Decker. "What did you hear?"

"How do I know I can trust you?" said Cruz. "I don't even know who you work for."

"I can't tell you who I work for. All I can say is they play a powerful role in our government, and they want to get to the bottom of what happened out there. The bunker. The ambush. None of it makes sense. They're trying to figure it out before the situation gets worse," said Decker. "As far as trusting me? What do your ten years of law enforcement experience tell you?"

Cruz shook his head. "They tell me I owe you one, but they also say something's off here."

"I'm glad to hear your ten years have paid off," said Decker. "We're the good guys, but it's complicated. What did you hear that nobody else heard?"

"Reception was spotty for most of what I heard. After they came across the kids, Pittman took off to try and find out where they came from. I heard bits and pieces of that. Nothing worth sending killers after us."

Decker nodded, not wanting to push him. Cruz continued after a deep breath.

"At some point, Pittman came back from his scouting trip and reported a group of soldiers around his vehicle. It sounded like he was on a hill observing the soldiers. I mean, that's the only way he could have transmitted that clearly."

"Soldiers?" said Decker, thinking that was an odd description. "What about Contreras?"

"I heard him on the main radio before it went to static," said Cruz. "Never really could tell what he was saying on the Motorola."

"What else?"

"Pittman stopped transmitting for maybe twenty seconds at one point, then he came back on the radio and said, 'Agents down. Ambushed by soldiers. Jacumba Wilderness Area.' But that's not what spooked me the most. After that, I heard voices—speaking perfect English. Pittman's radio was still transmitting somehow."

Decker presumed that the "soldiers" who killed Contreras and Pittman were cut from the same mold as the guy tied up in the back of their van. Mercenaries. Military contractors. Security officers. Whatever they liked to call themselves to avoid the truth. Paid killers.

"Did you hear what they said?"

"Not really. They were quiet, but it was clear that they weren't happy to discover his radio."

"I imagine they weren't," said Decker. "You're lucky they didn't come after you sooner."

"And I thought we were in the clear after nearly ten days," said Cruz. "Do you think Ocampo said something?"

"I don't know, but I highly doubt it," said Decker. "Is there anything else you can think of?"

"No. That's it. That's the big secret," said Cruz.

"I guess the big question now is where do you want to go?" said Decker. "We're not exactly a conventional arm of the law, so we don't have a base of operations or a headquarters. I can bring you somewhere very hidden and safe, but you'd have to stay there until we say otherwise. There's no telling when that might be."

"I think it would be better if we contacted my office and requested protective services," said Cruz. "If the cartel, or whoever is behind this, turned El Centro into a war zone, my guess is we'll be safe. Probably have to come clean about what we heard, but that sounds like the right thing to do."

"I'd keep that to myself, honestly," said Decker. "The evidence they gather from El Centro should be enough to jump-start an investigation. I think you'll be safe, but the offer still stands to join us. I'm looking at those two little girls and thinking I need to keep that offer on the table."

"I appreciate that, but I know the Border Patrol will take care of us," said Cruz. "We'll hang out in the shopping center. Grab lunch across the street with the family, then I'll call them. Say we called an Uber from a street over or something."

"It's better if you don't say how you got here," said Decker. "Leave it for them to fill in the blanks. The bottom line is you escaped when things went to hell on your street. Climbed over the fence and vanished."

"That sounds about right," said Cruz.

Decker glanced over his shoulder and saw that most of his team had converged on the table, delivering drinks and goodies to the kids. Harlow looked in his direction, and he motioned for the door.

"Al, I think this is where we say goodbye," said Decker. "Good luck and watch your back. Everything will be fine, but just be careful who you trust."

Cruz laughed. "You know how that sounds given these circumstances, right?"

"I do," said Decker. "Take care of those two young ladies, and the other young lady."

"Damn right I will," said Cruz, patting Decker's back. "Hope I can buy you a drink one day."

"Never know," said Decker, getting up to meet Harlow on her way out.

"How did it go?" said Harlow.

"Nothing earth-shattering. Pittman and Contreras weren't killed by a cartel posse, or whatever the military is claiming, but we pretty much knew that already."

"Who killed them?"

"English-speaking soldiers, according to the radio transmission they intercepted," said Decker. "Most likely mercenaries guarding the bunker who were out looking for their escaped entertainment."

"All the more reason to have a long, productive talk with our new friend," said Harlow.

"Yeah. I'm starting to reconsider what I said earlier."

"About what?" said Harlow.

"About the methods I'm willing to use to extract information."

Chapter Forty-Five

Nick Adler lay on his back in a shallow, yellow-brown-stained bathtub, his ankles zip-tied together and lashed tightly to the rusted handicap railing next to the water spout. His hands had been zip-tied to his belt individually, the plastic strips run through the belt loops in case he somehow managed to use his destroyed limbs to undo his belt. A bare fluorescent light fixture above the sink's mirror cast a sickly bluish-white hue over the bathroom. He deserved better. It was a shitty place to die. Even for him.

A few quick tugs on the handicap bar yielded nothing—except attention. Ryan Decker appeared in the bathroom doorway, sipping a Diet Coke.

"Ready to talk?" said Decker.

Not really, but he didn't see any other way to move this game forward, even if that meant the end of him. Adler nodded defiantly, if that was even possible given his circumstances. Decker turned to someone Adler couldn't see in the room.

"Are we ready?" said Decker, a wicked grin forming a few moments later. "Looks like we're ready."

Decker entered the bathroom and reached for Adler's face. "This is going to hurt—but you already know that."

The tape probably took some of his skin off, possibly tore his lip. He knew this. Not because he'd ever had his mouth taped shut before, but because he'd been in Decker's position more times than he could count.

"Not too bad. Looks like you cut yourself shaving," said Decker, taking a seat on the toilet.

Brad Pierce joined them next, leaning back against the sink. Harlow Mackenzie stood in the doorway with her arms folded. She looked less than enthusiastic about what might go down in this shit-box hotel bathroom. Adler's money was on Decker being the one to kick off the festivities. Adler had done his research and knew the man's history. Decker was a man who couldn't possibly care about rules and restraint anymore. Adler wouldn't last very long if Decker tapped into that inner beast, which was fine by him. His prospects were grim after this botched mission, alive or dead.

"Here's the deal," said Decker. "You answer a few questions to our satisfaction, and we don't kill you."

"I don't care what you do to me," said Adler. "It's only pain. It'll suck, but it'll end."

Decker looked at Pierce, who shrugged. Harlow chuckled, which he had to admit was a little unexpected.

"What do you think is about to go down here?" said Decker.

"The usual," said Adler.

"Some questions, which you don't answer. A little torture. Maybe a beating. More questions. Rinse. Repeat," said Pierce. "Does that sound about right?"

"That about sums it up," said Adler. "The usual."

"Your usual," said Decker. "We're going to do this a little differently."

"Torture first. Then questions?" said Adler. "Same thing."

Harlow unfolded her arms. "I'm going to get something to eat. Let me know what he decides so we can plan the rest of the day."

She walked away, the motel door opening and shutting a few seconds later. What the hell was this?

"What am I deciding? To tell or not to tell? Quick death or slow death," said Adler. "The usual?"

"I guess we're not all that original," said Pierce. "We were going to give you the choice of a local ER or a hundred-mile desert walk with no food or water."

Unexpectedly, Adler found himself interested in hearing more.

"I don't like the desert," said Adler. "But showing up to an ER with a gunshot wound a few hours after that El Centro business probably isn't going to end any differently."

"I'd be willing to take you to Riverside," said Decker. "That's far enough away from this mess to keep you off the radar. It's either that or somewhere as far as I can drive on the Mojave National Preserve."

"What do you want to know?"

"Truthfully, I only have one question. Who sent you? And I don't mean the person you were arguing with on the satellite phone. She's dead. I want the person you referred to as 'our boss.'"

"Dead? How?"

"Car crash at the other site," said Decker. "I can show you the drone footage."

He hadn't expected to hear that. It was actually good news.

"I believe you," said Adler, considering his situation for a few seconds. "So I have your word that you'll take me to a hospital in Riverside."

"As long as you're telling the truth," said Pierce.

"And how are you supposed to determine that?"

"Our drones took high-resolution pictures of everyone on your team and the other team," said Decker. "We're running those pictures through a number of databases for identification, known associates, background information, employment history. We'll have a pretty good picture of your group within the hour."

Now for a little gamble. Neither Decker nor Pierce struck him as a killer. They definitely didn't have a problem killing—he'd witnessed that firsthand—but they weren't murderers. Adler was starting to see a way to salvage this mess and not have to sleep with one eye open for the rest of his life. A chance to whitewash the fiasco in El Centro. He just needed to be sure.

"Then what do you need me for?"

"We don't, really," said Decker. "But we'll all sleep a little better at night with a confession. And trust me when I say this—I could use a good night's sleep."

"And all I have to do is give you the name of the man who sent us."

"That's it. If the name checks out, you're a free man," said Decker. "Not a bad deal, given what you came here to do."

"He goes by the code name JUPITER."

Decker and Pierce looked at each other, each of them shaking their heads. Adler planned to string them along, just a little. Get a reaction. Maybe get a rise out of one of them.

"You'll have to do better than that," said Pierce. "I'm pretty well rested. Sleep's not so important to me."

"I'm going to be completely honest with you," said Adler. "I'm not one hundred percent sure who JUPITER is. The system was designed that way for obvious reasons."

"I have a confession to make," said Decker. "I never had any intention of dropping you off in the desert to die."

"You're going to shoot me in the bathtub?"

"No. Killing you wouldn't be great for my sleep, either," said Decker. "I'm going to call the Border Patrol and tell them where to find you. Provide them with some handy drone footage of you barreling out of that corner house with a rifle. Wonder what the police will find in that house?"

Clever. That would definitely be a showstopper, and a guaranteed life sentence, but Adler wasn't worried. He had no reason to withhold the name in question. They'd undoubtedly figure it out eventually.

"I'm pretty sure the man behind this is my former employer. Well, he didn't employ me directly. He owned the company," said Adler, drawing it out a little more. "You're not going to like this, given what I know about your history. And for the record, I had nothing to do with any of that past. I'm pretty sure you can look that up in the court filings."

Decker kept a stoic face, but Adler could tell that he'd already guessed the name. No point in dragging this out any further. He just hoped Decker didn't put a bullet through his head when he heard it spoken.

"Jacob Harcourt is JUPITER. Rumor has it he's down in Mexico somewhere, paying the Sinaloa Cartel to keep him safe. Supplying them with whatever weapons and intelligence he can still drag out of the few people still willing to do business with him."

"Like you?" said Decker.

"It's a paycheck. A very healthy one, when he has a job."

"All right. We'll start looking into this. Probably get on the road within the hour," said Decker, nodding at Pierce as he left the bathroom.

Pierce followed, stopping briefly to pull on the handicap railing. "Just making sure."

"That's it?" said Adler.

"That's it."

CHAPTER FORTY-SIX

Ryan Decker struggled to keep his composure while storming out of the motel room. He glanced at Pam, who sat propped up on one of the beds with a Taser in her lap, and started to say something. Not a good idea right now. Just hearing Harcourt's name spoken in the context of someone who was still breathing oxygen pushed him over the edge. He needed to leave Adler with the impression that the name didn't bother him. They weren't done with Adler.

As he walked through the door, Pierce instructed Pam to resume her vigil. Harlow sat on the front bumper of their van, waiting for him with Katie and Sandra. Sophie emerged from the van's open sliding door to join them.

"Well?" said Harlow.

Decker waited for Pierce to close the motel door before he shared the news.

"It's possible that Jacob Harcourt is back," he said.

"Are you serious?" said Katie.

"Why doesn't this surprise me?" said Harlow.

"Because it's not surprising at all," said Decker. "I had my suspicions, mostly based on my hatred for the man. I wanted it to be him so badly, I think I would have been disappointed if that guy said anything different."

"His name is Nick Adler," said Sophie. "Josh and his team just found him in a federal security clearance database. He spent ten years working for Aegis Global. Same with the woman."

"You found her already?" said Pierce.

"Same database. Freya Walker. Did five years with Aegis Global before the crash."

"Sounds like he's putting the band back together," said Sandra. "Wonderful."

"Adler said everyone thinks Harcourt's in Mexico, cozied up to the Sinaloa Cartel," said Decker.

"Conforms with some of the rumors we've heard," said Pierce.

"I wonder how they'd feel about the fact that he's helping to arm rival cartels?" said Katie.

"I don't trust Adler, so I'm not going to put a ton of stock into which cartel or even which country," said Decker. "And there's a possibility that Adler chose to give me Harcourt's name because he read my file and knew this could be his ticket out. Most hard-core military contractors have worked for Aegis at one time or another."

"So. Where do we go from here?" said Harlow.

"I want to put a team on Adler. An outside team," said Decker. "This guy is seriously screwed, no matter who his boss turns out to be. His side of the operation was a colossal failure, and the fact that he's the sole survivor of his team doesn't look good. But his eyes lit up when I told him the woman was dead. My guess is he's going to reach out to his boss and blame this on Freya Walker. It's his only play, aside from disappearing for the rest of his life. Maybe he'll lead us to Harcourt, or whoever."

"I know a pair that could pull this off," said Harlow. "And they'll blend in if this leads to Mexico."

"Mr. and Mrs. Rivera?" said Sophie.

"Yep," said Harlow. "They know what to do. Buy airline tickets at every airport in and around Los Angeles so they can get past security and figure out where Adler is headed. They'll follow if they can get a ticket on the same flight. Worst-case scenario, we get a destination or connection city. Best case, the Riveras follow him right to the source."

"Do it," said Decker. "This all goes on the senator's tab, just so we're clear. She told us to spend her money. That's exactly what we're going to do."

"I'll call them," said Sophie, heading back into the van.

"At this point, I think we head back to Colorado and gather information. See if there's more to pursue—and if we want to pursue it," said Decker. "I need to drop Mr. Adler off near a hospital in Riverside."

"I'll help you with that," said Pierce.

"No. You head home with the rest of this motley crew," said Decker. "Harlow. You up for a ride?"

"Huh? I guess. Sure . . . sounds good. We'll take one of the SUVs. Just leave us a vehicle in Phoenix. We'll be two hours behind you."

Katie nodded. "Easy enough. The other thing we need to keep in mind is that we're pretty much mission critical on any gear we're not carrying with us. The spike strips and drones are gone. If we plan on pulling off anything like this again, we'll need to start sourcing that gear right away."

"Charge it to the senator," said Decker.

"I'm beginning to like the sound of that," said Sandra.

"Me, too," said Harlow. "We probably left forty thousand dollars of gear back in El Centro."

"She'll be happy to spend it, given what we may have discovered," said Decker. "If Harcourt is behind this, the senator will spend anything to bring him to justice."

He stopped short of saying, "And so would I," knowing it was a sore spot with Harlow.

"Ten-minute departure time?" said Pierce.

"I'll go distract the manager," said Sandra. "Transfer to the van in, say, three minutes?"

They'd parked the vehicles in a way that blocked most of the other rooms' views to the door they'd use to move Adler. The manager remained the only real liability. The five hundred dollars handed to him, in exchange for discretion, had so far done the trick, but Decker wasn't willing to bet his life or anyone else's on that five hundred. He'd come across men who would sell their daughters, and did, for far less than that.

CHAPTER
FORTY-SEVEN

Jacob Harcourt leaned over the thick marble balustrade framing his spacious veranda and took in the deep-orange sunset. Thick tendrils of bluish-purple shadow cast by the hilltops in front of him penetrated the lush river valley below his estate. He would have preferred an oceanside view, but this hillside luxury villa, deep in the heart of cartel country, better suited his security needs.

Only accessible to the world by a single winding road from Los Mochis and a concealed valley runway, the private, compact estate was an impenetrable fortress. Any approach by land would give him ample time to assess the situation and decide whether to stay and fight or slip away. If he suspected that the runway had been captured, unmarked valley trails gave him a few more discreet escape options. His Sinaloa Cartel associates would pick him up along the trail and spirit him to safety in that unlikely event.

They'd also respond by land, if summoned, and cut off the road. Anyone with the audacity to attack Harcourt's stronghold would quickly find themselves surrounded in hostile country, soon to pay the ultimate price. Overall, he was pleased with the arrangement, even if he felt more like a pampered hostage most of the time. He couldn't freely travel outside Mexico without risking capture by US authorities, which were actively looking for him. Even leaving Sinaloa territory carried significant risks, despite the money he paid the cartel to pave the way.

Corruption worked both ways, and the right price paid to the wrong official could put a CIA rendition team or an assassin in his path. Possibly even Decker. He hadn't thought about Decker for a number of months, while the pieces of Southern Cross started to come together. The final phase of the operation and the excitement of his impending, phoenixlike rise from the ashes had kept him distracted from the thought of the man who had singlehandedly dismantled his Aegis Global empire.

When Decker's name resurfaced a few days ago, he'd nearly choked on the Mazatlán swordfish his chef had prepared. He knew Senator Steele would take an interest in the border agents' disappearance, given the human-trafficking implications of the agent's last radio report, but he never suspected that the crazy bitch would send Ryan Decker to investigate.

Now he had a real problem on his hands. Far more than just Decker poking around the desert. News reports out of El Centro today suggested that Freya Walker's operation had gone entirely sideways. More than a dozen killed in a two-pronged attack that has left law enforcement authorities baffled. From what he saw on the television, there was nothing confusing about what had happened. Freya Walker had utterly failed to comprehend the danger Ryan Decker and his associates presented, walking her teams into a massacre.

Harcourt had no choice at this point but to assume that Decker knew he was directly connected to the border incident, leaving a few questions to be answered. How much does Decker know? What will he do with that information? And most important, what course of action should Harcourt take to protect Southern Cross?

Joint Task Force North was fully vested in the operation. Taking whatever scant information Decker possessed up the chain of command to US Northern Command would go nowhere. Senator Duncan and Congressman Saling were unlikely to crack. They had too much money on the line, not to mention the multiple life sentences they'd face if their involvement were revealed. Decker was effectively untouchable, his crew having no doubt vanished once again.

That left one real point of vulnerability—Senator Steele. Armed with the right information, she might be able to raise enough alarms in Congress or at the Pentagon to postpone or possibly sink Southern Cross. The team of Lithuanian hackers in control of the rootkit virus installed on her office computer network hadn't uncovered anything alarming—yet.

Harcourt took a long sip of scotch from the thick crystal tumbler in his hand and let it work its magic. He had to do something about Steele. She was just too influential to ignore, and he'd be damned if he was going to let her bring him down a second time. Unfortunately, the solution to his Steele problem would have to come sooner rather than later, and he didn't like to rush things—especially something as sensitive as potentially taking out a US senator.

"Jefe? Sorry to disturb you."

He turned to face Pedro, his estate security chief, who stood to one side of the cavernous opening that connected the veranda to the massive hacienda-style home. Unlike his former security chief, the bombastic, self-possessed tank Dutch Garraty, Pedro was soft-spoken, slim bodied, and unassuming—but he missed nothing. He seemed to be everywhere and nowhere at any given time, unobtrusively directing the estate's sizable but discreet security detachment.

The only group he didn't directly control was Harcourt's executive security team. Eight former Russian Special Forces soldiers bound to him by the promise of an excessive bonus at the end of their tour of duty. Enough money for each of them to retire more than comfortably in Mexico or wherever the hell they took it. Of course, each payment was contingent upon his approval, in person, at an undisclosed bank in Mexico City. One could never be too careful when dealing with mercenaries.

"It's fine, Pedro," said Harcourt. "What's up?"

He held out a satellite phone. "A call came in through the US network. Message from Nick Adler with a return number. I have the number ready to go on this phone."

Interesting. "Leave the phone with me. Thank you."

"*Sí*, Jefe," said Pedro, handing him the phone and disappearing into the house.

The lone Russian watching over him from the recesses of the veranda took leave as well, a procedure they'd established from the start. The less they knew about his business dealings, the safer for Harcourt. The sum of money promised to each of them was unheard of in the mercenary business, but it amounted to pocket change for the Sinaloa Cartel—who had undoubtedly planted a few informants among his house staff. If they caught wind of what he had planned for them, not even an army could protect him here.

He dialed the number and waited. Nick Adler, or someone claiming to be him, answered.

"Mr. Adler. How can I be sure this is you?" said Harcourt.

"I suppose you can't, sir. All I can do is verify the details of the mission you gave us. Verify the personnel roster. Payment methods. There has to be something only one of the team leaders can verify," he said.

"If that team leader was captured, there'd be nothing," said Harcourt.

"I wasn't captured. My entire team was wiped out, thanks to Freya Walker," he said.

"Then why didn't you die with them?"

"Because I refused her idiotic order, and she relieved me on the spot. Rawlings took charge and executed the order," said Adler. "She sent the entire team after Decker and Mackenzie the moment the two showed up. Didn't observe the target. Didn't analyze the situation.

Pushed them out the door as soon as they turned down the road. That move put the entire team on the street at the same time. Pierce was in the back of the SUV with a machine gun. Mowed everyone down in less than twenty seconds."

The story sounded sketchy to Harcourt. Freya Walker was far from impulsive, which was one of the reasons he'd picked her from a roster of several candidates. What she had lacked in tactical experience he'd hoped to gain with caution and deliberate planning. It obviously hadn't been enough, even though he now suspected that Adler had more to do with the mission failure than anything else.

"Except for you," said Harcourt, testing him a little further.

"I stayed back at the house to provide sniper support," said Adler. "But it was over before I could get into position on the porch. I got off a few shots, but the back of the SUV was somehow protected. Pierce lit me up after that. Got hit in the arm and hand."

"How the hell did you get out of there?" said a skeptical Harcourt.

"They left immediately. You could already hear the police sirens," said Adler. "I took off in one of the homeowner's cars and kept driving."

"Where are you now?"

"Parkview Community Hospital in Riverside, California," said Adler.

Harcourt was about to ask him how he managed to drive to Riverside from El Centro with two bullet wounds, but decided against it. He preferred to ask him in person. Too many pointed questions might spook him.

"Do they have a police officer watching you?" said Harcourt.

"No. I figured Riverside was far enough away from that mess to buy me some time," said Adler.

"I need to get you off the streets," said Harcourt. "The last thing I need is a direct link right now. Are you capable of air travel?"

"Yes. The hospital patched up my hand. I can wrap a few more bandages around it," said Adler. "Same with the arm. How long of a flight?"

"Four hours total," said Harcourt. "I'll call you back in fifteen minutes with flight details. For now, get clear of the hospital."

"I have money to move around, but I don't have a passport or any form of ID that will work at the airport," said Adler. "We sanitized prior to leaving for El Centro."

"This will be more of a private flight," said Harcourt.

One that couldn't be followed or traced to its destination. The last thing he needed was Decker asking the wrong kind of questions in or around Los Mochis.

"I'll be ready," said Adler, and Harcourt disconnected the call.

Not for what Harcourt had planned for him. He needed to be sure that Adler wasn't working some kind of double cross. Until then, he had some calls to make. The cartels needed to start moving the weapons away from the border to their forward staging areas. With Decker and Steele sniffing around, each cartel needed to be ready for an expedited timeline.

Joint Task Force North and the two useful idiots in DC had already played their roles. Nothing north of the border could stop the war Harcourt had set in motion at this point, but the revenue stream he stood to secure in its aftermath was a totally different story.

Assisted by sophisticated weapons he wrangled out of JTF North and the collaboration he brokered between cartel leadership, the New Jalisco Generation, Juárez, and Los Zetas cartels would soon deliver a mortal blow to the now dominant Sinaloa Cartel. The US-Mexico border territory currently controlled by the Sinaloa would be split up between the three cartels, drastically increasing their revenues, and a small percentage of the new business, representing a few hundred million dollars annually, would go to Harcourt. Unless the conspiracy was exposed too early.

If the connection between JTF North leadership, Harcourt, and the cartels were somehow effectively exposed, the complicit senior military officers would be fired, and the free flow of drugs and migrants through the new border corridors would vanish with them—along with most of the cash he stood to make from his arrangement with the three cartels. That was the best-case scenario if things went sideways. He didn't want to think about what would happen if the new leadership carried through with a real crackdown along the border.

Harcourt would probably have to find a new home, on another continent, where nobody spoke a lick of Spanish.

PART FOUR

CHAPTER FORTY-EIGHT

Senator Steele had chosen to participate in the videoconference from the wine cellar in the basement of her Annapolis home. It was the only room in her house without a window—safe from laser microphone surveillance. A countersurveillance team she hired had verified that the vibrations from her voice could not be detected through any of the windows facing either the Severn River or Weems Creek, where a boat or riverfront trespasser could easily go unnoticed.

The same team had scanned her home for electronic listening devices, declaring it clean before they assembled the equipment that would connect the videoconference to an encrypted satellite link. Despite assurances that her Senate office had been swept for bugs, she didn't trust the Hart Senate Office Building's data network, no matter what they did to secure the connection. Conducting the conference here, more or less without warning, felt like the securest option given what they needed to discuss.

She sat at the circular, antique French wine-tasting table and took long, deep breaths, waiting for the feed to go live. News out of the El Centro area strongly suggested that Decker and his team had touched a raw nerve. The people behind the disappearance of the Border Patrol agents and the weapons buried in the bunker had wanted nothing more than to close the loop on her informal investigation.

Unfortunately for them, underestimating Decker's crew had proven to be a costly mistake. Steele just hoped it had been worth the price of turning El Centro into a shooting gallery. Authorities reported that hundreds of bullets had been fired in the gun battle outside Agent Ocampo's house and dozens more just down the street from Agent Cruz's. The fact that no civilians had been killed or injured that morning was a miracle. Faced with a similar decision in the future, she was not inclined to turn Decker loose on the street again.

The head of the countersurveillance team, a tall woman dressed in a gray business suit, opened the door to the cellar.

"Senator Steele, we're connected to the encrypted link. I've communicated with all parties involved, and they are standing by for you to initiate the conference," said the woman. "All you have to do is click the green 'Start' button at the top right of the screen."

"That's it?"

"That's it," said the woman. "If you experience a problem with the feed, I'll be on the patio just off the game room. Give a quick holler and I'll take care of it."

She appreciated the steps that had been taken to ensure her privacy.

"Thank you," said Steele, and the woman left, pulling the door closed behind her.

She clicked the green button on the screen, and the team appeared in front of her.

"Oh. Here we go!" said Joshua. "Sorry about the zero warning thing."

"Better than last time," said Pierce. "Decker was three Special Agent Reeves jokes in before we knew we were live."

"Funny," said Reeves. "You keep hanging out with Decker, and I'll have to remove you from my Christmas card list."

"I think we'd all prefer not to be on any of your lists!" said Decker, eliciting a round of laughs—even from Senator Steele.

"I'm glad to see everyone in somewhat good spirits after what you've been through," said Steele. "The reports I'm getting out of El Centro, in addition to what's been reported in the news, paint a rather disturbing picture of the lengths this shadow organization will go to protect their secret—and their reach.

"Fourteen former military contractors were found dead on the streets near the two Border Patrol agents' houses. That number has not been released to the public, by the way. Police chased a hijacked car carrying five men away from Agent Cruz's street. That chase ended in a gun battle at a roadblock set up a few miles away, killing all five men and six El Centro police officers. Several more officers were wounded. These people clearly did not want to be taken alive. On top of that, they found a recently murdered couple in a home near Agent Ocampo's house. Most likely related."

"Probably the corner house," said Decker. "The nine killed on Agent Ocampo's street came running out after us. They didn't leave us much choice in our response."

"I think it's a miracle you're all still alive," said Steele.

"We had a solid plan," said Pierce. "And good people to execute it."

"I share your assessment, Mr. Pierce," said Steele. "But nine heavily armed, well trained ex-military contractors? A lot could and probably should have gone wrong. Same with whatever happened on the other street. Looks like you barely got out of that one."

"We had a few close calls," said Katie. "Nothing several thousand dollars' worth of drones, some talented pilots, and a Benelli shotgun couldn't handle."

"And some red-hot driving," said Sandra, high-fiving Katie.

Senator Steele broke into a grin. "I certainly commend you all on a job well done, but I think it's prudent to keep you off the streets moving forward. The public attention generated by the El Centro mission could prove to be counterproductive in the long run. This mystery group may very well withdraw and sink even farther back into the shadows, where we'll never find them in time to stop whatever conspiracy they've hatched."

"Senator Steele," said Decker, "I had meant to bring something up with you before this meeting, for reasons that will be obvious, but we really needed a secure setup for this information—and frankly, I've been dreading it."

"Mr. Decker, if this is related to what we're working on, I can't see any reason not to share it in committee."

"There's no easy way to say this. So here it is," said Decker. "We're more or less convinced that Jacob Harcourt is behind all of this. The weapons in the bunker. The Border Patrol agent killings. El Centro. All of it."

Senator Steele remained silent and very still for several seconds. Just hearing the man's name still paralyzed her with anger. She'd been mistaken on two counts when she insisted that Decker leave Harcourt trapped in his Virginia mansion for the authorities to arrest.

First, she had asked too much of Decker, especially considering what Harcourt had inflicted on him. She'd come to understand that too late, though Decker never mentioned it. He'd been surprisingly gracious when it came to the subject. Her second mistake had been assuming that Harcourt would be apprehended in the aftermath of Decker's assault on his house and the near complete destruction of the small army guarding him.

In an unexpected twist, Harcourt had shot Senator Frist, his coconspirator, and escaped with the help of the few surviving Aegis Global military contractors on the estate, robbing her of seeing the two of them stand trial for murder and treason. Leaving Harcourt's fate to chance was a mistake she wouldn't make again if given the chance.

What Harcourt had done to her was beyond the pale. He'd orchestrated the kidnapping and murder of her only child, Meghan, simply to distract her from paying too close attention to a Senate bill that would further line the coffers of his bloated military contracting corporation, Aegis Global. Her daughter hadn't been the only victim of his treachery. Her husband, who couldn't live with the grief of what had happened to their daughter, took his own life shortly after her death. And that was only a small part of the horror Harcourt had unleashed in his perverse quest for money and power. He was a monster who should have died along with Senator Frist that day. She chose her words carefully, trying to remain composed.

"I can't say it surprises me," said Steele, pursing her lips. "What makes you so sure, and what is he up to?"

"I really shouldn't say in front of Special Agent Reeves," said Decker. She cocked her head. *Interesting.*

"Should I turn the volume off for a few minutes?" said Reeves.

"Can you read lips?" said Decker.

"No. And I'm not recording our meeting," said Reeves. "This whole videoconference is about as unofficial as it gets. I'm muting my end."

"I'll wave when it's time for you to come back," said Decker.

A few seconds later, Reeves tapped his ear and gave them a thumbs-up.

"All right. What exactly couldn't you say in front of Reeves?" said Steele.

"I'm not even sure we should be saying this in front of you," said Decker.

"This conversation never took place. Tell me."

"We managed to capture one of the mercenaries in El Centro— Nick Adler. One of the team leaders. He swore he never met Harcourt face-to-face but strongly suspected that Harcourt, going by the code name JUPITER, had hired them for the job. He also said that Harcourt was rumored to be in Mexico, cozied up to the Sinaloa Cartel. I've heard the same rumors through some of my deep contacts."

"Not conclusive, but definitely worth pursuing," said Steele, trying not to sound excited by the prospect of finding Harcourt. "What did you do with the mercenary?"

"That's where it gets a little more conclusive," said Decker. "We let him go—"

"You did what?" said Steele, pounding the table.

"His release had a purpose," said Decker. "We hired a trusted private investigative team to follow him after we delivered him to a hospital in Riverside, California. He spent a few hours in the hospital, presumably seeking treatment for the two bullet holes I gave him, before skipping out on the bill and proceeding to Ontario International Airport."

"He could get around on his own?"

"I only shot him in the hand and arm," said Decker, getting a few uncomfortable laughs. "He boarded a privately arranged flight at the airport—which the team couldn't follow. They did, however, manage to determine the aircraft's destination: Los Mochis, Mexico. A Sinaloa stronghold. El Chapo was captured there—the second time around."

"I remember," said Steele. "So. You think Harcourt provided safe harbor to Adler by flying him down to Mexico?"

"I think Adler is going to end up fertilizing a garden somewhere in Los Mochis," said Decker. "He represents an extreme liability to Harcourt, and judging by his performance in El Centro, his skills do not outweigh the risks of keeping him around."

"Can we bring Joseph back into the conversation?" said Steele.

"Yes," said Decker, waving toward the camera.

"Joe, we've identified a likely associate of Jacob Harcourt, who was flown by private jet from Riverside, California, to Los Mochis, Mexico—deep in the heart of Sinaloa country. Is there any way we can use that information to track down Harcourt?" said Steele.

"Nothing that's going to move very quickly. Do you have evidence directly linking this associate to Harcourt's current operation?"

"He told us he suspected that Harcourt hired his team," said Decker.

"Was this information obtained illegally?"

"He freely gave us the information," said Pierce.

"He just walked up to you and offered the information?" said Reeves, raising an eyebrow.

"I think it's fair to say that the statement would have to stand on its own," said Harlow. "Without describing how the information came to be in our possession."

"At this point, all I can really do is refer the lead to our fugitive task force liaison. Give it a medium confidence rating and—"

"Medium?" said the senator.

"Without tangible evidence or a confirmed source, I'd be hard-pressed to classify it any higher," said Reeves.

"Consider yourself hard-pressed, Joe," said Steele.

"Yes, ma'am," he said. "I'll submit it as high confidence and keep myself in the loop. Even so, they'll move slowly and cautiously on this. If Harcourt made his home anywhere near Los Mochis, he did it with the Sinaloa Cartel's blessing. One misstep or misspoken word, and Harcourt will vanish."

"It's the best we can do right now with the information we have," said Steele. "Which begs the question—what else do we know and what can we do with it?"

Reeves interjected. "I confirmed the existence of two more military exclusion zones. One to the west of El Paso and the other north of Laredo."

"Which cartels control those areas?" said Harlow, beating Decker to the question.

"The border around El Paso falls under Juárez Cartel control, and the area north of Laredo is run by Los Zetas—two cartels in direct competition with the Sinaloa," said Reeves.

"Does anyone have a phone number for the head of the Sinaloa Cartel?" said Pierce. "I think we could solve our Harcourt problem with a single call. I can't imagine they'd be happy to learn that he's involved in shipping sophisticated weapons to rival cartels."

"I imagine not," said the senator. "Is there any way to make that happen?"

"Given the fact that nobody here or in Mexico knows where to find Damaso Casales, I can't see any way to place that call, or bring it to light in any way that would draw his attention without tipping off Harcourt," said Reeves.

Harlow started to raise her hand but dropped it back in her lap—shaking her head.

"Ms. Mackenzie? You looked like you had an idea," said Steele.

"What if we gathered conclusive evidence that these weapons existed and were in the hands of these rival cartels? Could we feed the information to some major newspapers? I think a few well-placed, speculative stories might be enough to spur this Casales guy into action. Maybe these media outlets reach out to counterparts in Mexico and leak the contents of the story in advance? A leak like that would certainly reach Casales before Harcourt, and even if it didn't, it would put a bull's-eye on Harcourt's back that could be seen from space."

Steele liked the way Harlow Mackenzie was thinking.

"I don't think any credible news outlet would bite on the photos you snapped of the spider robots and the side of the Javelin crate," said Reeves. "Just saying."

"I tend to agree," said Steele. "There's no way to vet the information."

"I'm talking about new evidence," said Harlow, glancing at Decker, who nodded like he'd just figured out where she was going with this.

"How would we acquire this evidence?" said Steele.

"We investigate one of the other two sites."

"That sounds incredibly dangerous," said Steele. "Especially with Harcourt, and presumably the cartels, on high alert for you."

"With the right approach, and the right investment," said Decker, "we can mitigate a lot of the risk."

Now they were talking.

"How much of an investment?" said Steele.

She didn't care what it cost to get Harcourt.

"I'd want to use the same outfit we hired to take down Harcourt last year," said Decker. "Plus enough to hire at least two more ground operators."

"Sounds a little crowded on the ground," said Pierce. "I don't think we need more than three total."

"Then we go with two. The best available," said Decker. "Preferably Spanish speakers, in case we run into anyone that might be able to answer some questions for us."

"We'd only need one," said Pierce. "Unless you plan on leaving me behind."

"That's exactly what I plan on doing," said Decker. "You've risked enough."

Pierce stood up, and for a brief moment, Steele thought he was going to hit Decker.

"Not a chance I'm staying behind," said Pierce. "I'm just as vested in taking down Harcourt as you are."

"I don't know about that," muttered Decker.

"I didn't mean it that way, and you know it," said Pierce. "I'd like to wake up one day not worrying about stepping out on the deck and eating a sniper bullet. Better yet, I'd like to sleep through the night again, not thinking that every creak in the house was a hit team sent to kill my family in front of me."

"Sorry for that. I just can't ask you to do more than you've already done," said Decker, turning to face the rest of the team. "Or any of you, for that matter. It's been a long year looking over our shoulders."

"We've been looking over our shoulders for years," said Katie. "Harcourt wasn't the first and certainly won't be the last dangerous asshole we piss off."

"You're not getting rid of us that easy," said Harlow.

"Ma'am, we'll get the ball rolling," said Pierce. "I'd conservatively estimate three-quarters of a million dollars to make it happen."

"Done. And there's plenty more to spend if necessary. I'll leave it to your judgment to decide what's necessary," said Steele. "What is our lead time on this?"

"I think I can scare up one Spanish-speaking operator pretty quickly. I actually have someone in mind," said Pierce. "The rest depends on the pilot's availability. I'd say five days at the most."

"That's too long," said Steele. "Harcourt won't sit still after El Centro. Will offering this pilot more money improve our chances of bumping up the mission timeline?"

"I'd say it would definitely improve our chances," said Pierce.

"Then you have my permission to offer whatever it takes to get this done in the next twenty-four to forty-eight hours."

"Copy that," said Pierce.

"Senator Steele?" said Harlow, waving at the camera. "Joshua wanted to brief you on the counter-rootkit operation."

"Certainly. The whole thing had almost slipped my mind," said Steele.

Joshua turned his chair to face the camera. "It kind of slipped all of our minds for the past forty-eight hours."

"His team was busy keeping us alive," said Harlow.

"And doing a damn fine job," said Katie, drawing a quick round of applause.

"The good news is that my friends have successfully deployed the shadow network designed to mimic your office network, and they've triggered the rootkit virus back door," he said. "The bad news is the rootkit trace led back to a Lithuania-based hacker outfit, with no exploitable connection to Harcourt or Senator Duncan."

"A dead end," said Steele.

"Yes. But I wonder how you'd feel about running the same trick on Senator Duncan," said Joshua. "Pretend I didn't say that if I'm overstepping."

"You're not overstepping at all, Joshua," said Steele. "How would I do this? I can't imagine the good senator falling for the same trick he tried to play on me."

"I completely agree. I was thinking something a lot less overt. Can you send one of your staff to his office and ask the front desk to check the thumb drive he gave you? Maybe say it wasn't working, and that it's important. See if they'll stick it in one of the computers to verify?"

"I don't see any reason we couldn't try," said Steele.

"The other option is for someone to carry a specialized device into the office and try to crack their password using a brute-force decryption program. The only drawback to that is the person would need to remain in range of Senator Duncan's dedicated Wi-Fi signal until the system is breached—and stay while we install a backdoor virus."

"I don't expect to find much on his system," said Steele. "I presume he's smarter than that."

"If he's using a government phone to make calls or send messages, we'll be able to see that, too. That's a common cybersecurity error. Plus, I'll put my team to work uncovering links between all of the known parameters. Joint Task Force North. Harcourt. Congressman Saling. Border Patrol. It worked with Harcourt and Frist."

"It certainly did," said Steele.

"The other thing to consider is possibly entrapping Duncan," said Joshua. "Right now you look squeaky clean from Harcourt's perspective, but we can change that, and gauge how they react, by generating some email or text message traffic suggesting that you're onto something in Mexico. Maybe get Harcourt to send Duncan a message. Something incriminating. Maybe dig out anyone else involved."

"I like the sound of this. Thank you, Joshua. Let me know what I need to do," said Steele.

"We'll work on it and get in touch shortly," said Joshua. "That's all I had."

"I don't have anything else," said Harlow.

Decker shook his head. "I think we covered everything we learned."

"One of the three paths, if not all of them, should give us something," said Steele. "Be careful across the border. They'll be expecting you."

"Don't worry. We still have a few tricks up our sleeves," said Decker.

Steele didn't doubt it. She just hoped it would be enough to keep them alive and bring back the evidence needed to blow the lid off this conspiracy.

CHAPTER

FORTY-NINE

Senator Paul Duncan had just bitten into the warm Maryland crab cake sandwich dropped off by some lobbyist's lackey when his personal cell phone rang. Recognizing the unique ringtone, he put down the fried sandwich and searched through the bag. *Idiot forgot the napkins!* Duncan finished chewing and grabbed the phone off his desk, leaving a greasy smudge on his phone screen when he pressed "Accept." He quickly navigated away from the call screen to a security application specifically designed to authenticate his presence.

"Paul Duncan," he said, waiting for the eerie, synthetic voice to prompt him.

"Voice and thumb recognition in three. Two. One."

Duncan pressed his index finger against the phone's fingerprint sensor and read the lines of text that scrolled across the screen.

"Identity verified," said the voice, followed by Jacob Harcourt's voice. "Senator, we have a problem."

"I'd say we do," said Duncan. "I didn't appreciate first hearing about the El Centro debacle from my chief of staff's Twitter feed. What the hell happened down there, and where have you been? I've left you several messages."

"I've been a little preoccupied with the fallout," said Harcourt.

"Fallout? How bad is it?"

"I'm not sure," said Harcourt. "But I've compressed Southern Cross's timeline. I firmly believe that Decker and his friends now have good reason to suspect I'm involved."

"Jesus. That's not good at all," said Duncan. "If Decker thinks you're behind any of the border stuff, that means Senator Steele knows."

"That's why I'm calling," said Harcourt. "The thumb drive you delivered paid off. My people just discovered that Steele typed up a memo that suggests both of your committees work together to launch a detailed investigation into the El Centro massacre and likely links to the border incident. Specifically, she recommends that the strongest measures possible be taken to pressure the Mexican government into digging up the bunker—even going so far as to propose the US launch a covert operation to dig it up if the Mexicans refuse. It's obvious Decker discovered more than we thought at the bunker site during his little foray—and Steele is intent on exposing it."

"Holy mother of Moses," said Duncan.

"I had a few more choice words when I read the contents of her draft memo," said Harcourt. "Paul, I'm going to need you to get your hands a little dirty here."

"What? How dirty? It's not like I can strangle her in my office and have her taken out with the trash," said Duncan.

"Sounds like you've given it some thought," said Harcourt.

"I'd gladly do it if I could get away with it," said Duncan.

"Then you'll have no problem with what I'm about to suggest," said Harcourt. "I need you to get her away from DC—out of her usual haunts. A private dinner away from the prying eyes of the Beltway, where the three of you can—"

"Three?"

"Sweeten the pot and bring Saling along," said Harcourt. "Propose a true across-the-aisle partnership on border security, encompassing all issues. It'll sound close enough to what she already plans to submit to you. I think she'll go for it."

"And what happens at dinner?" said Duncan.

"Nothing. She won't make it to dinner. She'll have a head-on collision with a drunk that will kill her and whatever security she brings along," said Harcourt. "You'll call her assistant, chief of staff, whoever, and ask why she's late. Say you'll wait. Eat a nice dinner, have a few drinks, and sleep sound that night, knowing that you're one step closer to Bill Gates money."

"What if she doesn't go for it?" said Duncan.

"Then I'll have to get even more creative," said Harcourt. "Let me know when you finalize dinner plans. I'll have a team standing by in a few hours to make this happen."

"This is crazy," said Duncan.

"You can always back out of Southern Cross," said Harcourt.

"And end up like Senator Frist?" said Duncan. "No. I'm in this until the bitter end."

"It's going to be a very sweet ending," said Harcourt. "For all of us."

"I hope so," said Duncan. "I'll call you with the details."

He ended the call and stared at the door for several moments before going back to his sandwich. Bill Gates money. He liked the sound of that.

CHAPTER FIFTY

Senator Steele opened her office door and nodded at Julie, who excused herself from a small gathering of legislative assistants and joined her in the office. Steele took a seat on the wide leather couch situated in front of the window framing the Supreme Court building and asked Julie to join her. Once they were both comfortably seated, Steele confided in her.

"I'd offer you a brandy or something stiffer, but it's still a little early," said Steele.

"Please tell me you're not retiring," said Julie, squeezing the armrest tightly.

"No. Nothing like that, though I suspect someone intends to retire me," said Steele.

"I don't . . . Wait. What?" said Julie.

"Remember when I said that if it ever gets to the level where you need to be concerned—I'd take care of it?" said Steele.

"I do," said Julie. "Senator Duncan appears to be the common link."

"He very well may be," said Steele. "I need to catch you up on a number of things I've regrettably kept from you. I apologize for keeping you in the dark this long, but I honestly never suspected the situation would get this far out of control."

She brought Julie up to speed on everything that had transpired since Decker had first discovered evidence of Javelin missiles buried in the bunker. The El Centro mission. Harcourt's likely involvement in everything. The counterhacking operation related to the original thumb drive given to them by Duncan, and how it resulted in the senator from Oklahoma's visit a few minutes ago. The agreed-upon dinner meeting to discuss Duncan's bipartisan proposal. When she finished, Julie didn't skip a beat.

"What do you think he has planned?" she said.

"I don't know, but I strongly suspect my night will not end with a quiet drive home—if I even make it to dinner. I just spoke with Decker, and he thinks they'll make a move before I reach the Point."

"Duncan suggested the restaurant?" said Julie. "It's located in a fairly secluded area."

"Yeah. That's what Decker said. Lots of twisty, suburban roads where I could be taken."

"I can't believe we're discussing this," said Julie.

"Neither can I," said Steele. "But we have to assume the worst."

"You should just cancel the dinner," said Julie. "Arrange an extra layer of security."

Steele shook her head. "No. Ms. Mackenzie said she would handle it. She had an idea that sounded just about perfect."

"Is Reeves involved?"

"No. What Mackenzie has in mind isn't exactly legal," said Steele. "I already spoke with Reeves and let him know he'd have to sit this one out."

Julie nodded. "And what can I do to help?"

"Two things," said Steele, producing a thumb drive. "First, I'd like you to walk this over to Duncan's office and ask one of his front office assistants to insert it in their computers. Say it's very important and it was just hand delivered by Duncan but doesn't appear to contain any files. You don't have to worry about him seeing you. He's headed to the Capitol for the rest of the afternoon."

"I assume you're giving him some of his own medicine with the thumb drive?" said Julie.

"Exactly. Harlow's team is going to scour his files for anything useful. Try to figure out how he's connected to Harcourt and whoever else might be behind this."

"No problem. Not sure if they'll go for it, but I'll figure something out," said Julie. "What's the second thing?"

"I'm going to arrange a discreet security detail to follow you and Scott. I want you to play nice with them," said Steele. "Let them do their job, regardless of the inconvenience. I wouldn't put anything past Harcourt at this point."

"I can live with that. Thank you," said Julie. "So. When is the dinner?"

"Tomorrow night. Nine thirty," said Steele. "Same night as Decker's next mission. Kind of a one-two punch."

"Dare I ask what he's up to?"

"Absolutely no good," said Steele. "Which is exactly what he's good at."

CHAPTER FIFTY-ONE

Decker sat on the hood of the SUV, not the least bit preoccupied with what lay ahead in Mexico. His mind was momentarily focused on Harlow and whether he should move his hand a few inches to the right and take hers. He urgently wanted to do it, but something held him back. Decker imperceptibly shook his head. What the hell was wrong with him? He could think of no logical reason why he shouldn't hold her hand and let her know how much she meant to him.

He strongly suspected she felt the same way about him, and it wasn't like their veiled attraction was a big secret. Pierce had his suspicions, and Harlow's crew had been dropping comments about their relationship for a few months—to the point where he had started to feel uncomfortable around them when Harlow was present. Another sign of just how ridiculous the situation had become between them. What was he waiting for?

Without giving it another thought, he placed his hand on top of hers and gently squeezed. He kept staring at the black outlines of the mountains, barely visible under the dark-blue night sky, anticipating her reaction. Harlow scooted closer, pressing a leg against his and resting her head on his shoulder. Months of agonizing and awkwardness vanished in an instant—the barrier finally gone.

"I really wish you didn't have to go," said Harlow. "I'm worried."

"We'll be fine," he said, leaning his head against hers. "It's a simple reconnaissance mission."

"That's what you said about the last bunker," said Harlow.

"Now we know what to expect," said Decker. "And if things get out of control, Bernie will scoop us out of there."

"You can't keep doing this," she said. "It's only a matter of time before something gets too far out of control for you to handle. You have a lot of people counting on you."

"I know," said Decker. "Just give me a little more time. If this doesn't bring down Harcourt, I'll back off."

"Backing off isn't good enough. The moment you smell blood, you'll be back in the hunt," said Harlow.

Decker nodded. She was right. Short of hiding in the mountains, with no television, internet, or phone, he'd always be looking for the next clue to find Harcourt.

"I don't know anything else right now. I've obsessed over revenge for close to three years. Every minute of every day—it's there. No matter where I am, or who I'm with," he said.

"I think if you spend a little more time with the right person, you'll find it easier to dial that back a few notches—to a point where it doesn't consume you," said Harlow.

"You mean like a girlfriend?" he said, leaning into her.

She squeezed his hand. "I'll get you set up on Match.com as soon as you get back."

"That should be a fun profile to write," said Decker.

"Yeah. Your past might raise a few red flags," said Harlow, laughing.

"Just a few," he said.

"No. I was thinking that—aside from the obvious candidate, sitting next to you on the hood of this car—you should spend some time with Riley, up in Idaho."

Harlow was right. He'd been up to visit her a few times, mostly staying away for security reasons, but it wasn't enough. Seeing Riley evoked painful memories for both of them, which were just as quickly washed away by the new memories they created together. He needed to spend more time with her, creating those new memories, for both of their sakes, but mostly hers. Decker took a deep breath and exhaled, neither of them speaking.

"I have an idea," said Decker. "When I get back from this little soiree, I want to bring you up to Idaho to meet some people."

"Meet some people? Sounds like you're introducing me to your mob contacts."

"Funny. To meet Riley and my parents," said Decker.

"I'd like that a lot," she said, lifting her head.

He turned toward her, their faces slowly drawing closer in the dark. A loud bang on the side of the SUV startled both of them, killing a moment that had been building for months.

This better be good.

"KILLER BEE is three minutes out," said Pierce.

"To be continued," said Decker, stroking her face. "Without interruptions."

She kissed him, lingering for a second before pulling away.

"Just get back in one piece."

"Sorry to break up this long overdue moment, but Bernie doesn't want to spend more than a minute on the runway. He likes to avoid drawing attention to his beloved C-123."

Decker hopped off the hood, then helped Harlow down.

"But he's fine with KILLER BEE as his call sign?" said Harlow. "Not exactly lying low with that one."

"It's better than his last call sign," said Pierce, getting in the back seat.

"What was that?" said Harlow, walking around the hood to the driver's side.

"Angry Jew," said Decker.

"How long ago was that?" she said.

"Not long enough."

Harlow drove them out of the parking lot and onto the tarmac, taking the taxiway to a point about a hundred feet from the runway. They wanted to give Bernstein plenty of room in case he couldn't stop the aircraft before the taxiway. The C-123 had a 110-foot wingspan, which would take up the entire width of the runway, extending a few feet past on each side. Better safe than sorry when it came to a forty-thousand-pound aircraft.

A few seconds after arriving, the deep buzz of the aircraft's two powerfully driven propellers washed through the SUV's open windows. The noise intensified as a dark shape displaying a red light and two white strobes came into view to the west. Decker tracked the aircraft as it banked and the green starboard wingtip light also came into view. When both red and green lights appeared evenly spaced between the center fuselage strobe, he knew the C-123 was headed straight for them. The aircraft descended at a frightening rate, headed for the single ground light indicating the southwest end of the runway.

The moment the darkened aircraft leveled, its nose lights illuminated the runway, tires screeching a few seconds later. The cargo aircraft slowed dramatically and could have stopped well short of the taxiway—its short landing distance one of the C-123's many selling points. Bernie rolled about fifty feet past them before stopping.

"That's it!" said Pierce. "Drive up to the ramp in back."

"He's not going to turn around?" said Harlow, speeding toward the runway.

"He says he has enough room to take off," said Pierce.

"I've seen him take off with half this much runway," said Decker.

Harry Bernstein met them at the edge of the cargo ramp.

"I knew you two would be back in business!" he said, shaking Decker's hand.

"Good to see you, Harry!" said Decker. "Thanks for fitting us in on such short notice."

"Thanks for paying me extra to do something I probably would have done anyway," said Bernstein, laughing.

"I'm spending someone else's money this time," said Decker.

"Even better!" said Bernstein before glancing at the pile of gear at the bottom of the ramp. "That's all you're bringing? What about parachutes?"

"I thought—" started Decker.

"Just kidding!" said Bernie. "I have everything you requested—including the Mexican bandito! Garza! Come out and say *hola!*"

"*No comprendo*, old man!" announced a voice deep inside the red-lit cargo bay.

"Sounds like the two of you have hit it off," said Pierce.

"We go way back," said Bernstein. "Good dude. Former Delta guy. Did some countercartel work with Delta that led to El Chapo's 2014 capture. He knows his way around Me-hi-co."

"Sounds good," said Decker, turning to Harlow. "I want to introduce you to Harlow Mackenzie. She's been the driving force behind both of these missions—and a lot more."

"Special lady kind of more?" said Bernstein.

"You could say that," said Decker.

"In that case," he said, shaking her hand, "it's both an honor and a pleasure to meet you."

"Likewise," she said. "Love your call sign, by the way."

"I don't like it as much as the last one," said Bernstein.

"Fifteen seconds!" said Quincy Rohm, his female crew chief, from the top of the ramp.

"She's always breaking my balls," said Bernstein. "Time to load up and roll out of here. And Ms. Harlow?"

"Yeah?"

"They're in good hands," he said. "I'll have them back in a few days."

"Thank you," she said, before nodding at Decker. "Watch yourself out there."

"I will," said Decker, heaving an overstuffed rucksack onto each shoulder. "Call you tomorrow."

"You better," she said, stepping back toward the SUV as the propeller blast intensified.

As Decker walked up the ramp, Pierce came around the other side of the hood, carrying two long nylon duffel bags containing their weapons.

"I'll make sure he doesn't do anything stupid!" said Pierce.

"I was just about to say the same thing," said Decker.

Harlow shook her head and got in the SUV, backing it up and reversing direction. Decker watched the vehicle's brake lights retreat down the runway, turning onto the taxiway moments before the ramp closed. He took a seat next to Pierce and scanned the cargo bay, noting several coffin-size plastic cases strapped to the deck. A short, stocky guy got up from the bench on the opposite side and approached them.

"Dave Garcia. It's an honor to be working with you guys," he said, shaking their hands. "Bernie calls me Garza. I'm good with whatever's easiest."

"Garza works," said Decker. "Sounds like Bernie picked the right guy for the job. Delta? El Chapo?"

"All of the above," said Garza. "Some crazy-ass stories."

"Well. We're going to have a lot of time to kill tomorrow," said Decker. "Plenty of time to pass a few crazy-ass stories around."

Bernie's voice squawked over the loudspeaker. "Hang on back there. We're going vertical as soon as this thing leaves the runway."

The crew chief shook her head before giving the flight attendant motion for buckling your seat belts. Decker tightened his lap belt and grabbed the bench strut behind his head as the aircraft picked up speed. He'd forgotten how flying with Bernie was like spending a day at a Six Flags amusement park.

CHAPTER FIFTY-TWO

Duncan remained seated when the restaurant's host, a serious-looking gentleman in an expensively cut suit, escorted Bob Saling to his table at the edge of the covered patio. The two men shook hands, and Saling took the seat next to him, his eyes darting nervously toward the marina beyond the patio.

He glanced over his shoulder, catching the green running light of a sailing boat headed out of the creek and away from the restaurant. Other than the occasional boat coming in or out of the creek, the restaurant's patio felt private enough for a quiet dinner among colleagues.

He'd intentionally made a nine thirty reservation, assuming most patrons would either be done with dinner and gone or just finishing up. The restaurant normally closed at ten but would remain open as long as they required. The perks of three influential lawmakers meeting in a DC-area restaurant.

"Senator Duncan. Congressman Saling," the host said, smiling deeply. "It's truly an honor and a privilege to have you dining with us tonight. You have the restaurant to yourselves, as requested. Will there be anyone joining you?"

"Yes. Senator Margaret Steele should be here any moment," said Duncan.

"Would you like to order drinks before she arrives?"

"Yes. Hold off on the menus until she joins us."

"I'll send your waiter out immediately to take your drink order."

"No need. What kind of bourbon do you have?" said Duncan.

"I have an Elijah Craig Small Batch. It's excellent served neat, or mixed into an old-fashioned or Manhattan."

"How does that sound, Bob?" said Duncan.

"That's a nice bourbon. We should try it neat. Then move on from there," said Saling.

"Then it's settled. Give us a double, neat—to start—and I'll have a Manhattan, straight up," said Duncan.

"Ditto for me," said Saling.

Duncan glanced at his watch. The deed should be done at this point. He had no idea where they would do it, but part of him hoped he'd hear the sirens responding to Steele's "accident." Anything to confirm or even suggest that she was no longer a threat. They had to maintain the pretext of a dinner meeting gone terribly awry, and the likely scrutiny afterward. A search on his phone's internet browser for "Senator Margaret Steele car crash" before the accident hit the news would raise questions.

"Do you think it already went down?" said Saling.

"I sure as hell hope so. We're right on time, and she didn't indicate she was running late."

"Will they call when it's done?"

"No. No contact at all," said Duncan. "Nothing that can be traced back to us."

"I kinda feel bad for the dumb bitch," said Saling.

"Don't," said Duncan. "Look at it like we did her a favor. Now she's in heaven with her husband and daughter."

They burst into laughter.

"Good one, Paul," said Saling. "Just remind me not to get on your bad side."

"In a few weeks, I won't have a bad side," said Duncan. "Think Bill Gates money."

"Yeah. Hard to get cranky with that kind of money stuffed in the mattresses."

"How long do we have to wait before looking at the menus?" said Saling. "I'm starving."

"I think we should have our drinks first. Wait for thirty minutes," said Duncan. "Then inform our host that we'll go ahead with dinner, despite Senator Steele's unexplained absence. Maintain the illusion."

"I'll be eating my napkin before thirty minutes."

"You'll be on your second Manhattan. Maybe your third," said Duncan. "Feeling no pain."

Their drinks arrived a few minutes later, expertly placed on the table by their host. When he'd disappeared inside, Duncan raised the thick crystal tumbler filled halfway to the top with his favorite elixir and nodded.

"To Southern Cross," said Duncan.

"To getting rid of that pain in the ass for good," said Saling, clinking his glass.

"Hear, hear," said Duncan, taking a long pull of bourbon.

"What are we celebrating?"

Duncan turned toward the voice that posed the question and inhaled, sending the bourbon down the wrong pipe. He erupted in a coughing fit that lasted several seconds as Senator Margaret Steele approached their table from the dockside entrance. Several serious-looking men fanned out across the patio, taking positions at the various entry points. Duncan coughed intermittently as she took a seat across from them. Saling just stared at him like an idiot.

When Steele had settled into her chair, she touched her earlobe and nodded, like she'd received a message. Her hand seized Duncan's Manhattan, raising it above the table.

"To Southern Cross," she said, smiling wickedly.

When neither of them responded, she spoke again. "To getting rid of that pain in the ass for good?"

Duncan found himself speechless. Partly because he was afraid he'd start coughing again. Mostly because he couldn't believe he was looking at someone who should be mangled and dead in a car crash right now.

"Let's try this," she said. "To feeling sorry for that dumb bitch."

Jesus. She'd somehow heard everything. He opened his mouth.

"How?"

"How?" she said, taking a healthy sip of the confiscated drink. "How what?"

When he didn't answer right away, she continued. "How am I sitting here when I should be dead? How can I hear what you said in private just minutes ago? How did I figure out you planned to kill me in the first place?" she said, before glancing at Saling. "Bob. You look like you're about to cry. Have some dignity."

Saling indeed looked like he might burst into tears at any moment. In all truth, Duncan wanted to cry. Steele clearly had gotten the drop on them somehow, and her tone indicated that she wasn't fucking around.

"Since the two of you seem tongue-tied right now, I'll go ahead and explain exactly what is going to happen moving forward. I strongly suggest you listen, because I won't repeat this offer."

"Offer?" said Saling.

"Two words total so far. My nine-month-old grandnephew has more to say at the table than you two notorious windbags," she said. "Here's the limited-time offer. Expires in about ten minutes."

"Margaret, I don't know what you think is going on here, but—"

"Save it," she said, shutting him down instantly. "And before you get any funny ideas about escaping or calling the cavalry, take a look around you. My security team has the entire property locked down, including a sizable force at the entrance, in case your murder team decides to come looking for me."

"What do you want?" said Duncan. "Name your price."

She shook her head and took another drink. "My price is both of your resignations, effective tomorrow. Tonight, you're going to connect the few dots I haven't connected regarding Southern Cross. Give up the entire plan."

"I can't do that," said Duncan.

"You can and you will," she said. "Both of you will, or I'll go through back channels to make sure the Sinaloa Cartel knows you were instrumental in whatever plot unfolds against them. I'll make sure Jacob Harcourt understands that you're responsible for what's happening right now outside Ciudad Juárez, at the second weapons depot. And if you somehow survive the rest of the week, I'll make sure to put a permanent death marker on both of your heads. I'm done playing games with people like you."

"What do we get?" said Saling.

"Jesus," muttered Duncan.

"What do you get?" she said. "You get to live—with your fortunes intact—if you give me everything. Leave anything out, and the deal is off the table."

"It sounds like a reasonable deal," said Duncan, downing his entire drink.

"I suppose so," said Saling, pausing for a moment. "What's going on at the second site?"

She grinned and got up from the table. "Ryan Decker is what's going on."

Duncan's head started to swim, and it wasn't from the double bourbon he'd thrown back.

"Enjoy the dinner and drinks. They're on me. I reserved the entire restaurant for this very special occasion," she said. "When you're done, my people will transport you to a secure location, where you'll speak with my colleagues about Southern Cross. You'll stay there until the morning, for your own safety, and to give Decker more than enough time to take care of business at the second site."

Saling started to say something, but Steele cut him off. "Don't worry. I've arranged five-star accommodations, and we've already notified your wives that you'll be away. Remember. Don't leave anything out. The people you'll be talking to have already connected most of the dots."

Steele departed, leaving them momentarily speechless, until they saw her waving at them from a sizable powerboat that slipped away from the marina.

"Do you believe she'll honor her half of the deal?" said Saling. "Not turn us in?"

"Not here. They can obviously hear us."

"We have to talk about this!" said Saling.

"Not here!" said Duncan, before leaning closer to him and whispering, "I'm not too worried."

"Really?" said Saling, grabbing his bourbon. "Because I'm pretty fucking worried right now."

Duncan grabbed him by the collar of his jacket and pulled him close, whispering as quietly as possible.

"It doesn't matter what happens here or down there. Nothing can save the Sinaloa at this point. When they're gone, and the rest of the cartels start paying all of us out of their new profits, we'll have enough money to buy our way out of whatever trouble Steele thinks she can cause us. I'm still getting the all-you-can-eat crab, by the way. I suggest you do the same. Drag this night out as long as we can."

He deliberately left out the morose joke about it possibly being their last night—alive.

CHAPTER FIFTY-THREE

Decker stood at the top of the C-123's ramp, waiting for Bernstein to flip the jump indicator from red to green. A quick look beyond the ramp gave him zero reference. No lights on the ground. No visible horizon. Just an inky-black abyss waiting to swallow him.

"Fifteen seconds!" yelled the crew chief.

He glanced to the right and gave her a thumbs-up.

"Final comm check," said Decker.

They wore hands-free, voice-activated throat microphones, which converted vocal cord vibrations into words over the radio net.

"Pierce is good."

"Garza copies."

"I have everyone loud and clear," he said. "Check in again once your chute is open and you've stabilized your flight."

"I plan on talking the entire way down," said Pierce.

"Don't make me regret choosing a HAHO jump," said Decker.

"Any time you arrange for me to jump out of anything higher than the driver's seat of my Jeep, I'm going to make you regret it," said Pierce.

The indicator light flashed red twice before changing to green. He looked to the crew chief, who nodded.

"See you on the ground," said Decker, walking steadily down the ramp.

"Not if I see you first," said Pierce.

When Decker reached the edge, he leaned forward and dived into the darkness, spreading his arms and legs into a position that quickly stabilized his free fall from the aircraft. He mentally counted to fifteen before reaching into his harness and removing the pilot chute, which was ripped out of his hand by the force of his descent.

The RA-1 Intruder parachute instantly deployed, jolting him. For a brief moment, it felt like he'd stopped falling entirely, the relative difference in speed between free-falling and a gentle descent initially too stark for his brain to accurately process. Decker glanced up and determined that the rectangular black parachute appeared intact. He pulled his helmet-mounted night-vision goggles down over his face and took a closer look at the canopy and riser lines, confirming his initial assessment that the parachute had deployed without incident.

Decker reached up and grabbed the toggles, gently pulling each of them to test the parachute's maneuverability. When he was satisfied that the toggles worked as advertised, he lowered the navigation board attached to his chest and angled it so he could easily glance down for updates.

The backlit, GPS-linked map screen indicated he was facing the wrong direction, prompting him to execute a 180-degree turn to face due east. The change in direction brought two clusters of distant ground lights into view, which he assumed represented the only two notable population centers within forty miles. Columbus, Texas, to the north, and Puerto Palomas, Mexico, to the south. Their target lay roughly two miles beyond Puerto Palomas, along the border.

Bernstein had dropped them ten miles west at fifteen thousand feet, which would give them plenty of time and room to make any navigational adjustments required to safely reach the primary drop point. The RA-1 Intruder's easy descent rate would keep them in the air for thirty minutes, about eight minutes longer than it would take them to glide into position.

"Pierce checking in. Everything's good on my end."

"Copy that. Garza, you out there?" said Decker.

"Right above you. All good on my end," said Garza.

"Very well, gentlemen," said Decker, playing with the toggles to precisely match his direction with the drop zone indicator arrow. "Enjoy the very quiet ride down."

"You don't want to hear a few jokes?" said Pierce.

"No," said Decker and Garza simultaneously.

Thirty-three minutes later, Decker hit the desert floor running after a slightly mistimed parachute flare landing. After deftly coming to a stop without falling over, he quickly detached the parachute from the harness and stepped away from the risers before they could become tangled with his legs and sweep him off his feet.

"Not bad. You didn't pull a foot-ass-head landing this time," said Pierce. "I'm at your four o'clock."

"Funny," said Decker, looking over his shoulder to locate Pierce.

He spotted him about a hundred feet away.

"Right above you," said Garza.

A swooshing sound rustled above him, Garza's dark form gliding past. The former Delta Force operator hit the ground harder than Decker had expected, tumbling for a moment before standing up.

"That was graceful," said Garza.

"You okay?" said Decker, slipping out of his harness.

"I think I broke my fragile ego," said Garza.

All Decker heard at first was "I think I broke . . ."

"Can you put weight . . . Funny. You scared me for a second."

"Pierce said you like jokes," said Garza.

"I told you he doesn't have a sense of humor," said Pierce.

They moved into a dry riverbed a few hundred feet west of the drop point and removed the extra layer of clothing they had worn for their time at higher altitudes. At fifteen thousand feet, the air temperature hovered just below freezing, sixty degrees colder than the air on the ground. Decker had started sweating profusely several thousand feet before hitting the drop point. By the time he landed, he felt like he might self-combust.

With the cold-weather layers removed, they prepped what little extra gear they had brought for the mission. The most important piece of equipment they carried, aside from their rifles, was the hand-portable radio frequency detector. The device had undoubtedly saved their lives at the first bunker, providing the only warning that some form of electronic surveillance device was active in the area.

Neither of them could have ever guessed that device would turn out to be a pair of suicide bomb–equipped spider bots. Decker doubted they would run into anything like that at an active bunker site. His best guess was that the two spiders had been left behind at the collapsed bunker to deter the casual intruder—and kill a more persistent one. Regardless, he wasn't about to take any chances.

The most exotic item they carried was the Zeus thermal-imaging scope attached to each of their rifles, always a handy piece of gear in a desert environment. The rest of their load out was fairly standard for an armed reconnaissance mission. Ballistic helmet with mounted night-vision goggles. No-frills plate carrier vests, housing front and back Level-IIIA body armor. Triple-stacked rifle magazine pouches attached to the carrier vest. Twelve magazines of thirty rounds each. Thigh-mounted pistol-holster rig. A shoulder-slung, hip-level pouch containing a smoke grenade, a block of C4 explosives with detonator, digital SLR camera with zoom, and a few emergency first aid items. Pierce wore an additional pouch stuffed with two sixty-round drums of ammunition. He would reprise his role as machine gunner if the situation significantly deteriorated.

Decker checked his handheld GPS receiver. "One-point-one-five miles. Heading zero-eight-four. Everyone hydrate and make any last adjustments to your rig."

"Not much cover out here," said Pierce.

"Yeah. It's completely different than last time," said Decker. "We'll have to lean heavily on the scopes. If anything stands out at all, no matter how small—we stop and observe."

He raised his rifle, nudging the night-vision goggles out of the way with the scope. A long scan of the eastern horizon beyond the riverbed raised no alarms.

"All clear for now. What do you think? Wedge or online?" said Decker.

"Online," said Pierce. "Fifty-foot separation. Maximize our ability to scan the threat axis."

"Heading out," said Garza.

They formed a line on Decker—Pierce and Garza each fifty feet to his sides—and started to walk toward the suspected bunker site.

CHAPTER
FIFTY-FOUR

After a long trek across mercifully easy terrain, they reached a thick stand of bushes a few hundred feet from the southern entrance of the presumed bunker. A skeptical Decker stared through his scope at the flat, scrub-infested ground. Unless the cartel had built an in-earth ramp leading down into the bunker, which was entirely possible, he didn't see any sign of regular human activity here.

"Anything on the RF detector?" said Decker.

"Not a single registered hit," said Pierce. "If something's out there, it's not transmitting regularly."

"Why would they put a bunker out here?" said Garza. "I mean, from what you've described, it made sense in the other location, with the hills and broken-up terrain. Mostly inaccessible by foot. Difficult to observe. Out here? Shit. You can see for fucking miles."

"Aerial photos showed a jeep trail approaching the US side of the border wall and disappearing," said Decker. "It reappears in Mexico, about a hundred yards south of the wall."

"It's really flat," said Pierce. "Those spiders will be on us in no time if they're out there."

"No cover from fragmentation," said Garza. "What's the estimated kill zone and casualty radius for one of those things?"

"I didn't get the impression the explosive charge was designed with fragmentation in mind," said Decker. "The overriding threat will come from blast pressure. If we see one, we drop down and hit it with a full magazine. Don't stop firing until it quits moving. The trick will be detecting it in time."

"Garza, I'm going to walk directly behind you with my hand on your vest," said Pierce. "I'm not taking my eyes off the RF detector's screen until we clear the area. It'll be the only early warning we get."

"Works for me," said Garza.

"If you get a signal, call out the relative direction," said Decker. "Then it's all guns up to face the threat."

Decker preceded them through the scrub, into the wide-open stretch that led to the suspected bunker. He walked forward slowly, scanning the ground ahead through his scope and occasionally checking the GPS unit.

"Anything?" said Decker when they reached the jeep trail.

"Nothing," said Pierce.

"Nada," added Garza. "You'd think they'd have a few sentries or something out here."

"Maybe this is the trick," said Decker. "To make it look like there's nothing out here, from the ground."

He lowered his night-vision goggles and followed the jeep trail north until it disappeared into the low-lying scrub about thirty feet away. If the cartel had camouflaged the entrance, they'd done one hell of a job.

"I'm going to check out the end of the jeep trail," said Decker. "Watch the RF detector and keep scanning for hostiles."

Decker walked down the center of the worn trail between the two wheel ruts, reaching the knee-high bushes. He kicked one of them, immediately determining that it wasn't part of the natural environment. The entire bush shifted a few inches and bounced back. *What the hell?*

He knelt next to the bush and grabbed it with his gloved hands, pulling it off the ground until something connected to its underside prevented him from lifting it. A few attempts to snap one of the branches yielded another discovery. The damn thing was plastic. The branches bent all the way back and snapped back into shape.

Further inspection of several more bushes revealed the same thing, prompting Decker to remove a flashlight and examine their anchoring system. A carabiner attached to the lowest part of the faux scrub was clipped to a stake driven deep into the hard desert ground. He rubbed his chin and surveyed the tightly planted field of plastic extending all the way to the pylon border wall.

"Gentlemen, unless I'm mistaken, which is entirely possible," said Decker, detaching one of the bushes and holding it up, "I don't think we're looking at a bunker here. I think it's just a road, hidden from sight by a few hundred plastic shrubs."

"What the hell?" said Pierce.

Decker stood up and stomped on one of the bushes, which had no lasting impact on its height or form.

"They could drive right over this and it springs back," said Decker. "Literally covering their tracks."

"Then where's the bunker?" said Pierce.

"Maybe there isn't one," said Garza. "And they just drive the weapons through to their destination. Hand that shit out on the streets."

"I highly doubt they're passing out Javelin missile systems on the corner of Revolución and Pico de Gallo," said Decker.

"I think that might be a racist statement," said Pierce.

"I like salsa enough to let it pass," said Garza.

"Careful, Brad. Garza's really starting to grow on me," said Decker.

"He can have the job. Please!" said Pierce.

"On a more serious note, should we do a full sweep of the area? Just to be sure?" said Decker.

"I think that would be prudent," said Garza. "But if they went to that much trouble to put down a field of fake plants over the jeep trail, I think we've found everything we're going to find."

"You're probably right, but let's be sure. Thirty minutes," said Decker. "If we don't find anything in thirty minutes, we'll call Bernie and ask for a surveillance run south of here. See where this jeep trail leads."

One very frustrating hour later, when Decker was convinced that a bunker didn't exist within the border area defined by the US military exclusion zone, he contacted KILLER BEE via satellite phone.

"Ready for pickup?" said Bernstein.

"Negative. We didn't find a bunker," said Decker. "We did discover a very well-camouflaged surface connection between the two jeep trails evident on the surveillance photos. On top of that, a vehicle-size section of border wall between the two trails has been modified to swing open on hinges. They just drove the shipments through and continued south on the jeep trail."

"You want me to take a look?" said Bernstein. "I'll have to file a flight plan with Mexican authorities, which shouldn't be a problem. Just an expensive one."

"Whatever it costs," said Decker.

"Don't tell me that," said Bernstein. "Makes me feel like I should be charging you more."

Decker laughed. "Repeat business, my friend. Think about all of the repeat business."

"Right. Right. I almost forgot," said Bernstein. "Hey. There's only one catch if I fly south. Once I'm in Mexican airspace, I can't fly back into the US right away. My flight pattern is suspicious enough as it is. Could be a few hours. Could be a few days. All depends on what the

FAA remembers about the last time my tail number came up in the system."

"I can live with spending some extra time in Mexico," said Decker. "We'll start walking south, along the trail, until you get back to me."

"All right. I'll be in touch shortly," said Bernstein. "You'd be surprised how fast I get calls when my text message starts with *twenty K USD in your pocket tonight*."

"That's all?" said Decker, ending the call and stuffing the phone in a cargo pocket.

"Sounds like we're taking a walk," said Pierce.

"More like a slow jog," said Decker. "From what I remember, the jeep trail intersects with the road coming out of Puerto Palomas about three miles from here. My guess is they're following a similar pattern and staging the weapons soon after they cross the border. Hopefully, Bernie will find an active site for us to explore."

"And if he doesn't?" said Pierce.

"Then he picks us up where the jeep trail ends," said Decker.

"After we jog three miles in all this gear," said Pierce.

"Garza, are you interested in a full-time position with our firm?" said Decker. "A job just opened up."

"You couldn't possibly carry on without me," said Pierce.

"I didn't say I was replacing you," said Decker, patting him on the back. "Just watering you down a little."

CHAPTER

FIFTY-FIVE

Juan Reyes stood in the middle of the warehouse's open bay door, justifiably nervous. The distant buzzing noise initially reported by one of his perimeter guards had returned. The sound had more of a deep rumble than the higher-pitched hum of a surveillance drone, leaving him unsure what to think. The Americans had flown drones in the area over the past few days, probably to make sure their precious shipment was under proper lock and key.

The double fiasco in California had obviously rattled everyone. He'd been sent by his boss to construct a rudimentary airfield and sit on the shipment with his best men until the weapons could be distributed to the various strongholds throughout Juárez Cartel territory. Launching points for the upcoming war against the Sinaloans.

Half of the weapons were already on their way, and in a few hours, a heavily guarded convoy of trucks would arrive to load the bulk of the remaining crates. Aircraft would start to land tomorrow morning to take what was left to a few sites deep inside Sinaloa territory.

Still, the sound above him, somewhere in the vast, star-filled sky, felt out of place. Several scenarios flashed through his alert and paranoid mind, the most dramatic involving a few hundred Mexican Army paratroopers landing on the hard-packed dirt airstrip just beyond the glow cast by the warehouse lights. Maybe he should turn them off. The building must look like a beacon in an otherwise darkened landscape—inviting trouble from the sky.

No. It didn't matter whether the lights were on or not. If the Mexican president decided to rain soldiers down on him from the sky, there was little he could do about it. The forty-odd men at his disposal would put up a good fight, but they were no match for the kind of men the military would send. The best he could hope to accomplish was to make it a costly operation for the army. With that in mind, he made a decision about his defensive posture at the warehouse.

"Quique!" he yelled.

A portly man came running out of the air-conditioned office, clumsily navigating his way between several hastily arrayed picnic tables that were crowded with heavily armed men. Enrique Valdez wasn't the picture of composure and strength one might expect from a cartel security head, but he had what most of the *soldados* down here lacked—a steel trap for a brain, forged by years of maneuvering and surviving with his wits.

"*Sí*, Jefe?" said Valdez, huffing a little from the sprint.

"Maybe we should pull the perimeter patrols closer to the warehouse," said Reyes. "In case we're attacked. Give us a better chance of inflicting maximum death and mayhem when they land."

Valdez looked up at the dark sky. "If they drop paratroopers on us, they'll pick a drop zone several hundred meters away, where they can land uncontested and organize before hitting the warehouse. If we keep the men out there, we might get lucky and cause some havoc with the landing. Either way, we're pretty much screwed."

"If the result is the same, I'd feel better dying among company," said Reyes. "Bring half of the perimeter guards in. We'll hold our breath until the trucks arrive in a few hours."

"Sounds good, jefe," said Valdez. "I'll bring them in immediately. If it's not the army up there, what could it be?"

Reyes cupped his ears, no longer hearing the sound. He shook his head.

"Whatever it is, it's gone for now," he said. "No sense in worrying about something out of our control."

CHAPTER FIFTY-SIX

Sweating profusely and nearly out of breath, Decker entered the coordinates he'd written on a small notepad into his GPS receiver and pointed it in the direction it indicated—noting a faint glow in the distance.

"The good news is that our target is a half mile away," said Decker. "A single warehouse with a dirt airstrip running in front of it. A new airstrip, possibly still under construction, from what Bernstein could tell. It doesn't show up on Google Maps, and he identified a small fleet of graders, bulldozers, and compactors parked next to a construction trailer."

"The bad news?" said Pierce.

"Thermal imaging indicates it's a very active site. Twenty-four hostiles on patrol, evenly spread in every direction. Four of those are positioned about a hundred yards from the warehouse, along the dirt road connecting the site to the main road leaving town. He made a second run at a lower altitude to get a look inside the warehouse. At least a dozen more are clustered around a set of picnic tables on the southern side. Several rows of crates fill most of the warehouse."

"Forty or so hostiles, most of them spread out all over the place?" said Garza. "This should be fun."

"Any chance he got some close-up shots of the crates?" said Pierce. "Save us a trip?"

"No such luck," said Decker. "There's one more piece of bad news. He had to drop the Fulton rigs pretty far away from the site to avoid detection by the patrols."

"The fact that you didn't give us a number tells me it's really bad news," said Pierce.

"Am I that easy to read?"

"Takes a little while to crack the code," said Pierce, turning to Garza. "But once you do, he's around the *See Spot Run* level."

"Funny," said Decker. "A thousand yards beyond each end of the airstrip, straight north or south."

"How long is the strip?" said Garza.

"Estimated fifteen hundred feet," said Decker. "We're looking at a twelve-hundred-yard trek to either of the recovery packages."

"Three-quarters of a mile," said Pierce. "Possibly under fire. That's a stretch."

"We've done it before," said Decker.

"Not on foot."

"Bernstein identified several SUVs parked behind the warehouse," said Decker. "Maybe we'll get lucky and find a set of keys."

"Not much of a strategy," said Pierce.

"If the op goes sideways, we can shake down some of the corpses until we find a set of keys," said Garza. "Use the fob to locate it."

"Still not feeling it," said Pierce.

"These are contingencies," said Decker. "If we can get inside the warehouse without drawing attention, we'll snap some photos and slip away. Meet up at whichever end of the runway looks the quietest."

"Meet up?" said Pierce.

Decker crouched low and opened his notebook, cupping his flashlight to direct a small beam at a crude drawing he'd created while listening to Bernstein's description of the site.

"Here's what we have. Airstrip runs north-south in front of the warehouse, which faces east," said Decker, pointing at the drawing. "Vehicles here, behind the warehouse. Construction stuff by the south end, along with the trailer. The *X*s represent sentries. Circled *X*s appear to be static sentries."

"Lots of room to slip through," said Garza. "Except for the guy behind the warehouse."

"Yeah. One way or the other, we'll have to deal with him," said Decker, pointing at another guy situated fifty yards west of the vehicles. "Same with this one."

"Lots of guys on patrol," said Pierce. "It'll require us to constantly reassess the approach."

"Right. And just in case things go sideways on that approach, or once we reach the site," said Decker, "I think you should take a position across the airstrip, directly in front of the warehouse bay door. At roughly a hundred yards, you'll be able to wreak havoc on the group inside. Fortunately, the ground cleared to flatten the airstrip has been piled up in several berms along the runway, giving you cover from warehouse gunfire if you have to make a quick escape. You could even set up between two berms to give you cover from any fire originating from the far perimeter guards east of the strip."

"That certainly falls in the good news category," said Pierce.

"Well, don't celebrate yet," said Decker. "It appears that they've posted two sentries on the berms, spaced about five hundred feet apart. You'd have to deal with them before you start shooting."

"Could be worse," said Pierce. "Tell me it doesn't get worse?"

"It doesn't," said Decker. "Unless they all have night vision. The cartels are extremely well funded."

"They're not as well equipped or organized as they're often made out to be," said Garza. "I can't remember one instance of them using night-vision equipment during my time down here. That said, we need to consider the possibility that some of them might have it, especially given the treasure they're guarding. Something to keep in mind when crossing a dark stretch where you'd normally feel safe."

"We'll put our suppressors to good use in that case," said Decker.

"With that cheery piece of advice in mind," said Pierce, "I think it's fair to assume that I'll need a good hour or more to get into position once we reach the site."

"Whatever it takes. We're not in a hurry." Decker stood up. "Check and recheck your gear. We'll head out in a few minutes."

"I thought we weren't in a hurry," said Pierce, patting his shoulder.

"*Hurry* is a relative term," said Decker.

While Pierce and Garza made final adjustments to their gear, he raised his rifle and pointed it toward the light, seeing the outline of a structure in the distance. A few hot spots stood between his team and the warehouse, which they'd either evade or eliminate. It all depended on how the situation unfolded. He slowly shifted the rifle to the right, spotting the four-man roadblock. The group was definitely something to keep in mind if a gun battle erupted—among a hundred other variables that could derail their escape.

Chapter Fifty-Seven

Decker centered the thermal sight's digital crosshairs on the sentry's upper chest and slowed his breathing just enough to cut down on the subtle movement his body would impart to the rifle. When the stock recoiled into his shoulder, Decker knew instinctively that it had been an accurate shot. He just needed to verify it—Garza was busy watching the next closest sentry for a response.

A quick search with the sight found the sentry motionless on the ground between two of the SUVs. A sizable hot spot on the hood and windshield next to him indicated that the bullet had found its mark.

"No reaction from the other guard," said Garza, who lay a few feet behind him.

"Copy that," said Decker. "Looks like a clean hit on my target. Pierce?"

"Nobody moved inside or outside of the warehouse."

"Did you hear it?" said Decker.

"Barely," said Pierce. "Wasn't distinctive at all."

Decker felt relieved. The suppressors they had chosen were top-of-the-line, and the magazine he had loaded for the warehouse approach contained subsonic ammunition, but the rifle still made enough noise to be heard from a distance—particularly to a trained ear. Fortunately, the number of sentries out here had been significantly reduced since Bernie passed along his observations. The downside was that Pierce reported twice the original number of men inside the warehouse, making the most important part of their job even more difficult.

"Moving up to the vehicles," said Decker, stepping forward.

He swept his rifle back and forth across the back of the warehouse as they approached the line of SUVs and Jeeps. When they reached the vehicles, Garza turned and faced the nearest guard, who sat on a rock a hundred yards to the south. Decker examined the sentry he'd shot, immediately determining he was dead. His bullet had struck the top of his sternum, likely killing him instantly. Lifeless eyes stared up at him, a grim reminder that this was all too real. One mistake and that could be him.

"Sentry confirmed KIA," said Decker. "Help me stuff him in the back of the Jeep."

Decker and Garza lifted him up and dumped him in the back of the open Jeep, taking his radio before covering him with a thin serape blanket they found in the back seat. They scanned the visible area around them with their thermal rifle scopes, verifying that nothing had changed.

"How is it looking out front?" said Decker.

"No change," said Pierce.

"Can you see the sides of the warehouse?"

"Negative. I can just barely see the northern side," said Pierce. "Best I could do without losing sight of both."

"Copy," said Decker, turning to Garza. "We need to clear that."

"I got it," said Garza, moving swiftly and silently behind the SUVs.

Decker covered the guard on the rock as Garza edged toward the warehouse corner. After a quick peek, Garza returned and crouched next to Decker between two of the vehicles.

"It's clear. I saw a window air conditioner and heard it running," said Garza. "Someone important must be here. In an office or something."

"I'd love to get my hands on someone important," said Decker. "Someone we can deliver to the FBI or Congress to shed some more light on this conspiracy."

"Don't get any ideas," said Pierce. "Snap some pictures, plant the C4, and get the fuck out of there."

Decker was intrigued by the idea but immediately aware of its shortcomings. The Fulton Recovery packages, like the one he'd used to escape Harcourt's estate nearly a year ago, were designed to extract three people—and three was pushing it. That left an odd man out, which was a veritable death sentence under the circumstances. Unless the odd man out could make it to the other Fulton rig. Bernie had dropped two, each nearly a mile away in opposite directions.

"Decker, do I have to spell out the obvious?" said Pierce.

"Three to a Fulton rig," said Decker. "But can Bernie grab two?"

"No. The anchor mechanism on the nose of the aircraft is spring loaded to grab one line," said Pierce. "I've gone over this with Bernstein before. There's no way to reset the mechanism without releasing the line."

"We could grab the head honcho and drive him out of here," said Decker, mostly just thinking out loud.

"How am I supposed to get across the airstrip in one piece?" said Pierce.

His question gave Decker an idea. One he'd have to arrange quickly. The timing would have to be perfect.

"I'm really concerned that you're taking so long to answer my question," said Pierce.

"I'm thinking."

"Garza, that usually means he's mulling over an exceedingly bad idea," said Pierce.

"I like the sound of that," said Garza.

"Trust me. You won't like what comes next," said Pierce.

"I need to call Bernie," said Decker. "I'm turning off my radio for a few minutes."

"That's even worse," said Pierce.

Chapter Fifty-Eight

The aircraft hum had once again drawn Reyes out of the air-conditioned office and into the sweltering-hot warehouse. He scanned the night sky, panning his head from left to right and back again. A futile gesture—but he was convinced it sounded closer this time. The men heard it, too, the mood around the crowded picnic tables taking on a tense vibe. The men had replaced loud, uneven banter with hushed conversations and an intense focus on their cigarettes.

A quick look at his watch momentarily gave him hope. The convoy would be here in less than an hour. Or was the aircraft waiting for the convoy? He folded his arms and stared into the darkness, silently cursing a sound that most certainly did not belong in the air above his warehouse.

"Jefe? Jefe?"

Reyes turned toward the office. Quique Valdez walked hurriedly in his direction. The man appeared to have broken into a full flop sweat, the thinning black hair on his head matted down on one side.

"What is it?" said Reyes.

The fact that Valdez didn't answer by yelling across the two dozen or so men who had immediately craned their heads toward him was not a good sign. Valdez skirted the tables and joined him at the corner of the bay door.

"Julio isn't answering his radio," said Valdez. "And Cesar doesn't see him by the SUVs."

"That's it?" said Reyes. "One guy didn't announce to the entire group that he's taking a dump? He's probably squatting out in the bushes somewhere."

"Julio is one of our best men," said Valdez. "That's why I put him at the back door. He follows procedures, and announcing that you're leaving your post, for whatever reason, is one of the most important procedures."

"Why are you bringing this to me?" said Reyes. "Figure out where he is. That's your job."

"I brought this to you because I'm concerned," said Valdez. "And I think we should put the security team on alert. I didn't want to do that without consulting you. We have twenty-plus nervous trigger fingers seated at those tables."

Reyes considered the implications of what his security chief had just told him. If he was right and something was amiss, it would be prudent to have everyone ready. Likewise, if Julio had just gone off to use the bushes and forgot to bring his radio, they'd have a warehouse full of twitchy *cabrones*. The men were already jumpy enough.

"Take one guy and check it out," said Reyes. "I'll be in the office."

"*Sí*, Jefe," said Valdez.

CHAPTER
FIFTY-NINE

Decker stood on his toes to push the one-and-a-quarter-pound block of C4 out of sight on top of a crate. Three rows over, Garza attempted the same trick but was unable to place the explosives package that high. Decker held up his index finger, signaling for him to wait, but the former Delta operator ignored him and gently tossed it the rest of the way. He froze in place, fully expecting the block and its attached detonator to tumble over the side and hit the dirt floor, drawing attention.

He shook his head and gave Garza the finger, getting a wink and an exaggerated thumbs-up in response. He was definitely growing on Decker. Bernstein hadn't steered them wrong with this guy. A short string of more serious back-and-forth hand signals set in motion the rest of Decker's highly improvised plan—move unobserved to the southern end of the warehouse and look for the office.

Decker peeked around the crates, seeing nothing beyond the long aisle between the stacks but the darkness swirling around the warehouse. He swiftly moved to the back of the next stack and crouched, nodding at Garza. Before Garza reacted, Decker's earpiece crackled, followed by Pierce's urgent voice.

"You have two men headed in your direction. One armed with an AK-47. No obvious weapon on the other," said Pierce. "They were just talking with the boss."

"Posture?"

"In a hurry, but not overly alarmed," said Pierce. "My guess is they're going to check on the sentry you nixed."

"Copy that. Talk us through it," said Decker, carefully letting his rifle hang by its sling. "We have nowhere to hide."

Garza met his glance, and they both drew fixed, double-edged blades from scabbards attached to their belts. He cursed himself for not insisting on a suppressed pistol. A semiautomatic .22 with a high-end suppressor would sound like a whisper. Now things were about to get up close and very messy. Knife messy. Not something he had a lot of experience with.

"They're headed into the row next to Garza. To the south. Round, unarmed guy first. AK-47 guy following," said Pierce.

"Am I clear to move back one stack?" said Decker.

Pierce had a straight-on view of this stretch of crates.

"You're clear."

Decker slid across the opening and stood across from Garza, who winked at him—looking entirely comfortable with the situation. They both knew how this would have to play out. Decker had drawn the short end of the stick and would have to deal with the second guy.

"Three. Two. One," said Pierce.

The first guy broke the plane of the crates and immediately turned right without looking in Decker's direction. He never really saw what happened to the man. His eyes were focused on the corner, body tensed for violent action. A rifle barrel appeared at waist level a few moments later, the rest of the man materializing behind it. Decker lunged at him, pushing the rifle aside and stabbing at the man's neck. The surprised Mexican instinctively flailed his arms, pitching the rifle but miraculously blocking the lethal jab. He screamed for help and stumbled backward, tripping over a crate.

Decker dropped the knife and raised his rifle. A single suppressed shot to the forehead collapsed the man onto his back. He turned to Garza, who whispered forcefully.

"Drag his ass back here," he said. "I'll create a diversion."

He lurched forward and grabbed the man's ankles, pulling him behind the stack of crates as the warehouse erupted with shouts.

"Pierce. What are they doing?" said Garza.

"Looks like most of them are waiting for instructions. A few have started to wander in your direction."

"I got this," said Garza, taking off for the back door.

When he got halfway there, he yelled in Spanish and sprinted back. All Decker understood was *ayuda*, or help.

"Looks like that worked," said Pierce. "Most of them are running across the warehouse toward the door."

Decker sneaked a peek. Several figures raced past the row, rifles and submachine guns pointed toward the northern end of the warehouse. He still wasn't sure how they were going to move south. If one guy noticed them sneaking from stack to stack, the diversion would backfire. They'd face gunfire from two directions instead of one. Not that any level of gunfire was advisable in a warehouse filled with antitank weapons, grenade launchers, and mines.

"I still see guys running by," said Decker. "It's too risky to move."

"We need to get out of sight before they reach the door," said Garza.

"You need a bigger diversion," said Pierce. "I think it's time for me to do my thing."

"A little earlier than I hoped, but that should do the trick," said Decker. "Make sure the boss man doesn't slip away. And that doesn't mean shoot him."

"Beggars can't be choosers in a gun battle," said Pierce.

"Just what we need right now," said Decker. "Confucius with a machine gun."

CHAPTER SIXTY

Brad Pierce had mere seconds to act. Not enough time to take care of the sentries perched on the berms a few hundred feet to his left and right. He'd have to deal with them later. Pierce flipped the two quick-release latches holding the thermal scope tightly to the rifle's top rail and yanked the scope free, tossing the ten-thousand-dollar device into the dirt without an afterthought. He flipped up the rifle's front and rear iron sights, centering them on the men who had run headlong into the crate aisle two down from Garza.

"Rounds out," he said, pressing the trigger.

Pierce sent three short bursts between the stacks, knocking the men flat, before shifting to a cluster of men who had almost reached the northernmost crates. Fearing they might effectively take cover behind them and reach the door, where they could shoot across the length of the warehouse at Decker and Garza, he unleashed a longer, sustained burst. Three of the Mexicans tumbled to the ground while the fourth turned to fire through the warehouse door. A single short burst shoved him against the stack of crates, momentarily pinning him against a bright-red mosaic of his own blood and tissue.

Gunfire erupted inside the warehouse as the cartel posse responded wildly to Pierce's fire. Bullets snapped overhead and thunked into the thick dirt berms on both sides of him, but none of it appeared to be directed at him. They were firing blindly into the darkness, Pierce's suppressor having done its primary job of concealing his precise location. Logically, they knew the bullets had come through the warehouse bay door, from the east, but that was it. Hopefully, the sentries on his flanks were just as clueless. He wasn't done with the warehouse.

"Pierce. This is Decker. We're on the southern wall of the warehouse."

"Copy that," said Pierce. "I need a few seconds to clear the berm."

"Hurry it up," said Decker. "KILLER BEE is two minutes out."

Pierce scanned his left flank for a few seconds, finally locating the cartel sentry, who lay flat on top of the berm, rifle pointed into the darkness to the east. The guy on the right flank was easy to locate and clearly confused, crouching on the eastern side of the berm, aiming west. Pierce activated the infrared pointer attached to the hand guard's rail and aligned the green laser with the first sentry's head. Visible only to night-vision devices, the sentry was unaware Pierce had targeted him. A single, suppressed shot kept it that way. He turned to the guy on his right flank and hit him twice in the side.

"All clear. Time to turn off the lights," said Pierce.

He aimed at the fluorescent lighting fixtures visible just below the top of the bay door and fired short bursts, moving from left to right until the warehouse was pitch-dark. Decker and Garza had simultaneously hit the lights he couldn't see from his position.

With bullets striking a little closer to home around him, Pierce detached the mostly expended sixty-round drum and replaced it with one of his two spares, intent on emptying it into the cartel posse as quickly and efficiently as possible.

CHAPTER SIXTY-ONE

Decker edged along the tall stack of crates facing the southern wall, his rifle pointed at its corner. The office wall stood directly ahead of him, his quarry possibly inside. At this point he had no idea what to expect when he rounded the corner. Hopefully, every ounce of the cartel's attention would be on the machine gun tearing the warehouse apart, allowing them to slip inside the office undetected. How they escaped the office with a prisoner was still an open question.

"Stand by for round two," said Pierce, and Decker moved the rest of the way.

The first few automatic bursts created a new round of chaos among the cartel gunmen, and Decker waited a few seconds for them to start firing back. When the staccato fire of a dozen or more uncoordinated shooters peaked, he activated his rifle's IR laser and rounded the corner, heading straight to the office wall. Garza remained at the edge of the crates, covering him during the short trip, his rifle cracking twice.

Decker gave him the signal and leaned around the wall, not identifying any immediate threat to Garza. The gunmen appeared entirely focused on Pierce's gunfire, which tore into the few men confused or stupid enough to be standing in the open, exposed to his gun. Pierce's

IR laser moved from man to man, a lethal fusillade of bullets following it. Not one to waste an opportunity to even the odds, Decker targeted a head with the green laser and fired a single shot that went unheard against the undisciplined cartel gunfire.

Garza fired on the run, hitting one of them in the back and knocking him forward, drawing the attention of the gunmen flanking him. Decker quickly drilled one of them through the face, but the second guy touched off a long burst of automatic gunfire with his submachine gun before Garza and Decker dropped him to the ground. The man's bullets struck the front corner of the office, most of them stopped by the corner beam. The few that passed through struck Decker like a hammer, knocking him into Garza.

"Son of a mother!" said Decker, his arm hanging limp at his side.

Garza pushed him out of the way and fired the rest of his rifle magazine into the warehouse within seconds.

"Can you move?" said Garza. "We need to roll."

Decker took a quick inventory of his body. Everything felt fine, except for his left arm and the hammer blows he'd taken to his upper and lower chest. He could barely draw enough air to answer Garza's question.

"Fine. Left arm is fucked," said Decker.

Garza tossed a smoke grenade about fifteen feet into the warehouse and reloaded, keeping a hand pressed against Decker to keep him in place. A hollow thump, followed by a hiss, spurred Garza into action.

"You still want the boss man?"

Decker nodded.

"Switch to your pistol and cover me," said Garza, disappearing around the corner.

Decker released his rifle and drew the Sig 320 from the holster on his thigh, following Garza to the office door. A gunman rushed out of the expanding chemical cloud, firing at the empty corner. He aligned the glowing tritium pistol sights center mass and fired three times, spinning him into a picnic table. A second man emerged from the smoke, squinting to see in the dark, his weapon pointing several feet to Decker's left. He pressed the trigger and knocked the man flat.

"Ready?" said Garza, perched in front of the door.

"Do it."

"Don't forget to duck," said Garza before kicking in the flimsy door.

They both dropped to the ground, the impact sending a shock wave of pain up Decker's arm. Dozens of bullet holes stitched the doorframe and wall, each releasing a beam of bright-green light as they punched through. When the shooting stopped, Garza hopped to his feet and peeked inside, firing a single shot with his rifle before turning to pull Decker into the office by his good hand.

The "boss" stood bent over in the far corner of the sparsely furnished office, gripping his right arm and moaning. Garza fired two more shots, killing the lights.

"Cover the door," said Garza, pushing a chair aside to get to the leader. "I don't think they'll shoot at the office with him in here."

Decker took a knee and aimed at the door, lifting his wounded arm far enough to check his stopwatch. Thirty-five seconds until Bernie landed. Smoke poured through the door, obscuring his view of the warehouse, but nearby voices, overcompensating for the gunfire-induced hearing loss, gave him the impression that the surviving cartel guards had surrounded the door. He glanced around the office, his eyes settling on the defiantly humming air conditioner.

"Buy us some time," said Decker, standing up. "Create a hostage situation."

Garza nodded and yelled something rapid and completely unintelligible to him, as Decker centered himself on the window. When he was lined up, he burst forward and front kicked the air conditioner clean out of the window.

"That's our exit," said Decker. "Toss him through."

Decker resumed his watch of the door while Garza manhandled the Mexican across the room and shoved him halfway through the window before pushing him all the way out.

"I'll help you through," said Garza before squirming through the open window and disappearing.

A murky shadow materialized in the doorway, moving slowly into the office. Decker remained perfectly still as two more slipped inside.

"*¡La ventana!*" yelled one of them.

Decker emptied the rest of his pistol magazine before diving headfirst through the window—and landing flat on his left side. The pain of impact knocked him senseless. All he could determine at the moment was that Garza stood several feet away, firing repeatedly at the wall above him, hopefully killing anyone who had tried to follow him to the window.

When Decker regained his senses several seconds later, he became acutely aware that Bernstein was on final approach—and they were still on the wrong side of the warehouse. He'd grossly underestimated the time it would take them to get through the warehouse and grab the cartel boss. He dug the satellite phone out of his pocket and called Bernie, who picked up almost instantly.

"Ten seconds out," he announced.

"How long would it take you to approach from the other side?" said Decker.

"Too long," said Bernie.

"All right. We need you to pick us up just south of the warehouse," said Decker. "We're in a bad way here."

"Make sure Pierce keeps that gun talking," said Bernie. "Or we'll never get off the ground. Start moving your ass right now."

"On the move," said Decker, signaling for Garza to take their prisoner diagonally toward the runway.

CHAPTER SIXTY-TWO

Pierce chucked his last ammunition drum out of the way and replaced it with a thirty-round magazine from his vest. He removed five additional magazines and placed them on the ground next to him for easy access so he could keep up the high rate of fire. Before the final festivities kicked off, he took another look behind him with the detached thermal scope—just to be sure none of the perimeter sentries had changed their minds. The three he spotted earlier had banded together after the shooting started and headed northwest toward Puerto Palomas. The area still looked clear.

As the deep thrum of KILLER BEE's engines intensified, he probed the warehouse's smoky interior with the infrared beam, not detecting any targets. The cartel guys had eventually figured out what he could and couldn't hit from his position between the berms, paying dearly for that knowledge. Of course, with Decker and Garza out of the way, he could stretch those limits by firing through the wall next to the open bay door. The bullets would pass right through.

Pierce didn't see a reason to aggravate them—yet. With their leader abducted, maybe the survivors would just keep their heads down and wait for everything to get quiet again. Go home alive. Movement near the left corner of the open bay door told him the last few seconds of the night would not go down as he hoped.

The aircraft engine noise crescendoed into an angry buzz somewhere on the southern side of the runway, indicating that KILLER BEE had landed and was reversing thrust to slow down. The sudden reverse of the propeller pitch always sounded like the damn thing was going to explode.

Almost on cue, several flashes erupted from inside the hazy warehouse. A torrent of bullets zipped past his head, thumping into the dirt a feet away. Way too close for comfort. There was something entirely different about that last barrage. Like they'd finally gotten their shit together—and were about to make a move.

He fired the entire magazine at the corner of the bay door, hoping to knock some sense into the group huddled behind it. He quickly reloaded and started to target single flashes deep inside the maze of crates. After two short bursts, a bullet ricocheted off the front of his helmet, shattering his night-vision goggles.

Pierce now stood on equal footing with the guys inside the warehouse. Actually, he was behind the curve, having relied on the night vision. Another bullet zipped inches from his head, reinforcing that theory. He grabbed the thermal scope from the dirt and scooted behind the berm, moments before a third and fourth bullet struck the ground he'd vacated. He definitely wouldn't tell Anna about this part of the operation.

"This is Pierce. Lost my night vision. One of those fuckers has me zeroed in. Moving down the berm to reengage with thermal scope."

A few extremely long seconds passed without a response as he jogged south toward the next break in the berm.

"Copy that. KILLER BEE is taxiing north. Almost to our position," said Decker. "He'll keep rolling down the runway and pick you up."

"Negative. Negative. We have a sharpshooter in the warehouse," said Pierce. "I need some time to take him out."

An argument broke out over the radio net between Decker and a member of the crew, lasting entirely too long.

"At least tell Bernie to slow down!" said Pierce, turning to climb up the berm.

Pierce detected a slight reduction in engine power by the time he'd reattached the thermal scope.

"Ten seconds," said Decker. "Then full throttle. Either you nail the sharpshooter, or you and I are hitchhiking home. I won't leave you behind."

"Ditto," said Garza.

Pierce slowly peeked over the top of the dirt ridge with the rifle, eye pressed into the scope. Pierce found the marksman immediately, a white-hot torso against a backdrop of dark gray. A flash obscured most of the figure, followed by an overhead snap. The guy must have a night-vision scope. There was no other explanation for how quickly he'd reacquired Pierce.

A two-sentence exchange between Decker and Garza came across the radio, momentarily distracting him. A second flash erupted before he could line up the shot, grazing the soft armor on his right shoulder.

"Son of a mother—"

Pierce pressed the trigger before the marksman could fire a third time. A beach ball–size hot spot appeared behind the marksman's body. The shooter somehow remained upright. Pierce fired again, knocking the man out of sight. The moment the gunman's thermal aura vanished, Pierce leaped up and crested the berm, sprinting toward KILLER BEE. He'd more than fulfilled his end of the bargain on this trip.

CHAPTER
SIXTY-THREE

Decker stood at the very edge of the C-123's ramp and tightened his grip on the aircraft's frame as Bernie increased speed. So much for ten seconds. He crouched, extending his good arm as far as it would go so he could gauge Pierce's progress. He'd meant what he said about not leaving Brad behind. If Decker determined he wasn't going to make it, he'd step off the ramp and take his chances on the ground with his best friend. He owed Pierce's family that much.

Garza sat cross-legged next to him on the ramp, bracing his elbows against his knees to create a stable firing platform for his rifle. He adjusted himself until he could point the rifle to the side of the aircraft. Decker hadn't seen that shooting position used since his days in the Marine Corps.

Decker backed up a little and took a seat next to Garza, pulling his knees up to his chest. He drew his pistol and ejected the magazine, letting it fall to the ramp before jamming the pistol between his thighs, grip facing upward. After slapping a spare magazine from a pouch on his belt into the magazine well, he took the pistol and assumed a firing grip.

A single gunshot echoed across the runway, drawing their attention to the berm on the starboard side of the aircraft. Decker peered into the furious dust storm kicked up by the C-123's powerful propellers, searching for Pierce, but came up empty. The monochromatic image created by his night-vision goggles was a washout. He could barely see past the wingtips.

A quick glance on the other side of the lumbering aircraft painted a grim picture. They rapidly approached the warehouse, which was where Bernstein would push the throttle to maximum power—a necessity to reach takeoff speed by the northern end of the runway.

"Pierce. What's your status?" said Decker.

"Running through a sandstorm—in the dark!" said Pierce. "Care to light the way?"

Decker dropped the pistol in his lap and scrambled to find the flashlight in his cargo pockets. After a few frustrating seconds, he felt its sharp beveled end and yanked it free—activating the six-hundred-lumen light.

"Got it!" said Pierce. "I'm almost there."

Decker pushed his night vision out of the way and waved the light back and forth until a shadowy figure lurched out of the dark, barely missing the ramp. Pierce vanished in the dusty murk behind the aircraft before reemerging a few moments later. His friend pumped his arms and legs but started to fade back. Gunfire erupted from the warehouse at the same time, bullets snapping past the ramp and pinging off the fuselage. Decker turned to the crew chief standing just inside the plane.

"Tell Bernie to slow down for two seconds!"

She spoke rapidly into her headset, shaking her head and gesturing with her hands while bullets ricocheted inside the cargo bay.

"Garza. Help me up," said Decker. "I'm getting off."

Garza hopped up and started to pull Decker to his feet when the aircraft slowed significantly—and Pierce rocketed out of the darkness. He collided with Decker and Garza, knocking them flat on the ramp.

Decker slid halfway down, his feet and legs dragging along the runway. The friction between the ground and his body slowly pulled him out of the aircraft until Garza grabbed the collar of his tactical vest with one hand and tried to scoot them up the ramp with the other.

The plane accelerated, nearly yanking him free of Garza's grasp. He was about to tell Garza to let go, to keep them both from being pulled onto the runway, when the ramp began to rise. The moment his feet and legs left the ground, someone easily hauled him into the aircraft. He remained on his back for a moment, listening to the hollow metallic thunks of bullets striking the fuselage with his eyes closed as the plane raced down the rough airstrip. When he opened them, Pierce loomed over him, shaking his head.

"C4?" said Pierce.

"Shit," said Decker, digging the detonator out of the pouch on his hip.

He opened the red trigger safety and armed the detonator, waiting for the small green light before toggling the trigger. A deep crunch penetrated the fuselage, the aircraft shaking for a moment before stabilizing on its high-speed run. The C4 hadn't been enough to completely obliterate the warehouse, but it would damage the more sophisticated gear, like the Javelin missile guidance units.

"Are all of your ops like this?" said Garza, lying faceup next to him.

"We do this once a year!" said Decker.

"This is our second annual outing," said Pierce.

A loud crack passed overhead, causing both of them to flinch.

"Bernie is not going to be happy about this," said Decker.

"Every one of those pops is a minimum five-hundred-dollar repair!" said the crew chief, crouching next to Pierce. "It ain't cheap to get recertified for full cabin pressurization."

"We're good for it," said Decker.

Bernie's voice came over the loudspeaker. "I'm charging you a thousand per bullet hole, Decker, plus emotional damages."

They all laughed as he continued.

"Hang on to your fucking hats back there. This is about to get interesting."

Decker started to respond when the deck pressed hard against his back, momentarily pinning him down. As the C-123's angle of climb increased, he slid against the ramp, which had already locked shut. The three of them pressed against the angled metal slab for what felt like an eternity until the aircraft leveled out and he could feel his face again. He'd almost forgotten about his arm, until it very acutely and painfully reminded him that he'd been shot.

"Did they fall out the back?" said Bernie.

Bernie's crew chief, who had somehow managed to buckle herself into one of the nearby cargo seats, shook her head.

"No. They're still here."

"Not even one of them?" said Bernie. "Like maybe the ugly one?"

"No such luck."

"Maybe next time," said Bernie.

They all looked at each other.

"Pretty sure he means you," said Pierce.

"Sure as shit ain't me," said Garza.

"I think I need to find new friends," said Decker.

CHAPTER
SIXTY-FOUR

Decker contemplated the man sitting across from him in the C-123's cargo bay, a sense of helplessness creeping over him. The cartel leader had been nothing short of defiant, arrogant, and confident since they started questioning him. Not at all what Decker had expected. He'd just assumed that the sudden and dramatic abduction, combined with the threat of extrajudicial extradition, would scare the hell out of him. Instead, it had somehow emboldened him.

Maybe it was time to transition from verbal interrogation to something a little more physical. The man somehow read his face and started to chuckle. Garza translated as he spoke.

"There it is," he said. "I recognize that look. Been there a hundred times myself. When words fail—time to make it hurt. Ha! Well. Everyone has their breaking point, and I'm certainly no exception. I just don't see why you'd waste the time. Your government is behind everything you saw down there. Your politicians. Your military. Call them and ask the questions. See how fast you lose your jobs."

"Unfortunately for you," said Decker, "we're not with the government."

"Seriously?" said the man, laughing again. "I don't expect you to understand why, but that's the best news I've heard all day. I was convinced the Americans had screwed us over."

"No. That's our job," said Decker. "Starting with you."

"We'll see," said the man smugly. "This isn't some back-channel, slip-a-few-crates-of-guns-across-the-border deal we're talking here. You'll be lucky if they don't disappear you—or hire us to do it. Do your family, too."

Decker started to get up, his injured arm swinging back against the fuselage. He winced in pain and sat down again. One of Bernie's crew members, a Special Forces medic in another life, had cleaned and stitched the wound. The bullet had passed through his upper forearm, tearing muscle and ripping key tendons before exiting.

No arteries or major veins had been damaged, so bleeding had been easily controllable. A small miracle. He'd require surgery and extensive physical therapy when he got back, but that was the extent of it. Good as new in six months—or so. Until then he needed to keep his limitations in mind.

"I'm sure you'll pop up on the DEA or FBI's arrest list," said Pierce. "You'll be taken into custody as soon as we turn you in. I'm sure that kind of press will buy us some goodwill."

"And how exactly is that going to work? Are you going to tie a red bow around me and drop me off at one of their field offices, with a note explaining how you kidnapped me from Mexico, killed dozens of Mexican nationals in the process, destroyed property, and committed only God knows how many other transnational crimes flying in and out of the country?"

"We're still over Mexico," said Decker.

The comment had a cooling effect on their prisoner, which Decker found interesting. The man had actually hoped they were over the United States, where he clearly felt he might be safer than in his home country. He had an idea.

"Maybe we're barking up the wrong tree here," said Decker, waiting for Garza to translate.

"I don't think that translates very well," said Garza.

"Try this. Maybe we should deliver you to the Mexican attorney general," said Decker. "I know for a fact that her office would take you into custody without any questions asked. I imagine if we gave them our theory about the weapons shipments delivered to the Jalisco New Generation, Juárez, and Los Zetas cartels, they might be interested in stopping a near civil war on the border."

The man shook his head, a patronizing smile spreading across his face.

"Maybe it's time I introduced myself. Juan Reyes. Right-hand man to Sergio Cuevas, head of the Juárez Cartel."

"So?" said Decker.

"So it's obvious to me that you have no clue how things work in Mexico," said Reyes. "Do you really think the Mexican government is unaware of what we're doing? That they would lift a finger to help the Sinaloa, their longest sworn enemy, when the new financial arrangements that will emerge in a few weeks will be far more profitable? That you wouldn't be arrested the second you landed in Mexico City, only to disappear shortly after that?"

Decker didn't believe him. He'd most certainly seen fear in his eyes when Decker stated they were still in Mexican airspace. Why?

"You're done no matter what you do," said Reyes. "The moment you hit that warehouse, you signed your own death warrants. All of you. Kidnapping me extended it to your families. I'll make sure of that, unless you bring me back."

"Wait. If we bring you back, you'll forget about this?" said Decker.

"I'll leave your families out of it," said Reyes. "It's too late for all of you."

"What if we just push you out of the aircraft right now?" said Pierce. "How would anyone know we were involved?"

"I suppose nobody would," said Reyes. "Which brings us full circle back to where we started. The Juárez Cartel wins—regardless of whether I live or die."

And so did Harcourt. There had to be another way, and Decker felt it was connected to something Reyes had said earlier, or his odd response to Decker's Mexican airspace comment. He was afraid of something more than his own death—same as Decker. It was that simple.

"Mr. Reyes?" said Decker.

"*¿Sí?*"

"How many children do you have?"

The man's face went dead before Garza translated, his eyes morphing into reptilian slits. Decker had solved the riddle.

"Maybe we should bring you to the Sinaloa Cartel," said Decker. "Hear what they have to say about this supposedly unstoppable plan to wipe them out and take over their territory."

No response. Just a murderous look that made Decker want to recheck the zip ties holding Reyes to the seat.

"Mr. Sulu, set a course for Los Mochis," said Pierce.

Reyes cocked his head toward Pierce.

"It's a *Star Wars* joke," said Decker.

"*Star Trek*," said Pierce.

"*Star* something." Decker turned to Garza. "I wonder how hard it would be to set up an appointment with the head of the Sinaloa Cartel?"

Bernstein answered the question over the intercom. "No appointment necessary. The Sinaloa watch everything that comes in and out of that airport. This baby, with its extensive cargo-carrying capacity, guarantees us a welcoming committee. They've been trying to hire me for years."

"I assume you've said no?" said Decker.

"You don't tell the Sinaloa Cartel no, which is why I avoid landing anywhere they have a big presence," said Bernstein.

"Then how will you say no this time?" said Decker.

"Normally you buy a no with a six-figure payoff," said Bernstein. "But in this case, I think giving them Mr. Reyes will suffice. Might even buy us some credit."

"Pinche cabrones," hissed Reyes.

"No need to translate. Even I know what that means," said Decker. "Bernie, how much will it cost to divert to Los Mochis?"

"A shrimp dinner for me and the crew on the coast," said Bernstein.

"Sold," said Decker.

CHAPTER SIXTY-FIVE

Senator Steele took Decker's call, despite the late hour. The evening had taken a frustrating turn with Duncan and Saling, neither of whom had cooperated to the level she'd expected. She needed some good news, and to brainstorm a new approach.

"Ryan. Please tell me you have the evidence," said Steele. "And that everyone is all right. Sorry. I should have said that first. I'm just a little agitated right now."

"The team is fine. We took about a hundred pictures inside the warehouse," said Decker. "And brought back a souvenir."

"Direct evidence is even better," said Steele. "Duncan and Saling haven't coughed up anything. They're not as stupid as I had hoped. I should have gone through with the decoy idea and grabbed the team hired to kill me."

"Ma'am, you made the right decision with that," said Decker. "Someone completely uninvolved in this could have been killed."

"But now the case we have against them is circumstantial at best. They made a few incriminating comments at the restaurant, under surveillance that won't hold up in an investigation, but their computer systems are clean. Harlow's team couldn't find anything we can use.

Aside from several trips to Fort Bliss over the past year, which could easily be explained by their committee leadership roles, the only link we have between them and Joint Task Force North is West Point. Paul Duncan and Jeffrey McCall graduated from the United States Military Academy in 1987. Not much of a case."

"You know who else graduated from West Point in 1987?" said Decker. "Jacob Harcourt."

"No way."

"Doesn't prove a conspiracy," said Decker. "But it might not be a bad thing to throw at Duncan. See if it rattles him a bit."

"I'll try anything at this point," said Steele. "I'm not sure how much longer I can compel them to answer questions. I think they've accurately concluded that much of tonight was a bluff. The whole operation is called Southern Cross, by the way. One of them let that slip. Very appropriate, I suppose."

"Try this approach," said Decker. "Tell them that I raided the warehouse south of Puerto Palomas, destroyed the weapons, and grabbed Juan Reyes, the Juárez Cartel's number-two guy—and I'm taking him to the Sinaloa Cartel to explain Southern Cross. If they don't start talking, we'll have to include their names prominently in the discussion with the Sinaloans."

"I don't know if they'll buy it," said Steele.

"They'll buy it, because it's one hundred percent true," said Decker. "Juan Reyes is the souvenir I managed to grab, and he doesn't look happy about our new destination."

"Jesus. I assume you've considered the consequences of delivering him to the Sinaloa Cartel and exposing Southern Cross?" said Steele, excited about the prospect.

"We have, and I think it's the only way to stop Harcourt from rebuilding his criminal empire at this point," said Decker. "Reyes indicated that the Mexican government was very aware of the impending cartel war and that they would look the other way until it was finished—embracing the new order that emerged. Our only hope of stopping Harcourt lies with the Sinaloa Cartel."

"Isn't he living in Sinaloa territory, under their protection?" said Steele.

"That's the sweet irony of this," said Decker.

"Sweet indeed. Keep me in the loop," said Steele. "I need to have one last talk with Senator Duncan and Congressman Saling. See if revealing your new destination changes their attitude about cooperating."

PART FIVE

CHAPTER
SIXTY-SIX

Jacob Harcourt woke to someone hurrying into his bedroom from the open veranda. His hand instinctively grabbed the MP5K submachine gun hidden between the bed and the nightstand, pulled it clear, and flipped the weapon's selector switch to automatic.

"Mr. Harcourt," said a Russian-accented voice, "we have a problem. Time to go."

The voice belonged to Viktor Borodin, one of his personal security guards.

"Time to go where?" he said, reaching for the lamp.

"Don't do that," said the Russian. "Not a good idea. Fifteen vehicles are headed up the road from Los Mochis. They've already passed the first security checkpoint."

"That's impossible. We would have heard—"

"There was no shooting," said the Russian.

Which could only mean one thing. Someone had sold him out to the Sinaloa Cartel—and his Mexican security detail had stood down.

"All right. Get Feliks down to the airfield to prep the aircraft. That's our only way out of here. The escape trails will be crawling with Mexicans," said Harcourt. "Assemble the rest of your team outside this bedroom. I want to be on the way down to the airstrip in two minutes. Have you seen Pedro?"

"None of the Mexicans are where they're supposed to be," said Borodin.

"If you see him," said Harcourt, "kill him. Quietly, if possible. Kill any Mexicans you come across. Assume they're all in on this."

"Understood," said Borodin.

Harcourt walked barefoot across the cool marble floor, headed for his expansive, custom-crafted walk-in closet, where he slipped on clothes and boots and armed himself with something that packed a little more punch than this nine-millimeter submachine gun. He emerged a minute later dressed in jungle boots, cargo shorts, and a T-shirt—under a tactical vest loaded with 5.56-millimeter magazines. A leather messenger bag containing passports, credit cards, and wads of cash hung across his body. Night-vision goggles attached by a head strap and a compact, suppressed rifle held in the ready position completed the load out.

He was literally about to flee a multimillion-dollar estate with the clothes on his back—and one hundred thousand dollars in a mix of twenties and hundreds. More than enough to get him situated somewhere safe, as far away from Mexico as possible.

Outside the bedroom, he linked up with Borodin, who had sent two men ahead to clear the quarter-mile trail leading to the airstrip. Three of them, including Borodin, would accompany him to the plane, and two would follow a hundred feet behind to prevent an attack from the rear. Anything could happen on the trail, especially with Pedro's men unaccounted for, but the Mexicans were no match for Borodin's seasoned professionals.

The bugs attacked him the moment he stepped onto the trail, biting him mercilessly as the Russians moved slowly and methodically down the narrow path, panning their weapons back and forth to scan the dense foliage. Halfway to the airstrip, Harcourt heard suppressed gunfire. Four shots followed by silence—somewhere ahead of them.

They crouched below the level of the surrounding brush while Borodin spoke softly into his headset, still upright.

Harcourt reached up to pull down on his vest, not the least bit surprised when a warm spray hit his face and Borodin dropped like he'd been switched off. Had the Americans turned on him? Cut him out of the equation for some reason? This didn't feel like a cartel operation.

A bullet zipped past his head, striking the Russian behind him with a wet thud. He crawled over to examine the Russian, finding him face-down with a hole in the back of his head, legs twitching in the bushes. His last bodyguard fired more than a dozen suppressed shots down the trail, moving his rifle from left to right, before a single bullet caught him in the throat.

Harcourt didn't wait around to watch him die. He took off sprinting toward the house and the two remaining Russians—who would serve as little more than a speed bump for whoever was out there. Bullets chased him up the winding trail, snapping overhead. He didn't bother to fire back, knowing it would only slow him down. When he reached the two Russians, he suddenly understood that the bullets hadn't been chasing him. They'd killed the last two men on earth paid to protect him.

He knelt on the path, scanning the green image displayed by his night-vision goggles, unable to detect the assassins who had dispatched his entire personal security detail in under a minute. Still alive a few very long seconds later, Harcourt leveled his rifle with the tops of the bushes and flipped the selector switch to automatic—emptying the weapon in one long, deafening fusillade.

When no return fire reached out to touch him, he made a quick determination. They had no intention of killing him right away, or they would have done so already. The team that had so effortlessly killed his Russian bodyguards had been sent to prevent his escape from the Sinaloa.

"To hell with this," he muttered, reloading the rifle.

If this was the end, he was going down with a bellyful of the best scotch money could buy. He had no idea what the team out there had in store for him, and he had no intention of finding out—sober. Harcourt turned and ran for the house, his desire to access the Mexican teak liquor cabinet in his study burning bright.

When Harcourt arrived at the back patio, he ducked inside the door they had left open on the way out and hurriedly navigated the dark home to reach his place of refuge. He removed the night-vision goggles as he entered the study and tossed them aside, heading straight for the cabinet behind his desk.

Through the ceiling-to-floor windows overlooking the valley, he observed headlights weaving in and out of the distant trees. No doubt an emissary from Damaso Casales—on his way to pass judgment. Let them come. He'd be pleasantly drunk by the time the Mexicans reached the house, ready to turn the rifle on himself.

Chasing the exquisite scotch with a high-velocity rifle bullet made infinitely more sense than the alternative. The very recent memory of Nick Adler's protracted torture and interrogation at Borodin's hands sealed the decision. He'd lock the study and wait, pulling the trigger when they made a serious effort to breach the room.

He leaned the rifle against the desk and opened both of the cabinet doors, activating the soft lights inside. Harcourt instantly settled on a bottle that had never let him down—the Dalmore fifty-year-old. It had been one of the first things he replaced after he'd fled his Virginia estate in the wake of Decker's unforgivable attack. He stood there, holding the bottle. Could Decker be responsible again? It didn't make a difference. The end was the end, no matter how you got there. He reached for a tumbler on the shelf in front of him when a familiar voice interrupted his train of thought.

"Looks expensive."

Startled by the voice, Harcourt dropped the bottle, which shattered on the marble floor, inches from his feet. He turned slowly to face the impossible. Ryan Decker stepped into the glow cast by the cabinet lights, one arm in a sling, the other pointing a suppressed pistol at his face.

"You?"

"Me," said Decker. "And I've waited a long time for this."

"Then get it over with," said Harcourt. "I don't have anything to say to you."

Decker nodded slowly. "There's nothing you *can* say."

"Then do it. I've come to my end," said Harcourt, wondering if he could get a shot off with his rifle either before or after Decker filled him with holes.

"As much as I'd like that," said Decker, "this isn't the end for you."

"It certainly would appear that way," said Harcourt, glancing at the headlights.

"Actually, it's just the beginning. I made a deal with the Sinaloa," said Decker. "I gave them Juan Reyes, whom I grabbed from the Juárez weapons stash last night, along with a detailed summary of Southern Cross. Compliments of Senator Paul Duncan."

"And you get to watch them lower me inch by inch into an acid bath?" said Harcourt, slowly shifting his weight to make a move for the rifle. "That's the deal?"

"That does sound nice—but I asked for something entirely different."

"Skinned alive?" said Harcourt, focused on the rifle leaning against his desk.

"Nothing like that," said Decker, stepping forward.

"What? Money?"

"No. I got you," said Decker. "You're headed back to the United States—to stand trial."

"I'm afraid that's not going to happen," said Harcourt, reaching for his rifle.

A shadow moved in the study doorway, and his arm locked in place, a paralyzing pain immediately spreading across his body. Harcourt dropped unceremoniously to the scotch-soaked floor, despite every desire to remain standing. His brain simply couldn't override the electrical current short-circuiting his muscles. When the pain finally stopped, he lay facedown in the middle of the office, a knee in his back and his hands held firmly in place behind him.

"Up you go," said another familiar voice. "We have a plane to catch."

He craned his head upward, barely recognizing the face under the camouflage paint. Brad Pierce. Jesus. Decker was serious. They were rendering him to the United States.

"Happy to see me?" said Pierce.

"Not really," muttered Harcourt, earning a kick to the left kidney.

Pierce and a Mexican-looking operative lifted him to his feet and wrestled him into an unusual full-body harness. When they finished, Pierce zip-tied Harcourt's hands in front of him. He examined the rig, which resembled a parachute harness—without the parachute.

"What is this thing?" said Harcourt.

Decker walked over and yanked him forward by the harness.

"You're going to fly."

"I don't get it," said Harcourt. "Fly in a plane? Why do I need this?"

"You'll find out soon enough," said Decker. "Time to meet the US attorney for the Southern District of California."

As they carried him down the trail toward the airfield, the deep buzz of a powerful aircraft echoed across the valley. He'd heard that same sound a year ago at his wrecked estate in Virginia, suddenly realizing what they had planned for him.

CHAPTER

SIXTY-SEVEN

Supervisory Special Agent Reeves finished the last of the lukewarm coffee in his worn travel mug and stared out the window. The landscape hadn't changed much since they drove north out of the San Bernardino Mountains. Two hours of brown, broken up by different shades of brown. He couldn't think of any other way to describe it. He glanced at his phone, checking the navigation app.

"Passing through Bagdad," said Reeves.

"I'm pretty sure Baghdad is greener," said Special Agent Matt Kincaid. "Tigris River and all."

"Bagdad, California," said Reeves. "Without the *h*. We're a few minutes out from the airport."

Kincaid stretched in the passenger seat, picking up his coffee cup and realizing it was empty for the tenth time since they drove away from the Barstow Starbucks.

"Think they have a Starbucks in Amboy?" said Kincaid.

"The picture of Amboy on Google Maps looks like it was taken in 1955," said Decker. "So I'm going to guess no."

"No coffee and no idea why I'm out in the middle of nowhere—first thing in the morning."

"I told you," said Reeves. "I got a tip."

"A tip," said Kincaid.

"From a very reliable source," said Reeves.

"And I don't need to worry about this being some kind of ambush," said Kincaid.

"Right. The only threat to our safety out here is a rattlesnake or two."

Kincaid shook his head. "You're really not going to tell me, are you?"

"I want it to be a surprise," said Reeves.

"I'm not a toddler," said Kincaid. "I don't need to be surprised to be happy."

"Trust me on this one."

"Yep," said Kincaid, leaning his head against the window.

Route 66 curved north before crossing a triple set of railroad tracks and heading east again. Reeves slowed after coming out of the second curve, searching for the dirt road he had spotted on Google Maps. The Amboy airfield was little more than a three-thousand-foot-long stretch of sand to the north.

He found what amounted to a rutted jeep trail where the dirt road should be and turned his SUV north, hoping for the best. The images on the internet had looked so old, he wouldn't have been surprised if the entire place had been wiped off the map.

The vehicle bounced up and down on the trail, drawing concerned looks from Kincaid, until they broke onto a flat, cleared surface. Reeves glanced left and right, confirming that they had driven onto the runway. He turned left and drove toward the northwest end of the runway, close to a half mile away.

"There's something out there," said Kincaid.

"Someone," said Reeves, grinning.

He pulled up next to the seated someone and got out of the SUV, joining Kincaid, who cast him a skeptical glare. The person sat cross-legged on a wooden pallet, zip-tied in place—a tan hood pulled over his head.

"Care to do the honors and remove the hood?" said Reeves.

"As long as this is legal."

"It's all perfectly legal," said Reeves. "I got an anonymous tip."

"I thought it was a reliable source," said Kincaid, reaching for the hood.

Reeves shrugged, and Kincaid yanked the hood free. Jacob Harcourt twisted his head toward them and squinted.

"Holy mother of anonymous tips," said Kincaid. "Jackpot."

Harcourt started to say something, but Reeves cut him off.

"Jacob Harcourt, you're under arrest for murder, kidnapping, and a whole host of other charges that will be explained to you in detail upon your imminent arrival at the US attorney's office in Los Angeles."

Chapter

Sixty-Eight

Jeffrey McCall hung up the phone and frowned. Big Jim hadn't made much sense, talking a mile a minute about the parking lot, some kind of double cross, and how they would all go down together no matter what. He sat there for a moment, trying to unpack the colonel's words. He was just as deeply embroiled in Southern Cross as Colonel Souza and General Hooper.

His motivation for taking part in Harcourt's scheme was different from theirs, but it was arguably a much bigger betrayal of his country, putting him in even more peril. He'd done it purely for the cartel money promised to him by Harcourt, where the two senior officers saw it as an opportunity to militarize the border. The brutal cartel war they'd been promised along the border would convince the American people to support a new round of border security legislation—which would focus on military intervention.

McCall rolled his chair over to the window and froze. Shit. Big Jim wasn't kidding. A small army of men and women dressed in suits and military police uniforms converged on the Joint Task Force North headquarters building from the parking lot. Double cross? Did Souza and Hooper think he'd turned on them? Where would they get that idea?

He considered calling his wife to let her know that he wouldn't be home for dinner tonight—or possibly ever again—but he didn't know how to even begin that conversation. Darlene had absolutely no idea what he'd done. All she knew was that their retirement had been on shaky ground until recently.

He lowered his head and took a deep breath. This was going to tear them apart, far beyond the physical separation of prison. His military pension was unlikely to survive the ordeal, particularly in light of the national security implications of the charges that would be leveled against him. They barely got by on his pension, and there was little in the way of savings after Aegis Global's implosion. She'd never forgive him for this.

A gunshot boomed, followed by a discordance of screams. McCall raced to his open door and peeked outside in both directions. Two doors away, Major General Colin Hooper's executive assistant stood in front of the general's office screaming hysterically. Son of a bitch took the easy way out.

He walked down the shiny linoleum-tiled hallway, taking a quick peek inside. The general's head lay flat on his desk, a crimson pool spreading around it. A bright-red, chunky mosaic covered the American flag hanging from the wall behind his desk. He turned to console Gabby Roy and usher her away from the ghastly scene, instead coming face-to-face with Colonel James "Big Jim" Souza, who placed the cold metal barrel of a gun under McCall's chin.

"This is for the general," said Souza, leaving McCall utterly confused for the last second of his life.

CHAPTER SIXTY-NINE

Rafael Guzmán, head of the Jalisco New Generation Cartel, got up from the table and shook hands with Carlo, the elderly owner of his favorite taco shop. El Taco Pescado barely qualified as a restaurant. Six scratched-up, wobbly plastic tables, surrounded by even flimsier white plastic chairs—some so brittle that Guzmán's men had to test them before he took a seat.

Nobody on the street gave the dingy place a second look, and no matter what time of day he stopped by, not a single customer sat inside. He was fairly convinced the place had one customer, Rafael Guzmán, and that suited him just fine. Hands down, Carlo served the best fish tacos on the Baja Peninsula. Guzmán was happy to have it to himself.

He slipped Carlo two hundred-dollar bills with the handshake, to show his appreciation for the old man's taco-making magic and to make sure he could afford to keep El Taco Pescado open for his biweekly visits. The old man thanked him profusely, holding on to his hand until Guzmán patted him on the shoulder—their long-established routine. He nodded over his shoulder at Javier Correa, his bodyguard, who left the restaurant to clear the street for their short walk back to his Ensenada office building.

A cool ocean breeze fanned him when he stepped onto the sidewalk, the crisp air a refreshing change from the stale heat inside the restaurant. That was his only complaint with the place. He made a mental note to take care of that for Carlo and have one of those wall-mounted units installed.

As he strolled with Javier and a small crew of trusted cartel soldiers, a convoy of three vehicles approached the intersection of Avenida Rayo and Calle Tercera. Javier was already speaking into his handheld radio, having seen them first. His bodyguard slipped between two parked cars and stood in the street, presumably communicating with the trio of armed cartel soldiers diverting traffic away from Avenida Rayo.

Javier returned to the sidewalk and shrugged. "It's Antonio. He says it's urgent. Something about the shipment from the US."

Antonio Lacayo, his right-hand man, could be a little impatient at times.

"Can it wait until we're back at the office?" said Guzmán.

Javier radioed the question as they walked, relaying the answer a few seconds later. "He said it might not be safe to return to the office. There's room in the SUVs for all of us."

Guzmán thought it over. The Americans had delivered the replacement shipment two days ago. Did he mean they wanted it back? Why couldn't any of his people accurately pass along a message these days?

"All right," said Guzmán. "Send him through."

Javier radioed the message, and they walked to an empty parking space along the street to wait for Lacayo's convoy. The vehicles pulled up several seconds later with all the windows down. Lacayo smiled at him from the back seat of the middle SUV. Guzmán walked toward the oversize white Suburban.

"What's this about the shipment?" said Guzmán.

"It's no longer ours," said Lacayo, a gun muzzle appearing beneath his smile.

Guzmán turned his head, finding that Javier and the rest of his bodyguards had cleared the sidewalk like rats fleeing a sinking ship. When he returned his gaze to Lacayo, he noticed more gun barrels protruding from the open windows.

"They insisted you get to enjoy your tacos pescados one more time," said Lacayo. "Don't worry about the old man. I'll be sure to frequent his shop and keep slipping him hundreds."

"He needs a new air conditioner," said Guzmán.

Lacayo nodded, an apologetic look on his face.

"Why?" said Guzmán.

"Someone tipped off the Sinaloa," said Lacayo. "This is the only way to keep our cartel alive."

Guzmán closed his eyes and nodded—hearing only the first few seconds of gunfire that riddled his body.

CHAPTER SEVENTY

Bob Saling sat in his four-door Jeep Wrangler, thumbing through the news on his smartphone. So far the violence south of the border had been limited to several targeted cartel assassinations. Nothing newsworthy for the folks up here, but down in Mexico, it was a big deal. Leadership of three of the five border cartels had changed hands almost overnight. The only Mexican crime syndicates that hadn't been touched were the Sinaloa and Gulf cartels, which wasn't a surprise.

Sinaloa leadership wouldn't let the attempted coup d'état go unanswered. The price would be a new arrangement, favoring the Sinaloa. Nothing drastically different, but significant enough to prevent all-out war in the face of a thwarted conspiracy to destroy them. Nobody would go broke.

Saling removed the key from the ignition, stopping the engine. The Jeep started to heat up immediately. At nine o'clock in the morning, on the Texas A&M San Antonio campus, it was already ninety-eight degrees Fahrenheit, with clear skies. A scorcher by any standards.

He grabbed the leather satchel from the passenger seat and opened the door, reaching back inside with his empty hand to retrieve his silver-belly Stetson cowboy hat. He donned the four-thousand-dollar hat, adjusting its tilt—just right—before shutting the door and heading for his office in the Patriots' Casa.

"Señor?"

He pretended not to hear the voice. He wasn't in the mood for a parking lot ambush by one of his constituents. Particularly one speaking Es-pan-yol.

"Señor. *Es muy importante.*"

It's always important. He turned to find a filthy-looking Mexican, with a ripped straw hat, standing at the back of his Jeep.

"*¿Sí?*" said Saling.

"Are you Congressman Saling?" said the man.

Saling nodded. *"Sí, soy Congressman Saling."*

"Bueno," said the man, taking a step to the side to expose the squat submachine gun he had been concealing behind the Jeep.

"Whoa! Whoa! Amigo. You don't—"

Within the span of two seconds, twenty-one of the thirty .45-caliber bullets fired from the Mexican's MAC-10 struck the Twenty-Third District's congressman—killing him instantly.

CHAPTER
SEVENTY-ONE

Senator Steele clicked on the various news articles she'd bookmarked, piecing together a final picture of what had transpired over the past seventy-two hours. Overall, she was satisfied with the end result, though a few events remained unexplained. Dark events she had some trouble reconciling.

The suicide-homicide inside Joint Task Force North's headquarters at Fort Bliss stood out as one of them. General Hooper's suicide sadly fit the pattern of a career soldier facing an indisputable and overwhelming disgrace after thirty-plus years of honorable service—but the cold-blooded murder of Jeffrey McCall didn't sit well with her.

Witness testimony suggested that the unit's second in command, Colonel James Souza, had accused McCall of "screwing them over" just before shooting him in the face. Steele found it strange that Souza had jumped to the conclusion that McCall had double-crossed them. Particularly because she knew it wasn't true at all.

Paul Duncan's testimony, along with the photographic evidence supplied by Decker's team, had sealed Joint Task Force North's fate. It would have been impossible for General Hooper to explain away the missing Javelin missiles and various other lethal weapons photographed in Mexico. The evidence, along with Duncan's statement, clearly proved that JTF North's brass had been covertly supplying the cartels for months.

Then there was Bob Saling—gunned down in front of his office on the San Antonio Texas A&M campus. Unless Steele had missed something, there was no way the Sinaloa Cartel could have known he had been involved in Southern Cross. She had honored her word and kept quiet, even giving Duncan and Saling a week to get their affairs in order before resigning.

Admittedly, Saling had been the less cooperative of the two, giving her pause more than a few times during their pointed discussions, but she would never have followed through on her original threat to expose him to the Sinaloa or put a marker on his head. Like the fiasco at Joint Task Force North, the circumstances of his death led her to suspect a little bird had sung a deadly song.

Beyond the two inexplicable killings, everything else had fallen into place. The weapons funneled to the three cartels had been recovered. Mexican authorities, responding to an anonymous tip, had found hundreds of unopened crates containing a variety of sophisticated US weapons in a massive Nogales warehouse.

The Sinaloa apparently had no intention of keeping the weapons in Mexico and incurring the wrath of the US government. She had to hand it to the Mexicans—returning the weapons and keeping the transition of power among the cartels relatively bloodless was a testament to their understanding of the bigger picture. Keep the US government happy and nothing significant changed at the border. The money kept flowing, and it was back to business as usual.

The next article hit hard on a number of levels. Jacob Harcourt was in federal custody, facing close to nine consecutive life sentences for dozens of murders attributable to his orders—including Meghan's. The list of charges against him read like a Tolstoy novel. Seemingly endless, but ultimately satisfying. To a point.

Harcourt's apparently generous fate, in light of his crimes, surfaced a bitter question. Why did Decker spare Harcourt while throwing McCall and Saling to the wolves? Steele knew Decker was the "little bird." She knew it because he was the only other person who shared her same level of anguish. Because of this, she also understood why he had done it this way.

Harcourt was the kingpin of two unfathomable criminal schemes. His very public trial and life imprisonment would serve as a perpetual warning for the next generation of self-entitled, corporate scumbags who fancied themselves above the law. A lighthouse built on the rocky shoals of unrestrained greed. McCall and Saling merely served as visceral, temporary reminders that collaborating with someone like Harcourt came with a very real price.

Steele knew the decision hadn't been easy for Decker, and she couldn't imagine the level of restraint he'd exercised to physically apprehend and deliver Harcourt into custody without killing him. All she had thought about for the past year was driving the steel Montblanc pen on her desk through one of Harcourt's eyes—clear to the brain stem. Steele was deeply grateful for what Decker had done, regardless of his methods and motives.

She picked up the phone and dialed the only number she had for him, figuring it would go to voice mail or be disconnected. Decker answered immediately.

"Senator."

He sounded distant. Possibly distracted.

"Ryan. How are you doing?" she said. "And I'm not talking about your arm."

"The arm is good, and I'm okay. Fair to middling, some might say," said Decker. "And you?"

"After careful consideration, I've come to the conclusion that I hate closure," said Steele.

Decker laughed. "It hurts more than whatever they call not having closure. Something to do with moving on?"

Steele teared up, unable to respond. When Decker stayed quiet, she guessed he was in the same boat.

"Thank you again," she said. "For everything."

Decker sniffled, confirming her suspicion. "I wanted to kill him— so badly," he said. "I'm sorry I didn't."

"You're a better person than I am," she said. "But you did the right thing."

"There's no better or worse when it comes to dealing with someone like Harcourt," said Decker. "No right or wrong."

"Trust me. You did good," said Steele.

"Thank you, Senator. I'll take what I can get at this point."

"That's about all we can do," said Steele, changing the subject before she lost it again. "I trust you're going to spend some time with Riley and your parents in Idaho while you recover?"

"Yes. I'm actually on my way to Idaho right now."

"Is Ms. Mackenzie with you? Sorry if I sound like I'm prying. I really like her."

"Me, too," said Decker. "And yes. She's here."

"I'm very happy to hear that," she said. "Rest up and stay in touch. I still consider our working arrangement to be intact."

"So do I," said Decker. "I'll check in with Reeves when I'm back in circulation. Might be a while."

"Enjoy the time you have with the people that care about you, Ryan. Never regret it," she said, abruptly ending the call.

She sat at her desk, looking at a picture of her late husband and daughter, feeling like they could all finally rest.

Chapter Seventy-Two

Decker placed his phone on the plastic table and lifted his beer, holding it up for a toast.

"Senator Steele says hi," he said. "We're still on her Christmas list, apparently."

"That's good news," said Harlow, clinking his pint glass with her own. "You had me a little worried there—not that those dirtbags didn't deserve what they got."

"Someone had to pay for the Border Patrol agents," said Decker.

"Should have been Harcourt," she said, taking a sip.

"It's better this way. So I keep telling myself," said Decker before tipping his bottle back.

"What's done is done," said Harlow, finishing her beer. "Another round?"

"I'm not driving," he said, tapping his sling with the bottom of his empty glass.

"Neither am I," she said. "We walked here."

When Harlow caught their server's attention, they ordered two more local microbrews and too many appetizers. He planned to stretch their evening on this patio as long as possible. The air was warm but not humid. The view of the mountains towering over the lake was majestic. The beer was ice-cold. And most important, he was enjoying it all with Harlow. Decker wasn't going anywhere.

"We make a pretty good team," said Decker, taking her hand.

"I get the impression you have a better time with Brad," she said. "I'm a little jealous."

"When I'm healed up, we'll get you free-fall parachute qualified and spend a few hundred hours on the firing range so you can replace him," said Decker.

"Is that all it would take?" said Harlow. "Sign me up."

"Anna and the kids looked relieved to know it's over," said Decker.

"Where do you think they'll go?" said Harlow.

"Good question. Anna wants to get the kids settled somewhere before school starts in a few months, but Brad's advocating a more cautious approach," said Decker. "We've tangled with the Russian *mafiya*, Mexican drug cartels, and one of the most dangerous men alive—all within the span of a few weeks. I'm kind of in his camp on this one. Don't tell Anna."

Harlow laughed. "I won't. What about Riley and your parents? I'm just a little bit nervous to meet them, by the way."

"I couldn't tell," he said, laughing for a moment. "Everyone is looking forward to meeting you."

"Even Riley?" she said.

"I'm not worried about Riley. I've spoken with her about you a few times already. I promise this won't be awkward," said Decker.

"Wait. You've talked to Riley about me?" she said. "When?"

"Ever since I started coming up here," he said. "She doesn't know the full picture, but you're no stranger here."

"What's the full picture?" she said, glancing at him.

Decker squeezed her hand and smiled. "It's still developing, but I like where it's headed."

Harlow leaned over and gave him a quick kiss. "They have to be excited to get out of here."

"My parents love it, but Riley doesn't. Things might get a little tense over the next few days. I'm going to insist that they stay up here," said Decker. "I'd just like them to stay off the grid a little longer. Until we know for sure that Harcourt no longer wields influence in the world—and the Sinaloa are worth their word."

A look passed across her face that he recognized well.

"I know. Trust me," said Decker. "I know. I was two-point-five pounds of trigger pressure away from erasing him from the planet."

"How many pounds of pressure is the trigger?"

"Five-point-five," he said. "If I had hiccuped, he'd be gone."

"Why do you know the exact trigger-pull specifications of your pistol?" said Harlow.

Before he could answer, their server placed two pint glasses of Broken Horn IPA on the table between them. Decker took his glass before answering her question as honestly as he could.

"I have no idea."

"That's deep," she said, raising her glass. "To two-point-five pounds of pressure. May they always separate right from wrong."

Decker paused before clinking her glass. Under any other circumstance, he might think she was playing with him. Making light of the weapons details he obsessed over for no practical reason. But her face was dead serious. She'd obviously internalized his conversation with Senator Steele, despite hearing only one side, and distilled its core essence—even if he didn't fully believe he'd made the right decision. Harlow never ceased to amaze him.

"Now that's deep," he said, immediately regretting his flippant-sounding response.

"I mean it," said Harlow. "You did the right thing."

He took a deep breath and actually thought about what to say next—a somewhat new experience for him.

"You have no idea how much that means to me," he said, even though he was pretty sure she did.

Acknowledgments

Good thing the acknowledgments are not tied directly to the first draft deadline—or I'd never turn in a book on time. This really is the hardest part. Not because I don't want to write it, but because so many amazing people contributed in one way or another to the book you've just read.

I always start out with the readers. Without them, I'm not sure where I'd be right now. Certainly not on my tenth year of creating stories! Thank you for your unwavering support and continued trust in my work. I've thrown pretty much every type of story at you by this point, and you keep coming back. For that I'm wholeheartedly grateful.

To the entire Thomas & Mercer team for turning the Ryan Decker books into the kind of success I could only dream of. To say that Thomas & Mercer exceeded all expectations as a publisher doesn't do the sentiment justice. I look forward to a long and prosperous partnership.

To Megha Parekh, who once again kept me focused on the right balance between Decker and Harlow, which I think is the key to this series. Her big-picture recommendations and their impact on the story can't be overstated. We're already hard at work to make book three even more satisfying than the previous two.

To Kevin Smith, my new developmental editor, for a painless edit. *Painless* doesn't mean we didn't work hard to smooth out the story and make some entirely satisfying changes to several scenes. One in particular stands out—the third spider bot. We had a lot of fun with that.

To the advanced readers, who weren't shy with feedback but were very generous with their time.

To a number of sources who will remain unnamed. You know who you are and what parts of the story you breathed to life—and that I embellished. Nothing makes me smile more than when readers ask if some of the more far-fetched technology in my stories actually exists. You'd be surprised what's out there. That's all I'll say.

Finally, to my wife and very first reader. None of this would be possible without her.

ABOUT THE AUTHOR

Steven Konkoly is a graduate of the US Naval Academy and a veteran of several regular and elite US Navy and Marine Corps units. He has brought his in-depth military experience to bear in his fiction. Konkoly is the *USA Today* bestselling author of more than twenty novels and short stories, including the Black Flagged thrillers; the Alex Fletcher books; the Fractured State series; and the Ryan Decker novels, *The Raid* and *The Rescue.* Konkoly lives in central Indiana with his family. For more information, visit www.stevenkonkoly.com.